The Vengeful Dead

John James Minster

DEDICATION

With all my heart, soul, and mind to Ιησούς Χριστός. Also with love and reverence to my brother-from-another-mother, Edgar Allan Poe, the unequivocable master of the horror short story.

CONTENTS

Acknowledgments   i

1   Snuff   1

2   Book of the Dead   23

3   Son of a Ghoul   51

4   Magic 8 Ball   75

5   Corpsicle   98

6   Magus   115

7   Family Plot   139

8   Yoyo the Clown   164

9   Dog   183

10   Casilda   205

11   Death Macabre   234

About the Author   256

ACKNOWLEDGMENTS

John and Leona, my parents, encouraged John Jr's appetite for reading horror and for all things bizarre; dead a long time, a nod to them here will have to suffice. By far the deepest gratitude is for my readers: welcome to my nightmares, happy to share, with love. Stay spooky!

Snuff

"How much money can you pitch in, Liam?" Blake asked.

"Eighty bucks, from mowing four lawns on my street. The rest I need."

"José, how about you?"

"Flat broke. What about you, Blake?"

"I can scrounge together forty. That totals a hundred twenty—not too shabby. I have old walkie-talkies that I'm willing to part with; haven't played with them in years."

"Are they loud?"

Blake snorted. "Dad got 'em from some military surplus seller. Cranked all the way up they're around eighty-eight decibels, same as a person shouting. We'll need a realistic female fashion mannequin. The anchor department store down the mall is going out of business and selling everything: steel shelves, mannequins, guest chairs, mirrors. Everything that isn't glued down must go. I'll go there tomorrow morning to see what kind of deal I can work."

"What else do we need?" asked José.

Blake paused to think. "Well, for the mannequin to appear totally normal, we'll need a wig, a dress and shoes, and some make-up. Bright red lips, eye-darkening shit, whatever they call it."

José smiled. "My sister has so much crap in her closets she won't even miss the dress, and that other junk, too; she has plastic boxes filled with it. I have a long black wig from Halloween years back. Got it covered."

"Liam, how can we be down on the street filming but somehow knock the thing off-balance so that it goes over the edge right when we need it to? You're the math and science nerd of this outfit. Figure it out."

Liam appeared thoughtful. "Online, I can get a radio-controlled model airplane transmitter, receiver, and a small motor with a propeller—for around sixty bucks—less if I use the bidding option and chase it hard. Everyone's into drones now, so you can get airplane stuff cheap. It has the range we'll need. She'll be up there; we'll be down here. This is all about balance. She's completely hollow, right? What does she weigh?"

Blake nodded. "Looked it up: about seventeen pounds; maybe twenty with the dress and shoes."

"Perfect. We'll balance her with a single ten-pound dumbbell plate, dead center, suspended from a string. I'll rig the motor to another string below the weight, to her front. Push the button: the weight suddenly jets forward at high-speed, slamming against her midsection. Bam! Over she goes. Simple, cheap. I got this, guys."

"Hey, José—your dad has spools of nylon rope in the garage. Think he'll miss a few hundred feet?"

"Nah, man. Those rolls are so big, he must've caught a sale or something when I was eleven. Even with all the trees he plants and uses rope to stake straight, I'm fourteen now and I've never noticed the roll get any smaller."

Blake smiled. "Gentlemen, start counting your money. This one's going viral and we're monetizing. Every click is money. Split three ways. Guys ready?"

Liam and José beamed and nodded.

The following Sunday, with everything in order and tested, the biggest hurdle in Blake's mind was how three fourteen-year-old boys would somehow manage to convey a life-size artificial woman into Center City, Philadelphia, up to the roof to set up, without being challenged by building security. They borrowed white landscaper coveralls and hats from José's father's stockpile which Blake had hidden in the garage. They used a ride-share from Blake's house, because his parents weren't home, as usual. It dropped them off at the office building service dock.

Blake stopped to consider all contingencies.

"José, you're the only one of us with a mustache. Since you look the oldest, I need you to knock on the door. When someone comes out, point to us. Say, 'Tomorrow, someone is giving a business presentation. Do you possibly have a cart or dolly we can use to bring up the materials?' If he gives you any shit, say, 'Look man, I'm paid nine-fifty an hour to set up these things. You want me to tell the boss 'No can do'—fine. Just give me your name and I'll lug this stuff back to the office with the news.' Okay, José? Got it?"

José smiled. "You are El Diablo himself, Blake."

Monday morning at six sharp, the three met early at Blake's and bought a ride into town. They disembarked directly across from the targeted building. Sunrise happened around five-thirty, but the ferocious morning commuter travel had not yet started. They stared at their creation, barely able to contain their excitement. There she stood, arms frozen in a pose, long brunette hair tousled by city summer breezes, a hangman's noose around her neck.

"Liam," said Blake. He pointed at a filthy, stinking dumpster in an alley behind the Chinese restaurant against whose brick wall it abutted. "Stand there. You can see her, and us, from there. Use your girl voice and shout loud, but don't let any pedestrians see or hear you do it."

Liam laughed. "Oh man, this is gonna be so cool!"

"José, you're in charge of photography. Use my dad's digital cam, it's so much better than a cell phone cam, plus you can zoom."

"Yeah man, I love that thing. Don't you worry, I'm handy with his cam, trust me."

By seven o'clock, rush hour had begun. City sounds swelled to a discordant roar of honking horns, delivery and garbage trucks backing up, and loud talking. Blake muttered that it was now, or never. He stood on the sidewalk under the woman, looked up, and pointed. "Human nature: you can set your clocks by it," he mumbled, as others joined in staring and pointing. Within fifteen minutes, a crowd of at least fifty had gathered. By seven-thirty, the number had swelled to over a hundred—and now included a Philly police cruiser, which stopped to investigate the situation. Blake cast a glance back at Liam, who nodded.

"Hey, if any cops try to come up to the roof, I'll jump!" Liam yelled into the walkie-talkie. Crowd noise diminished. Blake could not hear Liam, only the voice coming from above. Some onlookers led a movement to hush those still murmuring. "I can't go on. The crime; the hatred. I've decided not to stay."

"Jump!" shouted a group of older teen boys. Blake glanced over. *Muscle shirts and tattoo sleeves. Losers*, he thought.

One of the cops ran to the cruiser trunk and pulled out a bullhorn. "Miss, I'm sure that whatever you may be dealing with isn't so terrifying that together we can't solve. We will get you all the help you need."

Liam: "Fuck you, pigs! And fuck your mothers! I'm jumping!"

It required every ounce of self-possession for Blake not to burst out laughing at Liam's impromptu dialogue. He glanced at José, satisfied that he was capturing all of it: the dialogue, people's horrified facial expressions.

Love it when a plan comes together! Blake thought.

"Jump!" shouted the tough boys. The other officer pushed through the crowd until he stood before them. He glowered at the boys and said something Blake could not hear.

"Don't do it, lady!" others shouted. Again, the cop with the bullhorn, "Please, miss, I'm coming up to help you."

"Take one step towards that door, pig, and I jump!"

Blake thought he might burst a blood vessel from holding back laughter.

The police officer returned his bullhorn to the cruiser trunk and made strides toward the door. Blake looked over at Liam and nodded. Liam pushed the button. The mannequin plummeted.

Bystanders howled in horror. Full coffee cups exploded on the sidewalk. One female senior citizen dropped to the ground on her way to passing out. José seemed to be focused on the street drama, but then Blake watched him tilt the camera lens skyward to cover the dummy's long fall. Reaching the end of her rope, two stories above ground, the mannequin's body detached from the noosed head in the sudden jerk and inertia. The headless trunk hit the sidewalk. Horrified shrieks erupted as the head swayed in a five-foot arc.

Blake walked over to José and tapped him. José saw his expression, and followed his pointing finger to ten police vehicles, lights and sirens going full blast as they converged on the scene. José knew the mission was accomplished; now it was unsafe to tarry further. "Time to collect Liam and beat feet before cops start interrogating random passers-by," Blake said.

Back at Blake's, they broke loose with laughter, as each recalled specific viewpoints and details of the practical joke. Face red and tear-stained, Liam asked, "Can we call this the Practical Joker's Club, and sign our video with that moniker? I just think it'd be a cool story to tell our kids one day."

Blake smiled. "Sure, man, whatever's clever. How soon can you post the movie?"

"Give me an hour. I need to watch it first, see if it needs any editing. Has to. No offense, José, but even Hollywood film crews who do this for a living require editing. An hour, Blake. I have editing software."

Blake nodded.

The Practical Joker's Club video instantly went viral, and the clicks quickly mounted. Money poured into their account. Flush with success, they conceived and filmed a second gag. They decided that of the three, Liam appeared the least threatening. They bought a dozen straw brooms, which Liam held as he stood at the city bus stop.

José had boarded the SEPTA bus several blocks back, so that as people emptied out, he could work his way to the very back and save a seat for Liam. It arrived at Liam's stop. José started filming just as Liam boarded the bus, holding the brooms, which stuck out in many directions. As he walked, the brooms knocked off eyeglasses, poked heads, throats, and torsos. "Sorry! Excuse me! So sorry," Liam muttered. He absorbed fierce streams of profanity as he worked his way all the way back, where he sat next to José. At the next stop, he reversed direction up the aisle. All the same passengers suffered the same assault, this time to their ears, necks, and backs of their heads.

Liam had the rideshare waiting. As the bus pulled away, he jumped in. He told the driver to get ahead of the bus by a block and drop him off. José had never stopped filming; as Liam boarded the bus again, his brooms knocked around many of the same passengers. The vitriol was harsher than before. Death threats followed Liam. José captured it all. After antagonizing the same furious riders a third time, Liam feared for his safety; he grabbed José, left the brooms scattered on the floor, and ran off the bus. They cut through an alley to a parallel street and from there caught a ride back to Blake's house. Both boys' faces and shirts were wet with fear-sweat and tears of laughter.

This movie received even more clicks than the fake suicide video. By this point, the three had banked more money from the gag reels than some of their parents earned all year.

Blake, attempting to sound like the chairman of the board, said, "I hereby call to order this meeting of the Practical Joker's Club." José sniggered. He sat on the old paisley sleeper sofa that Blake's parents could not part with. Liam sat on a pile of tires and smiled contentedly. "Gents, I discovered that there is an even larger market than there is for joke reels."

Liam perked up. "Really? Hard to believe. What might that be, mister chairman?"

Blake smiled at the title. "Porn."

Liam and José exchanged terrified glances. José said, "No, man. Y'all's loco."

"Calm your tits, guys; I don't mean sex. There's a sub-genre I found on kink porn channels. Nobody has sex or gets naked. People out there pay a lot of money for faked death pics and vids. They call 'em 'snuff films.' But nobody really dies; it's all fake as shit. And weirdos with money just go apeshit over this stuff! Telling you, they eat it up. We can collect beaucoup crypto for every download; forget pennies per click."

Liam searched Blake's face for any change in demeanor. Finding none, he asked, "You're saying that we would need to stage a fake murder using a real girl this time, not a dummy?"

"Correct. Know any cute little actresses?"

Liam fake laughed. "You're the Casanova of the club, Blake. José's parents are so Catholic they don't let him date without a chaperone. I'm something of a celeb now, thanks to the broom vid. Out of nowhere, super-hot tenth grade girls are talking to me. But I haven't asked anybody out yet. So, no. Can't think of anyone."

"You haven't kissed a girl yet?"

Liam blushed. "No, okay? No."

Blake, seated in a flimsy lawn chair, tilted back. Liam and José studied his placid, thoughtful face. They saw him smile. He sat up. "Candy Angelo. She'd do it if I asked her to. She can wear a bathing suit or bra and panties. Make her look eighteen. Get around the underage laws."

"The witch? I mean, Wiccan goth girl, or whatever she claims to be?" asked José.

"Where can we do this? Can't use any of our houses," Liam said.

"The motor lodge. Fifty bucks a night. We'll need a good three-point lighting rig with silk filters. That'll be the biggest spend. My dad's movie cam will do fine. Oh, and some black candles, and a red bulb for effect. And a lighter or matches, something to light them with."

Liam frowned. "We'll only make money if it seems realistic, correct?"

Blake nodded.

Still frowning, "Well, it can't be a gun. Loud and too dangerous. Can't be another hanging; we might screw that up. A choking might work. Is

Candy a good actress?"

"She always pretends to cum when I've fucked her. But hey—she wasn't acting!"

All three laughed hard. "No but seriously, she could manage a scream and play dead. But a faked choking? I just can't see it. She's kinda-sorta dopey."

Liam thought about it, and the other two watched his wheels turning. "I've seen on websites these switchblade knives, stilettos, where you push a button just a little bit and a spring takes over. The blade shoots straight out the front of the handle and locks into place. Soldiers carry them. So, when you want to put the blade back inside, you push the same button and the blade glides back in. When the blade is out, it just looks like a mean-assed knife. So, imagine: if we start with blade out, then push the buttons when we fake-stab Candy, it'll seem like we are stabbing into her, but really, the blades are retracting back into the handles."

Blake stroked his chin. "Yeah. Totally can see that. Realistic fake blood is everywhere on the web, for the Halloween and cosplay crowd. We do a few rehearsals, make sure Candy doesn't royally fuck it up…yeah, this could work. But we'd need to cut her in. Four-way split. Her dad is drunk most of the time; they've even lived off food stamps sometimes. I'm sure she'd jump on it. Needs the money. So, members of the Practical Joker's Club: do we agree on this plan?"

Liam and José searched each other's faces; together they nodded. "We do, mister chairman."

"Liam, you get two knives. I'll get us a deal on a used three-point lighting system. José, you get a dozen black candles, a red bulb, a shit-ton of fake blood, two latex skull masks, and two cowled black robes. Make sure the blood is realistic. Read every review until you figure out the ultimate product. If it looks fake, we blew it. This meeting is hereby adjourned."

"Great! You are perfect for this role, Candy! Who knows, maybe it'll lead to bigger and better roles. Regardless, we each get a quarter share of the take. We're all using stage names. You need to think up a good one for yourself."

"My witch-name is Lilith."

"Great! Use that. Also, if you want to temporarily change your appearance, you know, like slather on a lot of makeup and rub in some pink or green hair powder that you can easily wash out after, so your rents don't throw a shit-fit, that'd be good too."

"Blake," she said, and batted her naturally long, thick eyelashes. "I miss you. Think afterwards, maybe you and I can hang out in the motel room awhile, after the other two leave?"

He grinned. Tenderly, he kissed her wrist and opened palm. "I wouldn't have it any other way, Candace my love. Oh, one thing: do NOT tell anyone about this. Seriously. Fake names and all—you're only fourteen, yadda-yadda. Liam will add one of those 'all actors were older than eighteen at the time of filming' blah-blah disclaimer statements in the beginning to make it seem totally legit. Tell no one."

"Tell who about what? I don't even know what you're talking about."
He smiled. "There she is. That's my girl."

They unloaded bags and boxes from the trunk of the rideshare. Blake eyed the motor lodge: an aged, unkempt rectangular building. Numbered doors faced the parking lot, and a small office sat at the end. It was in the worst section of town, less than a quarter mile from the stinking river. Two luxury cars sat in the lot outside the two right-most rooms nearest the office, backed into parking spaces to hide their license plates from the road.
Wife-cheaters, he thought.
Once again due to his facial hair, José received the assignment to enter the office and rent the room.
"I need I.D., and you need to fill out this form," said the clerk, a skinny, greasy-haired man perhaps ten years older than José.
"Señor, I'm meeting my woman. I got no I.D.," José said, affecting a Spanish accent. "Here," he said, and pushed two fifty-dollar bills under the safety plexiglass. "You gotta eat too, man." After a moment's hesitation, the clerk glanced over his shoulder, then snapped up the two bills. "My girl, she so berry loud. A real screamer. Got a room at the left end?"
The clerk turned and reached out to the pegboard behind him. He slid the key to the empty room furthest left through the slot. "Have a nice night," said the clerk. He snarked back mucus, no longer interested in José.
Inside the room, Candy sat on the bed. She watched as Blake unscrewed the light bulb in the room's single table lamp on the dresser across from the foot of the bed and replaced it with a sixty-watt red bulb. Liam popped open the three-point lighting umbrellas and plugged lamp cords into a surge protector. Blake unplugged the phone and deposited it in a dresser drawer; he divided twelve tall, thick black candles and placed six on each nightstand flanking the head of the bed. He lit them.
José turned on the camera and fiddled with low-light and night mode settings. Blake said, "Okay, team. I am your director, and I say it's time to rehearse. Would our star please lie on the bed, arms behind her head at either top corner, feet by the bottom two corners. Liam, is the lighting right where it needs to be? José, how does it look in the cam?"
"Looks washed out. Liam, kill the sidelights. I want to see it with top light, candles, and red bulb only." Liam did. "Still not right. Put the sides back on and kill the top light. Wait: no, not good." He searched through the lighting system packaging and retrieved a red silk filter along with a roll of

duct tape. He secured the filter over the top light, then did the same to both side lights. "Turn them all on, Liam." He looked through the camera and smiled. "Oh man, this is perfect."

"You rock, José!" said Blake. "Liam, grab the knives, show me how to work 'em." For a minute, each stood flicking out and retracting the sharp steel blades. "These are cool! Love the sound it makes. I'll carry mine with me every day after filming."

Liam nodded. "Yep. Totally badass. It's against the law in this Commonwealth to carry them, but like my dad says, 'Better to be judged by twelve than carried by six.' Come at me, bullies. I'll stick you like pigs."

Blake laughed at the tough talk coming from his diminutive friend whose high voice had yet to change from boy to man. "Okay, now we get in wardrobe. Candy, strip off all the bedclothes down to the white sheet, then strip yourself down to your undies. Liam—masks and robes for us."

"Candy, sorry to have to do this to you," said Blake, "but it's essential to the scene." Using lengths of José's father's rope, as gently as possible, he looped an ankle to the metal bed leg under the corner, then the other, and finally repeated the process with her wrists.

"You guys look really scary," she said, as Blake fluffed out her hair.

"Your bare-naked underarms and bare soles look so pink, tender, and ticklish," he said. Affecting a sardonic laugh, he wiggled his fingers close to her face.

"Don't! Don't you even think about it! I swear, Blake—I will kill you!"

"Okay guys, scene position. I'll stand on her left; Liam, you stand to her right. Hold the squeeze tubes of fake blood against the handle, like this," he said, and demonstrated for Liam. "When we press the retractor buttons, at the same time, we grip hard. Blood will shoot all over her belly. We do it all in one take."

"Got it," said Liam.

"Candy, this is the time to channel your inner actress. You need to appear scared. Terrified even. Think about it: if you were facing actual death right now, how would you feel? What would you be doing right now?"

"I'd be trying to get myself out of these ropes, pulling and twisting my body with all my strength. I'd beg for my life. I'd hyperventilate."

"Your eyes?"

"Wide open and scared. My head would thrash; neck muscles would pop out. For sure, I'd be screaming and crying."

"Can you make yourself cry?"

She hesitated. "I don't know. I can try. Can you slap me right before we get rolling? My dad slaps me sometimes and I cry every time."

"Geez, sorry. Okay, I will, but I don't like it. And yes, do all of that; do everything you just described. This must appear real or nobody's gonna buy it. Won't get many initial 'thumbs-up' or positive review comments, and that means no sales and no profits. It's all on you now, Candy," he said. "But I gotta tell you: excellent makeup job! You look old—like maybe twenty. You look beautiful and fantastic, doesn't she, guys?"

"Hell yes!" said Liam.

"Tu eres muy bonita, mami," said José.

"Hey, I took Spanish, thanks, José!" she said.

"Okay, get ready for action," said Blake. He took up his position to her left, knife and blood tube in hand. He leaned over and pressed his lips to her forehead for several seconds. "Sorry," he said, as he reached behind him and brought down a stinging slap to her right cheek, followed immediately by a vigorous backhand slap to her left. Candy started crying. "Action!" he shouted.

Blake and Liam held the knives with the points up to give José the opportunity to zoom in on them, showing viewers that these were in fact authentic, real sharp steel knives. Blake and Liam, black hoods over creepy skull masks, stood rigid. Candy cried and remembered what she had told Blake she would do if the threat of death had been real. She executed her role perfectly; she thrashed and pulled at her bonds.

They held the knife points down two inches over Candy's lower abdomen. Blake and Liam looked at each other. Blake nodded. Together they prepared to press the retractor buttons. They plunged down the knife points. At that exact moment, Candy twisted her body as if trying to squirm away from the awful conclusion. The sudden movement caused both boys to fumble the push-action.

Two five-inch blades pierced her skin and parted muscle, buried now to the handles deep inside her small intestine. José captured all of it; he thought Candy would be the next Hollywood 'scream queen.'

Damn! This is like…authentic! So real! It's like she's in agony with those panicked screeches, shrieks, and wails, he thought.

He zoomed in on her face, then onto the knives undulating with her violent, body-wracking sobs. That is when he realized everything was wrong. The knives were supposed to be gone from the scene by now.

"Holy shit! You guys really stabbed her!"

Blake and Liam stood in shock. José turned off the camera and bolted over. He pushed Blake aside, bent and held Candy's cheeks. "Candy! Listen to me! You're gonna be all right, I swear it! It was an accident, oh dear God, they didn't mean it! You're gonna be fine. I'm going to call 9-1-1 and…"

"No!" shouted Blake. He pulled off his hood and mask. "No, José. How's this gonna look? I mean, look around you. Assault, murder charges, video evidence. We'd be tried as adults for murder. Do you know what happens to guys our age in prison? Well do you, José?"

"Oh my God, Blake, what are we supposed to do?" Liam screamed.

The three boys were forced to shout at one another over Candy's tortured howling. "We can't just let her die!"

"Pull the knives out!" was all Blake could think of now. Liam and José stood immobilized with shock. Blake did the deed himself. Jets of dark warm blood splattered his face and arms as the steel shanks left her gut with two little 'slur-plop' sounds. "Quick, hand me that plastic bag," he commanded Liam, who still wore his skull mask and hood. "Do it now! Grab the fucking bag!" Jolted into action, Liam complied. Blake pushed the bag underneath Candy's back. "We can't leave a blood-soaked mattress. No blood evidence. So far, it's contained to right here. Give me the duct tape."

"What are you going to do with it?" Liam asked weakly.

"Give it to me!"

Liam handed the tape to Blake, who roughly and tightly wrapped it around her abdomen and trunk until most of the roll was spent. "Why'd you do that?" he asked Blake.

"The knives cut veins and maybe even an artery. Probably an artery. What jetted out was arterial blood, dark and fast-moving. I shouldn't have pulled them out. The blades acted like plugs. She was only bleeding internally until I did. Can't let the blood out; it needs to stay inside.

"I'm dying!" cried Candy. "Oh my goddess, don't let me bleed to death, Blake! Liam, José, please help me!"

"Don't you two move. Stay right where you are if you know what's good for you. Prison will ruin you; ruin me."

"This is loco, man!" screamed José. "This is so bad! Evil. I'd rather go to prison than to Hell!"

Gradually, Candy's energy bled out. High-pitched shouts became short barks, mewling yelps. She had lost strength now even to cry. Though it felt to the boys like far longer, it took fewer than twenty minutes for her to die, with eyes wide open.

"Liam, what time is it? Liam! What's the fucking time?"

"Nine-fifteen," he said, choked up, barely able to talk.

"My parents are wondering where I am right now," said José. "So bad."

"Make up some bullshit excuse. We went to the city and our rideshare broke down, whatever. Yeah, we'll all use that. We waited for the backup ride. It's dark out now. You guys, pack up all our shit."

"We're not going to leave her here, are we?" asked José.

"Get everything boxed first. Give me my dad's camera. Then we'll deal with her."

Liam was too morose to move. José moped through the task as though he was intoxicated. An impatient Blake ripped lamp cords out of the surge protector and stuffed them in a box, along with the lamps and red bulb, which shattered. Extinguished candles went in the box next. He snapped open the bedsheet over Candy and rolled her limp corpse until it was tightly wrapped. He checked to make sure none of her blood had soaked through to the mattress. He used the remaining duct tape to secure her shroud.

Satisfied with the progress, he said, "I need both of you to help me lug her through the woods to the river." Liam shook his head. Blake grabbed Liam's shirt, pulling him close. "Listen up. If you do exactly as I say, when I say it, we're going to get out of this mess."

Liam broke away, ran to the bathroom, and vomited. José and Blake heard him splash water on his face. He returned, ashen and defeated. "Okay. Fine. We do it your way."

Blake opened the door and walked outside. He was gone for over ten minutes. When he returned, he untied the ropes attached to the four bed legs and looped them over his neck. "Coast is clear, I found a path, let's go. Guys: use your right arm. We all need to be on the same side." He looped his arm under her neck; José under her waist; Liam under her legs. They lifted the seventy-pound package without any struggle.

By the light of the moon, they made their way down to the river's edge. All saw the piles of junk, illegally dumped and haphazardly strewn about, half buried in redolent river muck. Blake scanned the items, deep in thought. He pointed to a wooden pallet. "That's the ticket. The water's too shallow near the bank. We need to get her out to the channel where it's deep. We put her on the skid then push her off. Currents are rough out there after all this rain. The skid will flip. She'll slide off."

"Won't she float?" asked Liam.

"Hm. You're right. As her insides putrefy, it'll create gases. We need to perforate the shit out of her, let water into her internal cavities. She'll sink and won't ever rise."

"God save us," muttered José. Liam closed his eyes as Blake gouged and ripped into Candy's midsection, ribcage, throat. The grisly step completed, José freed the pallet from the mud with a sucking sound and dragged it to the water's edge. They took up positions as before and carried her to the pallet. Blake dropped her; her head hit the wood slats with a sickening thud. Liam and José gently lowered the rest of her down. All three boys pushed the pallet until it floated, then watched as the river's currents carried it forty percent of the distance across near the channel, where whirlpools and eddies upended it, precisely as Blake had described.

They watched Candy Angelo slide off. She bobbed like a ghost in the menacing, polluted black water for a few yards, until she sank into the dark, polluted depths feet first, down to the hideous murky bottom. Into the water they tossed in two open cardboard boxes filled with lighting equipment, rope sections, candles, bulbs, surge protector, silk filter, and a spent cardboard core of a duct tape roll. They watched the boxes floating eerily in the moonlight-dappled ebon black channel, until they took on water and plummeted down.

Back in the room, Liam and José took turns in the shower to clean mud from their sneakers and blood from their hands. Blake went last as his arms and face took longer to clean, while the two used soapy wet washcloths to wipe down every surface they might have touched, to remove fingerprints. Blake emerged. "Sometime tomorrow afternoon, the cleaner will vacuum in here and report a sheet missing. Just another day in a place like this. All trace evidence gone," he said.

He shut the door behind him using toilet paper as a barrier between his hand and the knob. He wiped the key, walked the building's length to the night drop-box and let it drop from the wadded paper into the slot. "Okay, drop a pin. Let's go home, guys. This meeting of the Practical Joker's Club is officially adjourned."

"Hi, it's Blake. May I speak with José, please?"

Silence. Then, "I'm afraid José isn't here. He spends all day in church now," his mother explained. "We don't know what's gotten into him lately. I don't know what's going to happen when school starts in a few weeks. Basically now, he lives at church. He's losing weight, too. Not eating as much. Blake, do you have any idea what's going on?"

His mind whirled in a struggle to process an appropriate response to the question.

Yes ma'am, I know exactly what's going on within the tortured soul of my friend. "Dunno. Maybe he's Born-Again, or something."

"Maybe. I'm worried. More so now that the Angelo girl turned out missing. All you kids need to be super careful out there. It's a sick, sick world these days. I'm serious. I worry about all of you."

"Please don't, ma'am. We're too smart to be victims, José and I. Don't you worry. I'm sure he'll come around. Please tell him I called."

Blake clicked off and called Liam. "Listen. Don't talk. Just come over. Don't say anything on the phone."

"I'll be there," he said.

Together in the garage, Liam on the couch, Blake in the lawn chair, they stared at each other. Neither would break the dolorous silence.

Blake asked, "Are you alright?"

Liam shook his head. "No, Blake! I'm not alright! Not even close. Not by a fucking mile. You do realize that you and I just murdered a girl. Don't you?"

"No, we didn't. She was a willing participant. It was, what do they call it: an industrial accident, pure and simple. Nothing more."

"It was. But she'd be alive right now if we'd called 9-1-1 right away."

Blake frowned. "No man, incorrect. She would've bled out in the ambulance even if it arrived in five minutes."

"We hid the body. That makes us criminals, Blake."

He nodded. "Yes, it does, Liam. Not murderers, but criminals for sure, yes. In prison, hard men rape boys like us. We'd become their pincushions. You'd learn to swallow cum just to save your own asshole. You seriously need to snap out of the self-guilt trip and move past it. I'm super worried about José."

Liam hesitated. "Are you having nightmares?"

"Nope. You?"

"Yeah. Bad ones."

Blake forced a grin of supreme confidence. "This too shall pass, my friend."

Three nights after the scene, lying in bed, Blake wrestled with the decision to publish the snuff movie to sell downloads.

The woman in the vid looks nothing like fourteen-year-old Candy, not even remotely. It would be the most realistic snuff film ever for the sickos to jerk-off to, watching her screaming and dying for real. Nothing to ID us except for José screaming "Holy shit! You guys really stabbed her!" but he was so worked up it didn't sound like him; sounded like a mouse huffing a helium balloon.

He stroked his chin.

Might as well profit from all this trouble. No police-types have asked any questions: so far so good. By now they've asked her parents for the names of everyone she has ever brought home, dates and friends, to interrogate. If they haven't questioned me by now, it means Candy never told her rents about the few times we hooked up. But she had to have told girlfriends. No woman can keep a secret. I need to have an alibi for that night. I was home, in my room the whole time. I always leave the stereo playing even when I'm not in there. My parents never know what's going on with me. They'll remember the music and the light from under my door. They'll back me up a hundred percent. They won't ask me any questions, either. They never do.

Blake fell asleep. He dreamed he was back at the river, alone this time, sitting on a rock overhanging a few feet above a deep, dark pool close to shore. His dreaming mind returned him to the place where he once went with a girlfriend who knew about the vista and loved it. She had jumped from the ledge into the river. When she resurfaced, she said excitedly, "Come on in, Blake! Feels good!"

He had screamed down at her, "No way! The water is filthy. You are gross! It'll take you a week's worth of hot showers before I even consider kissing you again, Wendy! I am so dead serious. Sewerage treatment plant right upriver—eight of them to this point. Mercury, PCBs, toxic chemicals, dead animals—probably even dead humans in there."

Now in the dream he found himself transported back to that ledge. He wondered what had ever happened to Wendy, who had attended a Catholic middle school. *She was so nice,* his dream-voice reflected.

He stared into the dark depths of the pool a few feet below the ledge. Moonlight reflected up from the serene surface. He thought he saw something under the water, something white. It grew larger. At first, the white shape broke the surface. It bobbed with the slow undercurrents. Hands—pruney, blistered and greenish black—reached up for him.

"Come on in, baby. Feels so good!" A mouth moved behind stretched white cloth. The voice sounded burbled, like when young kids discover the playful joy of talking to each other underwater in a swimming pool.

Blake jolted awake. His heart thudded, face and lower back slick with sweat. He blinked and rubbed his face. Light from the full moon streamed into his room through the metal insect screen, along with comfortable sixty-five-degree breezes. He scanned the dim room and saw his laptop, dad's camera tethered to it by a USB cord, exactly as he'd left it.

Propped on his elbows, he stared at the laptop, at the screensaver generating muted, erratic patterns of light. He failed to notice the slow increase of shadow blocking the moonlight. He shook his head, laid back against the pillow, and closed his eyes.

Can I get back to sleep after that whopper of a nightmare? Doubtful.

He opened them and stared straight ahead at the window. He thought he saw a flash of white as it dropped from sight.

My mind's playing tricks.

Half asleep, the secure chat client on his computer dinged loudly, and roused him. "Fuck! Forgot to mute," he said, and got up to do just that. He saw the message alert, that it was from Liam. Time in the lower right screen corner: 4:33 a.m. "What the…"

"She's floating outside my window. I'm looking straight at her."

Blake responded, "No, she isn't. Give it a rest, will you?"

He saw the tell-tale dots, evidence of Liam's typing. "Hurry it up!" Blake whispered at the screen.

The message: "Currents maybe dragged her along the bottom. Sheet in tatters. Face cut up. Skin green, black; lips swollen ten times their size. Eyes bulging. Hands wrinkled. Skin coming off. Can smell her through the screen. Rotten. Teeth pink. Hair gone in places. Tongue swollen out. I told her to leave. She won't. I don't know what to do. I'm so scared."

Blake typed. "You're imagining it, Liam, buddy. Like a nightmare except you're awake. Steal some of your dad's vodka, mix it with juice, then go back to bed. You'll see it was all only just a waking nightmare."

No response. As Blake was preparing to return to bed, he heard the ding. Angrily he returned his attention to the chat window. "Voice garbled; lungs filled with river muck. She told me I must stab myself in the gut, or else she will come in and do it for me. She said, 'Eye for an eye, law of the jungle, law of the river, law of the dead.' Blake, what should I do? She's clawing at the screen, rotten fingers. She smells so bad. If she can find me this far from the river, she can rip through the screen and get me.'

Irritated, Blake responded. "Then let her. Fucking nutcase."

He slammed down the laptop lid and returned to bed, though he could not fall asleep. Wide-eyed, he stared at the window.

The sound of the doorbell woke him. The digital clock showed 9:41 a.m. "God," he groaned. Sleeping in this late wasn't his thing, feeling like half the productive day is already gone.

"Blake? Come downstairs honey."

Another groan. He slipped on underwear, jeans, pair of socks and a light green polo that matched his eyes. A quick swish-swash of mouthwash, and he spirited down the stairs in a struggle to restore his lucid brain. He saw two uniformed police officers who stood with his parents at the bottom of the steps. He fought his own shocked reaction. He willed his face to remain peaceful in appearance. "Hi, what's going on, mom?"

"Blake, these detectives need to ask you a few questions. You need to answer them."

"Oookayy. What's this about?"

One asked, "Where were you last night?"

"Um…" he said, willing himself not to blink, and pointed straight up to his bedroom. "Why, did something happen?"

The detectives exchanged glances. The one who asked the question appeared to be the one elected to deliver the hard news. "What is your relationship to Liam Cappi?"

"My best friend since Kindergarten."

"Liam Cappi was found dead this morning in his bed. We have not ruled it a suicide, although signs suggest that his wounds were self-inflicted."

"Oh. My. God!" Blake shouted. Hands flew to his mouth, eyes watery and wide.

"Upon examination of his computer, we found an open chat window. Did you engage in an exchange with him this morning, around half past four?"

Blake nodded. "He dinged me awake. I was… pissed off. He was complaining about a nightmare, I told him that's what it was. He insisted it was real. Something about a monster scratching at his screen telling him to kill himself. Oh my God, Liam! --he *did* it?"

"We found muddy footprints on his carpet leading from the window to his bed, and back. Not his. Small, female. Window screen ripped inward from its frame. Lab guys took samples and are analyzing them now. He wrote to you about a 'she.' The description fits that of a drowning victim. What can you tell us about this?"

Blake shot a glance at his parents. They stared at him. He sensed mistrust. "I don't... nothing. Something his dreaming mind made up. How did he do it? Kill himself, I mean." His throat closed as he said it.

"Two deep stab wounds in his lower abdomen. Bled to death."

"Oh my dear Lord!" said Blake's mother. She started crying.

Blake shook his head. "Everybody loves Liam. His joke videos make everyone laugh. I can't imagine anyone breaking in and killing him."

Turning to leave, a detective asked, "Blake, one more question. Do you know a student named Candy Angelo?"

He felt his guts loosen. He held back a boiling-urgent toilet experience. "Yeah, sure, from school. Heard the name, can picture her face, but I don't know her."

"Thanks for your time, folks. Try to have a good day."

"José never called me back after I left the last message. Would it be okay if I come over?"

"No, Blake, that would be impossible."

"Oh wow—why, may I ask? Did something happen?"

He heard muffled crying. Then, "My son got admitted to the emergency room early yesterday morning. Then he was taken to the State mental hospital in the evening. Our priests could do nothing for him. My son—" she had to pause between sobs. "My son has renounced God altogether. He says Satan has him now, and that only Satan can save him. The priests recommended mental adjudication. Pray for him, Blake," then she openly burst into tears. "They have him sedated in a private room, a padded room. They took the laces from his shoes."

"Oh my God, why padded? Did he try to hurt himself?"

"Yes."

"How?"

Crying, "He tried pushing a knife into his stomach. He only got maybe a half inch inside. I knocked on his door, heard him crying, and he was talking to someone."

"Who?"

"I don't know. When he didn't answer, I kicked open the door and found him doing this terrible thing to himself. Oh my dear God in Heaven, our Father, please spare my son!"

Blake felt electric tingles of shock throughout his entire nervous system. "I am so sorry," he said, "Please take care of yourself, and José."

"Eye for an eye, law of the jungle, law of the river, law of the dead."

He studied these words in the chat window. It felt creepy and repugnant as he read his dead friend's final words. It caused him to wonder about Liam's final thoughts and feelings as he bled out.

Did he blame me? Blame Candy? Who or what left the footprints and tore up his window screen? Did he do all of that himself? Or was it all just part of his waking nightmare?

He stood with his parents at Liam's funeral, witnessing the emotional melt-down of Liam's mother and father, aunts and uncles, and two young sisters.

It was all just an accident, and nothing more. My decision to dispose of Candy's body was smart. If the corpse ever turned up and I got convicted, I'd get maybe a month or a few months of incarceration in a local light security prison for 'Abuse of Corpse' under State law. I am not a murderer; neither was Liam, his thoughts repeated.

Anxiety, paranoia, and now something like claustrophobia: he struggled against the cold, dark, leaden blanket that had settled over his heart and soul, heavier and tighter by the minute, making it increasingly more difficult to rationalize away his guilty conscience. At no time during his strenuous mental dialogue did he even remotely consider going to the police to confess everything.

Back home, he changed out his suit and tie to sit in his underwear and finish the job of posting the Candy video as-is, with zero editing, because that was Liam's department. He charged $49.95 per download. Almost immediately, someone downloaded. Cryptocurrency appeared in his wallet. Comment: "Best ever. So realistic, you'll believe it's real!" That one comment opened the floodgates. By nine that night, the video had enjoyed over seven-thousand downloads with no signs of slowing. He smiled.

If José makes it home, he'll get half. Still, though—I am rich! Screw college; to Hell with that garbage!

He decided to watch the video himself, something he had not yet gathered the courage to do. He locked his bedroom door and adjusted the laptop volume. He clicked 'Play.' There she was.

God, she was beautiful. Waifish body, silky-smooth skin. Crying from my slaps.

As she writhed and protested in her underwear, bathed in candlelight with reddish hues, he felt himself grow hard. He watched himself and Liam lower their knives to just above her belly; he hit 'Pause' long enough to freely access his boy-parts. He used his left hand on the mouse since his right was now full and took it off pause.

He watched the knives penetrate Candy's flat little belly.

I feel it. Muscle memory. How it felt in my hand when the blade slid inside. That brief whiff of perforated bowel. Blade parting flesh; the slippery resistance. José did such an excellent job, as with all the other videos. He captured her emotional reaction, and the gory substance of the 'practical joke' itself—immediately shifting zoom from the entry wound sites to her face. The shock in her eyes, forced all the way open by her own body's fight-or-flight mechanism. Her nervous system was telling her brain the body would soon be dead, but sensation and thought shall continue. You'll have to linger, and suffer, *came the autonomous messaging. Her wet, terrified eyes were a window into that internal communication. Mortal fear, unlike any other.*

Candy's sweet, delicious high-pitched screams went straight from his ears to his sexual organs. His eyes took in every muscle of her body as they tensed and rippled just underneath smooth, taut, unblemished skin. For the first time he took in the murder scene as a dispassionate observer versus active participant; watched her petite, tight little body as it bucked and convulsed helplessly as if laid upon a searing-hot barbeque grill.

Her screams! So desperate; so very afraid. The pain in her guts must have been unbearable! But my ropes prevented her from comforting herself. Trapped in Hell, she was consigned to suffer. Panic on the grandest scale. Look at her eyes! Those frenzied, dying eyes…

Blake experienced the most powerful climax ever, so acutely pleasurable it bordered on pain. Gobs of milky white liquid baptized his bare feet and carpet underneath his desk. It felt as though it might never end, though eventually, it did. Sensations returned to normal down below, and in his mind. He smiled.

Needed that. Under so much tension lately. This is worth fifty bucks. Now I see why I'll be a millionaire by this morning, or sometime this week at the latest.

His exertions left him completely exhausted. He lacked the energy to brush-rinse-floss as was his routine twice daily without fail. He flung himself into bed naked, pulled the sheet and blanket up to his neck, and almost immediately fell into deep sleep.

Awakened by a voice, he opened his eyes. Candy bobbed outside his second-floor bedroom window in an inhuman, unnatural motion.

Please let this be a nightmare, merely the product of an overstressed mind.

Partial skeletonization of the face; eyes that bulged far out of the sockets appeared to be attached to the skull by rubber-bands, movements inhuman. Liam had described lips ten times normal size and in between, a protruding swollen tongue: Tonight, after further putrefaction, only a skeleton's fleshless eternal smile remained. Scalp and neck were covered in a yellow-brown, waxy material. Hair clung in disparate patches at the back of the skull. "Are you a dream?"

"No," it said, drawing out the 'o.'

"Go away! Leave me alone! Leave *us* alone! God knows, it was only an accident!"

"No," it repeated. "Eye for an eye, law of the jungle, law of the river, law of the dead. Three" and it drew out the 'e' "must join us. Liam is here. José should have stayed in church. I cannot touch the faithful or cross hallowed ground. Now, I can get to him. Now—I will," it hissed.

"I'm alive! You hear me? I don't play by any laws of the jungle or river or dead. Go away!"

"Do to you what you did to me." He tried wishing it away with all his strength. The head, neck and trunk remained, moving as in a silent river-like current. Protruding eyes moved and rolled in impossible degrees left-right, up-down—yet both roughly came together into a stare when it spoke. For a moment his brain asked him to speculate on the condition of Candy's body from the neck down; he squeezed his eyes tightly to force away the thought.

Fear turned to anger. He glanced around the room. His eyes settled upon the replica Samurai sword his parents gave him last Christmas in support of his brief interest in a few karate classes. He leapt out of bed, grabbed the sword, unsheathed it, and held it out straight in front. He rushed toward the window at full charge. The blade parted the metal screen like it wasn't even there; the razor-sharp tip burst one of the Candy-thing's eyeballs. It released a foul and malodorous stench. He felt his stomach roll. The specter made no sound; also, it did not move. Blake dropped the sword, bent and vomited. Frightened and furious, he stood to face the screen and aimed to finish it off.

The shambling horror had disappeared.

He restored the sword back into its wall display holder and told himself it had all been a nocturnal vision. He noticed a waxy substance and dried ooze on the outermost blade tip. For the remainder of the night, Blake laid awake staring at the window, with the occasional glance over at the reassuring sword. He knew now with every certainty that he was not losing it, not cracking up.

The corpse is real. Candy's back, and she will never stop! She'll never let this go; not until I am dead.

At some point he decided that he would be safer in prison, scary though it may be.

Safer there than in my own bed. Even if I somehow manage to chop her into six or ten pieces—the pieces will come and get me. Powerful, rotten dead bitch!

When daybreak came, he showered, dressed, and made himself as presentable as possible. He downloaded the MP4 video file to a thirty-gig thumb-drive and pocketed it. He took a rideshare to the police station, where he asked for the two detectives who had visited his parents' home: Glenhold and Miller. It had been Miller who asked the most questions, and it was Miller who was already on duty at seven in the morning. He approached Blake. "Do you have new information for us?"

"Sir, yes. It's an unbelievable story, but it's true. Is there someplace we can sit down?"

In a private conference room, after Miller had read him his Miranda rights, Blake declined the need for an attorney present and granted Miller permission to record the conversation. Blake related every detail of the motel scene and aftermath. When he described the encounter with the corpse at his window, Sergeant Miller raised his hand in a Silence! Enough! movement.

"You say you have the video with you?"

"In my pocket."

"Take it out and put it on the table." Blake complied. "Wait here," he said, and snapped up the thumb-drive. Thirty minutes later, Miller returned with two uniformed officers. "You will be remanded into custody pending a bail hearing," and Blake was led away in handcuffs.

"Thank you, Sergeant Miller. I feel safer already."

Alone in a cell, he reviewed his situation.

Face my parents? Probably never again. Return to home and school after spending a few months in prison—nope. Not feeling it. Can't even imagine it. And what about the Candy-thing stalking around, little pieces dropping off as she goes? Now that the law knows Candy's dead, will they drag the river? Find out what section of river bottom it calls home, exactly where it slithers back to every night after terrorizing us? Might they put an end to this?

Money won't be a problem. Millionaire at age fourteen, in crypto. I can go anywhere! Leave the country even. Ibiza! Forever I've wanted to go there, dance the nights away at the electronic dance music concerts. Amsterdam, Copenhagen. They all speak English over there. I can buy a tricked-out mansion, throw massive parties, fuck every beautiful Euro chick I can lay my hands on.

He sat on the stainless-steel bunk topped with a thin foam pad covered by a sheet and blanket. He washed his face in the combination sink-toilet and dried it with the front of his polo shirt. He felt like the path out of this nightmare was clearer. Infused with hopeful emotions, he decided that since he'd vomited up his last meal, he was hungry; ravenous, in fact. "Hey! Somebody! I need food!" A functionary responded.

There were no windows in his cell and none within range. No clock on the wall. Having passed the empty dinner tray back, he wasn't sure if he would see anyone until morning. Deep-knee bends, push-ups, jumping-jacks: these he did to bleed off nervous energy. He thought of his crypto wallet swelling larger by the minute.

Money can't buy you love. Hah! Just something rich people tell poor people to keep 'em down. Sure, it can. It can buy anything and everything. He laughed out loud.

He found that staring at bars and three walls in a closet-sized room felt old, fast. Might as well sleep. He removed his shoes and the rest of his clothes. He slipped into the hardest, most unforgiving slab of a bed he had ever experienced. He closed his eyes and imagined himself in a sandwich between two European Czech nubiles, one blonde, one brunette, inside his Prague mansion. Focused on this vision, he drifted off.

Water dripped onto his face and woke him with a start. Though they had switched off the overhead light in his cell at some point after he was already asleep, hallway lamps burned brightly all night. He squinted.

A moldering, pale horror. One rubber-band eye lolled down at him. Skeleton teeth grinned. The hideous mouth opened. Sounds gurgled out.

Waxen-yellow fingers on which sloughed skin still clung in spots, as most of the digits were now bright white bone, clutched a steak knife. The belly distended out beyond the boundaries of a pregnant female, as though a pin would pop it, balloon-like. The bra was gone, burst away from the putrefying, bloated chest, just as Candy's tiny little panties had stood no chance against the distended, tumefied lower abdomen and groin. The stench of decomposition filled his nose to the point that he could taste the rot.

"Eye for eye," it gurgled.

"Guard! Help! Somebody, help me!" He meant to yell but, mouth cottony dry and throttled with fear, only managed a barely audible croak.

"You kill you." It sounded wet, like toilet sounds. It turned away from him, raised its right knee, and flopped down its loathsome, rancid groin onto his face. Muffled by rotting meat, only the powers in Heaven and Hell could hear the panicked fear vented in his screams. The Candy-thing pushed down the covers to expose his naked body. It laid the knife on his abdomen. He heard the repetition: "You kill you." Using all his strength, he bucked and contorted. He flailed his limbs and clutched at the thing, which did not move. His mind refused to acknowledge the horrifying spoiled pork-fetid fish flaps which now completely covered his mouth and nose. Rancid black and yellow waxy ichor leaked into his nostrils and down his throat. He gagged and threw up in his mouth. Thus sealed, it was now impossible to breathe. "You kill you." Nothing he did, no matter how hard he fought, made even the slightest improvement to his situation.

He grasped the knife handle. Gingerly he grazed his abdominal skin with the sharp point. He positioned it against the same spot where he had plunged a knife into Candy Angelo. He swallowed his vomit but could no longer breathe. He coughed, but the precious little air that remained in his lungs went nowhere.

His mind replayed the video of her agonies.

How beautiful she had been. This thing that had once been she, a gorgeous middle-school student whom I had repeatedly tasted with all the burning passions of my forefathers.

There is no escape. She will not let me live.

He pushed down against the handle, but the pain caused him to stop. He tried again and stopped. He wept. His brain swam down into a dark river pool from lack of oxygen. The Candy-thing grabbed his right hand and pushed the blade all the way into Blake's small intestine, withdrew it, and pushed it in on the left side, where Liam had originally cut her. "It is finished," burbled the thing. The last words Blake ever heard.

Officers who found him in the morning worried that they would be fired for somehow allowing a prisoner to lay hands on a steak knife. The following week, José was found dead in his padded cell with similar self-inflicted wounds to the abdomen, much to the dismay of facility officials. Despite international authorities continuing to force Web hosts to remove it, only to watch it pop up in a week on some other site, Interrogation of Witch Lilith remains the number one most downloaded fetish film of all time.

Over forty Practical Jokers Clubs have sprung up internationally, more than half in the United States, all of which pay homage to its deceased original founders. After investing two thousand manhours including a dive team, boat operators, shoreline searchers, incident command, side-scan sonar operators, sonar interpreters, cadaver dogs, and ringing up one hundred thousand dollars in expenses, law enforcement had given up the search for Candy Angelo. Her disappearance remains a cold case file. Sergeant Miller is convinced that the boy's hysterical story was nothing but a sick, twisted mind giving vent, and he assumes that eventually the student's body will turn up. "Given time, they usually do," he told a reporter.

Miller could not know at that moment the awful truth of his prediction; nor would he ever connect tens of thousands of dual lower abdominal stabbing suicides happening regularly all over the world to this unsolved case.

Book of the Dead

"Merrick Arthur Bicko," the Judge decreed, "you are hereby stripped of your medical board certifications and license to practice medicine in the State of New York. Have you anything to say before this court passes sentence?"

The lead defense attorney steeled herself for the death-stare from her client, having failed at her mission to exonerate him. Rather, Bicko focused his gaze solely on the judge, his gravelly tenor voice perfectly even. His face revealed no emotion.

"Your Honor, please note that not one family member of the deceased is here today. Not one. Why do you suppose that is so? It is because I acted at their request, with full patient and familial consent. We were all in this together. They are my witnesses, yet this court denied their testimony in this trial. Think of yourself, Your Honor. Not that I wish this upon you and yours: please understand, however, that it is an absolute mathematical certainty that you or someone close to you will become a terminally ill patient. Not living—merely existing. Dulling the intolerable marrow-deep pain with morphine." As Bicko spoke, the judge's face remained patient and placid. Sometimes, Bicko flicked glances at the jury.

"Perhaps your once-sharp mind will go first. Family will consign you to a memory care unit with other terminal dementia patients. Maybe you will recognize the family member who dutifully visits you; imagine his or her embarrassment and grief at seeing your once-proud self in these awful stages of dependent decomposition. Perhaps you'll be lucky and will no longer recognize your loved one, now a stranger to you, this person who comes and goes. But your two new best friends will never leave you: physical pain, and shame. These two will torture you every moment, asleep and awake, with no end in sight. Time will draw out for you like a scalpel. Is that fair to yourself? To your family?"

The judge did not respond. Bicko could tell his impassioned logic was falling on deaf ears. "You must sentence me; I understand. You have a job to do. But Your Honor, is the end I described a fair sentence from Mother Nature?"

"Mr. Bicko—Dr. Bicko—this court would appreciate no further personalization applied by you to its members."

"Yes, Your Honor. I'll close my statement with this: the right to choose one's location, method, and time of dying is inalienable; not a crime. Physician-assisted suicide is the kindest, least painful exit any terminal patient can experience. Every one of my patients begged me for release. Also, it is legal in many nations and in fact encouraged by their health systems. I wish only health and long life for all members of the court and everyone in this room, including Your Honor, and my legal defense team."

The judge studied the defendant. Satisfied that Bicko's statement had concluded, he said, "However, doctor, it is not legal in New York State, despite what may be compassionate motives on your part. The maximum penalty for your crime would involve hundreds of years should each conviction run consecutively. The court hereby sentences you to a minimum of ten years, maximum of twenty-five years, eligible for parole in eight years. You will be remanded to the Otisville Correctional Facility in Orange County, New York." With one sharp rap of his gavel, the judge said, "Court adjourned."

Eight years' worth of dust to clean from surfaces, filmy build-up on windows to wash, and general repairs for Bicko to make all by himself—though he would have it no other way. "For an academic, I'm pretty handy." This mantra he now recited daily as his sense of autonomy and self-worth slowly returned. Otisville had changed wardens twice during his stay; all three had seen fit to assign him a residency in the prison infirmary, to assist those licensed medical professionals in and out on rotation whose job it was to stitch up the wounded, pronounce death, and deal with the usual illnesses.

Fine by me, he thought. *I've heard prison abuse stories. No prisoners bothered me. I was a top member of the Elite Protected Class; me and the mob bosses. Board exams were harder than the easy time I did in OCF. They all viewed me as an essential player in their dolorous ecosystem. Bet I'm sorely missed.*

Satisfied with all the inside work and roof repairs, he opened windows to air out the musty staleness and sharp tang of cleaning chemicals. Refreshed, he decided to focus his energies on the property. Under deep blue, clear October skies, crisp cool air permeated with the delightful aromas of burning leaves and woodsmoke. He set to work clearing dead trees and limbs. He purchased a gasoline-powered chainsaw and watched online videos to learn how to operate it safely. Other videos taught him how to 'top' trees and cut them so that they would fall away from the house, not onto it.

After a few weeks of applied practice, he decided that he thoroughly enjoyed the work, which felt therapeutic, not like labor. A going-out-of-business landscaper advertised tools for sale, including a truck-trailer combo pulling a hand-fed disc-style commercial woodchipper designed for tree service professionals regularly hired for large tree takedowns. The chipper fascinated him, with its fifteen-by-twenty-five-inch throat opening to easily accept multiple branches and whole trees.

No problem pulling in big trees, crushing limby, forked branches, or processing multiple stems at once armed with this monster. I could do this work for others and charge for it. Wear a straw fedora or British mil-spec camo hat with neck flap; grow a goatee; nobody will recognize me.

It was decided. Although he had saved money, like everyone else he wanted to feel like a useful member of society. *Open a tree service, why not?* The next day, he took a taxi to the seller's location, who showed him how to work the woodchipper and maintain it. "Just curious, how much do you charge people for, say, taking out one large tree?"

"Depends on how busy I am. For a biggun, sixteen Bens or two large, there-bouts, dependin'. If they need me to grind the stump, I tack on seventy-five. That's if they pay by check. If cash, I discount it a percent or two, sometimes five if they're clever hard asses. If you get cash, come income tax report time, damned if I can recall how much I got," he said with a wink. "Cash leaves no trail, as they say."

Bicko negotiated a cash price and handed the landscaper a thick envelope. He drove home with the cumbersome rig and practiced backing it into his driveway.

He named his new small enterprise "Trees-Be-Gone," and advertised online using a simple strategy: shadow local handyman and driveway paver ad placements. The strategy worked. Immediately, he fielded two potential new customer calls. Both wanted medium-size dead trees cut into sixteen-inch lengths, stacked, to become weathered and dry enough to split into firewood. He did the jobs, enjoyed each, and pocketed over a thousand dollars in cash.

Gives me cardio and resistance exercise. Surely, I need both. And nobody recognized Doctor Death, as the media had labeled me eight years ago.

Word-of-mouth marketing resulted in a growing web of new customers. Long before radio, satellites, and television, there were whispers down the lane. He smiled as he counted out eleven thousand dollars in cash. As Halloween rolled into Thanksgiving, he felt good; alive again, mostly.

Though something felt missing. He'd read in psychology journals about physicians, especially cardiac surgeons experiencing a "God Complex," though he had never deeply internalized its meaning. After eight years trapped inside his own head with little else to do but ponder life's mysteries, he still never thought of himself as being more divine than others, though he readily acknowledged that some, possibly even himself, might consider themselves a little more gifted and powerful than mere mortals.

Missing until, surfing about his last home at Otisville Correctional, he happened upon an article about botched executions at prisons. Unskilled, non-medically licensed staff had been unable to locate suitable veins for proper insertion of two intravenous cannulas used to deliver lethal injections. These were not one-off failures, but rather a national problem.

The Bureau of Prisons apparently has no interest in finding qualified experts at venipuncture willing to end people's lives.

Taking the lives of trees could never deeply scratch the itch burning deeply within him, recalling now something he had said once to his "cellie"—the man with whom he shared his two-bunk prison cell—"Why should taking human lives remain the sole purview of God?"

God Complex. Now I get it. Finally, it resonates and hits close to home. I own it. He spent the next few troubled nights lying awake in bed attempting to self-psychoanalyze his core.

The id creates the demands, the ego adds the needs of reality, and the superego adds morality: somewhere between the three, I have a personality deficit, though I would not go so far as to label it a disorder. I was born to end lives. I'd label it a calling. The pope of death.

The next day, using certified mail, he sent twenty-five letters, identical except for inserting the names of each state's chief executioner. He didn't expect any responses, but doing it made him feel positive. He continued his "Tree-Be-Gone" work and checked his snail-mail and email twice daily for responses. None came. He ate Chinese take-out alone at home on Christmas Eve. One person called asking for two cords of firewood. "Sorry, I cut down trees and either leave sixteen-inch logs or grind whole trees in a woodchipper." Otherwise, there was nothing in the mailbox except Current Resident junk mail, and no other calls.

On New Year's Eve, he watched the ball-drop ceremony in Times Square on television, then went to bed. The first week of the new year felt like the lowest point of his life. He'd spent eight years with almost zero privacy, always hemmed in by men. To go from that to utter aloneness lowered a melancholy shroud over him, dense and novel, like a castaway on Enceladus, Saturn's sixth icy rock moon. Ever so fleetingly, thoughts of lethally injecting himself flickered in and out.

Dreadfully lonely, suffering from Major Depressive Disorder, wearing only a sweater he sat at his desk. It gave him a modicum of relief from dark feelings and self-destructive thoughts to pleasure himself; to remind him of the feeling of romance. The free pornography movies he watched led him to authentic torture porn movies from Budapest. For optimal immersion, he had the volume cranked high. With his right arm pumping furiously, he had nearly reached a crescendo when a startlingly loud 'ding' alerted him to the arrival of a new email, which interrupted his reveries. *Probably spam*, he thought angrily. He paused the porn movie and opened his email window.

It had a dot-gov address. His pulse quickened. He clicked it and started reading.

Dear Merrick Bicko,

Thank you for contacting our department. Regretfully, currently we have no job postings to align with your curriculum vitae and listed skills. Such positions come with various benefits, including salary with annual increases; full health insurance coverage; mileage reimbursement; health savings account; pension program; and paid time off. Following a review of your criminal background check, such positions shall remain unavailable to you.

However, if you would be interested in a contract position, compensation will be rendered on a per-job basis in the amount of $450, reported to the IRS via Form 1099-NEC, and we have two executions scheduled in January. Unfortunately, we cannot compensate you for travel expenses. If you are willing to accept these conditions, please complete and return the attached Form W-9. Once received, we will provide the date, time, and address for the first contract execution.

He recognized that the dot-gov address, prison emblem, and rank of the signatory were all legitimate. Naked from the waist down, his tumescent member bobbed and dripped as he printed the form, completed, signed, and scanned it, and replied with the attachment six minutes after hearing the ding. He had cc'd his parole officer, who called the following Monday to approve Bicko's crossing of the New York State line, given that the destination and timing were so easily verifiable through the officer's Bureau of Prisons In-Mail with the warden.

His body re-infused with endorphins and hormones quashed for nearly a decade, he hit 'Play' on the interrupted movie and soaked in the authentic, deeply suffering shrieks, sobbing, and wails as a pretty, young Hungarian woman gave vent to her very real agonies.

She consented to suffer authentic Inquisition-style tortures of the damned, for money. She deserves it. Every painful bit of it.

He carried these images to the shower, where he finished himself and watched his seed swirling down the drain.

Feeling better than he had in nearly a decade, he took a brisk, long walk facing a cold January sun. His sinuses welcomed the crisp infusion of frozen, lifeless, steel-scented winter air perfumed solely by the delightful fragrance of burning trees.

Chapman's lethal three-drug cocktail is inferior to my own. I pioneered the initial introduction of ketamine. Chapman; Kevorkian: only I had the cleverness to dose them with a dissociative anesthetic to induce a trance-like state. I relieved their pain and melted away anxiety and fear. Of course, laws will constrain me from adding ketamine to the cocktails I'll soon deliver. He thought of his remaining personal stash. Shelf-life warnings aside, it might remain potent.

Staff will remark on how peaceful and serene my condemned comported themselves compared to all other executions preceding my arrival. My reputation will spread throughout the Bureau of Prisons. I shall become the most sought-after executioner in history. Born to end lives: therein lies the truth, and the salvation of my reputation.

Redemption is now close at hand. Close enough to taste.

He spent more on food, fuel, and hotel lodging than his expected independent contractor agreement remuneration. "Doesn't matter. I'm on a mission," he muttered to himself. At 5:30 p.m., on the afternoon of the first execution scheduled for 6:00 p.m., in the maximum-security prison's Death Row, Bicko sat before the warden's desk. From a steaming paper cup too hot to hold, he sipped the worst coffee he had ever tasted. Underneath his white physician's lab coat, he wore a white shirt and solid black silk tie of outdated width, tied in a crooked single Windsor knot. The prison warden, a large, fit-looking African American retired law enforcement officer, with tinges of gray around his temples, registered the subtle changes in Bicko's face. "Sorry, doc. Budget cuts. Wakes you up though, doesn't it?"

With one nod and a bright smile, he said, "I'm grateful for the coffee, more so for the opportunity to serve. Thank you again."

The warden leaned into a conspiratorial posture and practically whispered in a low baritone. "Confidentially, doc, at the time of your felony conviction in New York, my mother was on her way out with acute myelogenous leukemia. The poor old girl's liver and spleen were so swollen she looked about to burst. God bless her. In so much pain and for so long until she finally went out hard. I was following your story at the time. Not that it means much now, but I was one hundred percent on your side. If doc-assisted suicide were legal, she would've jumped at it; and I would've swallowed my bile and gone along with it. I'm the reason you're here. No person should leave this world violently. Jesus knows, I believe that as deeply in my bones as she felt the leukemia bedded in hers."

Bicko nodded somberly. "At the time, using a drug combo of my own design, all one hundred thirty-one patients I assisted felt more comfortable before and during their transition than anyone departing under Chapman's strict three-injection sequence of sodium thiopental to induce coma, pancuronium bromide inducing complete paralysis, including that of the lungs and diaphragm, then stopping the heart with potassium chloride."

The warden's eyebrows went up. "Do tell."

Bicko leaned in as well and kept his volume low. "Warden, what would you say if I told you that mentally, these poor souls were already out-of-body before the thiopental hit their brains? Might you be interested in possibly allowing me this modicum of flexibility?"

The warden's lips pressed together, and he shook his head. "Sorry, doc. We must strictly follow the three-injection protocol. The law's the law."

"Yes, yes, of course, and I will follow it. I would have it no other way. What I'm suggesting is that a few minutes before you strap the condemned onto the gurney," as he spoke, he reached into his pocket and placed the ketamine inhaler on the desk, "squirt three aerosol doses into each nostril, asking him to snort back hard with each dose. From that moment forward, his mind will disassociate from his body. He will feel completely relaxed, yet still able to say his last words, or whatever standard operating procedures you follow here."

"Not him, doc: her. The condemned is a 'she.' Her last words."

"A female." He ignored the low electric tingle in his groin. "I see. May I ask her name, and for what crime was she convicted?"

"Veronica Rodriguez. She and her boyfriend tortured their infant son to death."

"Yikes."

"Happens more often than you'd think."

"Yes, yes. Most unfortunate."

The warden glanced at his atomic watch to the WWVB time signal radio station near Fort Collins, Colorado, with an error margin of only one second to one hundred million years. "Show-time, doc. You're on in ten." With the stealth of a shoplifter, he scooped up Bicko's inhaler and spirited it deep down in his pants pocket.

Intravenous tubing led to a room next to the execution chamber, separated from the condemned by a curtain. As a prison employee prepared to load the three drugs into lethal injection syringes, Bicko tapped his shoulder. "Please allow me. I am—was—a licensed physician. The government is paying me for a specific result, not for a best effort. The only way I can guarantee said result is if I fully control all steps in the process. Do you mind?"

"Not at all, doc. We've had a few botches here. I don't like the pressure and responsibility, truth be told. Now it's all on you." The officer stepped aside.

A thought struck Bicko. "When life leaves the body, all its muscles relax completely. This includes involuntary and smooth muscles. I'm sure you know this. How do you deal with it, put a diaper on the condemned?"

The employee nodded. "And an entire box of tampons up her ass. They don't pay us enough to deal with that mess and stink."

Bicko nodded. The tingle ran from his privates to his prostate, so strong this time that he was forced to consciously acknowledge it. "Also, I need to observe the patient—I mean, the condemned. Would you mind pulling back the curtain to afford me unobstructed visual access?" With a shrug, the officer walked over and wheeled away the free-standing curtain that separated the executioner's anti-room from the death chamber.

Bicko deftly managed each step himself. Satisfied, he turned to face the chamber, his face and posture a picture of serenity. He awaited the arrival of his first customer. A curtain over an observation window separated the condemned from a witness room. From his current angle through a side gap, he counted a full gallery. A sobbing Hispanic woman who appeared to be roughly his own age, early sixties, whom he assumed to be the condemned woman's mother. Several field reporters with PRESS badge lanyards around their necks commingled with uniformed prison personnel.

Double side doors swung inward. Bicko watched two uniformed employees holding the arms of the walking condemned, with the warden out in front and an officer behind. They led her to the stationary gurney. She wore a short-sleeved orange prison jumpsuit and blue medical booties. Bicko noticed her thick black hair appeared damp from her final shower.

The two men guided Veronica down onto the light blue vinyl gurney. They secured her ankles, calves, and waist with three-inch wide black buckled straps. Her arms were the last to get strapped onto outstretched projections. *Like a crucifixion*, Bicko thought. The warden looked at the prisoner, then at Bicko. He nodded. On top of a stainless-steel tray stand beside the gurney, Bicko noted an antiseptic swab, rolls of white medical tape, safety scissors to cut the tape, and two intravenous cannulas. He walked to her and closely examined her inner arms. He thumped and squeezed them. *No question they're amply feeding this evil little chunky monkey. No pronounced veins, given her percentage of body fat. This is precisely why they hired me.*

Highly skilled at venipuncture, he quickly identified a vein in her left arm. With wry amusement, he swabbed her with antiseptic. *Wouldn't want her dying of infection*, he thought, battling back a smile. He inserted the first cannula. He repeated the procedure on her right arm, inserting the back-up cannula to guard against any potential malfunction of the first. He opened her jumpsuit and exposed her naked breasts. He adhered five electrocardiogram leads to her torso, signals from which he would use to pronounce death. He closed her orange jumpsuit. He leaned close to her head. "How do you feel, Miss Rodriguez?"

"Okay."

Mission accomplished. *The warden took our last-minute exchange to heart. Her placid response proves two things: the warden had made proper use of the aerosolized ketamine, and my last remaining stock remains potent after eight years. So far, so good.*

A uniformed officer pressed buttons until the top portion of the motorized gurney tilted Veronica's face and upper body toward the observation window at a forty-five-degree angle. The warden gave a nod; the two who had led her in moved to either side of the curtains and parted them. The warden's tinny electronic voice addressed the gallery through speakers. "Observers are cautioned to maintain silence," he reminded them. He paused to briefly inspect each member of the gallery. "Veronica Rodriguez, before your sentence is carried out according to State law, do you have any last words?"

A dozen pairs of eyes drilled into hers as she panned the witnesses left to right. Her gaze fell on her mother. "I'm sorry, mama. May God forgive me. Please pray the Lord lets me be with my little Edwin in Heaven. I want to tell him how sorry I am about what happened to him…and that I love him so, so very much."

Hate to be the one to tell you, Veronica: after the body dies, there's nothing more, Bicko thought.

The warden nodded at him. Patently distrusting the prison's electronic drug delivery system, slowly he depressed the canister containing sodium thiopental. He studied Veronica's eyes as they closed. Glancing at his watch, patiently he ticked off a full minute to allow the drug to disperse throughout her system. She was fully unconscious. He pushed the pancuronium bromide into her, eyes fixed on her chest. Satisfied she had taken her final breath; he delivered the final death blow. His push of potassium chloride put an end to her cardiovascular function, forever. As he watched the electrocardiogram slip from arrhythmia to flat line, he pronounced her dead. The warden informed the gallery.

Bicko watched the hysterical mother's complete meltdown. Then he acknowledged the turgid swelling in his underwear, caused by it.

As the two officers closed the curtains, the warden approached him. "Doc, you did so very well! Six-and-a-half minutes—that, sir, is a new record time! And not one single hitch! Exactly the way these terrible episodes need to go and were meant to go. Can't tell you how grateful I am." Bicko made brief eye contact with all the nodding staff members. "I mean, how grateful we are, the entire team, for your work here today."

Bicko acknowledged the compliment with a curt nod. "Your staff are obviously very capable and experienced. I compliment you all as well," he said, his face a mask of false modesty. He drew closer to the warden. "What did she choose for her last meal? Just curious."

"Vaca frita and sticky toffee pudding. Said it wasn't bad. I'll need to inform the prisoner who prepared it. The State-appointed Chaplain thought it smelled good."

"What will become of Veronica's body?"

"The Rodriguez family will send a mortician to claim her body. Those without families get buried in the prison cemetery. Simple concrete headstones with names, birth and death dates, made here by inmates in the masonry shop. If the condemned were famously known for something, say, for example a nickname, sometimes they'll add it on their own accord. With my permission, of course. Anyway, thank you again, doc. I do hope you're available for next week's execution. I'll call the head of the Bureau and negotiate travel expenses and higher pay for you or at least give it my best shot. Your services are worth far more than scheduled contractor rates."

As the staff unstrapped Veronica's body and moved her to a standard wheeled gurney for transport, the warden reached out his hand. Bicko shook it. "Yes, Warden. You can count on it. Also, if you would be so kind, please share today's success story, including the ketamine aerosol, with your colleagues at the twenty-four other prisons. It's not about the pay. Please understand, this is about showing kindness and mercy to those who probably never received much throughout their entire lives." The warden slipped the aerosol spray bottle into his right hand.

Alone in the hallway, from his right lab coat pocket, Bicko pulled out a black gel pen and his old Moleskine classic ruled-lined hardcover little black pocket notebook. He thumbed past more than a dozen pages filled with one hundred thirty-one names, dates, and times. Under the last name entered over a decade ago, he wrote Veronica Rodriguez's name along with the date and time, accurate to the precise second her heart monitor first flatlined, as well as what she had eaten.

Bicko arrived home to a maxed-out voicemail folder and a full email inbox. Only four percent were about tree removal. The lion's share were inquiries from prison wardens and high-level functionaries communicating on their behalf. Grinning and tumescent, he indulged in a microwave dinner and a bit of self-release in the shower as he recalled Veronica's eyes at the exact moment he closed them with his heart-stopper death blow, the aggrieved mother's hopeless wails ringing in his head. He fell into bed and slept soundly the entire night.

He spent the next few days relearning how to manage a busy schedule; how to use Web meeting software as required by several wardens; how to book his own low-fare flights and discount hotels. He accepted every tree-cutting job.

Exercise. After eight years of having sex only with myself, I need to shape up and go seduce a few ladies.

By ten that evening, instead of the usual yawns and sleepiness, he felt completely wired. He put on his walking shoes and headed out into the invigorating New York January cold, dark night.

Cloud cover suggested a possible snowstorm coming. He walked to one of the seldom-traveled unlit roads a mile from his house, surrounded by woodland on both sides. Under a starless, moonless obsidian sky, barely able to see the road beneath his feet with any surety, he decided he'd had enough and turned around.

Before taking his second step toward home, he stopped cold, when he heard a voice not his own. A woman's voice. In the vacuum-like silence of the windless outdoors, he would have recognized a normal speaking voice from perhaps a few hundred yards away. This sounded far closer. Quite close. Almost as though the voice had come from somewhere overhead. He strained listening. Hearing nothing, he set his mind on solving the riddle of the voice.

Female, Mezzo-soprano. One word—can't make it out. Sounded like 'good' or 'gut.' A low cloud ceiling; a fragment of a conversation repercussed from a source miles away and bounced to my ear. It is decided. Satisfied with his own sagacity, he retraced his former course back home.

He took a long hot soaking bath first, an indulgence he always found very relaxing, followed by a quick shower. Hair damp, he climbed into bed. Even thus, it still took some time for him to transition his brain from wake to sleep. Hours later he awoke from a highly poignant and life-like dream.

I never remember dreams for long. Why does this one persist? It's as though my brain insists on replaying the memory of an actual event. Veronica Rodriguez in my living room power recliner adjusted to a forty-five-degree elevation exactly as she was on her gurney of death. Eyes open but not like before. Unnatural. The eyes of a vulture, brown irises now jetty black, including the sclera which should be white, with a cataract-like death glaze over them.

He shivered. No matter how hard he tried, Veronica's doomy, dead eyes remain fixed on him. His dreaming mind noticed that her hair, by now, had dried. *Unbrushed. Looks like a rat's nest. Barefoot, a manila cardstock tag dangled motionlessly from the big toe of her right foot. Zero movement, frozen in place.*

"Hello, Miss Rodriguez," he watched himself say. "How do you feel?"

Nothing. Only then, the rigor-mortis mouth slowly opened, lips purple and rubbery, tongue blue. "Good," came the reply, though he knew it could not have issued from her non-functioning diaphragm. Rather the sound had come up from dead lungs, like an echo in the woods under a low cloud ceiling.

In a chilling mockery of the living, the corners of its open mouth upturned ever so slightly. Frozen cheek flesh rippled almost imperceptibly into a grotesque parody of a smile.

Dear Heavens. Is my brain broken?

There would be no more sleep tonight, of that he was certain. He dressed and reluctantly tip-toed down to his living room. He flicked on the light switch. A sigh when he found the recliner positioned bolt upright just as he'd left it.

I needed to see it. Not sure why, but I did.

He poured grape juice into a large mug of ice, placed it atop the circular cork mat on his heavy dark-walnut desk, and pulled up a browser. He searched on 'Scholarly Articles for Psychological Effects on Executioners.' Before hitting ENTER, he contemplated the one hundred thirty-one patients he had 'executed' across earlier decades, after which nary a dream had ever plagued him.

Merely a one-off incident.

The first title arrested his attention. 'Flashbacks, nightmares and other post-traumatic stress related symptoms are frequently seen in prison wardens, executioners, and corrections officers… thirty-one percent will suffer from PTSD."

Weak men invent trauma to excuse themselves.

The next few hours he spent poring over peer-reviewed articles.

Head-shrinkers: a branch of medicine about which I have many doubts.

He concluded that there is absolutely no PTSD manifesting within himself.

I am mentally awake, aware, and healthy am I. Only just a bad dream. Happens to the best of us.

The following week, after a two-hour flight and rental car drive to the prison, the same warden met him with a huge warm smile. He enclosed Bicko's right hand inside both of his. He followed the warden inside where, during the next hour, he ushered convicted serial killer, Morris Johnson, out of this world. Quickly he dropped off the rental and boarded another flight to the West Coast, armed with a fresh new ketamine inhaler bottle from his private stock. At San Quentin State Prison, he repeated his manual procedure for a different warden and staff. Convicted pedophile and murderer, Ines Barrera, was strapped to the light blue gurney. Bicko asked how he felt. A baritone version of Veronica Rodriguez, same accent and identical answer: "Okay."

Alone in the rental car, he entered Morris Johnson and Ines Barrera, along with their exact moments of cardiac stoppages and last meal choices into his little black book.

From there, he flew to the Texas State Penitentiary at Huntsville, where he spent an awful night lying fitfully upon the most uncomfortable hotel room mattress he'd ever experienced, the atmosphere perfumed with the bitter-sharp tang of old mildew. At 12:33 p.m., sipping coffee in the Warden's office, he pulled the ketamine from his lab coat pocket.

The inhaler I used on Ines Barrera. Why should I worry about spreading germs? They're dead in a few minutes anyway. Now that I've lost scrip-writing privileges, I need to maximize what supply I have left.

He placed the bottle on the warden's desk and recited his now polished sales pitch in favor of the drug. The warden eyed the ketamine with curiosity.

"Convict's name is Violet Roxie."

"May I ask her age, and for what she was convicted?"

"Twenty-four, convicted of a horrendous murder. She and another girl broke into an old man's house demanding money. He didn't have much. So she tortured him to death. Poked him deep, sixty-seven times in the abdomen with an ice pick. All that perforation didn't kill him straight off. Took the lid off a live table lamp, broke the bulb, and shoved that electrified socket with jagged glass edges straight down the poor old bastard's throat. A decorated Korean War veteran died slow, in agonizing pain. Medical examiner said it probably took his old heart fifty minutes to bleed him out, not seven feet from the freedom of his own front door. The other girl testified against her for a lighter sentence."

"Wow. So young. Life about to end before it even began."

The warden nodded. "When the judge pronounced sentence, before he banged his gavel, he closed with this sentence: 'Rarely has it been my misfortune to witness such depravity and maliciousness of disposition.' I read her file. One hundred thirty-eight IQ, intelligent and lucid. No hard criminal record. I wouldn't describe Violet Roxie as a model prisoner, either. Normally they find God, or He finds them—however it works. Most are repentant and compliant, consumed with regret and sorrow. But oh no, doc, not this one. Not by a damned sight. The prison chaplain explained to her that human life consists of membership in a society of equals and consists of nothing more than a series of decisions large and small. Her accumulated decisions are what led to the State's revocation of her human privileges. He implored her to confess, to repent. She screamed out her innocence to the bitter end. Tragic. I have a girl of my own, exact same age."

Thinking of his gentle daughter, he grabbed and examined the ketamine squeeze bottle and gave it a reassuring shake before dropping it into his right front pants pocket. As the warden walked, Bicko could see its outline through the tight cloth. "You sure this'll calm her down?" asked the Warden, patting the bulge. "She won't be scared, pissed off, or feel anything?"

Bicko grinned. "A hundred percent. Thank me later."

The warden entered first and moved to the side of the gallery window. Behind him, two officers tightly held the condemned woman. Bicko's first look at Violet Roxie caught him completely off-guard.

He could not tear his eyes from the contour of the widow's peak above the lofty and pale forehead. *In beauty of face, few maidens could ever equal her! Faultless! Unblemished taut young skin rivaling the purest ivory; the commanding extent and repose; the gentle prominence of the regions above the temples. Long blonde tresses glossy and luxuriant, naturally-curling with life of their own. Orange jumpsuit form-fitted over her lithe, petite body. The smallness of her breasts, narrow waist, angular hips. A woman in a child-like body.*

Only with ample force of will did he finally succeed in averting his gaze.

He flicked a glance at the warden who stared at him with an expression Bicko perceived as, 'Remember what she did to the old man…depravity and maliciousness of disposition.' Nevertheless, his pulse raced. He felt dew forming in his underwear, cold and wet in the air-conditioned executioner's room.

At the warden's blink and nod, Bicko approached her. *Like buttered velvet,* he thought, as his fingers almost fully encircled her tiny bicep as he wiped antiseptic onto her skin. Gently and skillfully, he inserted the two cannulas.

He opened her top and laid bare a chest of arrested development, like that of a pre-teen. Pressing the adhesive electrodes to her petite ribcage felt like sex, to him. He deliberately grazed a nipple. Acutely aware of his full, wet erection, he leaned down. "Good evening, Violet, I'm Doctor Bicko. How do you feel?"

She didn't answer immediately. After a few seconds, she said, "I did not murder the old man. She did. You're murdering me for someone else's sin. I'll be back to see you out, pervert. I see right through you, Bicko the Sicko. I had pizza. Put that in your little black book. Abandon all hope, ye who enter here."

Did the warden skip the ketamine? he wondered, eyeing the warden with a questioning glance. The warden gave a nearly imperceptible shrug and tapped the Ketamine bulge in his pants pocket. Bicko walked away to take up his task with the canisters. Defenses obliterated, now he could think of nothing apart from Violet's memorial eyes.

Beautiful, bitter child with otherworldly insight. Somehow just now, she peered deeply into the darkest recesses of my personality. She read into me. She perceived the parts of me I conceal from the world and most of the time, even to myself. She probed my world with those hypnotic green eyes, of a wild and ghastly vivacity. Those cat eyes gleam with the lurid luster of a fire not of this earth; even now she continues to stare into me. Most unsettling. Get hold of yourself, Arthur.

"Violet Roxie," said the Warden, "before your sentence is carried out according to State law, do you have any last words?"

At no time did she break eye contact with her executioner. "I did not do the things of which I am accused and convicted. Further investigation will reveal this. Too late! By then your sin will be unforgiveable. I see the bulge under your zipper. And I'll be back real soon to escort you to Hell, you sadistic murderer, you apostate of Satan. Until then, sweet dreams, sicko-Bicko."

The warden met his gaze, shrugged, shook his head in disgust, and motioned with his finger. Bicko's face felt sunburnt. He might as well have stood there naked from the waist down for all to see what somehow only she could. Her words aroused in him new, novel, exceedingly dark emotions.

She exposed me to the world…and to myself.

Angry and vindictive, with a faster-heavier push than usual he jammed the anesthetic into Violet's blood stream. Her eyes fixed on his, he figured she recognized the nearly imperceptible smile at the corners of his mouth. Instead of waiting one full minute for the anesthetic to take effect, thirty-seven seconds later he pushed the pancuronium bromide.

How do you like that, you little cunt? Loving that intense pain deep inside your organs? At this moment you're experiencing the precise sensation of being disemboweled. Unparalleled agony. If only you could scream, ha-ha-ha! I made that impossible with the first push. If you could scream right now you would rupture eardrums. Reading me now? I do hope so. Bitch.

Due to the paralyzing effect of the chemical, her body merely spasmed. Weakly she coughed, eyelids closed. *Fun part's over.* He ended her brief life with a heart-stopper push. The cardiac monitor showed a weak sine wave. *Hm. Longer than I've ever seen. Spirited little she-devil; she sure is a fighter. I could almost admire her for that,* he thought. At 1:37 p.m., Violet Roxie flatlined. He pronounced her dead then turned to leave.

"Where's the fire, doc?" asked the warden. Bicko barely heard him.

I need to be alone. No time to inquire about her last meal. Wait—she told *me pizza! How did she know about my book? Oh God, what I have done—what have I tapped into here? I just lost control. She really saw me; saw right through me; exposed me. God damn it, this feels so humiliating. This was never part of the plan. Pull it together, doctor.*

"Um, sorry. Business is booming, warden, sad to report. Busy, busy, busy. I'm confident our paths will cross again."

"Doctor, what you just did, I believe, is a new world record. Five minutes-five seconds. You, sir, were born to this work. You really are that good surprise, surprise! Not that I don't place full faith in my colleagues' references but seriously, just wow. Exceptional! Can't thank you enough. Please make yourself available soon. We need you."

His ego, along with all sense of false modesty and professional bearing, just got shredded by Violet Roxie. He had never felt so humiliated and raw, his entire body one big, exposed nerve. "Thanks, warden, for the opportunity. Have a good evening." He scampered away without returning the courtesy of shaking the Warden's extended hand.

As Texas was the last job for the week, also for the month of February, he took a direct flight to La Guardia airport; from there, a connecting puddle-jumper conveyed him to Stewart International in Orange County, New York, where his vehicle awaited him in long-term parking.

He entered his home at an unfriendly 2:38 a.m.

Exhausted from overthinking the embarrassing scene in Huntsville, he ate a ripe banana in three bites, showered quickly to wash off any travel germs, and went to bed. He fell asleep almost immediately. He did not dream.

Normally up and out of bed before seven-thirty, given it was Saturday, aware that a massive Nor'easter snowstorm was certain to hit his area, Bicko slept in. At 1:07 p.m., the loud and steady percussion of ice pounding against his bedroom window roused him. His first thought: Violet's pretty face; her haunting green eyes. Her words. 'I'll be back to see you out. Pervert. Sicko.' *Somehow, she saw all the way into me.*

He threw on warm flannel pants, a comfy old sweatshirt, stepped into fleece-lined moccasins, and walked down through the living room to his study. At his desk, he entered Violet Roxie and the time of death into his little black book. He entered his password, opened a search engine and entered 'Demonic Possession.' The dominant perspicacious portion of his mind, a state of lucid reason which ruled him since childhood, was by no measure in dispute. It was only that yesterday's exchange with the condemned had cast within him a bleak condition of shadow and doubt that no matter what distractions he pursued, he could not shake. A pall had closed down upon him, like the storm raging outside that very minute.

In one psychiatry journal, his attention was drawn to a high-resolution photograph taken inside a mental hospital that fully arrested his attention. He saved the photo and zoomed in to the disjointed charcoal scribbling made by an adjudicated criminally insane patient on padded white walls. Some of the symbols he captured, saved, and did reverse-image searches. This brought him to nearly identical carvings and sketches made by peoples of ancient cultures, some etched in stone tablets. Ancient desert gods from polytheistic pagans. The more modern '666' from the Book of Revelations in the New Testament. *How could such anthropologically accurate knowledge of ancient cultures even be possible, given this mentally handicapped patient's lifelong mental deficiencies?*

After an hour of online research, mostly reading peer-reviewed PhD psychologist articles, his stomach finally awoke. At the kitchen sink, through a slim clear area of window not opaque with ice, he observed the woodchipper wearing a foot-thick hat of snow and ice. *Brutal storm.* With a pot of water on the natural gas burner, he prepared ingredients for a fresh Italian pasta salad.

Dicing green and red bell peppers into miniscule pieces, he thought he heard the machination of his electric recliner motor. He froze and listened. It felt like every hair on his body was attempting escape. He peered around the kitchen corner, cognizant of the quickened pulse squish-squashing deep in his inner ears.

The recliner appeared unmoved. *Could it have opened and closed on its own?* He shook his head. *The storm; nothing more. Keep your head, Arthur. Under way too much strain lately. Learn to relax.*

After the meal, he thought of the delicious dichotomy of drawing a very hot bath with the master bathroom window cracked, icy air against the water generating relaxing steam. His core temp would be toasty warm while his face remained comfortably cool and dry. *Light some candles, turn off the lights.* It was decided.

Languid in the tub, master bath illuminated by six beeswax pillar candles, fierce winds whipped ice and snow against the house. Steam ghosts haunted the water then got sucked out into the storm. The peace of it lulled him into sound sleep. After a time, he dreamed.

Veronica Rodriguez on my recliner—again. Vulture-eyes. Mouth frozen open in a ghoulish yawp. No chest movement. Dead by my hand. That awful mouth—is it moving? 'You sent us from this world. We cannot cross over to the warm place. Better…on the other side. Why do you hold us here?'

'My dear woman, how is it then that I, who dwelleth here on this rotating rock, trapped inside this mortal engine, can in any way influence whither it is you seek to go?' Rational mind: please reassure me this is a dream; that I'm not currently conversing with an animated cadaver; that I will awaken and shrug off this nonsense; assign it to prison-induced PTSD. But oh, Veronica, you seem so real, so vigorous, so very poignant.

As if the filmy dead eyes were not adequately creepy and disturbing, the index finger of the right hand slowly rose. With machine-like efficiency, it pointed at him. *'You sent us here to this cold, dark, lifeless Purgatory. Only you can lead us across to the warmth…to the life.'*

'I-I…cannot. I have a very important function to perform here, in the mortal realm.'

'Doctor, you violated your Hippocratic Oath one hundred thirty-five times, as many times as you have violated the Sixth Commandment: Thou Shalt Not Kill. For which you are not contrite. We can live in the warmth, only when you lead us across.'

'Madam, this is madness. I know you don't exist outside of dreams. How can I lead you?'

Oh, that smile. The most dreadful, the most gruesome image ever. 'You must join us.' Her finger lowered. Not sure why, but the fact that she points at me no longer is indeed Balm in Gilead.

Wait…now she's gripping chair arms; elbows up: no! She means to stand! She's going to…touch me!

Startled awake, legs limp, his head slid underwater. He inhaled a bit of it. He spent the next seven minutes coughing. Resolved to self-diagnose whatever might be awry with his psyche, he toweled off, dressed, and slowly walked downstairs.

I might genuinely be cracking up here.

He flicked on living room lights enroute to his study. He stopped cold. Blinked hard. Slapped his own face, first one cheek then the other. The image of Violet Roxie remained. Wearing nothing but a smile, it struck a seductive pose on his brown leather sofa. He could see the folded blanket through the body, though not clearly.

Violet Roxie winked.

"Told you I'd come back for you, doctor." She tilted her head, studying him with unsettling patience. "You keep records, don't you? Names. Times. Last meals." A faint smile. "Pizza."

He recalled the articles. Within a few seconds he mentally scanned dozens of PTSD treatment protocols. *The best self-therapy is to confront my fears head on,* he remembered. He recalled Violet's last words, spoken in the prison execution chamber. He took two steps toward his couch upon which lie the specter he believed was a mental projection, only this. Nothing to fear. "Hello, Violet. Are you here to see me out like you promised? You really don't look strong enough to do much of anything. You said you could see right through me? Now I can see right through you."

The figure of Violet Roxie traced translucent fingertips along its ethereal taut stomach. It rubbed and tugged its pert, tiny breasts. She shifted slightly, though nothing in the room seemed to move with her. "You're wondering if this is real." A pause. "It is real enough. Yes," drawing out the 's'. "You sent me out of one place," she said softly. "You can take me into another. How delicious!" It drew out the 's' like a snake.

"What if I don't want to lead you across?"

"Well, doctor, you know how it is: everything is free will. You can have me now, if you want. A little taste of everlastingness and infinitude. Come over, sit down. Kick off your slippers. Stay awhile. Oh, and please lose the pants and the shirt."

Am I dreaming? I must still be dreaming. If so, I'm compelled to play along.

He complied with the Violet figure's command. He stood before it naked, nerves jumping.

Why am I afraid? It's a dream. What's the worst that can happen? I wake up and snap to; the return of lucid reason; the whole notion flies out the window like a steam ghost from a hot bath. That's what.

He pressed himself into the corner of the sofa. The Violet thing appeared to slide toward him weightlessly. He felt the weight of ankles on his thighs as petite silken feet dug at his crotch. "I can feel that!" he said.

Her fingers traced the air just above her body, not quite touching. "Where I am… there is no decay. No ending. Only continuation." Her eyes lifted to his. "You would not be alone there. And no, doctor, you are not dreaming. We are both present. This is as real as real gets."

"I-I…I can smell your body. Breath, crotch, feet, underarms; your unique pheromones. Just as if you were here!"

A slight smile—not warm. "You don't have to pretend with me, doctor. I've already seen what you hide."

His tumescence increased to the point of throbbing. "This can't be. You're only a figment of my imagination."

She leaned closer, voice lowering—not intimate, but *certain.* "You opened the door when you ended me. That does not close on its own."

Bicko rubbed his face hard. He opened his eyes and blinked. "Why are you still here?"

It giggled mirthlessly. "A figment, am I? We'll just see about that." It sat up and straddled his lap, kissed him hard, and ground itself down on him.

He broke away and gulped air. "I can taste your mouth! I can feel your weight on me, and friction down there!"

It threw back its head in raucous laughter. Through the diaphanous chest he saw long blonde hair spilling down its back and saw his empty recliner and the room.

But her vagina grips me like a thousand silk fists. How can I see through her? Hands clutching the sofa cushions, he climaxed like never before, coating the carpet, cushion, and tops of his feet in pearly muck to a soundtrack of loud satisfied groans. He smiled; eyes closed. So good it was almost painful.

Best sex I ever had, bar none.

"When you take a life, you own it. When you save a life, you own it. Guess that means you half-own me, good doctor."

"Half?"

Green eyes narrowed. It hugged his neck. In a whisper, "You must lead me across if you want to have all of me. There is a threshold," she said. "You stand on one side of it. We do not."

His mind drifted.

Twelve years since my last sexual intercourse; that girl on my staff about Violet's age at the time. What was it, Mandy? Sandy? Seems my addled brain has formed a mental block. Giving her the wine spiked with Flunitrazepam was a stroke of genius. She seemed unconscious, head resting against the passenger window when driving her home from the holiday office party. But didn't she moan when I fingered her? Another smart bit was wearing a wool cap, a condom, and remaining fully dressed except for the unzipping. Left no DNA. Woke up in her own bed, slightly disheveled and sore down there with no memory of the time between the party and awakening at home. What a tasty daughter she was! Yet nothing was ever as good or as exciting as what just happened.

A spirit-lifting aura of ecstasy consumed every cell of his being. But then that tiresome rational part of him poked at his gray matter.

A wet dream; nothing more. How is it that I can still smell her musk? Taste her mouth and sweat on my tongue?

Your imagination is more powerful than you ever thought possible, Merrick, he answered himself.

He opened his eyes. He was alone.

Oh yes. I'm losing my marbles.

Cleaned up and redressed, at the computer he read an interview with a former State executioner. "It's a big thing to carry inside. The executions will haunt me for as long as I live."

Next, he looked up Violet Roxie.

BREAKING NEWS: DNA EVIDENCE CLEARS YOUNG WOMAN EXECUTED LAST WEEK.

Something inside him snapped. He imagined he could audibly hear it—like a timing belt inside the engine of his mind had finally succumbed to wear, tear, and powerful new tensile forces.

Elbows on the desk, face in hands, Merrick Bicko imagined his mind a gray gearbox, like the transmission of an automobile stopped midway up a steep hill which had slipped a few cogs. It ground noisily, but nothing happened, no movement. A doomed and helpless passenger in a downhill backslide toward certain disaster.

The cacophony of images and voices had become unbearable. In desperation, he reached for the last unopened aerosol bottle of ketamine. He squeezed five sprays into each nostril, far more than any prescribed dosage. He tilted back in the chair, enjoying the immediate dissociative effect; how in a rush it started to put distance between his lucid mind and the anguished, bitter moat of thoughts, identity, and memory. *I'm free! Though for only as long as the drug lasts… but for now, feeling no PTSD must be good enough. How do you feel, Merrick, old boy?*

"Okayyyy," came the voice of Veronica Rodriguez from somewhere behind him.

He sat up straight. He did not want to look. Electrons in his bedeviled brain resisted. *I will not succumb to this trick of the mind. Ignore. Ignore.*

Something more powerful compelled him. He swiveled his chair to face the source of the sound. From the recliner, filmy black vulture eyes bored into his. At once, they reminded him of shark eyes. The longer he stared, he imagined two nuggets of coal stuck in rancid dough shaped like a fiendish face, now stretched into an obscene parody of a smile.

On the sofa, a naked Violet Roxie shot him a glance. It smiled prettily; nodded perkily. It appeared to chew gum and pop the bubbles, a sound he clearly heard, as it absently fingered itself. Behind them, Ines Barrera and Morris Johnson in their orange jumpsuits stood still as statues. Eyes stared blankly ahead.

Veronica's arms splayed open with a machine-like motion. "A hundred-thirty-one more of your victims stand in your kitchen, on your bed, in the bathrooms. They look and smell even worse than I do. They seek justice, doctor. We asked them to wait, at least until we had a chance to speak with you."

"I, uh, wait for what? Speak with me about what, madam?"

The chilling smile broadened, forcing the rigor-mortis facial muscles and dead skin to pinch up like stop-motion animated clay. "Why, about leading us across, of course."

He groaned. "This again. Miss Rodriguez, again I must beg your pardon. I live here, now, in the corporeal world. You aren't real! You do not exist. You are merely a symptom of post-traumatic stress disorder."

"Am I? When you were in Otisville, a prisoner named Malcolm Blakely pulled your lab coat lapel down to whisper something private. Only you could hear. Do you remember what he said?"

He shook his head. "No, I do not. Many men died in my presence there. It all runs together."

"Blakely said, 'Jesus saves.' Remember now?"

He closed his eyes.

Yes, I remember that. But since I don't believe in that religious mumbo-jumbo, it passed out of my brain as quickly as it had entered.

"Yes, I recall now. So what?"

"I only knew that because I came here from that other place. Nobody but you and Mr. Blakely knew this. How could I, unless I am returned from another realm?"

"Bullshit! Repressed memory is all it is! You aren't real!" He shifted his gaze to Violet. "None of you are! You are projections from my traumatized mind." He closed his eyes. He decided to seek professional help.

I don't put much stock in head-shrinkers, but self-treatment is not efficacious—that much is evident. Perhaps they have a drug and therapy protocol that can help.

"Doctor? Merrick? You think what just happened between us wasn't real? Felt super real when you came inside me."

His face flushed. "Wet dream!"

Violet giggled. "I came, too. Wasn't a dream, doctor." With that, the violet figure arose, padded silently across the room, and knelt between his legs. It gazed up at him with long lashes framing wide green eyes. It made a pouty face. "Don't you want me?"

He reached down. He felt resistance as his hand passed through lush blonde hair.

"Yes, child," he said softly. "So very much. Like I've never wanted anyone else. I want you until time runs out. I owe you my life. You were innocent! I killed a completely blameless young woman. I owe you everything. I am so inexpressibly sorry."

"Merrick," it said. He felt Violet Roxie's hand cover his own with crackling electric warmth. "I have completely forgiven you. And where you're taking me, our time together will never ever run out. I promise. You will cross eventually." A pause. "The only question is whether you go willingly... or empty."

Ketamine inhaler in hand, he snorted another five sprays into each nostril, though he knew it was a dangerously high dose when added to what already circulated through his bloodstream. The dissociative effect was now total. His mind separated from his body, like Carlos Castaneda flying over mountains on peyote buttons. Real and unreal had become one. He gazed gratefully down upon the radiant face of Violet. "All right: suppose I believe you. What would you have me do?"

It smiled. "First, I need you to take off all these pesky clothes."

"With them watching?"

"Shh. Hush. The blonde head turned over its shoulder. "You there, all of you: close your eyes 'til I say you can open 'em." He watched as Barrera,

Johnson, and Rodriguez complied. Corpse eyelids seemed glued down, as in death. "Now, let's see, where were we. Oh yes. You won't need those clothes," she said, almost gently. When he hesitated, her expression didn't change. "You're already past the point of modesty."

On his knees at the foot of his desk chair, he humped the air to a powerful second orgasm. Face down on the floor, content and at peace, he sensed Violet straddling his back, could feel it kneading tense muscles. He moaned in pleasure. This continued for over half an hour. He felt it dismount. He wriggled onto his back. He looked up to find it seated in his chair.

"Her gaze settled on him. "You feel that now. The time is now for you to lead us over into the warmth, lover. Your earthly life is but a brief series of hellos and goodbyes, and yours is way out of balance: far too many goodbyes. Today is the day to take some reasonable account for yourself. To say hello to me forever, in paradise."

Her smile…the most perfect creature I have ever seen. Society misjudged her; used me to kill her under a false conviction. Such injustice. The system failed her…but it was I who killed her. I am the instrument of corruption. Whatever she asks of me that is mine to give, I shall give. "How do I do that?"

"Well first, you must join us. Everyone, open your eyes."

As he grabbed his sweatshirt to cover his privates, he turned and watched three pairs of eyes-glued-shut slowly motor open.

"I'm sorry, Violet, but I'd have to be dead to join you. You'll have to wait."

It grinned, all teeth and all-knowing. "It's only bodily death. We know you science-types like to think you're all-powerful masters of the universe but here you are a perfidious pariah, a cast-off from society. In the warm place, you will be a king! Lead us over now, and you get me! Your animated meat will soon revert to dust anyway. Gone—poof! — in a snap!" Clearly, he heard sound waves emanating from her limpid hand and reverberating briefly through the room. "Best to get it over with now: for if you do, once you cross over, you will be truly special! Receive knowledge of all things. Think about it! All your deepest curiosities, the desires of your heart, and needs of your new immortal body satisfied. This is the real treasure, Merrick. It waits for you and for us all in a warm, red, enduring place, where I'll be bound to you for all eternity. But only if you decide to move on right now, today, this very minute. Otherwise, if you wait for natural death, our door, *my door*, will be long closed and locked."

"But I'm scared!"

It laughed. The sound struck him as that of a teen girl joking with friends at a sleepover. "Do you think we weren't scared? Each of us was terrified. But in a blink, it was over; lights out. We awoke in limbo, this place of shadow and doubt, where we'll stay, until you to take us all the way to paradise."

Veronica spoke with an edge to its hideous, inhuman tone. "As I've told you before, Dr. Bicko, you have sinned beyond the pale. Your mortal end, therefore, must be something spectacularly grisly, to make amends. Also, you must confess your sins now, to us, if you hope to enjoin with the warmth, and go forward with Violet." At the mention of its name, Violet smiled and waved playfully, stood, and reached down to him.

His hand passed through it as he struggled to rise, and stand before it, lost in the heart-melting emerald eyes. Again, he reached for its hand and felt something like static electricity. Enchanted, no longer self-conscious about his nakedness, he saw himself cascading down an impossibly long, pink, velveteen slide, propelled by gravity atop a ceaseless stream of tiny pink beads causing delicious, insulated friction all over his body. Novel new sensations lathered him into a full, dripping froth, into a pique of sexual stimulation unlike anything ever felt before. There was naked Violet, knees drawn back to either side of its thin chest, splayed and smiling, positioned to receive him at the bottom of the slide. He felt blood rush to his nethers. "Kiss me down there." He did.

Abruptly, Violet pulled his head back from its groin. It pulled him, crawling on all fours, until he knelt two feet from the recliner, four from Barrera and Johnson. The Violet thing released its grip. "What waits on the other side isn't like this," she said. "No bodies failing. No time running out."

She watched him carefully. "Desire doesn't fade there. It doesn't weaken. It doesn't end." A pause. Then, quieter: "You wouldn't have to fight yourself anymore. "Merrick," it said. "Confess your sins to us."

His mind whirled. Warm salty tears flowed freely. "I-I…killed all of you. I confess too…that in each case, I-I… I enjoyed it. It gave me powerful tingles all over, in my privates, my chest, my belly, and most poignantly—in my soul. I felt like a god when I wielded the power of life and death in my hand! I chose to kill you: not because it was my job, but because I liked it; a lot! Too much, I'm afraid. I broke my oath. And for this I am guilty, and so very sorry. I repent, not for killing you people, but for so ardently coveting the stimulation it brought to me. I feel like something less than a man. The spirit of perversity made its home in me long ago, and I never fought it, not one jot or tittle. Please forgive me."

Veronica Rodriguez smiled. "We forgive you, good doctor. If not for you, our inferior lives here in the brutal, corrupt, unjust world of flesh would still go on, with zero knowledge of something far, far better. But doctor, please know that you must transition over in a most magnificent fashion, so that many hearts and minds of this earth shall know the depth of your contrition. You must prove fealty to the higher spirits who rule the warm place, to receive your eternal reward."

"But I'm SCARED!"

"You'll be more scared if you choose to remain in this realm. Know that wherever you go, whatever you do, we will never leave you alone. Then your flesh will expire naturally, and you will awaken in a cold place, all alone for eternity, in a refrigerator with no door."

"And I will never touch you again," added Violet, as it sashayed to the couch. "Here," it said, patting the cushion. He heard the thumps. "I will remain right here, and the others where they stand now, until the day your body dies of natural causes, and by that time we will be too angry to let you lead us. Someone else will; somebody more…deserving of the honor. Also, doctor, know that I will tease you day and night but never grant you relief."

"Authorities of this realm will lock you in an asylum," said Veronica. "But don't think for one second that any concrete wall or iron bars will separate you from us. When you take a life, it's yours forever. When you take a life," she said, almost absently, "it doesn't end where you think it does."

With tear-reddened eyes, he plodded to the couch and faced Violet. He felt one scintillating hand squeeze and tug his scrotum, as the other stroked and tugged his member back to full ardor. Her gaze settled on him. "You feel that now." A faint tilt of her head. "That means you belong to it… at least in part."

"I don't know…"

"Go over and snort more of that wonder-drug. It made me feel all relaxed and chill before you stuck me with poison!"

Obediently, he trotted over to the desk and dosed six sprays per nostril.

"How do you feel?" asked Veronica.

"Good!" he replied, and the word echoed in his mind like Déjà vu. He felt the drug fill him with courage, optimism, and warmth.

"Now you know how we felt just before you shut our eyes, forever," said Violet. "Now let's get this show on the road. "Come," she said.

No urgency. No excitement. Only certainty. At the door, she waited— not turning back. "You've already decided. Your body just hasn't followed yet."

"Mm, my dear Violet. Nothing in this world or the next could possibly make me happier."

"Great!" said the Violet thing.

"Where are we going?"

"Outside, silly! You'll see."

"Okay, but I'm completely naked. Let me get dressed."

"Nope! Just grab your little spray bottle." He did. The hand took his. It led him to the front door and pointed at the knob. He opened it to a blast of frigid air that instantly lowered the temperature in the living room by ten degrees. It hit him like a dive into a glacial bay. Immediately his genitals retreated up inside his trunk, though because of the ketamine, the temperature barely registered in his brain.

He crunched barefoot through nearly two feet of snow and ice behind the specters. His core body temperature quickly plummeted to hypothermia level. There was still enough light filtered through dark and menacing mid-afternoon clouds for him to see his house through falling snow, steam rising from the chimney. He thought of the warmth promised to him by the goddess of beauty, Violet Roxie, as he walked further away from his toasty home. He shivered uncontrollably, his teeth chattered, though he barely noticed. All he could see now were emerald cat eyes, brighter than the warm South Pacific Ocean, filled with love, forgiveness, and just the right amount of mischief. He wondered where Violet was leading him.

Ahead he could see the big wood-enclosed truck, half filled with shredded tree wood. He saw the trailer, atop which sat the woodchipper. The feeding chute yawned at him like a big, dark, hungry mouth. He glanced at Violet's naked backside as it rose and fell. His mouth watered. It stopped walking. Thirty or so feet behind them, the other one-hundred-thirty-three also stopped.

He turned, beguiled completely by Violet's eyes and voice, captivated by the extraordinary beauty. When it smiled, he felt his whole soul captivated. All cold, all fears, and awful waves of guilt melted away.

She makes everything better. I repent, not to that false God who doesn't exist; only to her.

He felt young. "Ride your face until you drown in my juices, Merrick. Now, how do we turn this on?"

"The truck?"

"The chipper."

"Hold on. Wait a second. You don't mean…"

"Doctor, you understood," said the Veronica figure from a distance. "The manner of your exit serves multiple purposes. It must be commanding and transcendent."

He looked at the machine, then at Violet. "It will hurt."

"Yes," she said.

No comfort. No denial.

Then, after a pause, she said: "But not for long."

Violet cupped his cold-retreated manhood with its left hand and stroked his cheek with its right. His brain registered the sensation of silky-smooth, youthful warmth. "Over in a blink. Now start it up."

He crunched to the side panel, primed the choke, and pushed the electric starter motor button. With a black-smoking cough and banging noises due to dormancy and extreme cold, the powerful gasoline-powered engine kicked on with a sputter. Soon it ran normally, smooth and steady, as it warmed up. He backtracked through his steps in the deep snow until again he stood beside Violet. Together they watched the rotating cylinder covered with metal teeth, mesmerized. "Well?" asked the Violet Roxie thing.

"No. I can't. I'm too scared." A hand guided his own up to his face. He squeezed and inhaled switching from left to right nostrils until the bottle was empty.

He felt ethereal lips and tongue exploring his mouth. "Yes, you can. You will. You must. Don't you want me?"

"Violet, I am so scared Do you want me to enter headfirst or feet first?" he asked it, body trembling, teeth chattering from cold and mortal fear.

Violet turned to take visual cues from the older, wiser Veronica. "Feet first."

"I adore you, Violet Roxie. I think I may even love you."

"I *know* I love you, Merrick. You own me, remember? Together forever. She stepped close, her face inches from his. For a moment, she almost looked human again. "This is the only way you finish what you started." Her hand rested lightly against him. "Come with me."

He climbed onto the steel frame of the trailer and chipper housing. Merrick Arthur Bicko slid his feet and legs into the metal chute, legs bent, naked buttocks seated on the frozen steel edge, feet inches from the rotating grind cylinder. Violet climbed up beside him, her forehead lightly resting against his. "Want me to count backwards from ten like in the rocket launches?" it said.

He shivered. He tried to smile. "No, I'd rather you just kiss me and give me a little push."

It kissed him. He tasted the mouth, imagined the warmth. With both hands on his shoulders, it shoved hard.

If the chipper had only been more powerful, it would have shredded the aorta of his heart, and it all would have ended in only a minute or two— about the same amount of time it takes the chipper to shred a six-foot long tree branch. Metal shark teeth welded onto the cylinder bit deeply into his feet and sealed his fate. Tortured flesh immediately began to die due to cell disruption, lactic acid generated by damaged muscles and tendons, and released toxins.

Far more severe trauma slowly commenced. Direct soft tissue destruction, bony injury, and limb ischemia. Digital nerves, lateral and medial plantar nerves, medial calcaneal nerves, and common peroneal nerves in his mangled feet did what nerves were designed to do—though never this many all at once—as electrical signals reached his ketamine-addled brain. Next-level pain on an inconceivable scale. The lucid physician who still existed, buried someplace deep inside his fatally overdosed brain, rationally informed him that this was only the beginning. The remorseless blades leisurely butchered the femoral, saphenous, obturator, and lateral femoral cutaneous nerves in both legs at the same time.

Piercing shrieks echoed about the snowy stillness. The woeful, wretched, high-volume howls of the condemned pushed wild animals and birds away from the property for a square mile. Now steel hit bone, three intelligible words bounced about for the briefest moment, then nothing but the uncontainable expressions of an overburdened sympathetic nervous system unable to process such agonizing pain. While his body would not fully die for some minutes, his brain was able to tell within twenty seconds that death was imminent. A sober person would have blacked out after only a few seconds, even though the brain would not yet have decided on death as the only possible outcome. Under this supreme level of trauma, the brain of a self-possessed person would have shut down all consciousness and voluntary nerve messages to save itself from going completely mad. The body would have been shredded without the cognitive brain knowing about it.

The drug in his system had disconnected nature's extreme pain shut-off switch, keeping him conscious. Genitals, rectum, colon, intestines, liver, pancreas, kidneys, lungs, spleen, spine—now a viscous purple gumbo. Until the chipper crushed his aorta long minutes later, exquisitely deranged, eardrum-piercing screams proved to the world he was feeling everything.

Each of the body's muscles, including the small muscles of the face, will immediately lose all tension when the brain governing them dies. During the French Revolution when the guillotine rose and fell without cessation, many eyewitnesses reported that, on heads severed only seconds before, faces that stared up from blood-soaked baskets had changed post-detachment, morphing into agonized, frightened and surprised expressions. Brains could still feel, even after decapitation.

So it was that the face of Arthur Merrick Bicko, after whirring steel blades diced his heart into chunks, still attempted to scream, mouth a rictus, tongue flat against the floor of his mouth, though he no longer had lungs to make such final, desperate pain abatement possible. It wasn't until the bladed cylinder stoved in his skull, when gray matter and bone shards splatted into blood-marinated wood chips inside the truck, that all feeling finally ended. Ketamine, the signature drug for which he had become known in Death Row circles, intended as a mercy to help ease fear and pain within the condemned—magnified and extended his conscious agonies beyond anything ever before experienced by a human. The drug had turned eight minutes of grind-time into what had felt like hours, to the condemned.

Investigators found only one set of footprints in the snow, and only his own fingerprints and DNA in the home. A more repugnant and unlikely suicide scene these career New York homicide detectives had never witnessed. Facts, however, were facts; and thus, their official report deemed Bicko had taken his own life. Nevertheless, to check boxes as they must to satisfy procedural requirements, they methodically interviewed every homeowner within a five-mile radius, asking about visitors or anything unusual, which is how they learned of three words screamed at the highest agitated human volume. Most area homesteaders claimed they thought it was a fisher cat screaming in the woods, a common sound in the area, otherwise they would have reported it. The detectives knew they were lying, to cover for their apathy. Cops know people rarely rise to intervene, investigate, get involved with helping people in mortal danger.

Three distinct words, heard by different people in different locations, along with prolonged, inhuman screaming.

Under certain atmospheric conditions, such as the low storm cloud ceiling oppressing New Yorkers on the afternoon that Merrick Arthur Bicko fed himself into his wood-chipper, it was akin to living under a big acoustic-tiled ceiling, against which sounds bounce up then back to earth; from there, words can carry for miles away from their source. As usual, the three words somehow got leaked from law enforcement to the Press, whose dramatic opinion pieces on the subject dominated news cycles for an entire week.

There was no corpse to bury. No family or friends interested in doing so even if there were. The warden at the prison where he delivered his first lethal injection had a soft spot for the killer-doctor. He had his inmates in the masonry shop make a headstone for Bicko, to honor him with a spot in the prison cemetery. The first line showed his name, the second gave his birth date and death date.

On the third line, separated from the upper two lines for emphasis, three words engraved into the stone, assumed by all accounts to be his last.

I Was Deceived

Son of a Ghoul

Graverobbing as a criminal profession does still exist. I should know. I rob graves for a living. Let me qualify that statement: I used to rob graves, several per week on average, until recently. Quite the profitable gig, and more organized than one might think. A substantial amount of planning and thought goes into it. Executing is the easiest part.

Ghouls. A few hundred years ago, that is what society labeled us, we who stole from the dead. Such a creepy and uncharitable title. Back then, the black market for fresh cadavers used by medical schools constituted the bulk of the supply chain. Today, it's about aggrieved loved ones burying family members with jewelry that held sentimental value for their deceased. With gold trading at nearly two thousand an ounce—need I say more. Precious gems can also fetch good returns. It's a business, nothing more. There's nothing creepy or psychotic about it. My former crew had families and attended church. No, it isn't legal, but nobody got hurt. Until somebody did, which is why I quit. Soberly, I pen these remembrances to document facts for the perfect sanity of the written record, should more hurt lead to even more unhappy endings. Also to serve as a warning, perhaps.

As to the business of graverobbing, if you want to excel at this game, you must focus your efforts on wealthy families. Study the obits. Attend viewings, sort of like in that hit movie about crashing weddings: you show up as a complete unknown but act super-friendly and empathetic to the aggrieved. When asked or challenged, drop a few names. For example, I'm a good friend of (insert-name of dead lady's high school friend you pulled off an online yearbook), here to pay my respects. She talks about her so much that I feel like I know her, like I'm part of the family. Since I live close, I thought I'd better stop and pay our respects.' The ability to summon tears on demand, like a professional actor, isn't critical though believe me, it truly does help. What famous guy said, 'The truth shall set you free: and when it doesn't—lie, but lie well?'

To speak the unfiltered truth would go like this: 'My dear melancholy friends, I'm here pretending to honor your dead loved one while taking mental inventory of jewelry draped thereupon, so that later I can dig her moldering ass up and steal it.'

Truth wouldn't go over so well, now, would it?

My name isn't Joe, but you can call me that. My partner's name wasn't Digger, but that's what I called him, and he was fine with it. I was the brains of the operation; he was the muscle. Digger and I were strictly nocturnal creatures. We worked nights and rested days. Some folks are plagued by Non-24-Hour Sleep-Wake Disorder, others by Shift Work Sleep Disorder.

In the very beginning it was an adjustment, but soon enough it normalized and became who we were. Eventually it felt completely natural; being awake during sunlight hours felt completely unnatural.

We lived near Philadelphia, Pennsylvania. During spring-summer-fall and most of the winter (except when the ground is too frozen to dig, which rarely happened) for me, life consisted of attending wakes which, ninety-eight times out of one hundred were scheduled for late afternoons and early evenings. Between midnight and four-thirty is when we followed our standard operating procedures.

One of my jobs was to spend all night shifts observing every cemetery in the area and finding a place for Digger and crew to park their innocuous white van all night where it wouldn't attract attention. I've found none thus far equipped with security cams. Some are police-patrolled; fewer still engage private security to drive through every so often. Knowing people are creatures of habit, I kept a log of what times uniformed types drove through cemetery roads. When Digger and his crew were engaged in their work, I kept a sharp eye on the cemetery ingress and warned him via walkie-talkie.

Digger was the most skilled and efficient graverobber who ever lived, I'm certain of it. He and his illegal aliens, Mexicans all, wore camo coveralls and British military camo hats with neck flaps to blend into backgrounds. They even wore camo face-paint. The few times cops or security came through; the crew would prostrate themselves flat behind headstones. Cruiser searchlights never once revealed them. Digger was neat and organized. Using spades, he and the boys carefully removed sod over the graves before he laid down camo tarps on both sides of the opening. Using shovels and pickaxes, they dug into soil still loose from recent burials. Hard enough work, but then they carefully placed the exhumed soil on the tarps so as not to besmirch the grassy sides of the grave. Using enormous heavy crowbars, they popped off coffin lids in under thirty seconds.

Since we already knew what jewelry the corpse wore from my viewing-crashing, Digger would jump in the hole with his small bolt-cutter tool. If his exertions met with any resistance, he'd lop off fingers to more easily pry off rings. Necklaces he attempted to remove by unfastening clasps; if he felt behind schedule, sometimes he'd use small diagonal cutters to separate chains and remove them. Watches always glided right off despite rigor mortis. Only three times did he need to hacksaw off hands to liberate bracelets or watches from some very thick-wristed, ham-handed gents who weren't about to part with them without a struggle.

While down there, Digger would pick pockets. It was always a nice bonus when he found something of value inside, although typically it was only photographs, cigarette packs, sleeves of nicotine gum, cans of snuff, flasks of alcohol, decks of lucky cards…whatever sentimental shit families thought would get their beloved dead through the night until Kingdom Come.

The Mexicans always gave him a hand up and out. They'd slap the lid back down not bothering to fasten it; they just made damned sure it was properly re-positioned to prevent the coffin from swallowing dirt, which would've caused a noticeably weird concave after replacing the sod. They backfilled every particle of the removed dirt. They used tampers to make it smooth and even before replacing the sod. Digger paid them in cash, thirty bucks an hour; also, he threw them the occasional bonus to keep their mouths shut. These Mexicans are so much harder-working than Americans, and they know the value of a closed mouth. We had put a premium on omertà, which means silence to the grave. High quality, loyal men. I miss them.

Sometimes, we'd give each man an expensive bottle of wine. Whenever there were pretty pieces of jewelry that we knew couldn't be fenced for any worthwhile sum, those pieces we'd give to the men, who in turn gifted them to their women. The chances of these mujeres mixing with the elite Main Line crowd of the deceased, where a custom-made heirloom jewelry piece might get spotted around a finger or neck by someone who might recognize it are about a billion to one. We considered it grease that kept this engine of ours humming along smoothly.

Although Digger's record is robbing five graves in one night, we tried to average two-to-three per night in the same cemetery. We had a guy located nearby who gave me fair prices for the loot. Peripherally, he's part of an organized crime family operation in Philadelphia. He likes to smoke real Cuban cigars, along with his potent home-grown weed. He has seven bullet wound scars. Once he took off his shirt and showed me. Each time, I hem and haw over cash amounts just to remind him that I am no pushover.

On a good night, after expenses, we'd clear anywhere from three-to-five grand. Sometimes we'd hit mother lode graves that yielded more. They boys only took Sundays and major holidays off to spend with their familiars; the other three hundred five nights multiplied by five large per night netted me and Digger over one and a half million dollars every year, split down the middle, untaxed. See what I mean now, about graverobbing being a very profitable gig?

Until it all quite abruptly ground to a halt—the night I learned a macabre and painful lesson that changed everything. Suddenly, the juice of crime was no longer worth the squeeze.

Digger's son was only eight years old that year, a skinny kid, height average for that age, with a mop of thick blond hair straight as a straw broom. Looked nothing like his mother and everything like papa ghoul. Digger's wife wasn't happy with the fact that her husband worked nights while she stayed home and lived a life with her son during normal hours, but she damned well-loved spending the bread he brought home. Lovely colonial-style brick house with black shutters and immaculate landscaping, driving around in her sexy little red Mercedes-Benz, oh yes, Mrs. Digger was quite content with all that. She and Junior understood that their father was paid 'under-the-table' as part of his job arrangement with PennDOT (Pennsylvania Department of Transportation—highly unionized) because none of the members had his skill set when it came to laying roads, and Digger wasn't into joining unions. I thought it was a lame story, maybe she did too—but whatever. That's how that family rolled. He took care of all the finances and income taxes (reported only enough 'tips' income to avoid suspicion) while she took giant wads of cash and figured out how best to spend it. On several occasions, I offered her some investment advice, which she summarily dismissed. She loved to overpay for ugly abstract original art, fancying herself a visionary investor. Also, she'd drag little Digger Junior to Atlantic City casinos every weekend to satisfy her lust for the high-roller craps tables. Last I recall she was nearly a quarter million in the red. Digger didn't care, so loving and easy-going. God, how I miss him.

Me, I traveled light. No wife, no kid. Thought better of it later, but I'll get to that. If I couldn't eat it, fill my old beater pick-up truck's fuel tank with it, or wear it until after many spin cycles it fell apart—I didn't buy it. My motto. I invested every hard-earned dollar in online equities trades, and my net worth had climbed to over five million, then. Slowly it keeps rising by about half a million per year, even though I'm no longer contributing to it currently. I only sell off little bits here and there to live off; otherwise, it rides a nice sine wave up and down yet always gently heads north. It'll reach ten million soon enough. My buy-and-hold, get-rich-slow method has made it so that I no longer need to work another day in my life.

There were other principal differences between my partner and I. Sometimes he'd invite me over for dinner, and sometimes I'd go, depending upon what his missus was cooking up. I'm a health nut, you see. Undoubtedly the only true vegan ghoul in all of history. When she'd make corn-on-the-cob, mashed potatoes with non-dairy margarine, milk-free crust sweet potato pie, then I'd come. Junior and I really hit it off. Maybe deep down inside I'd never grown up emotionally since I was his age. We'd shoot darts, have us a baseball catch or throw a football, toss Frisbees, race each other in his cool video games. I'd feel bad leaving those nights; hollow inside.

A life without having your own little progeny to play with had suddenly felt less real to me after hanging out for hours with Junior. His room was filled with horror movie crap. Posters, latex masks, fake blood capsules, action figures. And books—my gosh—this kid had read just about every horror anthology, collection, series, and novel ever published. He knew every character's name from every horror movie, and the names of the actors who played them. He even knew the names of horror producers and directors. Some kids do music or sports: this kid did horror.

If Junior had only known what his dad and 'Uncle Joe' did for a living, today he could become a bestselling author of shocking non-fiction simply by recounting an actual diary of our nocturnal work, in all of its grotesque detail.

Differences aside, one thing Digger and I shared: neither of us had ever felt one lick of guilt about our career choice. We know each other very well. Neither of us would ever steal from the living. If his kid were starving, Digger wouldn't shoplift a morsel of food to feed him. Too proud for that. Nor would he ever suckle the public teat by taking welfare. He'd work the worst job in the world to feed his family and himself before it ever came to that. Same with me. I don't steal from people who still breathe. Morally upright ghouls are we, and that's a fact. Is it not a sin to bury valuables with the dead—treasures that could be sold to help the living contend with earthly struggles? Woe to our critics! And, to the families of the dead; they who are the real criminals here, not us! Dead wealthy people feel no more. Worm-bait. Decaying matter in the ground is all they are. Their souls have moved on, like computer programs migrated from one physical machine to some ethereal new upgraded box that never wears out. Material wealth accumulated here won't buy them a drink of water in Hell, or an Admit One ticket to Heaven.

Such is what we believed at the time.

I had crashed the viewing of a dead man who—only later I learned after running online research, and I also ran his name past my fence—was an exceedingly sociopathic man given to the occasional caprice of animal rage. Alive, he'd been an absolute nightmare. I'll call him Tank for sake of accuracy, because he looked like a Panzer smooshed into the coffin. I know a little about coffins. I can tell you, his was the manufacturer's largest product if not a custom order. An organized crime figure, known thief, and ruthless murderer: Tank had been a man of notoriously vicious and intemperate disposition.

He'd started as a mob enforcer and debt collector, beating the shit out of people who owed his boss money until they paid up. If not, he'd kill them in ever more horrifying and darkly creative ways. Early victims were found stomped to death; but at some point, he'd developed a fondness for blowtorches and cutting weapons. Bones earned, he graduated to hit man. He eliminated whomever his boss wanted removed from the game. Old story and oft romanticized by Hollywood, except this guy was for real. I'd say Tank left a corpse that was probably six-foot-five, three-hundred-twenty pounds. His reputation among rival crime families instilled fear.

Tank was never into clean, tidy mob hits. Emotional and physical torture were his specialties. My fence told me one such story, gruesome as hell. A rival mobster in the Northeast, married with a son and daughter, encroached on the turf of Tank's former boss, and had ignored stern warnings. Tank was given the order to close the rival's eyes.

The boss had never said anything about the rival's wife and kids. Those gentle folk, Tank had considered bonuses, like sweet dessert treats.

While the family screamed their protests, Tank tied the mark to a chair in his own kitchen, then bound the arms and shins of the other three. He opened kitchen cabinets and placed one frying pan on each of the four lit stove burners. He drizzled olive oil into each pan, found a clove of garlic, and sliced off thin layers that he dropped into each pan. Satisfied, he used the largest knife in the block to slice off the wife's tits, then used the meat cleaver to chop both feet off the little girl, and the boy's hands. He dropped the grisly bits into the pans and sautéed them over everyone's agonized screams.

The mark was so horrified that Tank had to toss cold water on his face to bring him around. The guy had passed out cold, forced to watch his family slowly bleed to death, and watch Tank eat their body parts. When finished, Tank used a paper towel to wipe his mouth, and sprayed glass cleaner onto every knob, handle, and surface he'd touched. Then he earned his paycheck: slowly, he flayed the mark alive. He peeled the skin from the man's abdomen, chest, and back, up over his head, like pulling off a shirt. The face he skinned off last. By the time Tank had washed up, wiped every surface he'd touched to leave no partial fingerprints, and walked to the door, the victim was still alive. Tank broke open an ammonia inhaler and shoved the jagged glass vial into the opening where a nostril had been, to prevent the victim from lapsing into unconsciousness. Tank wanted him to feel everything right to the last second of life.

I hadn't known all this while I stared down at Tank's corpse; I learned about it after. Many people showed up for the viewing. Tank seemed a popular, well-liked guy—except to those targeted by his boss.

He also sported the thickest solid gold jewelry I had ever seen, positively dripping with it. Later, he was buried with no less than fifty grand's worth. Rolex watch, giant diamond and onyx pinkie ring. All-in I calculated seventy-five grand to split with Digger. (I only think in net figures after the fence rapes my wallet and we pay the boys.) Not bad for a few hours' work.

The ironic part: he was to be buried in a Catholic cemetery. I'm Catholic, and yes, I believe the guiltiest man can still be saved if he repents before dying. Except that Tank here caught a rival gang's nine-millimeter bullet through the heart, which means he crumpled to the earth like wheat in a hailstorm without time to repent of cannibalizing innocent women and children alive.

I thought about Digger's boy. The whole scene had made me cringe; made my skin crawl like nothing else ever had. I hate recalling it now, but the mission is to tell the whole story. I was sorry that I ever asked my fence about Tank. What has been seen (if only by the mind's eye) can never ever be unseen. I wish I didn't know now what I didn't know then. But I do, and a job's a job; and hey—we had work to do. Tank was a veritable gold mine.

I cased the Catholic cemetery. As far as jobs go, this would be a cinch. Zero cops or security passed through there. The cemetery abutted a busy highway, the periphery marked by a seven-foot-high wrought iron fence. Two points of ingress-egress protected by identical wrought-iron gates, both locked at night with a padlocked chain. Easy-peasy. Digger's bolt-cutters would make quick work of it. An ice-cream store sat by itself on the other side of the highway with two vans parked behind it all night: Digger's van would nestle right in with theirs without attracting one lick of attention. He and the crew needed to make sure no cars were coming when they crossed over, easy since the highway is flat like a board with no traffic lights for half a mile in both directions.

Since Tank was a once-in-a-lifetime opportunity, we scheduled no other digs for the night, only his. It was Saturday.

I'd had no inkling at the time that it would also be our very last.

After they tidied up their final dig, I met them in our typical secure rendezvous point to collect the loot. After he paid the boys and sent them home, an early night for a change, I asked Digger how the Tank job went.

"Fairly routine. Everything as you said." He handed me the small burlap coffee sack of loot. With a towel from the front passenger van seat, he wiped the camo paint off his face and simply stood there, blinking. I sensed an eerie, supernal vibe. I could see him struggling with what he would say next. "I found something weird in his right pants pocket. Here," he said, and handed me a calling-card size flat piece of solid gold.

"What is this?" I held my cell phone light onto the object. "Engraved. I can't read what it says. Some foreign language. Guessing Latin." It reads 'et non morieris tu et domus tua' on both the front and the back. I hefted it. Between one and two ounces of pure gold.

"What do you think it is?"

"I can't even guess. Never saw anything like it. But what I do see is at least two-grand. Glad you checked his pockets. Did you have to do any cutting?"

"Nope. Guy had fingers like sausages, but maybe they've desiccated already just a little. Rings came off without a struggle. On his road to Heaven, he'll have two thumbs to hitch a ride."

I shook my head. "That one is going straight down, pretty sure. Don't ask. Believe me, you don't want to know. Why do you look rattled, buddy?"

He stroked his temples. "God's honest truth, I have no idea. Just something about this job thoroughly creeped me out. And you know me, none of this ever gets under my skin. Don't know what to tell you. Just a super-bad feeling about this job."

"You need to go home, take a shower, wake up that pretty little wife of yours with tongue, and blow off some tension, partner. Tomorrow's our sabbath day. Rest up. Monday night will be here before we know it."

He nodded. "Yeah, right, about that. Hey, humor me; try to translate what's on that card.

"This job really has you spooked, doesn't it?"

"Yeah, man. Really, it does."

I got home and took a long hot shower, longer by twenty minutes than I ever allowed. Wide awake, after fixing myself a grilled cheese sandwich, I went out to the garage, emptied the loot bag onto a flattened cardboard box, and sprayed everything with disinfectant. I'm something of a Howard Hughes when it comes to handling objects taken from a decomposing corpse, though my brain told me it's probably cleaner than a door handle at the convenience store bathroom. After drying the gold calling card with a shop rag, I took it inside to my workstation. Guessing Latin, letter by letter, I typed the words engraved on the gold into an online Latin-to-English translator, fingers crossed that I'd been right.

'et non morieris tu et domus tua' translated to 'you will die with your family.'

Just, wow. This guy had the ego, the forethought, the temerity, to have an ancient Latin curse engraved—at great expense I might add—into precious material that never corrupts over time and managed to get himself buried with it. Like the curses carved or painted by ancient Egyptians all throughout Pharoah's tomb designed to dissuade would-be graverobbers, for time immemorial, from looting their demigod. Zero humility, this guy.

It did not work for the Egyptians, nor did it work for this evil clown. Graves got robbed, regardless. I found the curse at once absurd, amusing, and memorable. When you're in the crime business, I guess it's not too very dissimilar to being a priest, a detective, a lawyer…anyone who is professionally compelled to keep secrets. But inside you just want to explode and tell your crazy stories to anyone who'll listen. Which partially explains why I'm writing all this down.

If I should suddenly die under inexplicable causation, let this be the testimonial of a lucid man, not to be disputed.

I slept away most of that Sunday until mid-afternoon. Groggily, I checked my phone and saw Digger had tried to call every half hour. Heart racing, I called him back. Too late: I watched him on my porch cam monitor as he pounded down my door. I ran down and flung it open. A vision I shall never forget. Digger in that condition, completely bent out of shape, a mask of dreadful fear.

"Come in, buddy," I spoke calmly. "Get you a beer?"

Almost as though he did not hear the question, fifteen seconds later, "Yeah-yeah, sure, man. Thanks."

"Please sit down, mi casa su casa, take a load off," I said, and pointed to the most comfortable recliner of the lot. He chose to stand. I'm not a drinker but I always keep a six-pack of suds on hand; I walked to the kitchen and returned with two beers and handed him one. "By the way, sorry I didn't pick up. I never mute my phone, and I guess it buzzed each time you'd called, but I'd slept right through. Normally I lurch into the bathroom every few hours to empty my bladder, then struggle to get back to sleep. I must've been deeply exhausted. To the marrow, as they say."

"My wife and kid didn't sleep a wink last night. Remember I had a bad feeling about the Catholic cemetery job? My sixth sense told me something about it was entirely wrong, somehow."

"I remember."

"Tell me you haven't fenced the stuff yet."

"I have."

"SHIT! Go buy it back. Right now."

"What? You're joking. Either that, or you're a can short of a six-pack."

"I'm putting everything back exactly where we found it."

It's not often that I'm speechless. I studied his eyes and body language. All I could think of to say was, "Dude, calm down. Talk to me." With deliberate movements, never dissevering eye contact, I lowered myself into one of the recliners. I took a large swig of beer and ripped a loud carbonation belch. At that point, Digger did take a seat. Heart racing and yet still sleep-hazed, putting on the most soothing tone I could muster, I said, "Whatever's ailing you, we'll get you through it, I promise."

A long draught and belch later, he sort of seemed to have come back to himself, at least a little. "Before I go on, I need you tell me if you translated that gold card I found in the last job."

Given my partner's presently unstable state-of-mind, I did the next best thing to telling the truth. I lied. "No, not yet. Probably an ancient Roman blessing or something. We Roman Catholics love that shit."

"I want you to translate it now."

"Digger, now? Right now, this instant? Said I would, and I will. Tell me, please: why did your family have a restless night?"

"Because Junior had really bad nightmares. Woke up screaming. I'm awake all night anyway, so I ran in first, then his mother joined me in his bedroom. Found him all crunched up in a ball in the corner, clutching a raggedy rabbit he used to hold all night when he was an infant. My wife asked him what was wrong. Get this: he saw a huge man with dark hair combed straight back, wearing a charcoal pinstripe suit and plain blue tie, standing outside his window."

"Holy crap, man!" I yelled. "Is this the first report of a pedo seen in the neighborhood? I assume you called 9-1-1 and reported it."

His face morphed back to rage. "Did you not listen to the description? My boy saw the last corpse we robbed standing outside his window! I know how that must sound…"

"Completely batshit cray-cray, bro, not gonna lie."

"I knew you'd say that. No, of course I didn't call it in. There's more. My wife is good at getting him to talk; kid has a memory like a supercomputer. She asked if the man was looking at him." At this point, Digger choked up. A violent full-body shiver wracked him. After a time, he continued, "She asked if the man was looking at him. My boy said, 'Mama, his eyes and mouth were shut tight, like they were glued together. His face looked like one of those wax people at the museum. He hammered at the glass. That's when I screamed."

I made a face. "Dude, did you happen to look around his room? Not one square inch of white space, only wall to wall horror shit. Horror movies, horror dolls, horror books, comics, video games. He dreamed the whole thing, partner! The dreaming mind, as far as my experience goes, is like a computer screensaver: it pulls out random images from memory, then weaves and smashes them together in nonsensical, random patterns when in sleep mode. The wax giant outside the window is probably somehow loosely based on something in his room. See? Aren't you glad you have such a knowledgeable, insightful friend?"

If looks could kill I would've been a red spot on my own carpet. Digger stood, pulled out his cell phone, thumbed through photos, stepped toward me, and thrust the phone to my face. "Yeah, okay, Einstein. Explain these two shoe prints, men's size fifteen, in the dirt outside his window. They weren't there yesterday."

Irrationally, I thought of the gold card—and of the death curse etched thereon. Not that I ever planned to tell him about it. Take care of the business and it'll take care of you. I had to make payroll or I'd lose my crew. Here's my partner wigging out, telling me to buy back the most profitable loot we ever hauled in a single night, so that he and the Mexicans can re-exhume the corpse and restore my—or should I say our—property, to its original owner. "I feel like I just awoke inside some parallel universe…some alternate reality."

"Joe, I want you to drive over to the fence now. Go get the stuff back. Or—I'm out. For good. I mean it. I don't give a rat's ass what you think of me right now."

"Digger, indulge me. I'll drive you out to the cemetery. We'll stop along the way and buy some flowers. We'll take my truck, I'll drive, c'mon let's get moving."

"What for?"

"What for, what for: because you're my partner for life, bro, and you're a bird on a wire right now. We're going to blend in with all the other Sunday mourners there when we put flowers on our dear friend Tank's grave. I think we'll find the grave in the same condition as we left it. Then, my treat: I'll have my expensive residential security service install outside cameras and start monitoring your grounds full time. They'll dispatch local police the next time mister size-fifteen shoe-guy stops by."

"I'll blow his fucking head off."

"No, you won't. We don't need that kind of scrutiny, bub. By this time tomorrow, you three will be as safe and secure as bedbugs in a whore motel. Obviously, some weirdo is creep-stalking your boy. We'll let the cops deal with it. How would Junior feel if you shotgun-blasted some guy's face while he watched? Trust me—we got this."

Digger yielded to the logic of my plan. I grabbed my truck keys off the hook, went outside, unlocked, sat behind the wheel and fired up the old girl. The day itself was sunny and warm, blue skies with fluffy clouds meandering overhead like spun sugar, casting huge, interesting shadows. High humidity, which I love. It felt good. Normally I don't get to experience the outdoors this early, even on Sundays. I handed Digger a twenty and sent him into a supermarket; he emerged with what appeared to be a thirty-dollar bouquet of varying summer colors, bright and cheery. Driving on, when I saw the ice cream parlor on the left, I slowed.

Front cemetery gates stood wide open. I made a right onto the main road. Everything appeared strange during the day, not quite like what I remember from when I cased the property at night. "Pretty place," I muttered. Digger pointed; I made a left, then a right. Ahead was one parked police patrol vehicle, roof lights off. I saw yellow tape strung across the road and between headstones. I stopped, turned off the engine, considered all options, and made a quick decision. "Stay here," I told Digger, as I snatched the flowers from his hands. "I'll walk to a grave close to Tank's but not too close which, if I remember correctly based on that family mausoleum as a benchmark, should be…"

"Right where the cop car is parked."

I grimaced. "We shall see." I slammed my door shut extra hard hoping the cops would hear it. Never sneak up on guys with guns. They should teach that, among other practical 'Rules We Live By' beginning in kindergarten. I moseyed over to a spot about parallel with them, maybe fifty paces south. I pretended to study names on headstones as I edged closer to the cops. Twenty paces away, I saw a grave, Carson Cassidy, born 1918, died nineteen-ninety, a U.S. Navy symbol etched on the stone. I dropped to both knees and positioned the flowers roughly center of the marble. I pressed my hand to Cassidy's stone, hung my head low, and prepared to summon fake tears. As expected, one of the officers jangled closer to me. I did not look up.

"Good afternoon," said the officer.

I didn't look at him right away. Slowly I turned my head toward him, my mouth moving a little as if in prayer, tears on my cheeks. "Oh. Hi, officer."

"Sorry to disturb you, sir. I was wondering if I could ask you a few questions."

Slowly, I stood and sniffed back the summoned nasal congestion. "My dad survived World War Two. Made it to age seventy-one before the cancer got him. Isn't that something? Hordes of little Jap killers tried their best to take him out and failed. It took the devil's disease to finally get him."

The officer, eyes shielded by his hat, shifted. "I'm…sorry for your loss, sir. I'm sure he is a hero to the nation."

I nodded. "So please: tell me how I can possibly help you, officer."

"Come with me please, sir. It will only take a moment. I assume you come here regularly?"

"Lately. This is the week of his passing. I was here last weekend, too. Lead on, sir."

I followed him over to where the police tape started, which he lifted for me so that I could duck under. Fifteen paces later, I found myself staring into a hole containing an empty coffin. Grave dirt was scattered helter-skelter, nothing like when Digger and the crew cracked a grave. The coffin lid was perhaps eighteen or twenty feet away cleaved in two. The halves abutted another headstone.

Like a bomb had gone off inside the coffin, baptizing a two-hundred-square-foot area with yards of loose soil and clods of earth. The lid had launched as though from a circus cannon. I saw a few inches of soil atop headstones, like it had rained down onto them, at least seven or eight like that. I swallowed a huge lump in my throat, but that only made the lump feel larger. "Dear Lord," I heard myself saying into the abyss. That's when everything changed. I felt my soul sink into that empty grave, from where it would never rise again.

I summoned every brain cell to restore some presence of mind. I wiped my cheeks and turned to the officer. "What happened here?"

"Graverobbers."

"Ew, seriously?" God knows how I struggled to project a bit of my normal glib self.

He asked if last weekend I happened to see anyone hanging around this grave, pointing at Tank's plot. "No, officer. I had this entire section to myself. Sorry I couldn't be of more help. I hope you catch the bastard who did this. That poor family, my God."

He thanked me and apologized again for disturbing my private moment. I thanked him for his service and wish him a blessed afternoon. The heaviest feet I had ever felt slowly shuffled back to the truck.

Once I had driven away from the cemetery on the highway, I said, "We have a problem, partner."

"FUCK! I fucking knew it! What'd you find?"

I told him. What choice did I have but to give him the whole fact set, which included my translation of the Latin death curse, and Tank's grave, where it appeared they had buried a sizeable bomb on a timer, instead of a corpse. About the cops having already decided that it was the crime of graverobbing. I ended with, "They'll have every cemetery under twenty-four-seven surveillance for miles around, because of it. You know what this means for our business? I don't have to tell you."

"Fuck the business! I have a wife and son scared half to death. I'm scared even more than they are! This is all my doing! Now—fuck! —I can't even undo it. I don't see how I can. This thing I did—that *we* did—will haunt me wherever I go!"

Panic rose in my throat like a mercury thermometer in Hell. I wanted so much to join Digger in his enraged venting, but being boss of the outfit afforded me no such luxury. Self-restraint and a cool, calculating head is what life-threatening situations require. I gave my hysterical partner a calming grin and soothing voice. "Whatever's going on here isn't magic. Someone is onto us. Might even be Tank's 'people' which is bad, partner, bad. Really bad. Beyond bad. First, I promised you security cameras and home security monitoring. Ought to make you feel safe."

He frowned. "I don't know…"

"But I do. Leave it up to me. You're up all night anyway, and you have a shotgun."

Violating any reasonable sense of personal space, he stood with his face only three or four inches from mine. "Go get the stuff back," he growled.

I nodded. "He'll know if Tank's syndicate somehow learned of our existence. You've never come with me to the fence. The fewer people who know his location, the better. But since it appears that for the time being we are out of business, at least until things settle down a bit, would you like to ride along? You can stay in the car while I go inside. It'll freak him out big-time if I bring another into his realm."

"Let's go," he said.

I zigzagged along small roads as was my habit, in case I should pick up a tail. We passed through a blighted urban area of old abandoned factories and warehouses near rusted-out railroad tracks, down by the Schuylkill River. Over a century ago, these places were brightly painted, alive and vibrant with men actively engaged in affairs of their own, conducting business upon their own responsibility. Now, these buildings stand as decrepit empty hulks, more windows broken than intact, graffiti serving as the only fresh paint they'd received in the past one-hundred-twenty years.

The perfect disguise, hiding in plain sight.

The concrete lot was deeply fractured with age, with nasty-looking Bull and Canada Thistle weeds growing from every crack. I parked. Digger sat in my truck, twitchy and bent out of shape. I stood outside facing a set of rusted battleship-gray graffitied double-doors. No need to knock. Though difficult to spot, cameras were there. The doors cracked open. I slipped inside, unseen.

Outside it was a scary-looking, depressing dump. Inside was a dichotomous scene altogether different, like a palatial estate, something a wealthy family would proudly show off to fellow elites. The flat roof fifty feet overhead had turned into one giant peaked skylight casting the sun over a veritable greenhouse on the ground level. The entire expanse was covered with many exotic plants small and large, even a few mature banana trees sixteen feet tall. The most abundant specimens were columns of enormous, sticky-budding, richly-fragrant sativa giants—his cash crop.

Water effects everywhere. Four convex footbridges crossed over a burbling brook in asymmetrical places. Dense humidity and pungent aromas delighted my senses as I followed him through this slice of paradise to another set of double doors. These he opened to an enormous, gray, neatly painted warehouse. Banks of overhead LED motion-sensor lights awoke upon our entry, illuminating rows and columns of sturdy steel shelving forty feet in height. The columns stretched back at least the length of a football field. Stereos, big screen TVs, computers—pricey gadgets galore. An area of bays to the right each contained a vehicle, including some expensive sporty Italian jobs, a newish Corvette, some high-end German luxury sedans, and a few Harley Davidson production bikes. Each gleamed from hand-polished care and tire shiner. Thirty paces in, from a shelf at eye-level, my fence grasped the plastic bin which he said contained everything taken from Tank's coffin, intact.

"You know, I've already spent money on appraisers. Then there's my time spent sanitizing and polishing this stuff for sale."

My eyes narrowed. "I understand. I know what appraisers charge, and unless you're a Hollywood divorce attorney which clearly you are not, then with a fair degree of accuracy I can guess their hourly rate. Also, I'm saving you the expense of having to find buyers, which more than cancels out your time investment."

I ended up paying him two-thousand out-of-pocket over what he had paid me for the loot to recover it. He placed the container in a brown paper double-sack with handles, a wry expression on his face as we shook hands. I wagged my head and puffed air through closed lips. "Don't even ask," I said, as I walked back into the urban-blighted outdoors.

Back in the truck, Digger appeared jubilant. "Thank you, brother!"

I shot him a quick polite grin, though inside, truly I felt like backhanding his face. "Now what, Digger? You can't return it to the grave because the occupant is currently missing."

"No, but don't you get it? When Tank comes around again, I can hand over his stuff. He should leave us alone after that."

I shook my head. "Digger: Tank is embalmed. As in rigor-mortis; stiff as a utility pole. Unless you're Jesus Christ, there ain't no coming back. Period; end of story. The corpse was stolen. Probably by some very bad guys, which does worry me. But if it makes you sleep better tonight, then by all means hang onto the loot."

"Did the fence say mobsters are onto us?"

I shook my head. "I asked; he said no way. Omerta, their code of silence, also extends to affiliates like him. They don't ask where he gets the stuff and he doesn't offer. Mostly he does narcotics stuff with them. No dots connect them to us, zero. But somebody out there is on to us. Somebody desecrated Tank's grave and is stalking your family. How much do you really know about the Mexicans? Any of 'em former cartel?"

"I know everything. Super-Catholic. And none of that Santa Muerte bullshit, either."

I reversed my small-roads course, mazy and confusing as it was, until thirty-five-minutes later, I stopped in front of Digger's house, engine running. Emotionally drained, my patience felt thinner than the swept-back hair on Tank's vexatious head. I was as done with Digger as I was with the entire mega-FUBAR day.

"Cost me twenty-five Bens to get this stuff back, you know. In the near future when we are back in business …"

"I always pay what I owe, and I'll gladly pay the piper for this. Take care, man," he said, as I watched him carry the paper sack to a double-steel-door cellar entrance on the side of the house until down he went.

'Take care, man' were the last words he would ever say to me.

Back home, after a luxurious soak in my huge tub, surrounded by CBD candles scented of rose, lavender, lemongrass and sandalwood, I took another long hot shower. Around 7:00 p.m. that Sunday evening, I fixed myself a hearty breakfast and prepared to face a night of zero activity. Went online, checked my investments; this elevated my spirit somewhat, having realized twenty-seven thousand dollars in one week's capital gains before markets had closed Friday afternoon. Unlike Junior with his horror obsession, I prefer action movies and old-timey comedies. By midnight, I had watched one of each.

"God, I'm so bored," I said aloud. Normally I am the happiest bachelor on earth. 'We're born alone; we die alone; we might as well spend every moment in between alone'—is my mantra. Only sometimes, like this night, I do speculate about not being alone. Though please: what woman would want to invest her future in a nocturnal ghoul? Cold reasoning always quickly severs these speculative daydreams, cleaner than Tank hacking off a child's hands or feet.

At 1:00 a.m. Monday, I surfed the Web. Properties for sale in Alaska arrested my attention. *Good place for a fresh start*, I'd thought. Then, from somewhere in my peripheral vision, I perceived movement. It came from one of the monitors lined up in a neat row in my office, each fed by an outdoor camera. My pulse quickened. I filled my lungs, then flung open my eyes wide to study the security monitor screens. Nothing. An occasional neighborhood cat on the prowl. But then I watched as a kid emerged from behind the Helleri holly hedge. I could hear blood rushing in my ears. Had to be a boy, short and skinny, head on a swivel, acting all herky-jerky and paranoid. Tentatively, he approached my side door.

I grabbed my .357 only as a reflex precaution and flew downstairs to the side door. I flung it open. I didn't want to turn on the outside light, something nosy neighbors would remember at that hour. Light from inside illuminated the boy's face just fine. "Junior! My God, kid, do you know what time it is? Does your father know you're here?"

Barefoot in pajamas, he ran into my arms, buried his face against my stomach, and cut loose crying and wailing in utter despair. I shut the door, hoping my neighbors heard none of it before I did. I'm not a 'hugger' but I consented to it, given his emotional state. I started to ask what on earth could possibly bring him out here to me at this hour, until intuition instructed me to zip it, and just let the boy have his cry. Shrieks slowed to piteous sobs. When his storm felt like it was finally starting to pass, I mussed his blond mop as I always do. I turned him facing away with his back to me and gently marched him into the living room. I guided him onto one of the recliners. I knelt on the floor, and patted his knee, "Okay Junior. Spill it. I'm about to go call your dad."

"He's DEAD!" The crying started all over again.

By that point, impatience rose in me like a hurricane. He pressed his red-hot, wet cheeks between my cool hands. "No, he isn't. Can't be."

He choked on phlegm as he tried to get the words out. "The wax man came in through the cellar doors. He came into my mom's room, with a knife…" The crying crescendo resumed back to piteous wails.

"Where is she now?"

"DEAD! He cut her boobies off! My dad heard the screams and jumped on him. The man stuck the knife in my dad's zipper and ripped all the way up to his boobies. His insides came out like sausages…" He threw up on my immaculate light-colored Berber wall-to-wall carpeting.

For once, I found myself unable to answer the question, What Do I Do Now? My logical brain kicked in. Tissues and a glass of water for the kid: I sprinted to the kitchen and returned with these. He blew his nose but was still crying too hard to drink. Call the cops? Would love to make this their problem! Not a chance. I asked him, "How is it that you escaped?"

"I opened my window and dropped down. Then I ran. I was scared. I knew the wax man would get me if I stayed, and I knew my neighbors were asleep, and that you are like my dad, awake all night..." As soon as he said 'dad,' furious crying ended his ability to speak.

"Junior! Junior, I need you to listen to me for a second." Between hitched breaths, his snot-runners pooled on my recliner seat. I wiped his nose. Red eyes met mine. He nodded. "I'm going over there now, to your house. You'll be perfectly safe here. You'll find soda, and milk and cereal in the kitchen if you get hungry."

"No! Don't leave me alone! The wax man will find me here!" he screamed, face a picture of ghastly terror.

I shook my head. "Son, you don't understand, so let me explain. Junior, this home is a fortress! Reinforced doors, shuttered windows, cameras outside. You are as safe here as you would be in Fort Knox."

"What's that place?"

"Where the government stores all the nation's gold. Never mind—just know that nothing can get to you here, I promise."

"Swear?"

"Yes. Swear on my life. Now please, you just sit tight. I'll be back before the clock chimes two."

Keys in hand, I stepped into loafers, stuffed the S&W Model 327 Magnum revolver in my right sweatpants pocket, went outside, closed the door, and locked it behind me. A part of me patently rejected the kid's hysterical story. Another part had me scanning every shadow, every bush, every possible point where a large figure could burst out and lay hands on me. I fought to silence the *Am I fucking crazy?* thoughts by countering with real-world evidence, in a winner-take-all battle to dominate my lucid mind. I fired up the truck and forced myself to drive one mile-per-hour below every speed limit. Inside, it felt like my heart and guts would burst out like roiling eels. I crawled twelve blocks to Digger's home, parked, and got out. I shined my cell phone light at the cellar door entrance.

Both steel doors had been flung wide open and were open still.

I'd been down in Digger's mancave enough times to know where to find the three-way light switch. I flicked it on. Seven LED shop lights snapped on, so bright they made me squint. I inspected his dad's big black sea chest, protected by a combination lock. Eyeing bolt-cutters hung above his workbench; I cut the lock and looked inside. There sat the brown paper double-bag, loot undisturbed in the plastic container. I grabbed the bag, walked it back to the concrete steps I had just descended, and set it on the third step to grab on my way out which, nervously I suspected, would be part of a hasty retreat.

Every cell, every atom of my being cried out *You do not want to be here five minutes from now.*

I padded up creaky wooden stairs as softly as I could in my buffalo-hide loafers. I alighted into a dark kitchen. In the splash of cell phone light, I did notice the largest of the German steel kitchen knives missing from the block. Not encouraging. Cell light in my left hand, I walked toward the staircase holding the Magnum in my right, which fires eight hollow-point 125-grain rounds. These missiles leave the snub muzzle at nearly fifteen-hundred feet-per-second. Whatever target they kiss gets hit with nearly six-hundred foot-pounds of kinetic energy—enough to drop a fully-grown grizzly bear, or a charging bull. I shined the light up the stairs to the second-floor hallway, finger on the trigger. I would have to ascend and turn right, then make the first sharp left into their bedroom. I wondered if I might have a heart attack, soul-engine thud-thumping away in my ears and eyes.

I'll confess I was terrified. Not like that moment just before a fistfight or sitting in the hospital room waiting to be called in to pre-op for life-threatening surgery. This wave of fear was unlike anything I had ever felt, marrow deep. Fear of eternity; of Hell itself, and all the hungry, misshapen misanthropes and pale horrors consigned to eternal damnation lurking within it.

At the door to their bedroom, I paused to listen. I heard nothing but caught a whiff of bowel. Behind the cone of light from my cell phone, my shaky right hand attempting to steady the .357 hand-cannon, I finally screwed up the courage to enter the room.

Below the window, abutting the drywall, was the head of the bed. Atop the bed, the gore scene before me maybe could only be compared with the loathsome aftermath of a primeval sword battle. Surely, I am far from the first to witness such cruelty, of what man is sometimes eager to do to his fellow man, but this was a first, for me. I felt like the unluckiest man who ever lived. I grappled with wonderment. *How could any human being carry around such apathy, hate, and sadism—as some do?* What must it feel like to spend an entire lifetime battling the urge to give vent to these dark drives? A man however did not do this, as I would soon learn. Less than an hour ago, Junior had eye-witnessed in what form the eternal spirit of hate now presented itself.

Sanity is a fragile thing, something else I learned during that zero-dark-thirty-morning. Those who take it for granted, most people probably, have never had their holds on it tested. Mine was getting stretched to its maximum limit, forced to explore the very heart of evil and all its dark, diseased innermost recesses. I had completely forgotten the present. My responsibility to the boy felt like a distant memory.

Turning my back to the carnage, I shined the light out into the hall. I noticed the thin wood covering the hollow slab door to the boy's bedroom appeared split. It hung slightly ajar; the top and middle hinges ripped completely out of the door frame. I left the master bedroom and shined the light through the huge gap in the frame, into Junior's room. Satisfied that it was unoccupied, I eased aside the wounded door and quietly entered. In the closet, I found a rolling bag with cartoon action hero faces emblazoned thereon. Taking great care not to squeak wood or drop anything, I slid open drawers and grabbed whatever I found. I packed as many of Junior's clothes into that silly piece of luggage as it would hold. I knelt on it and brought my full two-hundred-pound body weight to bear down on it. With a struggle, I zippered it closed.

I tip-toed back to the kitchen, heart thudding away. My cotton mouth tasted like the underside of roadkill, and I felt dizzy. I eased opened the fridge. Two fingers of soda remained in a big two-liter bottle. I drained it. Unable to easily find a garbage can, I remembered spotting one in the basement. Why I cared about neatness in the moment, which I have puzzled over, remains a mystery. In a world spinning off axis and orbit faster than a meteorite., boring little routines help restore emotional order, maybe? I pinched the handle of the boy's rolling bag and the empty plastic bottle together in my left hand, clutched the gun in my right, flicked on the three-way basement light switch, and cautiously made my way back down the wooden stairs.

I heard something up there in the kitchen. Every hair on my body tried to push its way out. Bathed in bright white light standing below at the foot of the steps looking up, I saw only the dark open door. Maybe I disturbed something and it fell over; I recall my wishful thinking. I debated whether to ascend once more. But ultimately, I froze, paralyzed with fear, as a shadow in the door frame moved. The right leg of a pinstripe suit lurched down one step. A resounding thud. The first of the stairs groaned under the enormous muddy dress shoe. In an awkward, almost mechanical movement, the other leg joined it. The beam trembled when I shined my cell light higher.

I never again want to feel such abject panic and terror, what ripped through me at that moment, nor do I wish it on my worst enemy. Tank wore the identical expression as when I last saw him in the funeral home. Why wouldn't he? *Because he is fucking* dead! I'd thought, as I watched the unnatural descent of the right leg. The right foot joined the left on the first stair step. I was forced to make a hasty fight-or-flight decision. *If I run now, I'll be running forever*, I'd thought. My brain never worked so hard and so quickly for a solution.

And there it was, in my right hand, and on the floor beside the boy's luggage. I wedged the big empty soda bottle over the muzzle of my revolver. It took some work to stretch the thicker plastic mouth over the fixed titanium site. I stepped into my modified Weaver shooting stance. I aimed directly at the heart. Without the benefit of the fixed front site that was now buried in plastic, aiming was exceedingly difficult. Thank God, adrenaline and muscle memory did the rest. I fired. *Surely, I hit center mass. At this range, I could not possibly miss*, I'd thought, pulse pounding behind my eyes.

The bottom of the bottle had exploded; the home-made single-use noise suppressor did an adequate job of keeping the shot noise confined to the subterranean space. I watched the cloth of the suit over the heart puff out as microfibers either caught fire and burned up, or char-blackened around the small hole over the heart. The exit wound at the back would be about the size of a fifth-grader's fist—this I knew—and in that split second, I did notice a few drops of what must have been pink embalming fluid, along with darker bits of heart and lung tissue splatted against white-painted drywall to the right. A living man would have crumpled and plummeted head-first down the stairs, dead.

It just stood there. Until I saw the right leg in motion; heard and felt the thump of the shoe on the second step. The logical sections of my mind went bankrupt. Only the primitive lizard-brain remained to ensure survival of the organism that is me. Full panic mode. *Get out! Run!*

Supernatural panic.

I pocketed the gun, grabbed the superhero bag, ran to the concrete steps, grabbed the loot bag, flicked off the light, and bolted up through the open painted steel cellar doors. I closed them, not that I believed it would do much good, considering this thing had freed itself from a box under tons of tightly packed clay soil. I ferried the two bags into the passenger footwell and flopped the gun on the seat.

I took one last look at my dead friend's house. I tried to imagine it was daylight, his wife giving me a hug, Junior tugging on my shorts to come see a bumblebee hive, or a dead squirrel. Penning these remembrances now makes my head throb. I recall having momentary thoughts that this whole episode was merely a highly lifelike and lucid nightmare from which I would soon awaken, one that coffee would make me forget. Or that someone had slipped me a powerful hallucinogen, and that the strangest thing happening at Digger's place tonight was his business partner parked out front, staring at it like a mental patient. Any minute now I'd see a light go on inside and everything would be alright. I'll drive to my home and find it empty.

Steel doors exploded outward with a tremendous clang, like some bell atop the church of Satan.

Just then, a wonderment hit me: *Have I just spent decades living inside of a dream—a pleasant dream inside which I was just a normal workaday guy, making a semi-honest living, not hurting anyone, living a boring but stable life? Is that true—was my entire life merely a dream—or am I really a ghoul, condemned to die for my sins under some infernal curse, at the hands of a bedeviled corpse?*

Now the dream was over and, quite clearly and fully, the accursed ghoul was awake. I hit the accelerator pedal so hard that the ancient rear wheels chirped and left burnout marks on the asphalt.

Junior had passed out asleep on the recliner. Thank God, because I needed time to think. For the first time in a long time, I prayed the Our Father and begged for Heavenly guidance. Not that I deserved it—I, least of all God's creatures. Soon after, I did receive a mental image, like a sort of waking dream. I saw boundless ice and snow, polar bears, arctic wolves, seals, sea otters: creatures living their frolicking lives on floating rafts of bluish-white ice. I smelled rich woodsmoke. I saw single-engine aircraft buzzing by at eye level against snow-capped mountains so huge they made the Poconos seem like foothills by comparison, under a sky weakly brightened by a cold sun that remains overhead for eighty-two-days straight, never a dip below the horizon, until it glides into a month-long polar night.

Also why did I spend so much time searching on Alaska real estate? Never been there; never had a desire to go there. And now this detailed daydream. *Thank you, Lord.*

Methodically, I packed everything I needed, and a few items of sentimental value. Computers, monitors, accessories, routers packed in bubble wrap, boxed, sealed: check. Winter clothing in plastic bags; sea chest filled with valuables and memories; non-perishable food—check. Everything else I might need I'd buy online and have it delivered.

The bulk of my wealth resides in anonymized offshore accounts where all I am to these people is a long string of numerals, but no name. I only kept ten grand in a local credit union from which all my creditors withdrew receivables directly from it via ACH. I looked around and shrugged, realizing I was walking away from ten thousand and the house. Homicide detectives would consider me the top person of interest in the Digger murders. I'd just have to forfeit this bit of my property, mere peanuts in the grand scheme of things.

With my outdoor lights off, unwilling to risk attracting any neighborhood night owl's attention, gun in my right hand, I made multiple trips outside, head on a swivel and ears perked for the slightest movement, until everything was loaded. I covered my truck bed and locked the tonneau cover, went inside, drained a soda can, then knelt before the recliner. Junior was snoring. Gently I pressed my hand to his narrow chest. When this failed to rouse him, I shook him a little. It took a full minute for his eyes to open.

I smiled. In my hand a glass of cold water. He took it and drank. "I need to talk to you, son."

His eyes grew very wide. I suppose the repressed memory of the earlier horror re-cached in a rush. Tears welled. "I was dreaming of the wax man."

I nodded. "Unfortunately, Junior, he is anything but a dream."

"Y-you, believe me? I-I didn't think you d-did."

I nodded. "I believe you *so* much, Junior. Now please listen, because you have a very important decision to make, one that will affect the entire rest of your life. Do you understand? If you don't, ask me anything. If you do understand, I need you to say it."

"I-I, I understand," he said. At that moment he appeared older than his years.

"Good. Okay, here goes: if you want, I'll drive you over to the police station and drop you off. You can tell them what happened. They'll call your mom's sister in New York. She'll come and take you back with her to live." I watched his eyes as reality clasped his heart like a hydraulic claw.

"Or you leave with me this morning, right now, and I'll do my best to raise you right, as your mom and dad would've wanted. When we hit the Northwest, I'll drop an anonymous letter in the mail to your aunt explaining that I'm a dear old friend of one of your parents, and that, for your own safety, I cannot reveal your whereabouts, as those who attacked your family will never stop looking for you to finish the persecution they started."

"Will the wax man find us?" The fear in his eyes probably matched my own. It's only that I'm a better actor; I refused to let it show. I smiled.

"Not a chance, Junior. Not where we're going. Impossible." *So is a walking corpse*, but I bit my tongue. His eyes moved rapidly side-to-side, deep in thought. My heart felt torn in two, this sweet kid whose childhood didn't only just end—it died in bloody pieces and went to Hell. Gazing at Junior made me want to rip out my eyes, but the pragmatic little counselor in me again shrieked, *'Get out NOW! Tank's lumbering over here and may in fact BE here.'*

"I don't want to live with my aunt. She's weird. Her house smells funny. I want to go with you."

I nodded. "Do you need to use the bathroom? Hungry? Thirsty?" He shook his head. "I grabbed some of your clothes, they're in my truck. You can change at a rest stop. Let's get moving. We can't stay here. The wax man is coming."

My fence came through with two completely new identities for me and Junior. Social security cards, driver's licenses, passports. Cost me a hundred grand, and those were friend prices. For the first few weeks, the owner of a bed-and-breakfast bled me for two hundred a night; online I saw her advertised rate was three hundred per, so I'm not complaining. She's an odd person but very friendly, warm and polite. The same could be said of all the hard-scrabble citizens living in or near Barrow, Alaska, an alien landscape so cold, dark, and dangerous that people here haven't the luxury to be mean or impolite. It's all of us versus nature and the elements, never each other.

In our third week, I purchased one hundred sixty acres in North Slope Borough, and had contractors dig wells and septic, and tap the main electricity trunk with a very long buried cable. Another contractor built a large steel Quonset hut, parts of it pre-fab from Canada, but much of it customized to my design. I was thinking of the fence back home, how he converted the inside of that ugly warehouse into a warm, humid, sunny and fragrant utopia, which is precisely what I did here. Indoor swimming pool, indoor and outdoor hot tubs. Cut into the top-most sections of the steel hut are tons of thick convex glass, maintaining structural strength in the arch design yet it lets in so much light. I even have a banana tree. Eight cold-weather-proof outdoor cameras mounted on the structure feed my command center screens, and another one-hundred-sixty solar-powered motion sensor devices around the periphery activate cameras when anything moves within range. Thus far, plenty of wild animals large and small, but that's it. No humans. No demons.

Amka, a moon-faced Inuit woman twenty years younger than I, started cleaning my place for money. She answered an ad I had posted on the local Catholic church bulletin board. If there is anything one might consider an upside to this ill-fated macabre emprise, I truly feel born-again. I have given myself over completely to my deeply rooted core faith in the Lord. I no longer feel lonely. Sometimes, when it snows hard, Amka stays the night in my bed. Now she's here just about all the time. She satisfies most of my needs, and she dotes on Junior, who enrolled in the local schools where he excels. He's made lots of new friends. He calls me dad and refers to Amka as 'Aaka'—the northern Inuit equivalent of mom. Whenever I mention his formative years, it's as though his mind has formed a thick mental callous around it. Never, ever will he speak of the past, nor allow anyone else to, either.

If a creature were to totter along at one mile per hour, forced to travel only at night to avoid detection, mathematically speaking, it would take approximately two years for it to get from where we started to where we settled. It has now been two years since I abandoned my Pennsylvania home. If my security sensors pick it up, most definitely there will be time for my son and I to pull up stakes and relocate to Hawaii. *Good luck walking the Pacific Ocean floor, Tank. You inconceivable demon.*

Nevertheless, in case the worst happens, let this journal serve as my testimonial. What I related of the earlier period, believe; give only such credit as may seem due, or doubt it altogether, or, if doubt it you cannot, then play unto its mystery the eyewitness accounts of demonic possession, also death and bodily resurrection, recorded by civilized, highly intelligent people two millenniums ago who were no different, apart from technological advances, from people living today.

On the cover of the journal is my real name and original social security number. I keep it in a locked box in my office, along with the plastic container of loot which I keep as a sort of bribe, or talisman; a peace offering, maybe—although the bag of jewelry did nothing to protect Digger. If I die of natural causes at some ripe old age, everything is willed to my son, and therefore, this will never get read. For he will follow my written instructions to shred or burn the envelope and these contents therein, unread. I want him to forget the past entirely.

If my son and I are found dead, and you are the unfortunate law enforcement officer reading this upon discovery of our mutilated remains, then check the security cam footage and thus conclude that the cause of our deaths was anything but natural.

Magic 8 Ball

The Will

12 January, Year 2021—Philadelphia, Pennsylvania

Priscila Leone looked sharper than a blade in her brand-new black blazer and pencil skirt, sheer nylons, black high heels, and black cloth gloves. She reached for the door handle. "Pickmann, Levenstein, and Roth. Attorneys at Law. We have arrived."

Her companion, Cozbi Abital, wore close to the same outfit, though her blazer and skirt were not black, but charcoal gray. Both women wore black cloth facemasks as required by State law during the Covid-19 pandemic. "Thank Gaia. I'm freezing. Twenty-eight degrees wouldn't feel so bad except for the wind."

In the lobby they stood at the fifty-inch LED screen. Priscila used her knuckles to part brunette bangs whipped into her eyes by wind. She scrolled down alphabetically to the 'Ps' until she found Pickmann's law office on the seventeenth floor, the only name on the marquis for the entire floor, in contrast to all other floors listing multiple corporate names with suite numbers. "Hmm," she muttered. "These legal parasites must be fatter with blood than a tick in a coon dog's ear."

She punched in the floor number at a wall kiosk. An elevator door opened to their left. Inside, the doors closed behind them almost silently and the elevator whooshed them up at a speed neither had ever before experienced, fast as an amusement park ride. Both yawned and swallowed to crack the sudden pressure in their eustachian tubes and relax middle ear muscles. Seconds is all it took. Doors opened to a vestibule separated from the law office lobby by floor-to-ceiling, wall-to-wall glass, with a single pedestrian doorway to the right. The firm's name and brand logo, some avant-garde artist's take on the balanced Scales of Justice, occupied a large part of the middle glass in the form of an etching. Behind the reception desk burbled a water effect. Many plants in the lobby, and only six comfortable-looking pastel blue padded vinyl chairs, all of them unoccupied, save for one. A beefy uniformed law enforcement officer glared at them. The receptionist, an emaciated barely-twenty bottle blonde, wore what Priscila and Cozbi immediately recognized as a Neiman's Last Call clearance item, a pink-hued Veronica Beard fitted jacket and matching slacks, an outfit probably released as a new item three years ago. Her pinkish cloth facemask just about matched the outfit.

Cozbi, reading Priscila's face, whispered, "When you're that young and skinny you can wear a burlap sack and make it acceptable at Fashion

Week."

"Gaia knows, those were the days, sister," Priscila whispered back.

"Good morning!" squeaked the receptionist in a helium-huffing child's voice. Whom are you here to see?"

"Hi, my name is Priscila Leone, and this is Cozbi Abital, here to see Barry Levenstein. Our appointment is at nine." She glanced at her watch. "And we are right on time. Beautiful outfit. You may call me Pris, and her, Coz."

The receptionist beamed. "Thanks! I'm Brandi. Did you park downstairs? I can validate your parking ticket."

"No, we took a bus down from the Poconos, then a rideshare. Thanks though, for asking."

"Have either of you been here before?"

"No!" both answered.

"If you could both just sign in here," she said, pointing to a tiny console. Priscila went first, tapped in her name, phone, email address, hit next, until the device asked her to center her face in the window. Satisfied with the centering, she tapped next; her photo, along with her name, date, time, and Levenstein's name printed out onto a self-stick nametag, grainy but serviceable. Cozbi followed. Both pressed nametags onto blazer lapels.

Priscila managed to wrench her brown eyes away from the pretty blues of the gorgeous woman-child behind the reception counter long enough to glance at the policeman. *Still staring. Eerie. The unemotional nature of his interest kinda makes me feel like a virus under a microscope.*

"Great! Now if you follow me to the large conference room, there's coffee, bottled water, and breakfast croissants inside, be sure to help yourselves before Mister Levenstein enters, because then you must always wear masks. This way, please." They followed her down a hallway containing both empty offices and cubicles, once occupied with stylish young people. Priscila could sense the unsmiling eyes of the burly cop. She distracted herself by watching the silky-smooth calf muscle action of the receptionist. *Would love me a sip of this Brandi, mmm mm. Gaia knows, how I do covet young, innocent girl-flesh.*

The girl stopped at the restroom. "Yes!" said Coz, denying the receptionist a chance to ask. Both went in and emerged four minutes later. "Thanks for the pit stop, lead on, beautiful Brandi!"

"Brandi. Such a unique and pretty name. Magical, almost," said Priscila. She decided to creep-stalk her later.

"Really? Wow. That's like the nicest thing anyone's ever said to me!" *Issues. Lots of issues. Going to groom her right in.*

The lobby and hallway felt chilly compared to the conference room. Priscila figured that, with most employees working from home, it didn't make good business sense to raise the thermostat higher than the sixties.

The conference room, floor-to-ceiling glass on two walls at the building's corner, allowed enough weary winter sunlight to warm the room into the low seventies. Sipping coffee, the two sat together with their backs to the city outside the glass. They faced the door, anxious for the lawyer's arrival. Under the glass conference room table, they dared a handshake and squeezed each other's thighs in triumph. *Victory over the patriarchy. A major win for us, and for the goddess. A bright, deeply arousing future lies just ahead after this one final, necessary legal formality.*

Two sets of male footsteps approached. Quickly they re-donned their cloth facemasks. The door swung open. In walked an impeccably dressed masked man with male pattern baldness centered inside a shock of neatly combed black hair, followed by the hulking and ripped sinister-eyed policeman. "Madam Alaister, Madam Abital, my name is Barry Levenstein, Esquire. Please call me Barry. With me is Trooper Tyler from the State Police. We must follow State protocol during the pandemic; such an inconvenience to us all, need I even say it."

"Good morning, Mister…I mean, Barry. I'm Priscila Leone, and this is Cozbi Abital, here at your request. Please call me Priscila."

"Call me Cozbi."

"Very well, Priscila and Cozbi, thank you for making the long journey this morning. First, do you have something for me?"

Recognition in Priscila's eyes. She reached into her black designer quilted tote and withdrew what appeared to be a crumpled paper lunch bag with something round inside. She placed it on the immaculately clean, thick glass table before the lawyer. He quickly spirited it into the bag he was holding.

"Thank you. Now we all know why we are here. Let us commence with the reading of the last will and testament of one deceased Gabriel Inglebert Meshach, in which both of you are named.

Holding hands under the table, their grips tightened.

Levenstein sat across from them with his back to the door with Tyler standing behind him. He laid his smart black leather attorney messenger briefcase bearing the firm's logo in white embroidery onto the tabletop. From it, he withdrew two file folders, one yellow, one red. He pointed to the yellow folder. "In this contains the last will and testament of my client, Gabe Meshach. Let's begin there. A rather simple will, as they go. I should know I authored it."

Priscila and Cozbi could scarcely breathe. A risky plan, years in the making, had come together so neatly that neither had expected every facet to fall into place without a single hiccup.

Levenstein cleared his throat. He held what appeared to be only a few letter-sized papers bound with a large gold-colored paper clip, which he removed. Trooper Tyler blocked the door like a large stone gargoyle. His impassive eyes never left the faces of the two women.

"I, Gabriel Inglebert Meshach, domiciled and residing in Carbon County, Commonwealth of Pennsylvania, declare that this is my will. I revoke all my prior wills and codicils. I am unmarried. I have no children or heirs.

"I appoint Priscila Leone as the Executor of my Estate. If she becomes unable or unwilling to serve, I appoint Cozbi Abital to serve as successor or alternate Executor. I direct that no Executor appointed in this Article will be required to execute or file any bond, with or without sufficient surety, in any jurisdiction for the faithful performance of their duties as fiduciary.

"I direct my Executor to pay the medical, funeral, and estate administration expenses that are payable at or by reason of my death before making a final distribution of my estate." The women searched one another's eyes for signs of emotion. Tyler's eyes never left theirs.

Trooper Tyler, older than his unlined eyes and super-fit body might suggest, read this exchange for the open book that it was, to him. Thousands of guilty people had lied to him over the years. Nobody knew the 'tells' better than he. His eyes were drawn to the matching gold medallions both wore on chains about their necks. He had never seen anything like it. Round, with an Aztec interlocking daisy chain forming a circle close to the periphery. Inside the circle was a curious symbol which to him appeared to be a nude female with hands enjoined over her head, and some sort of germinating plant, wide hips coming together to a point instead of feet. Left and right of the woman hung opposing crescent moons, points facing outwards. So odd was the symbol that it transfixed him, which interrupted his body language read.

"There's a longer section authorizing the executor to pay all federal and state estate, inheritance, transfer, or succession taxes, including any interest or penalties thereon (herein "death taxes")—and it goes on like that. I think you understand.

Both nodded.

"Skipping to the substance of it: I give to Priscila Leone if she survives me all the tangible personal property that I may own at my death, including but not limited to all my household goods, appliances, tools, furniture and furnishings, silver, china, jewelry, books, photographs, documents, digital and electronic information, personal effects, wearing apparel, and any automobiles or other vehicles that I may own at my death.

"My "Residuary Estate" is all the property I may own at my death and that remains after payments are made under Article III and distributions are made under Article IV above, whether such property is real, personal, or mixed, and whenever obtained and wherever situated.

"I give all my Residuary Estate to Priscila Leone if she survives me. If Priscila Leone does not survive me, I direct my Executor give my Residuary Estate to Cozbi Abital, acting as Executor. Cozbi Abital is specifically empowered to distribute my Residuary Estate to herself, or to anyone else she may choose in her complete discretion to distribute to.

"If neither Priscila Leone or Cozbi Abital survives me, I direct that all of my Residuary Estate shall be distributed to Morfran Asra, Orusula Umbra, Abigor Moreau, and Zagan Alarie, who survive me and who would have taken my estate and in the shares they would have taken it, under the intestate laws of Pennsylvania in effect at my death."

Both felt the bolt of electricity from their brains to their tingling ears, aroused pudenda, and curling toes.

"Then a section on Definitions—just boilerplate stuff—and signature areas, and notary seal. Priscila, Cozbi: I wrote this simple will for Gabe in December, one of my last tasks before taking some time off for Hanukkah, so if you have any questions, please ask."

Priscila cleared her throat. "Gabe meant the world to me. My lover and my best friend. I spent the holidays grieving his absence. I set an empty place for him at the dinner table of our sisterhood. He seemed so happy! He and I were happy together! His self-emasculation and suicide make absolutely no sense. I do nothing but search my own mind, every day, even in my sleep, torturing myself trying to figure out where our love could have possibly gone so wrong without me recognizing signs. How did I fail him? He seemed so enraptured, so filled with passion and love, and pure joy. "And yet here we are, talking cold hard business," she said. Tyler studied her like an entomologist with a rare insect specimen. "I feel so vulgar asking. What exactly comprised Gabe's estate? I need to know what level of work I'm facing here in the weeks or months ahead, dealing with all of that." Trooper Tyler, as apoplectic as a statue, shifted himself at hearing the question.

"Precisely this: his cabin in the Poconos and all its contents. His red 1986 Ferrari Testarossa, black 2019 Nissan Titan pick-up truck, and…" he reached into his bag for a green folder from which he pulled two sheets of paper, "electronically traded funds, electronic stock shares, municipal bond funds both long and short term, also a checking account. Using yesterday's market valuations, Gabe's total net worth is just north of three million dollars."

Eyes widened and handhold tightened as whirling minds struggled to process the fact that, as of this moment, they were truly, filthy rich. They'd spend the rest of their lives farting through silk. "Any other questions about the will?"

"Do you have user I.D. and password access to his online trading and checking accounts?"

From his left jacket pocket, he extracted a thumb-drive. "Gabe stored all his impossible-to-remember, un-hackable I.D.s and passwords in a spreadsheet contained on this storage device. I made back-ups on our shared server should the drive malfunction. Following security protocols, handing this to you today would be most unwise. Bad things happen to nice people every day in this city. I would not wish to risk my client's personal information falling into criminal hands. Therefore, I have arranged a secure file transfer protocol site on our server where the file resides. I will send you an encrypted email containing the SFTP location, then another encrypted email giving you file access credentials. This you can accomplish from the safety of your own domicile. These emails are very secure. Our operation is ISO 27001 certified. We take information security very, very seriously here."

She nodded. "Yes-yes, smart, very smart. This city really has gone downhill fast."

She shot a glance at Cozbi. "No more questions. Should we go?"

Barry Levenstein glanced over his shoulder at Trooper Tyler. "Not just yet."

"There's more?"

The attorney nodded. "Gabe mailed something to me after I ratified the will. A daily journal of his final weeks."

Priscila and Cozbi exchanged quick nervous glances. This did not escape Trooper Tyler's notice. "A journal?"

Levenstein nodded. "Fairly detailed and articulately written. He enclosed a signed note instructing me to read aloud the journal at the reading of his will. This of course is not strictly required by law. However, it was the last wish of a dying man. Do either of you have any objection to my executing Gabe's final instruction?"

They searched each other's eyes. "No objections, Barry," said Priscila, glad for once to be wearing a mask. She now openly stared back at Trooper Tyler.

Magic 8 Ball

The Journal

3 October, Year 2020—Jim Thorpe, Pennsylvania
Journal entry. 9:00 a.m.

Nights are cool now, in the forties. Love it. Sleeping weather hath returned! Leaves about to explode in color, starting already, a little. Keep my bedroom window open. Priscila complained, especially when I peeled down the sheet, acrylic blanket, and thick down comforter an hour ago when I went down on her. The cool air made her nips hard and gave her gooseflesh. But I warmed her up nicely. :-)

Meeting her on social media was the single most life-changing event ever. She approached me first with a Friend invitation, then messaged me. So incredibly beautiful! She had me at 'Hello!' she did. Thirty-two, with the thin, lithe body of a twenty-two-year-old college athlete. Flat stomach, firm thighs and butt. All that aside, her almond-shaped face, huge brown eyes with lashes for miles, thin upper lip, pert nose, and unblemished pale skin— I don't know, what can I say—she just completely grabbed me. Captivated, enchanted, bespelled: insert adjective here. Objectively, I put her up there with the world's prettiest one percent.

At first, I thought she must be a scammer. But then we exchanged numbers and started texting each other, which led to conversations. Next thing I know, she's moved into my cabin with me! I've sort of stopped praying to God over the decades, so I can't rightly claim that Priscila Leone is the answer to my prayers. But to whatever force delivered her to me, I owe a gargantuan debt of gratitude.

Today her friend, Cozbi (weird name, makes me think of pudding and bad sweaters) is having some yard sale or something. Pris insists we go together. I'd rather stay in bed with her all day, slowly consuming her like I'm a big cat in the Serengeti who just took down prey. My passions will just have to simmer until she lets them boil over later tonight.

Journal entry. 12:00 Midnight

Pris is passed-out asleep. Made her cum six times. Same for me. Now that we've found our groove we cum at the same time, every time. Truly amazing. I should be exhausted but I'm not. I could go at her again. Figured I'd write.

The yard sale, summed up in one word: weird. Her bff Cozbi in a word: spooky. This was no run-of-the-mill yard sale. Not even close. Before moving in with me, Priscila lived with her 'sisters,' as she refers to them, lived in a big old rambling Victorian showing signs of disrepair, with an overgrown yard, located in Nesquehoning, not far from here.

First off, Pris introduced Cozbi as some sort of high priestess. Those two wear matching amulets around their necks. 'Coz,' as she likes to be called, is a stunner, like Priscila. Her eyes seem vaguely Middle Eastern though her skin, like Priscila's, is pale and unblemished. No moles or imperfections, at least that I could see. Pris's friends, or 'sisters' as she calls them milled about the yard answering questions from potential buyers. Abigor who goes by Abi; Orusula or 'Oru;' Morfran who goes by Morticia (don't ask me why, seems dumb), and Zagan, who apparently is a licensed medical doctor. Each is more beautiful than the next. Priscila sure can pick high-quality friends! Wowser. Confession: I wondered if their menstrual periods all synced up and fantasized about being the sole focus of an orgy. But I digress…

They conversed with each other, and with potential teenybopper customers, about love and reverence for the Earth Mother, which they interchanged with Goddess (whomever she is), which I found bizarre. Nor do I completely understand all the stuff they were selling. Artsy trinkets. Wood carvings of Aztec or Mayan figurines, maybe. Pre-Columbian stone heads purported to date back millenniums. Carved bowls, incense, oil lamps, hemp blouses. Middle and high school girls came by the carload to spend their bread on this crap, and to hang on every word spoken by the sisters. One rough-looking dude with muscles everywhere, in a brown leather biker vest with tassel fringe, picked up and examined a curiously shaped knife.

"What the heck is this for?" he asked Abigor.

In a deadpan way, she responded, "A gelding athame. Used to neuter big tough men, turn them into compliant eunuchs. Asking fifty, but I'll sell it to you for half price: twenty-five."

If looks could kill, Abi would've dropped dead.

"Ooookay… that's a no, then. May I interest you in this Damascus ceremonial gutting athame?"

The man's brow furrowed; head wagged. He motioned to the woman who made him bring her there and jerked his head toward his Harley Davidson. With a loud roar, they were gone.

I heard some of the women say to Priscila, "We miss you. Gaia knows. We really miss you."

***** Note for later: who or what is Gaia, the Goddess, the Earth Mother? *****

They don't seem to care much for men, but because I'm with Priscila, each sister warmed up to me just fine. Flirty, even. Some of them brushed against me when they came near, as if to gently move me aside, though in no way was I blocking anyone's way. Blinky eyes, long lashes, half smiles they give me. It's like they couldn't keep their eyes off me, but in a good way. Some outright told me that I'm cute. Zagan, the doctor, asked me questions about my diet and health; told me she liked my flat stomach and that I appear fit. She offered to examine me thoroughly for free if I ever wanted to, a twinkle in her eye. Getting a physical exam from her feels more like a fantasy than a chore. Might take her up on that. :-)

4 October, Year 2020—Jim Thorpe, Pennsylvania
Journal entry. 10:00 a.m.

Lazy Sunday. Pris woke me up today for a change by squatting over my face and six-nining me. Without a doubt the most deliciously passionate, amazing woman I have ever met.

Journal entry. 12:00 midnight

Except for meals and bathroom breaks, we stayed in bed all day. Neither of us wanted to shower. We wanted to smell like we've been non-stop fucking, and we do. Priscila doesn't believe in putting chemicals in or on her body. She's vegan. When she moved in, she went through my freezer and tossed out everything that had anything to do with an animal. Frozen meat, fish sticks, chicken tenders. Butter, cheese, coffee creamer, milk—all of it bagged and gone. Using her own money she had gone shopping and came back with hundreds of dollars' worth of soy cheese, plant-based imitation meat protein, sauces, pasta. She said it would make me feel better and give me unlimited sexual energy. Gotta say she was right! I do feel better! With energy to give her what she wants, any and every time she wants it. Amazing. I'm thirty-two but I feel fifteen years younger!

10 October, Year 2020—Jim Thorpe, Pennsylvania
Journal entry. 9:00 a.m.

Pretty sure I'm head-over-heels in love. Never felt like this before, not even with high school crushes, or my first real girlfriend as a teenager. Like, I would do anything for this woman. A few times when she climaxed, she called out that name: "Oh, Gaia!" I looked it up. Gaia is mother earth. She was the ancient Greek goddess of the earth, one of the primordial elemental deities (protogenoi) born at the dawn of creation, the ultimate goddess of raw, maternal power. I asked Priscila about it, who said "She is the reason that the mountains, seas, plains, rivers, the god Uranus, and the starry heavens were formed." I asked Priscila if she worships Gaia. "Oh, yes. So do all my friends at the house. This symbol I wear is to honor her and carry

83

her eternal spirit with me wherever I go."
Okey-Dokey.

Journal entry. 1:00 a.m.

I guess I'm a 'fallen-away' Christian. If anyone asked me what I believe, that's what I'd say. But this Gaia stuff that obsesses Priscila and friends is bizzarro-land. I've done more research. The pregnant Gaia long ago had spurred the druids to sacrifice human beings! What god would demand such an awful and immoral crime of its worshippers? Other cultures named her Cybele, who required her adherents to castrate men. Odd that anyone as beautiful and intelligent as Priscila and her friends, one a Board-certified physician, could possibly lend credence to any of that ancient hysteria. Hey, whatever floats her boat, as long as she keeps on floating me into pleasure zones I never knew existed.

11 October, Year 2020—Jim Thorpe, Pennsylvania
Journal entry. 9:00 a.m.

She's dragging me back to the house in Nesquehoning. Learned the sisters hold a yard sale there every weekend. It's how they pay for things, the five sisters (minus Priscila, who works from home doing accounting stuff, which she does at my kitchen table now). They use these yard sales to recruit younger women into their worship services. Priscila gives part of her earned income to the household. So does the doctor. As for Abi, Oru, Coz and Morticia, hell if I know what they do to contribute to the good and the welfare. They're all skinny. Not saying they're malnourished, but they sure are pale.

Journal entry. 12:30 a.m.

Best sex ever! The yard sale was the weirdest yet. Coz kept bugging me to buy this Magic 8 Ball, the kind you find in toy stores, for a hundred bucks! I was like "Sista you cray, or what?"
She said, "Gabriel, hear me now, believe me later: this Ball is very special. Not like any others. Buy it, take it home, and you will soon learn the vastness of Gaia, she who knows both the Alpha and Omega—both the beginning of time and end of time, and every moment in between."
I asked her if there's some special technique. She said "Yes, there is. Hold the Ball in both hands. Stare at the '8' and ask it a Yes or No question. Be sure to begin by saying, 'Magic 8 Ball…' then ask it a yes or no question. Turn it over the top one full rotation until the '8' passes again, then another quarter turn until the answer window faces up. If it gets caught on an edge

and doesn't give you an answer don't shake it! This only means the powers behind it did not like the question. It is important that you never tempt the magic inside by asking the exact same question twice. Change the question around slightly but never ask the same question a second time. Got it?"

I turned to Priscila for her reaction. She nodded. Given all the money she'd plunked down on getting me to eat healthily, her captivating eyes pushed me over the edge. I handed Coz five Thomas Jeffersons and took the Ball home. Tomorrow, I will put it to the test. If it doesn't work, Doc Zagan won't be the only cultist left in that house getting intimately acquainted with my physique. Coz, girlfriend, I'll take a hundred bucks' worth out of your tight white ass! A hundred bucks felt like a lot of money just then.

12 October, Year 2020—Jim Thorpe, Pennsylvania
Journal entry. 8:30 a.m.

Priscila is downstairs. I hear her tapping away at her laptop fully immersed in spreadsheets. After we had sex and she left the bed, I've lain here for half an hour thinking only of her eyes and perfect body. Given the fact that one, my employer's manufacturing plant remains closed; two, I'm making more collecting unemployment than I was working long-assed shifts; and three, Pris seems okay with me being a 'kept man,' figure that I am right where I belong. One-two-three.

But, figured I'd get up and put skin in the game when it came to this Magic 8 Ball Coz sold me. I logged into my online trading website. Only about five grand in my cash settlement fund to play with. I looked up what some of the blue chips were doing. Yawn. Then I looked at NASDAQ newbies, some of these tech start-ups. I mean, the big boys each had to start small sometime, right?

The name of a Silicon Valley software start-up appealed to me. Remembering Coz's instruction, I picked up the Ball and asked, "Should I invest in this company?"

I flipped it slowly, exactly as she had described. The answer window now faced up. The little white triangle floating in blue liquid showed, 'My Reply Is No.'

Scratch that company. I found another promising name and asked the Ball about it. 'Ask Again Later.'

Damn! Two strikes. I asked about another.

'You May Rely On It.'

Just for kicks I asked, "Should I put all five thousand into it?

'Signs Point To Yes.'

Figured if I lose money, I'll get to lay a massive guilt trip on Priscila, forcing her to acquiesce to some kinky stuff, and maybe too, realize my dream of a three-way sex marathon with sisters Pris and Coz. I will dig in on this if I lose my savings. "This will be the only way you two can ever make it up to me," I would say. I clicked on the company name, held my breath, and converted five thousand dollars into shares.

16 October, Year 2020—Jim Thorpe, Pennsylvania
Journal entry. 8:45 a.m.

Just logged in and checked my stock. Holy crap! Share prices doubled in four days with no signs of slowing! I sold half, grabbed the Ball and asked about a biotechnology company not even five years old, a team who completed all their animal testing and Phase I human safety testing and dosing studies, who filed an IND with the FDA, Phase II efficacy trials completed. They'd be hearing from the Agency any day now.
'It Is Decidedly So.'
"Should I invest the five thousand?"
'As I See It Yes.'
So I did. I'm so nervous!

27 October, Year 2020—Jim Thorpe, Pennsylvania
Journal entry. 10:00 a.m.

Markets are open for biz. Today, the FDA approved my biotech to run Phase III trials—my shares shot up in value four hundred percent! Praise Gaia! Praise Coz! Praise Priscila! This Ball really works! That's it. I'm selling off shares of the two companies I'd bought. I'd pay the short-term capital gains tax and invest the difference in whatever the Ball tells me to. How is this even possible? SO EXCITING! I could seriously get rich here without ever leaving my bedroom!
I've never felt better than I today. Priscila was over-the-moon when I told her we're about to be wealthy. She told me I needed to be healthy and strong, because it's one thing to amass wealth, but it requires self-discipline to keep it. Starting last week, Priscila switched up my diet. She started me on health shakes she mixes for me. Maybe my body needs time to adjust because, every day since she started me on the shakes, I've had this nagging ache in my gut. Otherwise, I do feel so much better. Everything else seems better: my sleep, our sex, my bowel movements. Might just have Doc Zagan look me over after all, though.

30 October, Year 2020—Jim Thorpe, Pennsylvania
Journal entry. 2:00 p.m.

Priscila and I just returned from Nesquehoning. The doc palpated and

86

pushed around my stomach, asked me a bunch of questions, and took a blood sample. She's sending it to a lab.

4 November, Year 2020—Jim Thorpe, Pennsylvania
Journal entry. 10:30 a.m.

Zagan called. Priscila and I put her on speaker. "Gabe, I could run more tests, but the results are clear. Stage Four pancreatic cancer."

I felt the world swim away from me, like tunnel vision. Started to black out. Saw black spots before my eyes. Broke out in a cold sweat. Priscila bent me over, pushed my head down between my knees. Doc Zagan spoke again. "I know honey, the worst news any man can get, and I had to be the one to give it to you. I am *so* sorry, love."

I raised my head. "Don't bullshit me. How long do I have?"

Silence. Then, "Good healthy time. I'd say until February, without treatment. By then, you won't feel much like eating, and the downhill spiral begins. You could spend your springtime in hospice, on opioids to ease the pain until you…move on. If you consent to chemotherapy, maybe it could buy you a bit more time, however you must understand, Gabe, the five-year relative survival rate for Stage Four pancreatic cancer is less than three percent. And that's with aggressive and painful treatment. This means that those with the disease have maybe a 2.9 percent chance of being alive five years after their diagnosis."

I felt like throwing up. "What do you think I should do, Doc?" I wept. So embarrassing.

"If it were me, I'd spend the next few months indulging every appetite I could reasonably afford until the pain gets too overwhelming, whenever that is. When it does, I'd check myself into this great hospice not too far from here and spend my days floating in a warm morphine sea. Exactly what I would do, unless a cure or a better offer comes along, since you asked. Or I'd stay at home with Pris. I'm sure Sis Pris can find ever more creative ways to distract you from pain. I can write a prescription for Tramadol when the time comes. Really does take the edge off without making you sleepy and stupid."

I started to feel pretty pissed off. I stood up and punched the shit out of a sofa pillow. "You know, this is some very fucked-up unfair repugnant shit. I'm only thirty-two! My whole life is still ahead of me! This can't be happening, Doc. You must've made a mistake. Tested the wrong guy's blood."

"I know you're angry, Gabe. I would be, too. Hell, I *am* angry. I like you so much. All the sisters do. We will do anything and everything in our power to ease your pain and see you out as the manly man you truly are. But there's been no mistake. Does your stomach hurt?"

"Every damned day."

"Now you know why. Priscila my love, I'm hanging up now. I'm sure you two have a lot to talk about."

Wow. Nuclear bomb. I broke away from Priscila and went upstairs to my study, gym room, man cave, whatever you want to call it. I got online, researched pancreatic cancer until I could read no more. Then I asked Magic 8 Ball if I'm really dying of cancer.

'Ask Again Later.'

Reticent little fucker.

I looked up clinical trials for pancreatic cancer, figuring that maybe now with the Right To Try law in effect there might be some new experimental drug or treatment. I found nothing. Though I did find a biotech team who submitted the results from a Phase III auto-immune disease clinical trial, just waiting on FDA approval. "Should I buy it?"

'You May Rely On It.'

"How much should I bet on this horse, everything?"

'Yes Definitely.'

"Should I buy right now?"

'Signs Point To Yes.'

Now there was a first. The Ball had never given me three affirmative responses in a row. I liquidated everything and put it all on this one stock play. Believing your days are numbered makes you think and do crazy shit, let me tell you. This damnable stomachache never leaves me now.

12 November, Year 2020—Jim Thorpe, Pennsylvania
Journal entry. 8:30 a.m.

Lying in bed. Priscila has been especially kind and generous to me lately, including sexually. In the beginning, during the 'feeling-each-other-out' stage, I had floated fantasies past her. Extreme Sex, we'll call it. She had poo-pooed all my ideas, but guess what we did around six this morning? SO AWESOME! She loved it too. Climaxed like gangbusters. If not for my gut ache it would've been the best sex of my life.

I just looked at my latest stock. FDA approved the drug! Pharma blogs were calling it the first blockbuster breakthrough drug approved for the condition in half a century. Suddenly, overnight really, I became a millionaire!

But then, the stomach pain throbbed which cut short my ebullience. I have no appetite for food. She's downstairs laboring to keep her income stream alive. But now that I have money she doesn't need to, not if she doesn't want to. I've decided not to tell her. Hey, I can't take the money with me, but at least this game serves as a distraction from my hideous reality. I'm so scared of dying.

I've decided to talk with Magic 8 Ball. A small, relatively new potential defense contractor company allegedly has produced a combat drone, powered by some new super-efficient battery. It runs silent and invisible under enemy radar, for a full day without a full recharge. Also, a cloaking device renders it invisible to human eyes, using some hell of a complex technology involving mini projectors and mirrors. But unless the Joint Chiefs say it's real and award billion-dollar contracts, then I couldn't care less. A Pentagon insider might know. Finding myself short any friends in D.C., I decided to ask the Ball. When it all sounds too good to be true, well, we know what they say about things like that.

"Should I invest in this stock?"

'It Is Decidedly So.'

"How much? All? Every penny?"

'As I See It Yes.'

Again, twice in one séance! I've come to call them séances, because seriously, Coz wasn't lying, this thing is powered by something out of this world, must be.

26 November, Year 2020—Jim Thorpe, Pennsylvania
Journal entry. 12:00 Midnight

Spent Thanksgiving at the ramshackle Victorian in Nesquehoning with the sisters. It's like a haunted house, I swear. But they sure livened up the place, singing songs to the Earth Mother, praising the goddess, wearing rings of flowers in their hair. Each wore sheer white garments, entirely naked underneath. Strangest, best Thanksgiving ever, if not for my throbbing gut, I mean.

This is when I sprung the good news on Priscila and the sisters. The Pentagon awarded a huge contract to my robotics firm, and my net worth had crested three million. They cheered and applauded. Every one of them kissed my mouth. Orusula gave me this sly look then slipped me the tongue! She's so delicate-looking, waifish little blonde, face and body like a runway model, only shorter. What an amazing night! Priscila and I had arrived in my 1986 Ferrari Testarossa, bright red, known as "The Flying Mirror," back in the day. Learned about it watching old Miami Vice television series re-runs on cable as a kid. The one in the show had gotten a white paint job, but the factory original paint was red, like mine. So cool-looking! Got it used from some Los Angeles movie guy for seventy thousand and paid to have it trucked out here. My dream car! And now dream girls were fawning all over me.

Hard to believe I'm quickly dying, that my days on earth are truly numbered. I read about the five stages of grief: I was still in the denial phase. Here comes the weirdest part. If anyone ever reads this, I will challenge the reader, seriously, to ask himself what he would do in my situation.

After dinner, with a big fire blazing away in the hearth, seated with my back to the warming flames, all six of them lounged seductively upon an expansive cloth symmetrical sectional. Priscila stood. She pulled her white shift over her head and stood there completely naked. Immediately I felt the familiar twinge of arousal. Then Cozbi stood and joined her. Two nude beauties, holding hands. Morfran disrobed next, followed by Abigor, Orusula, and finally my new doctor, Zagan. Aroused doesn't quite capture the wars fought in my mind, heart, spirit, and body. I completely forgot about my chronic stomach pain. Any hetero man would.

Priscila and Zagan approached and knelt before me. Morfran crept behind. Ever so tenderly she stroked and cupped my face between hands that felt like warm buttered velvet. She massaged my neck, trapezius, shoulders, and chest. Priscila spoke first.

"Gabriel, my angel. All of us want you. The goddess, Gaia, wants you, too. But in her own way. You see, her spirit must occasionally be refreshed through sacrifice. Do you understand?"

I was listening, but maybe I didn't hear, or want to, as I floated in a sea of distraction from gut pain, and a state of hypersexual arousal. Deep was I swallowed into a maelstrom of pure bliss. "Yes," I responded. "Sacrifice."

"Sacrifice, Gabe, yes. We prayed to the goddess tonight, and she answered our prayer. She gave us a path to blessings for us all, and a place in the eternal realm for you, a very special place. Imagine spending an eternity feeling as good as when you and I cum together. An eternity not only with me, but with all of us." Every woman in the room nodded and smiled. "Imagine all of us, Gabe, cumming together for all time, just as we are today, free of aging and disease."

I smiled languidly. "Beautiful. Perfect."

"Your body will quickly pass on, ours to follow later, then we will all be together. But first we demonstrate our true faith in the Divine Mother. If you will commit your body to us during the Festival of Yule, of Saturnalia, a few weeks from now, then you will never have to feel the pain of a slow, ignominious death from cancer."

"Instead of going out in agony," Doc Zagan cooed with a smile and nod, "you will go out like the beautiful, strong young man you are, giving your body and spirit to all of us, to distract you from your pain for the seven days and nights of the festival. Then at the end, after one last poignant release, you'll only feel a little tugging, and the knife. No pain. You won't even see blood, as we will be swarming all over your body with ours. Ceaseless, intoxicating pleasure right to the end. You'll fall asleep and wake up in the blessed realm where, in the blink of an eye as time moves differently there, we will join you for an eternity of mutual pleasure. You'll be a demigod there. We will be your eternal harem, and together we will be co-heirs to the throne, Gaia be praised."

Priscila looked up at me with lustrous, sensual eyes. "Will you give yourself to the goddess, and to us, lover?"

As if to sweeten and seal the deal, starting with Priscila, each of the sisters took turns sticking her tongue in my mouth. Each inhaled me while others squeezed away at my embattled crotch. It was the single most erotic moment of my life—up to that point. The decision came easily.

"Yes," I said.

"Yes, what?" Zagan asked.

"Yes, Zagan. I commit my body and soul to all of you, and to the goddess, Gaia." Into the unknowable eyes of Priscila, I said, "Thank you for loving me this much." She smiled and kissed me like it was the first time.

30 November, Year 2020—Jim Thorpe, Pennsylvania
Journal entry. 11:45 a.m.

The date of my send-off was set by Priscila: Friday, December the twenty-fifth, Christmas Day. Gaia worshippers hold the day in high esteem, a holdover from the Norse Yule, except that instead of celebrating the birth of Christ, Gaianists recognize the sun—its beauty, its light (literal and figurative), and Gaia's annual journey around it. This Winter Solstice, when the earth tilts furthest from the sun, to help Gaia on her journey around it, they plan on giving her the gift of energy.

Me.

So much to do between now and then. First thing's first: call Barry Levenstein, whom I've not seen since he was my dad's lawyer when I was a kid. Now he's a partner in a big firm in Philly. My dad trusted him implicitly. I never had much to leave behind until recently (thank you, Magic 8 Ball) and so never needed a will. I'll leave it all to Priscila and the sisters. Every time they won't have to sell junk in a yard sale, they'll think of me, LOL.

The pain in my stomach gradually worsens every week. At some point, if I'd let this cancer eat up my pancreas, pretty sure I'd lose my mind. I don't relish the thought of getting my junk cut and bleeding out, but they promised me no pain. I very much look forward to the girls coming here to stay with us beginning Saturday the nineteenth. Let the games begin. :-)

5 December, Year 2020—Jim Thorpe, Pennsylvania
Journal entry. 10:00 a.m.

Priscila was incredible in bed this morning. So generous. Each time is more intimate and ferocious than the last. I don't have much appetite. I'm losing weight.

5 December, Year 2020—Jim Thorpe, Pennsylvania
Journal entry. 12:00 Midnight

She just passed out after another incredible evening of sex. I can still smell and taste her essence on my face. I came downstairs for a sip of cold juice. She left her purse open on the kitchen table. I felt guilty about going through it, but the temptation was too much. The usual girl stuff: combs, lipsticks, spare tampon, cell phone. But also, two prescription bottles, one filled with liquid, the other with pills, both with her name on them. Weird. I know after spending months with her that she is a purist, a total health nut, staunchly against man-made treatments. Finding these bottles baffled me. Shocked me wide awake. So, I looked them up. Elixophyllin-Theophylline, Anhydrous Oral Sol: 15mL, 80mg in liquid form. The pills were Rosuvastatin 40 mg. The first is for emphysema, or COPD as they call it nowadays. The other is serious treatment for high cholesterol, requiring frequent blood tests to ensure the patient's liver doesn't explode by taking it. 40 mgs is considered a very high dose. Neither of us suffer from these diseases. I continued my research, hoping to solve the mystery. To figure out what both had in common.

And there it was. Both cause stomach pain. Taken together, the pain would be acute.

6 December, Year 2020—Jim Thorpe, Pennsylvania
Journal entry. 8:30 a.m.

She's in the shower. I searched the kitchen. I stood on a stepladder to see above the refrigerator. Way in the back I found a pewter mortar and pestle. NOT MINE. Inside I found yellow-colored powder matching the color of the Rosuvastatin tablets.

6 December, Year 2020—Jim Thorpe, Pennsylvania
Journal entry. 1:45 p.m.

I should've called Five-O. She's watching me all the time. She's not been out of the house shopping today, which is highly unusual for her. I hear movement downstairs, so it's safe, at least for the moment, for me to ask the Magic 8 Ball a question. Coz had adjured me to never ask the same question twice. If it doesn't like a question, it will tell me. A month ago, I asked the Ball if I'm really dying of cancer. It had replied 'Ask Again Later.' So now I'm going to ask it in a different way. This thing has never lied to

92

me. Maybe it's alive.

"Magic 8 Ball, do I have cancer?"

'Very Doubtful.'

6 December, Year 2020—Jim Thorpe, Pennsylvania
Journal entry. 3:35 p.m.

You know those house arrest ankle bracelets that courts lock onto sentenced prisoners to keep them home? She pulled off my pants. I thought we were going at it. Wrong. She strapped on an ankle tracker with 5G GPS linked to her phone. I don't know where she got it, but without the key to the locking device, I'd need sturdy tools to remove it. Even if I tried taking it off, she'd get an alarm. If I wander outside the house, she instantly knows. I was completely caught off guard by this. She read the surprise on my face.

"Gabe, sweetie. It's perfectly natural for someone on 'death row' so-to-speak to want to bolt. The goddess created each of us with fight-or-flight mechanisms for survival, even lower animals. The lives of six women—not to mention the goddess—are counting on finding you in 'scene position' on the twenty-fifth. If your instinct to run away kicks in, and you act on it, you'll ruin everything! For everyone! And it won't be your fault; it will be mine, for allowing it. Sorry, Gabe, but I cannot allow you to run. We hope that you'll comply with our every wish. Soon we'll restrain you not with ropes but with our naked bodies." She shot me that look of hers, those amazing bedroom eyes. She shrugged. "Although if you'd rather, I tightly cinch a retractable dog leash to your nuts and yank you back whenever you try to bolt…"

"No! No," I said.

"Great! Then it's settled. Just wear it, hon. You'll get used to it quickly, like wearing a watch.

16 December, Year 2020—Jim Thorpe, Pennsylvania
Journal entry. 10:00 a.m.

After issuing a stern warning not to remove the bracelet or leave the house, she left minutes ago for supplies, meaning enough veggie protein to feed seven people every day between the nineteenth and twenty-sixth. I asked her last night what will become of my body, and who will find it.

"Zagan and I will find you. She's a respected member of the local medical community. She'll call 9-1-1 and report an apparent suicide. When asked, I'll tell whomever that we had broken up, and I wasn't about to spend Christmas with you, so Zagan came with me for moral support the next morning, when I stopped over to get my car and the rest of my

93

things."

"I see. So, you'll be picking up the five sisters this Saturday morning and bringing them here, so that your car and mine will be the only two in the driveway for all that time."

She smirked. "You've got it, lover. All neat and tidy. None of us will leave the house until zero-dark-thirty on Yule night, the twenty-fifth. I'll drop them in Nesquehoning and be back here before any nosy neighbors even know I left."

I looked at her, tears in my eyes. "Will it hurt? I'm scared, Pris. Terrified."

She leaned over and kissed me, hard and long, her hand clasping at my jeans zipper. "Six beautiful women are going to make sure that throughout every millisecond of your sacrifice, you will only feel ceaseless emotional and physical pleasure, more than any man has ever felt before. I promise." She interlocked her fingers with mine. "Pinky-swear."

I don't have a landline phone, only a smartphone: she walked over to my desk and took it. Next, she disconnected my Internet router and took it. "Can't have you panicking while I'm at the store, lover." She left the room with every means I might have had for contacting the outside world.

When she's preparing my daily health shakes, I've stood at the sink. I pretend to sip them, but when she averts her gaze even for a moment, I pour more down the garbage disposal side of the sink. What do you know—all stomach pain gone.

18 December, Year 2020—Jim Thorpe, Pennsylvania
Journal entry. 1:00 a.m.

This is my final entry. Priscila is asleep. Yesterday she took every article of my clothing, even my underwear, stuffed them into plastic trash bags and locked them in her car. Said she would replace them after my 'scene' as she likes to call it. I'm naked all the time. She teases me sexually day and night, for over a week now, but only foreplay. Says she wants me to save up all my energy for the seven days and nights with her and the sisters. Zagan gave her a prescription for twenty-milligram Cialis. She wants me to be hard twenty-four seven, including and especially when they cut me.

I've just addressed a large mailing envelope to Barry, my attorney, and hid it under a rug. I'm enclosing this journal in a sealed envelope, and a note instructing him to read it aloud at the will proceeding. Also to include police at the meeting for his own safety—though I implored him not to read any of it until then. I ended the note with a request: ask Priscila to bring the Magic 8 Ball to the legal proceeding, for I am bequeathing it to Barry.

Which means, Barry—if you are now reading it—my escape attempt failed, and they've murdered me against my will. Repeat: if I am found dead, I DID NOT COMMIT SUICIDE. All together: Priscila Leone, Cozbi Abital, Morfran Azra, Orusula Umbra, Abigor Moreau, and Doctor Zagan Alarie—conspired to manipulate me with inconceivable deceit and premeditation. They unmanned me and bled me to death. They staged the scene to make the wound appear self-inflicted. They are not entitled to one red cent of my estate.

I have used enough Forever stamps to get this to you, Barry. The nearest blue public mailbox sits in a strip mall about a mile from here. I'm about to run to the box to drop the envelope. I'm naked. For once I hope—nay, I pray—that a cop, or any motorist or pedestrian capable of calling one sees me. I'll take the Indecent Exposure rap at this point. As soon as I'm out the door, her cell phone next to her head upstairs is going to blast her awake.

She'll throw on clothes, grab her phone and her 'athame'—what she calls her bone-handled ritual knife—an awful thing—with a razor-sharp curved karambit blade like a raptor's claw. They sell them at their yard sales. A hideous, ghastly thing—oh, mournful and terrible engine of my undoing! I should have known to avoid a woman who carries a ceremonial knife that the sisters told shoppers has only one use: castration ceremonies, which she now fully intends to use on me.

She'll drive around with the GPS looking for me. I plan to do my best to duck and hide, in a storm drain if I must. I'll make it difficult for her to get at me. But if her arm with that blade at the end can manage to reach me, she'll coax me into her car under penalty of horrible torture—which she will carry through without the slightest hesitation—to return me to this death row cell. I'll try my hardest to extricate myself from this terrifying nightmare.

I haven't had much of a tongue for prayer or great interest in the mysteries of The Christ, and God in Heaven. Right now, though, I'm regretting it. I believe. If I'd had the strength of God coursing through me from the beginning, that faith would have given me the strength to override hormones and to apply good judgment. I never would have allowed a coven of witches to allure, seduce, enchant and bespell me into this alarming predicament. Dear Lord, I repent. Please forgive me for my sins which are grievous and many. Please don't reject me if it comes to that. I pray that You get me out of this mess.

Whatever happens, I shall know that Your will, not mine, was done, on the birthday of Your Son.

Gotta run.

Magic 8 Ball

Grave Revenge

12 January, Year 2021—Philadelphia, Pennsylvania

At the reading of the late Gabriel Inglebert Meshach's journal, Barry Levenstein wept. Trooper Tyler launched into motion. He snapped cuffs around the wrists of Priscila Leone and Cozbi Avital behind their backs, and not gently. He smacked enormous hands onto their backs and pushed their stunned, teary-eyed faces against the thick conference room glass tabletop as he read them their Miranda Rights.

Levenstein collected himself as best he could. He wiped his eyes and honked into a monogramed silk handkerchief, once artfully folded into his left jacket lapel pocket. *Their faces must look like two pressed hams from underneath the table. Demonic pigs,* he thought. *Pack of hyenas. Dear God.*

Trooper Tyler pulled both to their feet. Priscila choked out, "What about the money?"

Hand on the door handle, the trooper froze. It seems he wanted to hear this, too.

"Ah yes, Ms. Avital. The money," Levenstein interrupted. "You'll likely need a lot of it after the bail hearing. I will immediately file to contest and revoke the will. To succeed, I must prove coercion, duress, diminished mental capacity, undue influence, menace, or outright fraud." Lips pressed together; he tapped the journal of his best childhood friend's murdered son. "This, along with the coroner's toxicology report which showed unusual liver enzymes and organ stress, no doubt caused by massive overdoses of theophylline, tadalafil and statins—prescribed for Priscila Leone by Zagan Alarie—I can assure you, Ms. Abital, that the D.A. can easily prove all of it. None of you will ever see any of his money."

"But…"

"Know too: the Carbon County coroner, as part of the test battery available to him, sent Gabe's blood samples to a DNA lab. Lo and behold, there was a hit for a young boy living in Shamokin. The coroner and police felt compelled to share his report with me, having investigated the boy's birth record. When Gabe and his long-time girlfriend split up in their early twenties, she was pregnant, though she deigned not to inform him. Therefore, completely unbeknownst to him, he did have an heir, living below the poverty line." Levenstein raised his head high. "I mean to change that."

"What will happen to us?" asked Priscila.

"Trooper, correct me if I'm wrong: you will radio in the names and address of the other four women living together in an old ramshackle Victorian in Nesquehoning. All will be arrested within the hour. Given the distance between Philly and the Carbon County jail on Broadway in Jim Thorpe, I expect your co-conspirators shall anxiously await your reunion behind bars."

Trooper Tyler had them halfway out the door; roughly he dragged them by their cuff chains. "No," Cozbi shouted. "She means, what will happen to us in court? You're a lawyer."

The Trooper stopped. This sort of outcome was way above his pay grade. He'd seen guilty people get mistrials on technicalities, and all manner of legal injustice. This too, he wanted to hear.

Barry's eyes narrowed. "My parents fled Germany while most of their relatives and friends perished under the Nazi program, *Lebensunwertes Leben*, which means 'life unworthy of life.' After the war ended, most of those Nazis were hunted down and executed or imprisoned. I would say to you what is in my heart, but professional restraint gets the better of me.

"Murder in the first degree is a capital offense in Pennsylvania. A capital offense is a crime punishable by death. Murder in the first degree carries a penalty of life in prison, or death. In my experience, there is more than sufficient evidence here to get a murder conviction, no question about it. The Carbon County District Attorney is a fair but hard man. Given the conspiratorial, premeditated and vicious nature of this crime, he will likely seek the death penalty. You could give full confessions, all six of you, and if all six confessions align, and you all plead guilty, perhaps the D.A. will ask for twenty-five years to life, in prison. Of course, all of this is up to a trial judge and jury. Therefore, I cannot answer with certainty."

Barry watched the women's eyes as he spoke. Rays of hope, clear as day, he recognized. Likely they were thinking that they will get away with murder, as so many do. None fit the killer profile. "But there's someone who does know exactly how this will end, for certain."

He reached into his satchel and liberated the Magic 8 Ball from the paper bag.

"Magic 8 Ball: will these two women die by lethal injection as convicted murderers?" He turned over the '8' until it came around again. The little window with blue liquid and white triangle now faced up.

'Outlook Good.'

Corpsicle

"Where's your faith in science, Uncle Herk?"

Francis Archibald Herkimer, otherwise known as Frank, called 'Herky' by his familiars, sat at the Italian designer table, ebony wood with inlay and edges in saddle leather, inside Cryothera Corporation's boardroom. Sitting across from him was his dead brother's son, Andrew Thaddeus Herkimer, called 'Tad' by his inner circle. Tad was his nephew, godson, and junior business partner. 'Truly, you can only trust blood' was his business mantra.

Affected grin, eyes lowered to hands folded before him, Herky retorted. "I never believed in anything, Tad. Not in God and Satan, Heaven and Hell, and all that other superstitious mumbo-jumbo. I believed humans created these characters as scapegoats for their own bad behavior... as tools to control people. I had no faith in larger spirits, the same way I still feel about political parties, which is why I donate to both in case I need legislative advantages for my businesses. I was as ambivalent about what happens after we die. But I've been reading the Gospels, which strike me in every way as authentic eyewitness testimony."

Tad blew out air, wagged his head, and laughed. "Trust in science, Herk. It's true because it works."

"Ah, I see. I'll bet you can't get through a single day without invoking Christ's name or calling on God. You say you're an atheist so, why is that? Because deep down, you know all this," he said with a sweeping hand gesture, "cannot be a cosmic accident. Listen, Tad, if you had tomorrow's newspaper you wouldn't need to work for a living. You could simply bet on the contests and outcomes you know will come true the next day. Horse races, stocks, currencies. But nobody knows what tomorrow will bring. I've spent a life serving only myself. Sure, I was charitable, but only for the tax write-offs. I've taken advantage of people for three quarters of a century. Now that I find myself in the final lustrum or two of life, you will simply have to excuse me whilst I also hedge my spiritual bets, if you will."

Tad smiled. He slapped the arms of the chair. "Got it! This is just me feeling jealous that The Little Voices speak only to you."

Herky regarded him with tight lips and furrowed brows. "I'm a businessman, Tad, and a highly successful one at that. You know how I got to the top?"

Tad shook his head. "Give the people what they want, yes-yes. Heard it from you a million times."

"I never once believed in this cryonics nonsense until you and your Ivy League brat-bros set before me an inarguably sound business and marketing plan. Would've been a fool not to invest in this grift. Only four providers serving thousands of desperately misguided consumers willing to drop six figures on this absurd fantasy. It's the biggest up-and-coming scam, so why not be an early investor? Wealthy rubes seeking eternal life through science. Preserve their dead bodies for a future when disease conditions can be treated or reversed. Banking on being resurrected, cured, and reborn into new lives where their vast experience will make them masters of the universe, demigods, or whatever. Tapping human ego. What could I say to such a beautiful flimflam but yes? No-brainer. Investing in a competitive field this small and tight was the easiest business decision I have ever made, bar none. But understand this, Tad: it's all bullshit. I want no part of it."

"So just sign the paper! Marketing insists!" He slid it across the glass at the old man, blue gel roller pen on top for the ride.

"So you can post my signed consent form all over social media. No can do, Tad. Consent denied. This service we provide is for sale; my core beliefs and values are not. I believe there may be something waiting on the other side. Maybe, just maybe, the God Squad got things right. To get frozen is to utterly reject even the possibility they're right." Herky slid the form and pen back across.

"Dammit uncle! You need to make me chairman so that I can sign for the firm.

"When I'm dead, you can be chairman. Not until. My interest is controlling. As the majority shareholder, what I say goes. You're trying my patience."

"Uncle, as President and CEO, I want my position put on record with the Board that it is my recommendation that you be replaced as Chairman under Article XII, section five point one: Should the Chairman become mentally or physically incapacitated, the Board shall vote on a Chairman in absentia."

Herky leaned toward the younger man. "You sure, Andrew? Are you absolutely certain you want to go to war with me over this?" Fierce baby blue eyes set deep inside crow's feet sockets, eyebags like steamer trunks.

He's nuts. That was when the seed of an idea germinated. Tad pushed against the back of his chair, hands steepled before his face. He stayed like that for half a minute. "No, uncle. Sorry. Sometimes I think testosterone overrides my better judgment."

The old man leaned back. "Runs in the family, kiddo. All is forgiven. Now, get to work. Do your job. You're good at it. Go sell subscriptions the old-fashioned way: burn some shoe leather. What I'm about to say may not make perfect sense to you now, but one day you'll understand and remember this little chat. Wealth must be earned, for it to feel like wealth."

Back in his office, Tad tapped away at a search engine. He stopped, suddenly remembering that its host collects and sells search data. He cleared his cache and cookies, leaned back into his Aeron chair, and played with his wavy dark brown hair.

Ah, right: why didn't I think of him first? Loyal to me as a dog. He slipped into his white lab coat and took the elevator down to the underground sciences floor.

"Matt!" he said, fist extended for a knuckle-bump. "How goes it down here?"

"Let me tell you, Tad, they say the dead don't talk, but sometimes I swear, not even joking I hear whispers downstairs. Especially in those shadowy parts, you know, where there are extra cold pockets?"

"Hah! Doc, you need to get topside more often. Drive over to La Jolla. Ogle Asian chicks on the beach or something. Remind yourself you're alive."

Matt Wu, PhD in chemistry, Master's in physiology, undergrad in biology, ethnically Chinese but born and raised here in San Diego, nodded and grinned. "Asian women are too controlling. Check your brain before doling out advice, round-eye. I've a thing for redheads anyway."

Tad smirked. "Come clubbing with me Saturday night, I'll introduce you to a few sexy gingers who, not to be demeaning, aren't the brightest bulbs, and who tend to be, how shall I say it: morally flexible? I assume you're not seeking wife material."

"Pfft. What's mine is hers? No thanks. Maybe I'll take you up on that offer. So what's up? How can I help?"

"Okay, yeah, sorry Matt, I know you're busy. This won't take long. Marketing shit again. If you had to explain what it is you guys do down here in a hundred words or fewer, how would you say it?" From the logo-adorned breast pocket he pulled out a notebook and pen.

"Only a hundred? That'd be tough."

"Give it your best go, Shakespeare."

"Okay. We remove the patient's fluids and replace them with a vitrification solution, a preservative cocktail of cryoprotectant chemicals such as dimethylsulfoxide, ethylene glycol, propylene glycol and glycerol which prevents ice crystal formation and reduces tissue damage after flesh is frozen. Perfusion replaces body water in cells and in the circulatory system. By perfusing vitrification solution into the blood stream it replaces all water inside veins and tissues by diffusion. Freezing means ice: we don't do ice. With vitrification solution we preserve the brain and tissues. The patient goes into a computer-controlled cooling box and brought to liquid nitrogen temperature—196°C."

Tad tapped the page with the pen tip. His lips moved. "A hundred words. Damn! You're like—spooky smart! PhD means 'Piled Higher And Deeper,' 'cept in your case. Thank you, doctor!"

"Sure. Anything else?"

"Yes. I've read the cryonicists' reports about storing a body at such a low temperature filled with toxic chemicals can damage a corpse."

"Factcheck: True. Sorry. I know that's not what marketing wants to hear."

"I need to hear it, Matt. A great man once said, 'The truth shall set you free, and when it doesn't—lie. But lie well. It begins with a thorough understanding of the actual truth. So which chemical causes the most damage?"

Matt stroked his chin. "I'd have to say the DMSO."

"The what?"

"Oh. Dimethylsulfoxide, probably. Crazy stuff. Whatever you mix in with it gets absorbed into tissue along with it."

"Really? That's crazy! So you mean that if you were to mix DMSO with cyanide and spill a little on your skin, you'd die in a few seconds?"

"Not in a few seconds, but yes, you'd die. DMSO takes fifteen minutes or so to work its way through the stratum corneum under the skin, called the 'brick wall,' but we all know brick-and-mortar walls leak and seep. We used to say skin is waterproof, but with DMSO, the best we can say is that it's water-repellent."

"Hm. Interesting stuff. What do I know: I got an MBA from Columbia and a J.D. from Villanova. Blood and guts scare the shit out of me."

"Hah! Yeah, so about those redheads…"

"We'll do it. Shoot me an email reminder."

Dr. Lee mailed him that evening. Tad Herkimer deleted it upon receipt. "Thanks for the DMSO tip, doc," he muttered. "Now you can just shut the fuck up."

He used a Tor browser to access the latest Silk Road on the Dark Web to locate the closest exotic illegal animal seller. It took hours. Using a burner email account on a burner phone, he asked a question. The dealer replied 'Mamba. Boomslang. Viper. If you have the coin.'

Now where do we keep the DMSO?

He visited a Halloween store and paid in cash. He rented a moving van with a ramp. Into it, he loaded his Harley Davidson motorcycle and roped it to wooden rails along both walls to prevent tipping over while turning. He unscrewed the Harley's license plate and replaced it with a realistic fake.

He drove the van forty miles east of San Diego into the Cuyamaca and Laguna Mountains. In Julian, California, he parked the truck in a guest lodge lot nestled in with RVs and service trucks. He freed the Harley. His helmet completely covered his head. From there, he used Waze on his smartphone to find the exotic pet dealer, located on some obscure, off-grid plot of scrubland somewhere in the Peninsular Ranges. When he got close, he pulled up a trail and changed his entire appearance. Long wig, fake mustache and beard, leather concealed-carry vest, classic black biker boots.

In this disguise, he pulled into a chip-and-oil driveway, leading through Jacaranda and Box Elder trees, to a cabin. Animal cages speckled the landscape. *Must be the place.*

"Trying to impress a girl? You do realize that if this snake bites you once, you're dead in a day."

"I think it's cool to own lethal things, that's all. If you ever need anything that goes bang, let me know," Tad replied. He expected the seller to be suspicious, given the illegality of owning, or especially selling, an African boomslang snake.

"You won't think it's cool when the antivenom and blood-thickeners fail to prevent bleeding from your eyes, lungs, kidneys, heart and brain. Not that any medical center in California would have antivenom, since these things only live in Africa." He tapped the steel mesh cage. "This little girl's venom is highly hemotoxic. Her kiss will make you bleed out internally and externally. Victims suffer extensive muscle and brain hemorrhaging, and on top of that, blood will start seeping out of every possible exit, including the gums and nostrils, and even the tiniest of cuts. Blood will also start passing through the body via the victim's stools, urine, saliva, and vomit, until they die. Bad, messy, exceedingly painful way to go. Accidents happen every day. Not that I don't want to take your money," he said, eyebrows raised, lips pursed, "but are you a thousand percent sure you want this thing?"

"Thanks, friend, I'll be sure to wear Kevlar riding gloves when cleaning her cage."

Back in his house on Tenth Street in Del Mar, Tad studied online videos to learn how to safely milk a snake of its venom. He managed to do it twice and fill up a vial. Nerves got the better of him. He refused to push his luck with a third milking. His Kevlar-covered right hand firmly grasped the neck just below the head. His unprotected left hand flipped on the kitchen garbage disposal. He fed the snake down into it tail-first. The grinding sound was louder than usual. The one-horsepower whirring blades had never been so challenged and yet still made quick work of it. "Twelve grand down the drain," he said. "Oh well. A wise investment in the firm's future, I'd say."

He switched to a pair of thick blue rubber gloves he'd pinched from the lab along with a small glass vial. He used a toothpick to stir a fifty-fifty cocktail of dimethylsulfoxide and freshly squeezed boomslang poison in the vial. He had tried removing and replacing the felt contents of a half-dozen different plastic highlighter pens and failed with each, though he did have better luck extracting and replacing the felt wick inside a metal-housed whiteboard pen. He had soaked the extracted felt piece in isopropyl until all the green-yellow color leeched from the felt piece into the bowl and left the wick on his balcony to dry under a hot sun. He inserted the bone-dry marker's felt into the most lethal vial of hemotoxin on earth. The thirsty felt material quickly wicked up every drop of the poison cocktail. Trying to keep his trembling hands still, with the most intense focus he could summon, he inserted the felt back into the metal dry-erase marker housing. He changed gloves, then clicked the cap over the wick. Four gloves in a plastic bag, he slipped on a third pair and thoroughly wiped the metal cylinder with isopropyl. *Not that I need to; I didn't spill a drop. But for some reason, a final sanitizing makes me feel more like a Boy Scout— Prepared. As for this plastic bag of death here, no, I can't dispose of it in any sort of trash. Could find it, and my fingerprints are inside the gloves. What if some schmuck accidentally gets hold of it and dies? No. If I burn it in the firepit out back, what if that venom vaporizes and I, or some downwind neighbor breathes it in?*

Bury it. But where? Ah. Under the firepit. Even if I sell this place, nobody'll bother to dig up and move the firepit. If they do, then the toxins will be leeched deep into the soil and harmless. If years from now somebody finds my prints, so what? I live here!

He finished the lethal dry-erase marker project on Wednesday evening. He spent Thursday and Friday evenings practicing how to forge Francis Herkimer's signature. Size and slope of the writing, pen pressure, pen lifts, the spacing between words and letters, the position of the writing on the baseline. *Harder than I thought.* By Saturday night he felt that his product would pass muster for anyone not a professional handwriting analyst, and possibly even get by them, too. At 9:56 Saturday night, Tad signed his uncle's name to the required consent forms. *Now, there can be no autopsy. A legal impossibility. The ultimate organ donor card.*

He spent all day from morning until after dinner rehearsing the scene in a mirror. *Must seem flawless, not only to the old bastard but also to his assistant, Annabel, and any other office staffer who happens to pass by. We're both long used to being stared at.* He imagined himself executing every muscle movement as though watching a movie.

Monday morning, he arrived at the office at 7:45. The executive assistant was typing at her desk. She heard his familiar footfalls in the antiseptic, stark white tiled hallway. "Mr. Herkimer, did you receive the first-class boarding pass on your phone?"

Tad checked. "Got it! Thanks for taking care of it, Annabel!"

She spared him a brief glance and smile, then resumed typing. The smile was rare and radiant and always reminded him of a popular young actress. *God, please let me fuck her. Excuse me, Annabel, but may I please kiss you where you pee? Hah. Think she'll go for the direct approach? Yeah, no. Better not even fantasize too loud around that one. The ultra-woke, litigious, Me-Too type. Oh, no. There I go again, using God's name in vain. Uncle Herky will think less of me in his final hours. Forget living your final lustrums you old demon. You're living your last few days and just don't know it yet.*

In his office, he left the folder bearing Francis Herkimer's name, which contained his forged consent to undergo cryopreservation, in a conspicuous location on his desk. He sat in his uncle's Aeron chair and considered the old man's habits. *What's the name of the group I'm supposedly going to meet with in Armonk, New York?* He searched files on the shared drive. He abandoned the search and was about to buzz Annabel, but then he found the email subfolder: Infinity Society. He laughed. *Such bullshit. Hey, I'll take your money. Armonk is where the old money wealth in New York lives. Rich dumb fucks. You can't take it with you, so you might as well give a sizeable chunk to Cryothera Corporation.* He glanced at his Rolex watch. *It's 8:26: in four minutes, Herky will go to the bistro for coffee. At 8:55, he'll go piss out the cup he had driving to the office. My flight's at 10:35, which means 8:30 is the opportunity.*

Back in his own office, he grabbed the marketing report due on Herky's desk this morning and walked it to his uncle's office. The door was open. *Nobody else but him wears neckties anymore. Hey, Uncle, 2003 called; they want their vintage cravat back.* Wearing a politician's smile he said, "Happy Monday, uncle!"

"Tad, I'm really busy, what is it?"

"Marketing report. You said—"

His hand went up. "Right-right, yes, I did. Just leave it on the guest chair. I need coffee before my 9:00 web meeting."

"Sure thing. I won't make the meeting."

"Oh? Why is that?"

"Two words: shoe, and leather. Your words. I've a flight in ninety minutes to White Plains Airport to meet with those rich fuckers."

"Infinity Society?"

He nodded. "I've read the marketing report. Pretty bleak quarter ahead if I don't slam home one or two fat contracts, which I will do."

Sagging gray skin on the old man's face tightened into a genuine smile, pallor suddenly radiant and sanguine. "Attaboy! Go get 'em!"

"Uncle, your meeting is in a half hour: your double Windsor knot is a bit off. Let me get behind you and fix it. I think I know the problem. Happens to me when there's a fold in the section around your neck. Bunches up." He strode behind the expensive leather and wood chair. "Flip your collar up for me? Great."

He reached into his right rear pocket for the dry erase marker. While the uncle turned up his collar, he uncapped it and lightly grazed the breadth of the neck, left to right, then right to left. He looked down at both hands to be certain he recapped the marker perfectly. He pulled a sandwich bag from his left rear pocket, inserted the marker, sealed the locking strip, and safely spirited the marker back to its pocket. He accomplished the move in under three seconds. He pretended to adjust the thin silk strip and smooth it against the white cotton dress shirt. "Voila! Good to go. You can flip it down now."

"Thanks, Tad! Fly safe and go break a leg!"

The flight from San Diego to Westchester County, New York lasted nearly seven hours. He eased back his window seat and tried to sleep, but found it impossible, mind awhirl with feelings and thoughts, mostly about how he would take Cryothera Corporation into a dominant market position once the old bastard was out of the way. *Like a rocket, we'll be! I'll be on the cover of Forbes and Time before the end of Q4!*

Touchdown. He turned on his smartphone. At least a hundred emails. Three missed calls from the office. *Annabel knows my departure-arrival times; did the bubblehead not tell everyone?* One text message from her stamped 5:37 p.m. local time: 'Call my cell.'

Standing in the aisle, he called her. "Hey Annabel, just landed; what's up?"

"Sorry to bother you, Mr. Herkimer. I wouldn't be stalking you if it wasn't top priority."

"What is it?"

A pregnant pause. A sniffle. "It's your uncle. He's…sick."

"Okay. Sorry to hear. He'll get better. The show will go on. Is that it?"

"You don't understand. He's sweating blood. It's pouring from his eyes, ears, mouth. His shirt is soaked. I found the consent form on your desk—"

"Uncle's consent form? Yes-yes, he signed it."

"And you signed as witness."

"Indeed, I did. Please tell me you didn't call an ambulance."

"No! Of course not! I know the process. I called the lab. They sent up the cryopreservation rapid response team. Before I texted you, I called down and spoke with the medical doctor on the team. He can't figure out what's wrong with your uncle. He said symptoms seem consistent with hemotoxic envenomation attributed to a snake bite, requiring monovalent antivenom, which he says is impossible to get. It is decidedly not viral, so, you're not in danger."

"Snake bite? My uncle is not the outdoorsy type. I think we all acknowledge that."

"Right? Which is why he's so confused. He examined his body head to toe. Zero puncture wounds. I'm scared, Tad."

She never called me that before. Is this a breakthrough moment? An opportunity?

The jet door opened. He grabbed his rolling bag from the overhead compartment and dragged it in his left hand. "Sorry about the noise. Tell me everything that happened."

"He started the marketing meeting at 9:00 sharp. Everyone was there, including me. He looked bad, Mr. Herkimer. I could tell he was nauseated. In front of everyone he vomited blood onto his desk. It was awful. I felt embarrassed for him more than anything. I rushed to his office. He was shivering. I felt his head: he was burning up with fever. He went to the bathroom. I ran to your office to grab towels from the gym bag I know you keep in there and found the form. If I hadn't, I would've called 9-1-1. So, I called down the team. The doc looked him over. Herky had just micturated blood, the doc said. He was covered in sweat. The team came up with a stretcher and started an I.V. before they took him down to the lab."

"Did you go see him?"

"Doc told me not to. At that point, he wasn't sure if whatever was affecting your uncle could be contagious, though thank God, it isn't. Tad…I am so very sorry to be the one to tell you. Your uncle passed away. Doc pronounced his death at 5:17 your time, not even an hour ago. He notified the coroner's office just before I texted you."

"Christ! What did he give as the cause of death?"

"Renal failure. Though I heard him say it was from disseminated intravascular coagulation."

"Say what?"

"He thinks that somehow, Herky ingested a powerful blood thinner. But to avoid a legal battle with the County over an autopsy court order, he basically told the coroner that the official cause of death was renal failure; that the old man's kidneys stopped working and he died from it."

Remind me to bonus that guy a Porsche this Christmas. Oh uncle, there I go again: I said Christ. Naughty me. Bad atheist, bad atheist.

He could hear Annabel's struggle against a full-blown cry. "Shh, none of that. You were brave and efficient and really, you saved the day. Perhaps our founding father will one day live again and give you his thanks for the graceful way you handled his mortal end. But until then, I'm in charge. You work for me, now. Please do one last thing for me before you leave?"

"Anything, Tad. Name it."

"Please arrange for an immediate return flight. Shoot a mail to the Infinity group with our sincerest apologies for missing the meeting due to an unforeseen death in the Cryothera family today."

"Will do," she snarked back snot.

He pulled his contact lens rewetting vial from his pocket and emptied it into each nostril. He made sure she heard him do some snarking and nose-blowing, and hard swallows, as though fighting against a full-blown cry. He affected a tremble to his voice. "I really don't want to be alone tonight. God. I miss him so much. Annabel, you have no idea what the man meant to me, my dad's big brother. I idolized him growing up. And now all his responsibilities fall on me. I'm scared."

Six seconds of dead air. "Texting you my apartment address. Please come over. I don't want to be alone, either."

Awakened at six AM Tuesday by alarm, they showered together. He dressed in pressed tan slacks, polo shirt and blue sport jacket from his rolling bag; she in a smart-looking summer dress. "I know you like bacon and eggs for breakfast, Tad, but I'm vegan. Best I can offer is steel-cut oatmeal with raisins and oat milk. I can add brown sugar or maple syrup too, if you like."

He walked behind her, wrapped his arms around her, and kissed her neck. "Annabel, my belle, I need you to listen carefully. I'm leaving now for the office. Bad enough that my Ferrari sat outside your apartment all night; nothing we can do about that now. When I get there, everyone will act differently. Conciliatory. 'So sorry for your loss,' yadda-yadda, like ten-thousand times. You need to keep your head cool and respond in kind, same tone, same facial expressions. Mimic them. Head down, hang-dog expression. Only look at me if there is an urgent piece of business. You cannot act any differently toward me. Same goes for me, too. In that building, you and I are strictly employee and boss. Not friendly, not flirty: strictly professional. Got it?"

Her green cat eyes glimmered. She nodded. "I understand," she said with a curt nod. He turned and walked to the door. "Tad," she said, and he stopped.

Over his shoulder, "Yeah, Belle?"

"Was last night a one-off? I mean, will I ever see you like that again?"

He turned to face her, hand on the doorknob. "God, I hope so. But strictly in secret, of course. Gotta keep up the appearance of propriety. Uncle Herky would kill me if he knew I was drinking our executive admin's bathwater." She grinned.

Also, he'd smirk at me with that condescending look of his about the fact that I can't seem to go an hour without invoking the name, God, in due course of daily communications.

He strode back to her, unzipped his fly, hiked up her dress, slid down her panties, and quickly relieved himself one last time, as she groaned in frustrated pleasure against the granite kitchen island countertop. By far and away the m*ost perfect woman I have ever had, bar none. Why do I feel like I'll never get this chance again? She's crazy about me! What gorgeous young woman wouldn't be? I'm rich!*

As predicted, the office staff grieved the loss and made a great show of it. With as much patience as he could muster, he shut his door and fielded dozens of obsequious calls from corporate employees who all now reported to him. "Annabel, could you please come to my office?" She opened the door. Their eyes locked. "Please come in and sit down," he said, loud enough for hallway skulkers to hear. "We need to edit marketing's press release about Uncle Francis and release it at 10:30."

"Let me print it out first," she said. "Also, I have purchase orders for you to sign." She disappeared for six minutes. She returned with a file folder.

"Please shut the door behind you," he said. She entered. He shot a wicked smirk and made a lock-in-key hand motion. She locked the door behind her. He pointed to the small round table with four padded rolling chairs near the window. She sat. "Okay, Annabel, first order of business: the press piece." He read it. He jotted several notes in the margins. "Done. Purchase orders for what?"

"Security and QA are worried about power-outages."

"But our data is cloud hosted. Secure as it gets."

She shook her head. "They mean down below, in storage. One of our competitors lost power. Nine cryonics patients were found in a state of decomposition. Our engineering team have competitively sourced a diesel-fueled back-up generator with automatic fail-over in cases of power interruptions."

He nodded gravely. "We thought of everything except for this, apparently. Good call." He signed the purchase order. "Anything else?"

Chin down, eyes fixed on his. "You left me unrelieved. Not fair."

He grinned and shrugged. "Not my fault it takes you so long to cum."

Shoe heels thumped his back as he leaned his face down into his work. Seven minutes later, she left his office with no need left unsatisfied.

After a quick dinner of Chinese take-out, alone back at his place, he changed into sweatpants and tee, grabbed a shovel and large prybar from hooks in his garage, lugged them to the backyard, and buried the plastic bag of toxic evidence under the firepit. Afterwards, he built a fire and sat before it, feet propped, soaking up aromatic wisps of mesquite smoke and comforting warmth on this cool, cloudless night. He felt better than he ever had in his life.

He thought hard on any possible misses; loose ends he might have overlooked. *Nope. Left no trail. Old fucker would've died soon anyway. I did him a solid. No long, lingering death from prostate cancer or some other killer disease. Here in the morning; gone by mid-afternoon, and relatively painlessly, at that. As he would say, 'Nothing personal; just business.'*

"We need to expand," he said aloud. *First things first: finish what I started. I'll have Belle reschedule the meeting in New York; start there. Networking is key. The Infinity Society will be connected to similar groups I've heard about in Milan, Paris, Barcelona, London, Madrid, and Taipei. Wouldn't she love a few exotic trips abroad! End the year twenty-million higher in new booked business than last year or die trying.*

He thought of wealth; of his equities portfolio. Absently he clutched at his crotch through the sweatpants. He thought of Annabel. *For sure, the best I've had; I went from minor league to the majors in one night. Should I keep things going with her? Why not? At least until something better comes my way.*

The lawyer in him reviewed the Annabel situation. *If I broom her from my bed, she'll do what any woman would do: cry foul. Make my work life a living hell. I'd have to fire her. She'd get some pro-bono Me-Too asshat attorney looking to make her bones to sue me. In this State for sure, I'd lose. Before all that happens, she'll accompany me on a business trip to someplace loaded with hemotoxic snakes; or better yet, hemorrhagic fever viral carriers.*

"Nothing personal, Annabel; just business," he muttered to the hypnotizing fire.

Wednesday and Thursday were the longest, busiest days he'd experienced since law school finals and run-up to the California bar exam. Annabel wisely left him completely to himself. *At least she's not up my ass like most chicks. Graciously low need for constant attention. Maybe this affair can last. We shall see.* Thursday night after work, he paid her a visit. After their three-hour wrestling match, seated in his car, he noticed that in the time he'd spent inside her apartment, dark, menacing storm clouds had settled over the area. *Hmm. Rare, but welcome. So damned dry here. But with torrential rain the mudslides come. The I-5 too, maybe. Tomorrow's gonna suck. Three TV interviews scheduled, plus all the normal nonsense. I should probably stop home, grab the cot, the pillow, a change of clothes, toiletry bag, and spend tonight in my office. The Five could be a parking lot in the morning; absolutely cannot be late for the first interview at 8:00 AM. That's the big one. I'll be invited into millions of viewer homes, exactly the free press we need to create maximum marketing buzz.*

In his office, at 9:32 p.m., he switched off the overhead LEDs and pulled the little brass chain on the green banker's lamp atop his desk, which he couldn't recall ever once using before, there only as an affectation. The soft, warm light created shadows inside the space he never knew existed. He lay on the soft foam of the cot and followed his thoughts.

I dreamed about you last night, Uncle Herky. Spent all day trying to forget the dream but failed to. Silly of me, right? Lying here, talking to a ghost I know doesn't exist, like people spending Sunday mornings in churches praying to a God that isn't real. Or weirdos dancing around a campfire worshipping the moon, or Satan, or whatever squeezes their grapes. Hey, Herk—you listening? Can you hear me? Talkin at you, muthufucka. Yeah you—you pathetic, self-righteous, overbearing, withered old dick, you. I bested you. No—permit a correction: you allowed yourself to be bested. The fault lies entirely with you.

Lightning outside for a fraction of second obliterated every shadow from his office, followed by a thundercrack so loud it rattled thick window glass. *Damn! Smart of me to come here tonight; people will wake up in the morning to a mud-block, for sure. Crews probably won't make the Five passable until midday, if that.* He thought of the current state of his uncle. *I've never seen your grave, and make no mistake, uncle: it's a grave. Only this, and nothing more. No second go-arounds.*

He wasn't sleepy. Curiosity got the better of him. He slipped into his loafers and walked out into the dark hallway. Lacking other human activity in the office or anywhere in the entire building, his footfalls sounded sharp like firecrackers. Inside the elevator, he pushed the lowest yellow button to launch the slow descent, down to the cryo-keep.

Motion sensors activated hallway rows of harsh white overhead LED lights the moment he stepped out of the elevator. To his right, columns of tall, gleaming-white cylindrical tanks bearing the Cryothera Corp logo, stretched back hundreds of feet, eight tanks to a row, two-hundred-thirty-seven of which contained human corpses, preserved at -320 Fahrenheit by liquid nitrogen. Electrical cables and flexible tubing extended from the top rear of each tank back into blue-white-painted walls.

Left of the elevator stood far smaller tanks. Some contained human heads. *What—did they think in the future, some ripped, young, virile bodybuilders with big dick energy would donate their bodies for head transplantations? Morons.* Other smaller cylinders contained beloved pets. *Now, would somebody please tell me who in the Mary-mother-fuck would spend a fortune to preserve a stupid animal? Hey uncle: at least you weren't as moronic as these saps. Excuse me: valuable paying clients.*

Francis Herkimer's new address he would never forget: *Section six, row six, number six. Six-six-six. Christians believe that is the number of the Anti-Christ, or Beast. Whatever. Fitting, uncle. You were a beast in your day.* He walked to cylinder six. He pressed his hands flat against the metal but yanked it back quickly. *Whew! Cold! You always thought Hell was fire and sulfur. Wrong. And so here we are, reunited at last: old beast—meet the new beast.*

He sat on the floor, leaning back against the base of his uncle's tank. Thinking of Annabel, he slipped his right hand into his pajama lounge pants, closed his eyes, and recalled the aromas, sensations, tastes, and views of her. Brain bewildered and intoxicated, he thought of her inevitable generosity when he would fly her to Paris. In Taipei, and at Taiwan's night markets, strangers would stop the couple to take selfies with them, like celebrities, as always happens whenever he visits there. *Putty in my hands. She'll let me do anything.*

It was at that moment that the building lost power. Startled, he thumped the back of his head against his uncle's steel cylinder. "Ow! What the—"

Two red emergency lights popped on at the far ends of each column separated by hundreds of feet, but to little effect. He sat at least one hundred feet from the closest red light. The mechanical-electrical thrumming in the subterranean space abruptly ceased. Hundreds of pop-hiss sounds happened all at once, as electricity ceased to power liquid nitrogen pumps, and the hermetic cylinder lock-seals. *Holy shit! The clients will warm up quickly and begin to decompose! If we don't get power restored immediately, we're out of business! Wait, fuck that: we'll be sued! Forced to declare bankruptcy! Oh my God!*

As the name left his lips, he thought he'd heard a thump from somewhere deep inside cylinder six-six-six. The red splash of light from the nearest emergency light barely penetrated the pervasive ebon blackness. Suddenly aware of his right hand, he released his now very shriveled soft bits and pushed himself to standing. He pounded both fists in tandem against his uncle's tank. "Fuck you, uncle Herky-Jerky. I'm not scared of you." Suddenly he never felt so cold in his life. His body shivered.

It was only your panicked imagination. Vibrations from his blows echoed hollowly and quickly subsided. Vacuumlike silence returned. He could hear circulation in his ears, his own breathing, and nothing more.

But then, and there could be no mistake this time, clearly, he heard—felt—a thump, followed by a clang, inside the cylinder. Another metallic clanging noise, this one louder.

Probably just machinery expanding. Cold and heat have curious contraction and expansion effects upon metal parts.

A loud crash from above the tank. Panic singed and tingled his nerves like thousands of tiny hot needles. *Not logical. Makes no sense.* He bolted toward the red light running at full speed, turned, and followed the column back to the elevator. Irrationally he pushed the button. *Fuck! No power, dammit!* He spotted the glowing red 'EXIT' sign which, like the emergency lights, remained lit under battery back-up power. He ran to the door and tried the steel handle. *Just fucking perfect. Goddamn security protocols! No one's supposed to be here at night. Electronic deadbolt was in the locked position when the power died.* "Hey! Any of you melting corpsicles happen to have an acetylene cutting torch?"

I may be stuck down here all night! I'll miss the interview! How's it going to look to the Board when they learn lab guys found me down here in pajamas? He slid to the floor, leaning back against the emergency door. He could picture the stair steps on the other side. *Should've brought my phone. Belle has keys; she could open this.* "Hey, San Diego Gas & Electric! I sign-off on your big fat monthly power payments—what the hell am I paying you for? Your service sucks ass and swallows."

Which brought Annabel back to mind. "Belle, I am so sorry for ever entertaining the thought of poisoning you someday. If you can feel me, I mean it. You're the best thing to happen to me in a long time." His voice echoed around until minor percussions made their way back to his ears. He also heard an unnatural sound. It reminded him of when he and his friend were eight, dropping water balloons from a hotel balcony onto patrons in the parking lot. *That hotel manager was such a dick; our dads grounded us for the entire summer break for that gag. So. What is that splat sound?*

The expansive and sterile cryo-keep had no smell. If anything, when he first alighted from the elevator, he thought he'd caught a faint whiff of antiseptic, perhaps leftover from the last janitorial floor mopping. Now he smelled his own fear, acrid and sharp, like the tang of rotting bologna. He stood and slowly walked back in the direction from which he had run. He looked down at each row, insofar as it was possible given the weak red light. Rows one, two, three, and four seemed still. He paused at row five. Nothing. Six strides carried him back to row six. He stared into the pervading gloom. All quiet. He let out a small sigh, though dare not ask himself why. He advanced two paces and stopped directly below the red emergency light fixed high overhead to the white-painted cinderblock wall. He picked up what felt like the sensation of the faintest cool breeze against the tiny cilia and sensitive nerves in the skin on the back of his neck. *Power's out, which means no HVAC, no fans, no AC…* With deep reluctance, he turned around.

Andrew Herkimer stared into the face of death. Violet death. Frozen death. Red light against blue flesh gave the corpse of Francis Herkimer a purple hue. Dark lips appeared frozen closed. Eyelids welded together. It stood statue-still. The young man's disbelief and terror found vent in one short scream, like the bark of a wounded dog. The sound of it bounced away and it came back to him.

"Oh God, no. This isn't real. Cannot be real. I'm hallucinating."

Icy eyelids slowly opened, like motorized patio awnings. Eyeballs, glassine and opaque, stared back. Corners of the mouth moved slowly, mechanically. So too did the eyes. The mouth curled into a sneer. Andrew 'Tad' Herkimer blinked three times. The apparition remained. "God no— am I going crazy?"

The awful head moved right three millimeters, back to center, left three more, and returned to center. "Oh, dear God, it shook its head no!" He glanced downward at the hideous naked purple body. *"Nooooooo!"*

Tad sprinted down row seven with all his strength. As red lights from the columns were too feeble to reach deeply, the middle of the row was completely dark. As he ran past the cryo-crypts toward the red light ahead in the distance on the opposite column, his shoulder clipped a canister. "Fuck!" As he emerged from shadow, he struggled to decide whether to run right along the far column, or left, back to row one, which leads close to the elevator. *Right*, instincts instructed. Twenty strides from the column, he stumbled and fell. Francis Herkimer stood blocking the end of row seven.

"But how—" The corpse did not bend its right knee. Stiffly it thrust the rigid leg forward as a man with two full-length plaster casts might attempt to walk. Right foot planted; it dragged the left up to meet it. "You can't run faster than I can!" Before it could manage its grotesque lurch toward him, he picked himself up and ran back toward the opposite column. He thought of the water he had seen under Herky, plainly visible when close to the red light. *Dripping condensation, like a glass of ice. Ghosts don't drip. Because they don't exist. Holy fuck.*

He neared the top of the row. *No sign of that thing. Go right.* He did. He ran straight into the frozen corpse. He screamed. Icy arms fired out like projectiles and clamped together around his shoulders. The squeeze felt almost hydraulic in its sheer force. His own face, and the face of the frozen mauve abomination that had once been his uncle Herky, were now separated by sixteen inches. Its left leg lurched backwards. Tad felt himself pulled down the column. When he got pulled down row six, *realization coiled around his pounding heart like a frozen steel noose. He means to pull me into his grave!* "God no! Let me go!" The harder he struggled the tighter the squeeze, like a Chinese finger trap. The sardonic smirk never left the ghastly, gruesome face, more purple than blue when dappled by faint red light. Slowly, mechanically, it shambled backwards between cryo-tubes five and six. When it contacted the wall behind the tubes, purple fingers closed around thick cables and tubes. Dark purple feet connected with the steel canister. It inched up, with Andrew pressed between the world's largest and coldest lobster claw of inanimate frozen flesh.

It took twenty minutes of the reverse rappelling for the corpse of Francis Herkimer to reach the open top of the canister, towing its godson-nephew, flailing and screaming piteously, imprisoned between its arms.

At the top of the canister, together, they plunged head-down into the black hole filled with liquid nitrogen. An arm reached up and pulled the seal down over them. Six minutes later, restored power resealed all four-hundred canisters within the cryo-crypt.

At 7:30 Friday morning, Annabel arrived at the office. She found Tad's cot and immediately concluded he had spent the night there. *Makes perfect sense*, she thought. *But where is he?* At 7:41, she called the network show producer to explain the situation and to fill his slot with another. At 7:55, she phoned local police. By 10:11, detectives had searched every inch of Cryothera Corporation's headquarters. One of them asked Matt Wu to open the canisters. "Sorry, officer. No employee is able to open the hermetically sealed cryo-canisters. A special electronic key code is programmed for each. The keys are stored in electronic and paper format in bank safe deposit boxes. Even loved ones can't access the keys. No, sir: to open any one canister would require a court order. Given the nature of operations and the complicated legal framework protecting the clients, I sincerely doubt any judge would grant the order. Issuance of nearly four hundred court orders? Think about it."

"Why? What's inside?"

"Human corpses, human heads, human brains, and animal corpses, preserved in liquid nitrogen. Think of it as a frozen cemetery for the wealthy. Once these canisters are sealed, only a far-distant-future court, centuries from now, could order their opening."

"Sick! I've heard people pay to get freeze-dried when they die. Never knew that's what goes on down here."

Matt narrowed his eyes, unamused at the simplistic comment. "One canister per customer, and I assure you, Tad Herkimer is not among them. Only his uncle. Have you tried his home?"

"We have. The team found a suspicious bag recently buried in his back yard. Dr. Wu, I disagree with your 'centuries from now' comment. We will return by end-of-business today with a court order to examine your team's post-mortem examination file on Francis Archibald Herkimer. An employee described his day-of-death symptoms which bear zero resemblance to 'renal failure.' Homicide will order the coroner to perform an autopsy. You might do the city a service, doctor, and commence the thawing process now."

Magus

An American Jew, walking alone in the West Bank, Palestinian Territories—or the magma chamber underneath Yellowstone erupting into a super-volcano this year. Which unlikely scenario has the better odds? Professional illusionist, Schmuel 'Sam' Hoffman, sensed eyes on him. *This trip is absurd. What the hell was I thinking?* The relentless June midday sun seemed intent on incinerating him. He compared his phone GPS with a storefront window's words, stenciled in both English and Arabic.

Ashkenazi features, designer-label clothing, gait, bearing, presence—everything together screamed 'American Jew.' If this were his hometown of Jericho, New York, stopping someone to ask directions would be a no-brainer. Here, in Bethlehem, West Bank, Occupied Palestinian Territories, he wouldn't dare.

At least it's nothing like Jew-hating Gaza forty-five miles west of here, but as we know: hate is viral and it spreads quickly. I look and feel like a target. Amir said it would be a falafel place near Manger Square. This area is super-touristy, but still, I wish I had a bodyguard with me. Okay, where the hell are you, Amir? This alleged juice of yours had damned well better be worth this squeeze.

Amir Al-Ghazzawi had answered Sam's globally advertised open offer to purchase new innovative illusions for his magic show. At age forty, decades of hard work in Tin Pan Alley had finally blossomed for Sam into a primary 'resident headliner' multiyear contract at a Vegas casino, also an award bestowed by the International Federation of Magic Societies.

None of this is enough. Not even close. I mean to destroy all competitors past, present, and future. To make myself into the biggest name in magic since Simon Magus left his indelible mark on history two thousand years ago, not far from where I now stand. Maybe he stood on this very spot.

Most especially, he sought to put his stiffest competitor and arch-nemesis, Ollie Lloyd, stage name 'Oliver Twisted,' out of business. *Clever and devious enough to reverse engineer and steal many of my own illusion innovations for his own shows. Twisted bastard.*

He did a double take. "And there it is," he muttered. He glanced down at his GPS to confirm. He stared down a narrow, steeply downslope street at a restaurant sign on the left, affronting the second structure down from the main thoroughfare upon which he stood. *Please let there be air conditioning.* Affable men stood outside, all smiles. One greeted him in English and ushered him inside. Outside was stone construction, almost medieval looking. Inside he found it well-appointed and tastefully decorated. Plenty of bright light through the front window illuminated clean white tablecloths and napkins, and yes: the AC hit him like a cool blessing.

A quick glance summed a clientele of families, couples, friends, but only one single: a swarthy-looking man wearing a black tee shirt with gold Arabic writing, thread-worn blue jeans, and no-name sneakers likely purchased in a mart. The man stared at him, back to the stone wall, seated at a small round table built for two. He raised his glass of water and smiled at Sam.

"Amir?"

"Hello! Come, please sit down, Mister Sam."

Sam did. Amir extended his right hand. Sam, a maximum germaphobe, offered a fist-bump in return. "Amir, don't know about you but I'm starving. If you recommend something fantastic off the menu, I'll buy lunch."

Amir nodded. "Shukran! Please try the falafel, hummus and tabouli wrap with Lebanese pickles. This you will love. I shall have the same." A nearby waiter overheard the exchange and said something to Amir in Arabic, who nodded. "He'll bring it right out along with ice water for you."

"Great. So let's get down to business, shall we?"

Amir's expression changed. To Sam, he seemed wounded. "It is with the heaviest heart that I am here today discussing the sale of a precious family heirloom, in my line for three hundred generations."

"Three hundred? You know this with absolute certainty?"

"Inshallah, yes, three hundred. On January 11, during Ramadan, in the Year 630—Makkah, or as people these days pronounce, it, Mecca, the Prophet Muhammad—peace be upon him—smashed the three hundred and sixty idols in the Ka'aba, a holy site protected by his tribe, the Banu Quraysh. This was the most magical time in the history of Arabia. Until the Prophet united all the tribes through his new religion, Islam, each tribe had worshipped their own gods or goddesses," said Amir. He leaned toward Sam. "I am a direct descendant of an ancestral family in the Banu Quraysh tribe."

Sam nodded. "Impressive, that your family has kept such scrupulous records. Now, about the magical time…"

Amir slowly closed his eyes and reopened them. "Yes, business, of course." The waiter interrupted with two platters and water glasses. Sam promptly drained his. The waiter refilled it.

"Shukran," Sam said to the waiter. Amir smiled.

"I see you have learned some Arabic."

Sam nodded. "I like to win people over. Let's say that it's a big part of what drives me. Learning languages helps attract people of all stripes. Puts them at ease, demonstrates respect. Don't you agree?"

"Yes, oh yes. I struggled with English in school, but it is the language of business. Now, please understand, I need to first explain the ancient history of the magic Baetylus, so that you fully understand the provenance."

"A magic what?"

Amir furrowed his brow and spoke in low tones. "Hāwlat: she is the Arabian goddess of magic and power, patron goddess of the oases that were Dumah, and Hejra. The name of the goddess means 'to change fortunes.' Then too, Ar-Rā'iyu, whose name means 'The One Who Sees' is the Arabian god of ru'ya"

"Ru'ya?"

"Dreams and prophecy. All dreams were messages from the gods in pre-Islamic Arabia. Soothsayers specialized in interpreting dreams. Ar-Rā'iyu is an all-seeing guardian, and had origins with the Hebrew El Roi, meaning 'The Seeing God,' who was believed to be the deity who protected Hagar, the mother of Ishmael and the ancestor of the Arabs, during her time in the desert.

"The third, Al-'Uzzā, is the Meccan goddess of power, and the planet Venus as the Evening Star. She was worshiped by the Arabian tribes of Banu Quraysh, Banu Sulaym, Banu Ghanim, Banu Ghatafan, Banu Khuza'a, Banu Thaqif, and Banu Kinãnah. The main idol of al-'Uzza, in which her spirit lived, was a cluster of three acacia trees that were situated in the valley of Nakhla, not far from the town of Mecca. Al-'Uzza had a second bayt in Mecca—"

"Bayt?"

"Temple, called Buss, which was made of brick, not far from her shrine at Nakhla. Inside the Buss temple was another important idol of al-'Uzza: a blood-stained slab of granite, shaped like a human thigh bone, which was venerated. Upon this slab, the pre-Islamic Arab tribes of the Hijaz offered blood sacrifices. They believed that the goddess herself spoke through the idol and would grant an oracle to the worshiper. Khalid ibn al-Walid, an early convert to Islam, cut down the sacred trees of the goddess, and destroyed her shrine, under orders from the Prophet Muhammad—peace be upon him. He crushed every pagan idol among the Arabs of the Hijaz. Followers of Al-'Uzzā sacrificed animals, sometimes human slaves, and prisoners of war, in exchange for her blessings."

"How civilized of them." Sam could not stop himself from getting in a snarky little dig. "Appreciate the backstory, but what is a magic Baetylus?"

Amir took a bite of his wrap and washed it down. "A Baetylus, or Baetyl, is a sacred stone. The power, the essence, the very spirits of gods and goddesses here on earth, are said to dwell for all time within these durable objects. Al-'Uzza chose to live in a white granite slab, and also inside three trees."

Sam polished off his wrap, grabbed one of the crisp thick linen napkins and dabbed his mouth. "Thanks, Amir, for the fascinating trip back in time. Do you have an illusion to sell me or don't you?"

Amir frowned. He shook his head. Sam sensed he had offended him. "No. Not illusion. Authentic supernatural magic."

Amir touched the back of his neck. He grasped the top of a clasp-less solid thick gold chain. With great difficulty, he worked the chain over his head. Sam noticed several patrons staring, fascinated by this remarkable struggle. Sam stared at the object dangling from the chain. At once he observed that the chain and the object were like one, meaning that, given the size of Amir's neck, a jeweler had fed the open chain of tiny gold links through a hole in the wood, and melted a link shut to create a single loop. Judging from Amir's painful exertion, the chain had been melted closed around his neck when he was a young man, never meant to be removed.

Breathing heavily, Amir laid it reverentially upon the white tablecloth. He did not release his grip on the chain. "You see three stones set vertically in wood. The top stone, red agate, is from the destroyed idol of the goddess, Hāwlat. The second stone, black, meteoric, is from the crushed baetyl of the god, Ar-Rā'iyu. The white stone at the bottom came from the sacrificial slab of the goddess, Al-'Uzza, the most powerful goddess in all Arabia. The wood in which the three stones are set is acacia, from one of her three trees."

"Beautiful. So?"

Amir locked eyes with him. "With this Baetylus, the owner can make anyone see anything he wants others to see."

Sam laughed. "Sure."

Amir's eyes opened very wide. "You don't believe me?"

"Ah, no, Amir. I think you've wasted my time." Sam tossed a folded wad of Israeli shekels on the table and stood.

Amir sulked. "How about if I give you proof?"

Sam stopped. "Okay, give it to me."

Amir glanced around. "Not here. Follow me over to the cafe bar in the hotel lobby, which is more promising. There, I will give you proof, absolutely."

Sam rolled his eyes. "In for a penny—in for a pound. Sure, why not. This trip's been a bust. The least you can do is buy me a big glass of Patron Blanco. Lead on, Amir."

After another hot walk, they arrived at the hotel. Sam's eyes fixed on a group of beautiful women half his age, flirting with young men seated at the bar. Some wore Canadian maple leaf symbols on their shoulder bags. *Students*, he thought. Amir led Sam to an unoccupied table and sat.

Unenthusiastically, Sam did also. *What a colossal waste of time this trip has been.*

"Do you see a girl that you like?"

Sam scanned the bar. "The little redhead. Interesting face."

Amir smiled. "Hold the Baetylus when you look at her. Imagine yourself beside her, kissing her. Picture your hands and mouth on her body. Seduce her. Make her climax. The fantasy must be clear in your mind."

"Amir—"

"You wanted proof? Proof you shall have. Just do it. Or I'll be the one to walk away this time."

Sam's eyes narrowed. "If it'll get me out of this oven any faster, sure." Holding the Baetylus, he stared at the redhead. A young man stood a foot away from the redhead, obviously putting the make on her. Sam imagined giving the boy a powerful shove aside; saw himself standing in the boy's spot. His intense brown eyes bored into her pretty green eyes. Wordlessly, he grabbed the back of her neck, pulled her face to his, and lightly kissed her mouth. He kissed up and down her long pale neck. Greedily, he teased open her lips with his tongue.

Both he and Amir saw the abrupt change in the woman's demeanor. So too did the young man. He appeared stunned. Sam watched himself massage her breasts, a firm grip on the crotch of her short shorts. Now in his mind he had yanked down her shorts and underwear in one smooth stroke. He watched himself pull her buttocks to the edge of the dark wooden bar stool, kneel between her legs, slurping and swirling away at her while his hands kneaded her breasts. The scene in his mind was so crystalline that it aroused him.

Suddenly the din in the room quieted to a hush. All anyone could hear were the woman's high-pitched squeals. Every eye in the room watched her squirm into a boisterous and very loud crescendo, her climactic explosion heard clearly by passers-by outside through thick glass.

As if freshly awakened from a trance, flushed with embarrassment like she never knew possible, she studied the stunned faces in the room, until she spotted Sam. Crotch soaking wet, no trace of shame or embarrassment, almost as if she had little memory of the event, she got up and walked over to the table. Sam beheld the face of enduring afterglow. In a shy, almost reverential manner, she said, "Oh my God, I know you somehow, don't I!"

Sam grinned modestly. "I'm famous in the USA. You're Canadian, yes?"

A nod and a smile as she reached into her bag. She took out a yellow sticky note and purple pen. She jotted her telephone and email information under her name, Victoria Pleasance, and ended with a smiley face. She handed it to Sam. "What's your name?"

He took the note. "People know me as Sam Magus."

He could smell the heat from her crotch. *Amir is legit. I feel like a sleep-deprived 8-year-old who just discovered sugar and free will. Tear yourself away from this beauty and get thy mind back on business.* He failed to notice the young man at the bar, furious from the loss of his *objet de désir*, stalking toward their table, fists balled. Amir noticed; he snatched up the charmed necklace.

The young man's eyes glazed over as Amir stared. He stopped dead in his tracks and threw up his hands in surrender. "As-salāmu alaykum, brother," he said. He took several steps backward.

Amir broke his focus on the boy. "Sam, please, let us leave this place quickly."

Back at the restaurant, the two split a plate of baklava. Sam broke the silence. "Proof positive. Sorry I ever doubted you, Amir. I don't know how it works, but I know that it does. Old desert magic, I guess. That is some serious snake-charmer stuff you have there."

Amir gave a polite close-lipped smile. "When my dying father bestowed the Baetylus to me on his deathbed, he told me that it would bring me luck, fortune, money, power, as it had throughout our enduring family branch." He shook his head, eyes luminous and watery. "But baba never saw this Satanic pandemic coming, now, did he? Our family business relies on tourism. When lockdowns and travel restrictions endured for over a year, Allah be praised, I could no longer afford to remain in business and pay my workers who are also my dear relatives. I am now forced to make a difficult choice. Feed, clothe, house, and educate my family—or cling to the Baetylus for sentimental reasons. Sentiment buys you nothing in Palestine, sadiq hamim." Sam raised his eyebrows. "I mean, brother."

Sam eyed him narrowly. "At lunch, if you had laid this story on me, I would've thought it a negotiation ploy to lower my offer. But I see now that everything you say is true. How much do you want for the Baetylus?"

I would've paid five mil for it. It's worth a hundred times that. Sam buckled in for the final flight of his journey back to LAS airport in Vegas. *I don't feel bad. Two mil over there, where the middle-class skilled laborer is lucky to earn the equivalent of twenty-five grand American dollars in a year, hell. Amir and his family are now likely among the wealthiest in Palestine. He'll never have to serve another tourist again, if he properly invests, and spends thriftily.* Through his shirt, he stroked the rectangle hanging from the gold chain, puzzling over Amir's peculiar stern warning.

"'Al-'Uzzā is the driving force of the Baetylus magic. I will now tell you what my baba told me: that unless her followers occasionally refresh her with meaningful, personal blood sacrifices, she will become wrathful. She will turn her magic against her host.'"

"Philistine pagans," he muttered.

The flight, a red eye, was darkened for passengers to sleep. Two rambunctious teen boys cavorted loudly a few rows up. *Bastards are ruining the flight for everyone in the cabin not wearing ear buds or headphones.* He stared at them. He imagined himself as Amir, seated in the row ahead of them, turning now to face them, his hand clutching the Baetylus. *My name is Jihad. If you fail to sit silently for the remainder of this flight, when we land, I will follow you tonight wherever you go. I will find you. I will slice the skin under your chin and peel the face away from each one of you. This is what I do. If you choose not to believe me, you will, later tonight. You will enter Hell, this very night, with no faces.*

The boys straightened in their seats. None dared look at one another or make a sound. In stunned stasis they remained for the next ninety minutes, including after touch-down and deplaning. Sam smirked. *I'll be greater even than Simon Magus. I shall take to wife my own version of his Helen, introduce her to my audience as a goddess, same as he did. Nah, to hell with that. With this thing, I can seduce any woman or girl I want, like Victoria the Canadian ginger. Why tie myself to one woman? Boorinnng.*

But then, his twenty-six-year-old assistant for the past four years, Rachel Haim, never left his mind for fewer than fifteen minutes. Jewish, parents tragically killed in a freakish condo building collapse while she attended university. Try though he might to keep his thoughts and interactions with her professional, he fantasized about the life they could have together. *A traditional marriage in a highly untraditional career trajectory. Could it work?*

Never had he desired intimacy with anyone as ardently as he ached for Rachel. *One of the reasons why proximity matters to attraction is that it breeds familiarity; people are more attracted to that which is familiar. Just being around someone or being repeatedly exposed to them increases the likelihood that we will be attracted to them.* His self-psychoanalysis sessions he realized were happening more frequently lately. The rational pro remained locked in a persistent struggle to diffuse the burning passion for the girl of his dreams, and to rationalize it away as a deceptive trick of his own mind and body; merely a biochemical swindle.

Seated in the hotel shuttle, he shifted to recalling imaginary sex with the girl at the Bethlehem hotel bar, Victoria. Only now did he realize when Amir had implored him to pick one why he had selected her. *She looks remarkably like the goy version of Rachel; drop-dead gorgeous, but also seems quick-minded and warm-hearted, qualities that explain why the crowds respond to Rachel's smiles and seductive movements with such enthusiasm. No. I dare never cross that line with Rachel Haim, a key ingredient of my successful stage act. Besides, she views me more like a substitute daddy, pretty sure.*

As he caressed his two-million-dollar Baetylus, an all-consuming, desperate, urgent longing crept in like some mindless selfish scarab in his ear, which can only crawl forward not backwards, and clawed its way deep inside his brain. An epiphany of epic scale: *I love her! I am hopelessly, deliriously in love with Rachel! The most ardent, the most abject worship and adoration a man can feel for woman. I'd give it all up, cash out, live well off my investments, give her anything and everything her little heart desires…and she would love me for it.* He imagined Rachel curled up his lap on the sofa after an entire afternoon of lovemaking. Through the window he saw his host hotel and casino loom large, his home for all intents and purposes, and felt deeply unsettled. *What, Sam, are you going to do now?*

While he imagined a future with his assistant, his hand never left the

Baetylus.

Back in his enormous penthouse suite at the casino, comped to him free of charge thanks to his almost full-house box office draws, having spent the day sleeping, instead of rehearsing with Rachel as planned, he texted her cell. "We have four hours before showtime. I want to lay a new trick on you. Come over?"

Ninety-seconds later, "Sure thing, boss!"

Rachel, in a simple floral summer dress over gold strappy sandals, red hair tied up in a bun, bopped in without knocking. "You really should keep your door locked. Remember that obsessive fan? Creep-stalker extraordinaire."

He beamed, as he always did whenever he saw her. "That's my girl. Always looking out for me."

She skipped to his refrigerator, poured herself a glass of grape juice, and demurely sipped from it. "Okay, so what's this new trick up your sleeve?"

"Please have a seat," which she did, her butt on the cushioned edge of his sumptuous black leather sectional sofa. The thick, black, faux fur area rug she found too appealing to resist: she unbuckled her sandals and buried hot, slick soles into its cool, plush depths. "Mm," she cooed. He cast a furtive glance at her flexing calves. He knew she caught him gawking, though he recovered quickly. "Please, Reychie, why don't you just make yourself at home," he quipped, and she laughed.

"Now, you are going to find this absolutely irrational, unreasonable, illogical, and by every measure of science and the laws of physics—wholly impossible."

"What? Come on, Sam! Tell me already!"

"Enough words. Better if I show you. I'm going to sit at the kitchen island where you can still see me." He walked over and took a seat. "Now, I want you to remain focused on me, your eyes on mine." She complied. He freed the Baetylus.

"Oh. Oh wow! OH MY GOD! Sam! How in the heck are you floating?"

"Eyes on me, don't even blink."

"Oh my God! Sam, you're flying! You *really are* flying! This is so cool! Fly over here and touch my nose." Pupils in her large and luminous brown irises involuntarily contracted. "How did you do that?" She watched him do a somersault in the air. She could still feel where his finger had touched her, like tingles of low voltage coursing through the skin of her nose.

He restored the Baetylus under his shirt, closed his eyes and broke the connection. "You like?"

She jumped up. "Sam, I'm scared! Not gonna lie. I am *really, really* scared."

He smiled and opened his arms at her. She ran into them. They hugged tightly. She gazed at him. "You're... amazing."

He laughed. "And you complete me, Rachel. I owe you so much more than a paycheck. I could spend the rest of my life repaying you, in every way a man can. One lifetime would never be long enough. I'd barely make a dent in what I owe you. Believe me when I say that you, little miss, are the amazing one of this duo."

She blushed. He wiped a tear from her cheek. "In many ways, you saved me. My grief was all-consuming. If hadn't answered that ad you placed for an assistant back when the people who knew your name numbered in the hundreds, I don't know where I'd be today. Dead, maybe? I considered ending it all, more than once." She lowered her eyes. "I never told that to anyone before. I'm sorry."

He leaned down and pressed a kiss to her forehead, and one to her nose. She stood on tiptoes, eyes open, when for the first time, she kissed his mouth.

Rachel glanced at the huge pendulum clock. She shrieked. "Oh my God! We only have an hour before show opening!"

He barely stirred, eyes closed, left cheek flattening what there was of her already flat right breast. She shook him. He jolted back to full consciousness. "Yes, you're right. The show must go on, lover."

She smiled. "You said love."

He smiled. "And I meant it."

"Do we have time for a quick shower? I mean, we smell like sex."

He grinned. "I love it. Love your bouquet. I want to snort your juices deep into my sinuses to keep you with me and keep Mr. Stiffy stiff twenty-four-seven." She blinked seductively. "No, just throw on your makeup and costume, I'll do the same. If we hurry, we can be backstage in thirty minutes, giving us time to get our heads back in the game."

He heard his stage name announced. It always gave him a low prickle in his prostate to hear it reverberate through the auditorium. Lights flashed from somewhere high up in the audio-visual booth like so many times before. Tonight, it felt different, more powerful. *Because of Rachel? Or is it the Baetylus?* Feeling reborn and high wattage electrified, glowing from inside out, Sam Magus burst onstage, cape flowing behind him to resounding applause. He always made it a point to stand as far forward as the stage permitted, shield his eyes with his right hand, and slowly make eye contact with every audience member—or so it seemed to them. Applause always continued while he did this. He claimed it established an intimate personal connection between him and each paying guest, so, even if he had an off night, they'd forgive him. *Tonight, they'll get their money's worth, and more.*

He opened with the tired old sword-box illusion. Rachel curled up at the bottom of the box and guided the authentic, very sharp swords past her body as he slowly inserted them. She arose out of the box unscathed to mediocre applause. In another box, he sawed her in half and separated the two halves of the box, her long, slender, wriggling painted toes out of one, her pretty, smiling face framed by long, luxurious red wavy hair from the other half, along with finger-wiggles. More polite applause.

He thought about the next illusion on his menu, rehearsed and performed many times, but then decided, now is the time.

"Ladies and gentlemen, thank you. I guess you know Rachel, my lovely assistant, was scrunched up inside both the sword box and the wooden coffin you watched me saw completely in half. The feet at the bottom half are remote-controlled robotic prosthetics."

Alarm registered on murmuring faces. A top magician had just given away community secrets. He grinned uncontrollably. "Yes, illusionists follow a process. We use expensive equipment. Practice makes perfect. Audiences pay hard-earned money, or hard-gambled winnings in some of your cases for a momentary escape from life's mundane routines. Secretly, audience members hope that somehow, somewhere on this miserable rotating rock in space, *real* magic does exist; and maybe, if they're lucky, some illusionist will leave them believing that it truly does. Well ladies and gentlemen, moms, dads, and kids, and let us not forget you wise old-heads still young at heart: tonight, real magic does exist. I'm about to give it to you. Now, I need you to turn off your cell phones. Do it now, please."

Alarm turned to excitement. He watched much movement wash through the dark rows and columns. Pointing up at the control booth, he said, "Turn on the house lights. I want it super bright in here." He imagined their confusion up there, and chuckled. They complied. "Now, I want each of you to watch my eyes. This is critical. Do not break eye contact. If you must sneeze, choke it back, do it later."

Heads turned to one another in search of an answer. Some stared at him, which caused others to follow suit, curious if nothing else. He repeated his orderly scan of the audience, slowly panning each column and row, to give the illusion of individual eye contact with fourteen hundred people. Now that all eyes were on him, he disrobed down to his white vee-neck undershirt and tight black pants. He reached between the buttons of his shirt and grasped the Baetylus.

That was when, for the first time, he started flying.

Sam Magus flew through the brightly lit auditorium. Cables, guy wires or harness quickly would have been spotted. He flew, arms and legs outstretched. He did somersaults. He affected a lounging position directly above the audience, head propped in elbow. He flew twelve inches above laps along every row, turning himself like a spit-roast as he did. He smiled at every face. He hovered at times in each row, stationary. He asked old ladies, nursing moms, teenage boys, and burly men wearing trucker's hats to please touch him. "Pass your hands above and underneath my outstretched body, check for wires or trickery. Just don't grab my crotch." Laughter. Locked in eye contact with a corpulent older woman, the audience heard him say, "Well, little miss… certainly you can check my crotch for wires or trickery." The room roared with laughter. Mindful of the time, he closed his eyes and palmed the Baetylus. Contact broken.

The audience erupted. Rachel, the only person behind him and thus not in eye contact, suddenly remembered to give her trademark smile and curtsy. Neither she, nor Sam, nor the AV guys up in the booth, nor the security guards who had also watched him fly had ever heard such a raucous, resounding audience reaction.

"You came here hoping real magic might exist in the world. So now that you know that it does, let me ask: would any of you like to fly, too?" Another outburst of cheers, whistles, and claps. "If you would like to fly right now, make some basic beginner moves, please raise your hand." The room quieted. Every hand went up. "Very well," he said. He cast a glance at Rachel, whose mouth hung ajar. "Eyes on my eyes, you know the drill. Don't even blink, and you too shall fly."

Baetylus in hand, he thought of all the faces he had scanned—imagined each levitating straight up above their seats, somersaulting one time, doing a reverse movement, heads thrown back, bodies in backflip rotation. He thought of them floating back down as softly as feathers in a room following a pillow fight, until seated. Then, he closed his eyes.

Rachel awoke in his arms atop black satin sheets. Head propped in hand, wide awake, she stared over at Sam's face. *No fine lines or wrinkles. No hair loss. An amazing, generous, hungry lover.* She knew then with absolute certainty that she was drowning in a warm, black, deep and silent tarn of emotion for this man, some of which she recognized and understood, along with novel new 'daddy' feelings. *My mom would've been proud of him; God rest her soul.* She wondered about last night. *How did he do it? How could he possibly hypnotize an entire roomful of average people to make each see the same illusion?* She wondered too why he wore that hideous necklace even in the shower, and while they made love. She could hardly wait for him to wake up to ask him about the thing. Quietly, she slipped out of bed, sat on the couch, turned on her phone, and read through headlines.

Sam Magus Really Can Fly! Illusionist Sam Magus Sends Audience Over The Moon! She scrolled through dozens of similar headlines in her media feed. She selected one she deemed reliable, posted by a respectable journalist in a mainstream e-zine, and read the full article. Eyewitness testimonials by the hundreds. Each aligned without deviation. Not one single negative review. Not only did illusionist Sam Magus actually fly, but so too did each witness. 'I never thought such a thing would ever be possible, but it is! I flew! Swear on my kids' lives, I flew up into the air, did two somersaults, and floated back to my seat!'

"Good morning, my love," came a voice from behind her. "Make us some coffee?"

Beaming. "There you go, using the 'L' word again, mister."

He grinned. "And I meant it again. Now come on, I need caffeine before I get a headache. Then it's back to bed. I'm hungry for breakfast."

"Want me to make you something, my scorpion king of kings?"

Grin morphed to a smirk. "I like the sound of that. No, you are my breakfast. All the nourishment I shall ever need is packed into a tiny hundred-pound red pepper omelet served to me on a black satin platter." He looked her up and down like a wolf in a rabbit hutch.

Next to each other at the island, before two steaming black mugs, she covered his hand. "Sam, seriously. I'm your assistant. Let me in on the mass hypnosis trick."

He swallowed hard. "It's not hypnosis, Rachel. It's authentic magic." She made a face at him. "Seriously, stab me in the heart if I lie." He smacked his chest for emphasis.

"What's with that hideous new amulet ya got there?"

His face grew stern. "It's…well. It's the source of my new magic. You wouldn't understand."

"Try me."

He related the entire story, from flying into Ben Gurion Airport in Tel Aviv, through his meeting with Amir in Bethlehem—though tactfully he changed a few key details about the beta test on Victoria Pleasance—and how he silenced the rambunctious teen boys on the return flight. He studied her reaction. Silence.

"Okay, someday you'll let me in on your hypnosis technique. Did you hypnotize me into bed with you?"

Appearing shocked, he said, "I assure you, Rachel Haim, that I used no such trickery to summon your ardor."

She smiled. "I know that much is true, lover." She took his wrist and pulled him back to the large, soft lake of satin.

During the show that evening, Sam did the first card trick he ever learned as a child as his warm-up segment. Comically, he bowed and flexed his biceps. "Please try to hold down the applause, you're confusing my hearing aid." The audience laughed harder than he had ever heard a comedian's audience laugh—and he knew precisely why, bleeding off the nervous anticipation of flying.

He spent the next hour standing at the edge of the stage in a sweep of every audience member's face. They watched him creatively murder and dismember his lovely assistant. She knelt near the edge of the stage. His first action was to behead her with one powerful stroke of a Samurai sword. In his right hand he lofted her head by its auburn locks, Baetylus in his left hand. The audience screamed. Several patrons splatted the red carpeting with vomit.

"Raise your hand if you would like to ask Rachel's severed head a question." Most hands went up. He projected one question into every person's head: What does it feel like to be dead? In their minds they asked it. The head responded. 'I sort of miss my body…I was a highly orgasmic lady, you know.' The audience roared with approval and mirth. They watched him spit into the gory neck and reattach the head to the body. He pulled twenty yards of white handkerchief from his left palm; this he used to clean imagined blood from her neck wound. He took Rachel's hand, raised it high into the air, and asked, "Would you like to watch me lop off my lovely assistant's hands and feet for you to pass up and down the rows?" Applause followed, so vigorously that it shook desert dust loose from atop the lighting banks.

Every night's show over the next fourteen followed the same successful pattern, until an incident caused a major policy change. A patron posted a selfie to social media taken during the eleventh performance. It captured an audience sitting in a starry-eyed, almost catatonic state, with Sam staring out at them. No one flew. No blood, no severed body parts; only Sam, with Rachel standing behind him. As a result the casino, at Sam's insistence, implemented and enforced a strict no cameras-no cell phones policy. While he had worried that the photo and these security shakedowns might negatively affect ticket sales, he felt ecstatic to learn that ticket sales were now booking six months in advance of his shows.

"Forbidden fruit tastes sweetest," he told Rachel.

She giggled. "The clown who posted the selfie collected nothing but negative comments against himself. Your audience is loyal, Sam! So is your perky little assistant."

All went well until the fifteenth performance ended in complete show business disaster. He stood and made eye contact—yet nothing happened. The audience stared back and commenced loud boos, cat-calls, profane insults, middle fingers, and walk-outs. Sam pulled Rachel backstage in fear for their safety.

"Sam, what happened?" she asked.

He appeared stunned. "Honestly, Reychie, I haven't a clue. Not one fucking clue."

But indeed, he did. *'Meaningful, personal blood sacrifices.'* Amir's words bounced in his brain. Red-hot iron pincers closed around his heart.

"Let's go upstairs," said Rachel. She took his hand. "You need cheering up."

He regarded her strangely as though absent, not fully present. "Rachel, sweetheart, I'm not good company tonight. I need to be alone. Be a dear, won't you? Give me some space. Only for tonight, I promise. I just want to work things out in my head. You still have your apartment." The expression on her face tightened like her grip on his hand. "Tonight only, lover. I swear it."

She studied his eyes. "Fine." He accompanied her to his suite. Both changed into street clothes. As she walked out the door, she turned. "Feel better, lover."

Alone, he took a hit from a bottle of single malt scotch whiskey. *No! I don't want to.* He struggled to push down old memories of going to synagogue with his parents, Psalm 28 on loop, feelings of moral certainty and conviction at once warm and comforting. *The Lord loves justice and will not leave those who worship Him. He will always protect them, but the children of the wicked will die.* He thought of Utilitarianism, learned in university psychology courses; the philosophy of Hegel. *The ends justify the means. What are the ends, here? I'm a two-bit entertainer. The ends will mean immortality, like Merlin, like Simon Magus. The wizard of my age. Surely if there is a God, He will understand. Surely He did not ascend to His current lofty throne by showing love and mercy all the damned time. Look at nature. Large eats small, strong eats weak, clever eats both.*

He dug through his closet until he found the new, sealed plastic shower curtain he had packed prior to move-in, not knowing the suite was equipped with an enormous walk-in shower featuring a sleek style frameless door of thick, tempered glass. He took the elevator to the lobby, waved at the bell captain on duty, who nodded collegially as Sam took a bell cart. Through doors inaccessible to the public, he wound his way backstage. Onto the red carpeted bell cart, he loaded the sword box illusion and pushed it to the elevator. He wheeled it into his suite.

Another shot of single-malt. He snapped open the shower curtain, shook it out, and pressed it into the sword box as a liner. He changed clothes again.

Pretty sharp, he thought as he stood before the mirrored closed door. White Novachek-collared Burberry polo over tan khakis and loafers. Elevator fob in his pocket, he went down to the casino floor. He walked around. *It's inevitable. Worthless whores. Absolutely worthless. God won't miss one.*

Eleven minutes later a pretty bottle blonde scoped him out. He guessed her to be around Rachel's age, though around his own height, five-feet-eleven-inches. "Hello, handsome!" she said, voice high, rough from too many cigarettes or bongs. He glanced at her cheap sequined reddish-gold evening dress and equally low-class peep-toe pumps. *Beyond worthless. What is lower than worthless? This black hole of human refuse right here. Can almost hear the genital lice jumping through her pubes like a flea circus. Disgusting flappy fish market.*

"Good evening, miss. You're looking sparkly tonight."

She smiled. "My name's Chrystal, spelled with an 'h.' I know who you are. Everybody knows Sam Magus, the world's greatest magician."

"Illusionist," he corrected.

She moved close to brush a non-existent fleck from his pink shirt collar. "I bet I know a few tricks that'll turn you inside out."

He laughed. "Of that I have no doubt. Ever been up to the penthouse floor?"

She raised her eyebrows. "You mean…"

He smiled. "Sure, why not? Here," he said. He handed her the spare elevator key she would need to access the secure top floor. "Give me a ten-minute head start. And Chrystal with an 'h'—not a word of this to anyone. I have very powerful friends in this town. Merciless friends. I'm sure you know the type. You'd lose all your Vegas privileges forever, and that's with them being kind, should you ever feel tempted to boast of your conquest."

"Relax, sweetie! I'm a pro! A deep ocean of secrets, and the ocean never gives up her secrets."

Nervously he inspected and re-inspected the sword box while his mind walked him through the next thirty-five minutes. Sharp door raps broke his reverie. He answered with a fake smile, ushered Chrystal inside, closed the door, and helped remove her shoes. "Who knows where those shoes have been?" he said. Barefoot, she held his hand as he led her to the kitchen. "Would you like a drink?"

She shook her head, "Believe it or not I don't touch the stuff, or drugs."

He smiled, poured himself a third of scotch into a glass tumbler etched with the casino's logo, and slammed it down in a single gulp. "I'll show you my tricks if you show me yours," he said. She beamed in triumph.

Eye to eye, she stroked his right cheek, as she cupped and squeezed his crotch. "I've always wanted to know how these tricks work. Deal. Show me yours."

He pointed to the sword box. "I'm sure you've seen this one, am I right?" She nodded. He lifted the lid, "Go ahead, take a look down inside. Let me know if you see any trap doors or mirrors, anything other than wood and plastic."

She did. "Seems like a solid basket to me."

He smiled. "Go ahead, climb in. You'll fit, just scrunch up a little." Holding his hand for balance, she lowered herself down inside. "I'm going to put on the lid now," he said, and locked it down. He could see flashes of red and gold sequins through sword slits on the sides and top.

"Comfortable?"

"Mm hm."

He dangled the Baetylus though a top slit. "Hold this object. I want you to think hard about a time in your life when you felt the safest, warmest, and most loved. I want you to remember every detail, as if you are back living in those scenes."

Silence for half a minute. "Oh wow! It's Christmas. My dad is still alive. I must only be eight, because he overdosed when I was nine. There's the model train running around the tracks with the cat going berserk trying to paw it off the track! We're laughing so hard at Bee cat! Wait… I'm opening a present. It's the doll I wanted so much! I'm crying tears of joy. I hugged my dad. I never felt so warm and secure as I did in his arms. This is incredible! I feel like I'm back with daddy! You don't understand, I ache for him every day, wish I could go back to where he would take care of me again. The only man I ever really trusted."

"You'll be with him again soon," said Sam, "And please believe me— it's nothing personal." He thrust a sword through a side slit. It pierced her flesh with little resistance, skewered her right kidney, gall bladder, left kidney, and emerged bloody through the opposing slit. Too shocked to scream at first, agonized shrieks and desperate pleas, unnatural sounds to most ears escaped through every slit.

"It'll be over soon," he said. In the moment that followed he could hear her breaths coming short and fast. Both hands firmly locked around the sword haft, with all his weight, he bore down on another sword through the top on an angle. The tip broke the skin of her lower abdomen. Smoothly, as a hot knife dices a cold butter stick, it hewed through her uterus, vagina, and reappeared from her rectum out the bottom slit. The quality of her sounds changed. Hysterical, angry, manic, panicked, savage: a discordant, indignant roar shook the box.

"Only three more." He found himself forced to yell over the excruciating high-pitched wailing. He did not enjoy this at any level. "I swear to you I am *not* a murderer! Not a sadist! The end justifies the means!" He felt no guilt or remorse, because he knew this heinous action was required to maintain and grow a career. His overarching emotion was pity. Truly he did not want the woman to suffer.

"Remain focused on daddy." He pushed the third sword through her liver, stomach, and spleen. Despite thick soundproofed walls and floors, he worried about her noise making it to the air conditioning ducts. The fourth sword pierced both lungs. Shrill squawks and whoops degraded into burbling, choking, drowning sounds. The fifth and final sword pierced her heart, severed her aorta, and blessedly killed her almost instantaneously.

He withdrew the Baetylus. Satisfied that it was well baptized with sacrificial blood, he returned it to his neck and tucked it underneath his shirt. *No time to waste. If I remove the swords here, some blood will drip through cuts in the plastic liner. There's a rinse hose down by the dumpsters; that's the ticket.* He wheeled the effect to the suite door, slipped into his twelve-hundred-dollar loafers, and pushed the wheeled box into the elevator. It opened into the lobby facing gamblers, inebriates, and uniformed security guards. Left hand around the blood-bespattered Baetylus, using his hips and right hand, he pushed the now heavily laden bell cart while keeping a clear image fixed in his mind. Those who glanced at him saw a smiling, very tall broad and fit African American staff member in hotel uniform pushing a cart to the service elevator, a familiar and instantly forgettable sight.

He boarded the second elevator leading down to the parking levels and pressed P5. It carried him down to the lowest underground deck. He pushed the warm corpse of Chrystal to the dumpster area and worked quickly. Soaked in sweat, a bit dizzy from unventilated vehicle exhaust fumes commingled with high anxiety, he removed the swords and top basket cover. He tilted the box onto its side to make things easier. With great effort, he dragged out the dead prostitute encased within her ready-made plastic shroud. Hoisting her dead weight up to the dumpster's top opening proved to be the most difficult physical challenge of his life. *Never saw myself as a weakling but holy shit—I might as well be military pressing a dead cow.*

With one final push and spring from his legs, the semi-wrapped corpse dropped into the dumpster atop plastic trash bags. Holding his breath against the stink of rotting organic material, he climbed up, reached down, and moved as many bags on top of her as he could reach. Satisfied that his plastic-shrouded mummy appeared well-disguised, not that anyone would climb up as he did and look inside—*better safe than sorry*—he used the auto-wash hose in the nearby bay to spray blood from the swords, drips from the illusion box, and a trail of red splotches from the smooth painted concrete floor. He used a wad of wet and dry paper towels to clean blood that had dripped by the dumpster.

Back in the suite, he took the longest, hottest shower of his life. He still wore the Baetylus.

The following evening's show was a resounding success. Back in the suite, he and Rachel showered together. He sponged suds over her back. Infused with confidence over his relationship with the Baetylus, with more vigor than usual, he took Rachel from behind. She flattened her forehead and palms against the tile wall and filled the humid echo chamber with delighted squeals.

All seemed well. Until it didn't.

Three performances later, things fell flat again. Attempts to soothe his wounded ego only made it worse. "Leave me alone!" he bellowed at Rachel.

Tears welled in her eyes.

"I quit!" she snapped. As she turned to leave, Amir's words looped: Personal blood sacrifices.' *The hooker meant nothing to me. It wasn't personal.*

"Wait, Rachel, please. Wait up," he said in a hot trot toward her. "God, I am so sorry, lover. You were only trying to help. I didn't mean to direct my pain at you. It just…came out at the wrong time, at the wrong person." He called upon his inner thespian to summon a few real tears. She watched them roll down both cheeks. "I've lost my touch, lost my audience: I cannot possibly bear losing you, too."

She turned back, stepped close, and gently wiped away his tears. "I love you, Sam." She pressed herself against him. His arms encircled her. He rested his cheek against her auburn scalp.

She had him lie naked face-down upon the plush terry hotel-monogrammed robe atop the black satin sheets. She drizzled warm Argan oil onto his back and massaged his knotted trapezius, the full length of his back, buttocks, hamstrings, feet. He felt tension drain out of him. She reached under and patiently oiled his boy parts, squeezing, tugging, until a different form of tension returned to him. Six-nine and reverse cowboy brought them both to a shuddering climax. She collapsed on top of him, face nuzzled against his neck. She fell asleep.

Awake, he pondered the mysteries of the Baetylus, his professional future, and the value of human life. *Perhaps it's true what the Christians say. Maybe for some, it's better on the other side, where evil cannot reach.* Tomorrow, Tuesday, will be his day and night off.

He spent Tuesday completely enraptured. Greedily he indulged in the mysteries and captivating pheromones and textures of Rachel's taut young body.

"My heavens, tiger. What's gotten into you? It almost feels—and I know this is crazy—like this is our last night together before you sail off to distant shores, never to be seen or heard from again. You've squeezed a lifetime's worth of love into the span of a single day! Believe me though," she said with a mischievous smirk, "I'm not complaining."

"Rachel, do you ever think about Sheol? About life after mortal death?"

She gave him a curious look. "Hey, now. You're not thinking of—"

"No! Certainly not. So what, I've had another bomb of a show. I could always go back to sawing you in half and having audience members pick cards out of decks. Make little wadded up balls of paper appear to dance around audience heads, lights low, so they can't spot the wires. I made a good living doing those illusions." He tapped her nose. "No, lover. I'm not the type to off myself. Hear me now believe me later, if you ever find me dead, it wasn't me who did it."

"Stop! All this talk of death is icky. Can't you just lick me some more?"

He did.

Wednesday night's show marked a return to his former routine. Members of the audience shouted, "I wanna fly!" "C'mon, Magus! Make us fly!" "Cut the girl's head off!" He ground his teeth, affected a fake smile, and pressed ahead with his traditional routine to lukewarm applause. He watched the capacity-filled room slowly empty into dark nothingness.

"Well, boss. We gave them their money's worth. That's all the contract requires. Cheer up. Let's go upstairs. I want to fuck your brains out." She gave him an innocent batting of eyelashes.

In the shower, Baetylus on the tiled floor atop the gold-colored metal drain cover, her front pressed flat against floor tiles as languidly he penetrated her. Warm water cascaded over them, relaxing and yet invigorating. She had no knowledge of the razor blade clasped between his right index and middle fingers. She barely felt the cut as he opened her right carotid artery. Eyes closed, she did not feel her life's blood swirling quickly down the drain, pumped out more furiously from her sexual exertions. As their passions reached a crescendo and point of no return, she opened her eyes and saw blood. Panicked, she attempted a push-up move to dislodge him, but the blood loss was too great. She was too weak to do much of anything. As he released, he watched Rachel's heart stop when blood ceased to flow. She died atop the Baetylus with her eyes open.

He rode the elevator down to the common floor, not caring who recognized him, and grabbed a bell cart. He wheeled it backstage, where he found a large enough cardboard box. He reversed course back to the suite. With respectful care, he arranged the livid, naked body of Rachel inside the box. Wet hair clung to her now pallid face, blue lips frozen partway open. Tenderly he brushed hair from her face and took one last look. He collapsed to the travertine tile bathroom floor. Piteously and uncontrollably, he wept. For half an hour, Schmuel Hoffman became a kid again, free of all utilitarian checks and balances developed in adults, helplessly denuded of the cold-hearted pragmatism considered by many to mark emotional maturity. He completely lost it.

Piqued emotions now out his system, down on P5, he hoisted Rachel Haim's cardboard coffin over the dumpster's ledge and covered it with white plastic garbage bags. He dropped off the bell cart at the captain's stand. As he did, the uniformed hotel employee, a large fit native of Mexico, wished Sam a good evening. "You're working late, Mr. Sam! Much respect, sir. Say, Mr. Sam: can you really make people fly?"

He questioned the man's eyes. "Would you like to take a quick flight right here, right now?"

The man glanced about and saw no one else in the immediate vicinity. "Okay! Let's do it!"

Sam held the Baetylus and maintained eye contact. He imagined the man rising five feet, doing one forward somersault in the air, followed by a backflip. His mind's eye watched him float gently back to where he now stood. He released his grip on the infernal object, and the bell captain returned to himself. "Oh, my Dear Jesus! I feel dizzy! That was…amazing! You have powers I cannot understand!"

A furtive glance down at the nametag, Sam leaned toward him conspiratorially. "Let you in on a little secret, Carlos: I don't understand them, either."

He showered off dumpster germs and climbed into bed. Emotionally drained, sleep took him almost immediately. That was when the dreams first started. Nightmares of epic derangement, detailed, and in lurid color.

A disfigured body enshrouded in plastic, yet still palpitating, still alive somehow! Somewhere past the Las Vegas Speedway on the I-15, near the Apex Landfill, the corpse of Chrystal lurched towards him in the dark of night, across rough desert terrain. Even in sleep, his body hair stood on end. The scene changed to bright daylight. Atop the landfill he recognized the box, the final resting place of his beloved Rachel Haim, decomposing rapidly within her cardboard coffin under the relentless Nevada sun, body beginning to bloat from internal gases. A malodorous fetor hung about her, a sulfurous, vinegary stench. Her eyes were just as he had seen them last, clear brown irises, but now covered by a dull film. Black pupils that were almost as large as the irises; between the two there was no distinction. Maggots tumbled from her open mouth as a low, granulated groan issued forth, speech attempted through a mouthful of insects. 'Dieeee for meeee,' it sounded like. 'Sheol awaits us.'

After a fitful night, managing only three hours' sleep, Sam stood backstage minutes before curtain opening. Desperately he craved caffeine but was unwilling to endure the urgent need to urinate that follows the drinking of it. He peered out at the audience. The sight of many unfilled seats, pre-purchased by patrons months in advance, struck him harshly. At the sound of his name, he feigned energy, more muscle memory than enthusiasm, as he burst onstage and walked to the edge.

"Ladies and gentlemen, good evening. You may notice that my lovely assistant, Rachel, is not with us tonight. Sadly, she will be with us no longer, called to a greater purpose somewhere out there on this big blue marble of ours. With love, we wish her only the best. Friends, this evening is an especially intimate event. But first I must ask please raise your hand if you have a fear of flying!"

The audience cheered, whooped and stomped, not a single hand raised. Later, interviewed by trade magazine and mainstream media publication journalists, audience member quotes included, "Best night of my entire life!" and "There is no way Magus is only just a mere mortal" and "Supernatural!" Hundreds of testimonials like these went viral across the Internet at the speed of electricity.

Back in his suite, he found the yellow sticky note given to him in the hotel bar. He texted Victoria Pleasance. She called within sixty seconds. "Due to a wholly unexpected vacancy," he said, and went on to describe the assistant position, generous salary, and all-expenses-paid trip down from Canada.

"I'll need to run this past my parents!" came the enthusiastic response. She called back to accept and arrived with suitcases the following afternoon. She spent the night in a comped standard room. The following morning, together for the first time backstage, he helped her to understand the role and duties. He provided her with Rachel's outfits, which fit perfectly.

"My-my! Dearest Victoria. Your beauty is that of the Seraphim. Unparalleled. The audience will adore you, but not as deeply as I will." What he had done to her at the bar had never left her mind. She approached him.

"Put your hands and mouth on me, Sam. For real, this time." He spent the remainder of the day exploring the innermost recesses of her body, captivated and intoxicated by aromas and textures uniquely her own. More sexually reserved and inhibited than the open-minded, wildly experimental Rachel, he found it even more enjoyable to peel away Victoria's inhibitions like layers of onion. She excited the passions of his forefathers to next-level satisfaction.

Long red waves of hair leisurely splayed across his bare chest as they rested. "You are the boldest, most skilled lover I have ever known, Sam. You make me feel, I don't know…more wanted, more worshipped than I have ever felt before. I don't ever want this feeling right now to end."

Sam did not answer. He worried that the powerful, eldritch spirits, Hāwlat, Ar-Rā'iyu, and most especially, the great and terrible, al-'Uzza might grow jealous, about having to share his worship with a mere mortal. He fell asleep.

Chrystal had reached the city. Her plastic-wrapped, barefoot form shambled through an alley in the dark shadows of a small dumpster. Rachel, eyes now completely gone, smiled a skeletal grin. Decayed, yellow-tinged mottled gray skin clung tightly to facial bones like peeling wallpaper. 'Dieeee for meeee' hissed the Rachel-thing.

Startled awake, body hair erect, middle of his back coated in cold, slimy sweat, he shivered, body wracked from feelings of true terror that had consumed his soul at rest, and lately while awake. Minutes later he could not shake it. In these nightmares, his true core was laid bare, stripped of the waking armor of rationalizations and reasons applied as justifications for his pique evil, unforgiveable actions. Guilt permeated his heart and soul to the crux. *So much for resting up to be sharp for the show.*

The evening's performance, to Sam, felt remarkably equivalent in all ways to the former shows with Rachel. The audience thrilled to Victoria's talking severed head. After, backstage, "How do you do it, Sam?" she asked. "Will you ever let me in on your secret?"

He kissed her cheek. "One of these nights. Can't say precisely when. But be sure, Victoria, that, like my last assistant, you will soon know more than any mere mortal can ever know."

"Promise?"

In his mind, he snaked his tongue into her mouth. He pulled back to look into her eyes. As he held the Baetylus, Victoria Pleasance flew. She soared high above Las Vegas at night, gazing down at all the lights, until she landed back in his bed, where she allowed him to do experimental things to her, deviations from normal vaginal intercourse, moves to which he sensed normally she would never consent. Corrupting her thrilled him far more than his relationship with Rachel.

He closed his eyes and broke the spiritual circuit flowing between them. She smiled. "Let's go upstairs. Now, Sam."

The next five shows followed the success of Sam and Victoria's first. Not one empty seat followed by glowing reviews. It lulled Sam into believing that the 'personal blood sacrifice' of Rachel had sufficiently sated the bloodlust of the mysterious powers living beyond the corporeal membrane, insofar as he could understand Amir's explanation. As his emotional investment in Victoria grew, for how could it not, given they were together every day and night? —even more lurid nightmares haunted him. The harder he tried to distance his feelings from Victoria, the deeper he felt pulled into her emotional event horizon, deeper into the murky depths of her heart. None of it made sense to him.

She's not Jewish. Not even American. Nearly a generation separates us. We have so little in common, he thought as he watched her sleep. *I can't feel for her, or anyone, even close to what I felt for Rachel, whom I loved with a love that is more than love. Only Rachel could have lifted this evil shadow blanketing my spirit.* His emotional state degraded deeper by the hour into a miasmal sewer of fear, regret, and unrelenting remorse.

The evening's performance started off normally. The audience thrilled to the severed talking head of Victoria. Each asked the head a question; each received a personalized response. But then, when it came time for the flying segment, the booing started.

Am I doing anything different tonight? His mind quickly replayed every detail of the prior five shows. *No, truly I am not*, he decided. As the theater emptied prematurely, he walked backstage. Victoria followed in dejected silence. She regarded him with an expression of curiosity and concern.

"Victoria, let's go up."

Back in the suite, together in the shower, she fondled his manhood to no effect. "Sam, I'm so sorry about tonight," she cooed. "Try to let it go.

Put it behind you. There's always tomorrow—"

"Not so sure about that," he snapped. Her stunned expression of disappointment broke his heart. "I'm sorry." His gaze fell to the shower floor. Again, he watched Rachel's dark arterial blood as it swirled down the drain. He raised his eyes to hers. "I'm trapped, you see."

"What do you mean?"

He wept. Silently she held him, until his emotions settled.

"You cannot know the full extent—cannot possibly comprehend—the vastness and certainty of my inveiglement. Even I can't, so how can anyone else? Suffice it to say, the God of my youth to Whom I prayed, Who watched over me and my family: He is real. I believe this. He created me, created you; made other spirits that dwell only in this earthly realm, spirits no longer invited to trouble the dead in Sheol who await the day of rebirth. Maybe too, the Messiah did visit, the Savior of my people. I was raised to believe that Jesus of Nazareth was a sorcerer, a fraud. Now I'm thinking that I may have been misled by the community who raised me. Maybe there really is a Heaven and a Hell, and a narrow path to salvation. Right now, I expect that I've allowed myself to become massively deceived."

"Sam, I—"

"Shh," he said. He pressed his right forefinger to her dripping lips. "Let me think a moment." She held him, cheek upon his shoulder, hands behind his back. She pulled him tightly to her. Feminine, protective love dulled his delirious edge. They stayed like that for a quarter hour.

It was decided.

"I need to confront something tonight. This thing I do—I must do alone," he said. He turned off the water. "Dry off, get dressed. I'll give you a fat wad of American currency. Ask the hotel shuttle driver to take you to the nicest place in town. Slip him a hundred-dollar bill. Tell him Sam Magus is asking. He'll do it. Then rent the nicest room, and order room service for dinner. Stay there until I call. Will you do this for me, Victoria?"

She gazed into the two black holes of his eyes. In them, she recognized a desperate vacancy. She shivered violently once, then nodded. "Wanna know how I'm sure this'll all turn out okay?" She said it more to assuage and tamp down her own inexplicable wave of fear, than his.

"No, tell me, how do you know?"

Her face broke into a gentle smile, so warm, so pure white and beautiful that it pierced his heart. "Because I love you, Schmuel Hoffman. That's why it's okay."

Alone, dressed again in his stage outfit and cape, he stared out of the floor-to-ceiling window at the bright lights of Las Vegas. His right hand tightly clutched the Baetylus. The suite he had darkened, save for every lit black candle spread about the space in clusters of six. The word 'séance' flitted across his mind. *Is that what this is?* he wondered.

Loudly, eyes closed, he called upon his new gods. "Hāwlat, Ar-Rā'iyu, and al-'Uzza—rulers of this realm. I throw myself at your feet, in tears. Somehow, though try as I may, I have disappointed you. I have bled unto you one life that meant little to me, one that meant the whole world to me, and now, I fear, you immediately demand a third of me, that I may receive your continued blessings. I beseech you, please, show me what you demand of me."

Hours passed until he saw the first muted rays of sunlight spark off building windows. From somewhere below his window, Rachel Haim arose, beautiful and resplendent, dressed in an outfit of gold, as beautiful as the day he had first laid eyes on her. She hovered outside the glass. She smiled at him. She did her trademark curtsy. With both arms she motioned for him to join her in the air. Never releasing his tight grip on the Baetylus, he felt himself floating.

Inside the yellow taped rectangle, shattered limbs bent at impossible angles. Gray brain matter matched the color of the cement. Shards of glass bespeckled the entire protected area like a pop-up hailstorm. A detective from the Las Vegas Metropolitan Police Department wore latex gloves to touch Schmuel Hoffman's naked, barely recognizable face. He picked up and briefly examined the talisman, or whatever it was, attached to a solid gold rope chain around the broken neck. With a shrug, he laid it back against the exploded ribcage.

In the weeks that followed, the detective received tip calls from the sanitation department that led him to the bodies of Rachel Haim, and a prostitute who had run away from a broken Missouri home ten years prior, Carol 'Chrystal' Martins. These he ruled homicides. His official report named Hoffman as the only possible murder suspect. Using Luminol and DNA collected from his suite and down in parking deck five, it was a certainty. Hoffman's reputation was forever destroyed, which at least provided detectives with some measure of justice served. Hoffman's death they ruled a suicide.

Within the month of his death, the Baetylus, along with all remaining property belonging to illusionist Sam Magus's worldly estate, having left behind no heirs, relatives, or last will and testament, went up for auction by the casino. Oliver Twisted, the celebrated illusionist, out-bid all. He purchased the entire lot at a bargain price just north of one hundred thousand dollars.

By December, his audiences had learned to fly.

Family Plot

Jayden Bonner, now thirty-two, sat at his kitchen table adding rows to a spreadsheet containing names, ages, and locations of single young women from wealthy old money families across the United States. His father's sage wisdom twenty-four years earlier flashed to mind: "The world is divided into two basic personality types: planners, and wingers. Planners dominate the wingers."

He grinned, remembering how overtly jealous all the second-grade boys acted towards him when he received all the valentines every February 14th. Wide-set brown eyes, impossibly long, thick lashes, sensuous rubicund lips, pale unblemished skin, thick wavy brown hair down past his shoulders when all the other boys had short haircuts. Gifted with natural charm, extreme confidence, and impressive schoolyard skills. Like balancing a spinning red rubber Greek dodge ball on his forefinger, juggling three baseballs without a drop, drumming, and mimicking Bruce Lee's Jeet Kune Do movements. His parents had two boys, he and his older brother, Hamilton. Although at some point, Jayden had realized that his parents had always wanted a boy and a girl. One day, it dawned on him why they gave him a gender-neutral name, encouraged him to wear his hair long, and fussed over him so.

As he researched wealthy young heiresses, inevitably his mind flashed back to his first sexual experience at age twelve with a high school senior, a neighbor, whose beauty inspired stares from every male student in her grade, in the school, and anyone anywhere who laid eyes on her. *Could any woman thrill me anywhere close to what I felt that night on Daria's couch? Doubtful. If it hasn't happened by now, like, it ain't never gonna. One's as good as another, except when it comes to money. I'll pick one with the means necessary to let me live the way I deserve.*

He stopped at one hundred names, a nice even number to break it off, and made himself dinner, which stunk up his one-bedroom apartment in downtown Philly with the aromas of exotic spices and slightly overcooked meat. His living room was a fully equipped free-weight gym with dumbbell rack and simple lever machines. His bedroom was empty save for thick foam padding on the floor, that he one day carefully sliced to fit all corners and around baseboard electric radiators. The room consisted of a pad and a pillow. He had few male friends, but those who espied this arrangement asked him where he sleeps. "On the floor, duh. Push on it, it's super comfortable." They asked him why. "Because when girls look in the bedroom, immediately they know what they're in for."

He took a pause to pop the top from a cold bottle of imported beer, from which he took a long, pleasantly numbing swallow. He felt refreshed on a delightfully mild Friday night in March, windows wide open, and returned to his task. Social media, image searches. He had sorted the list alphabetically by last name, and by 11:00 p.m. he was down in the 'P' rows. He entered a name into the search field. Eyes widened; pulse quickened. "Hell-ooo, Arabella Pendleman. Well-well. So nice to meet you, miss," he said, absently stroking his long hair with his left hand as he clicked through photos. He squeezed himself through his underwear.

"Mm-hm, yes, oh yesss. You'll do. Thirty, never married, heiress to the Tyler Pendleman pharmaceutical fortune," he said aloud. Studying her social media, quickly he judged her mistrustful of men overall, spiritually bound to this world, atheist, exceedingly liberal, who believes this world is all there is; that mortal death is the end of the line. He reviewed each of her meme posts going back years. 'Live for Now' and "Self-Love' themes dominated. "Wants to save the earth and all humanity from itself. Bitch wants to change the world but can't even change herself," he muttered. *Hates The Patriarchy, whatever the fuck that is.* The only photos of her with other males showed the most callow, obsequious specimens he had ever seen, none of them fit or attractive. *Yes-men pulled behind her by the balls.*

None of her personality traits appealed to him. *But I would rank her face and body among the top half a percent in all the world. I mean, wow. I could never tire of looking at her.*

From her posted photos, he was able to discern that she must live over in Gladwyne, where much of Philly's Main Line 'old money' going back generations tended to live in big old stone mansions with indoor and outdoor heated swimming pools, helicopter ports, wrought iron fences and gates, and more money than any reasonable person could spend in a lifetime. Reading about her father, aloud he said, "Ah, just as I thought. Trust-fund mutant. Inherited wealth. Never built anything on his own, just dozes during board meetings while smart people run his great-grandfather's legacy. Oh, this guy would, like, absolutely *hate* me. I come from nothing. He wants to marry her off to a mutant similar in all ways to himself."

Long, beautifully coiffured sandy blonde hair, flawless skin like bone china, no retouching of any photos: a very truly natural beauty. Wide forehead, pert aristocratic nose, thin lips when closed forming a unique and attractive shape. Small, perfectly shaped white teeth showing in some photos. "No makeup needed. Goddamn this girl is gifted."

Father be damned, he decided to make the seduction of Arabella Pendleman his mission without moving further down the list.

Creep stalking her every action on social media, which included live video postings, from his own experiences he recognized every bar and nightclub where she hung out. One of them was a favorite of his, where even internationally renowned dance music DJs always recognized him, smiled, and often waived him up to join them, knowing his ability to attract young ladies would introduce them to their bedmates for the night following their shows.

Showered, dressed in his white hand-made monogrammed dress shirt, black tailored Canali suit with a thick roll of twenties in the right pants pocket, skinny black cravat tied in a perfect double-Windsor knot, and pointy black shoes, at 10:00 PM, he headed over to the club. The usual employees greeted him with smiles, stamped his hand, and ushered him inside ahead of a long line of hopefuls waiting to be admitted. At six feet four inches, two-hundred-twenty pounds, he was used to being stared at, and adept at not making eye contact while searching faces.

She's not on the main floor. He walked through a short hallway that connects the main stage area to a large room, and faced a long, avant-garde bar. At the center of a gaggle of giggling cocktail girls, there stood Arabella Pendleman. He felt his pulse quicken. Although he knew it was bad form, he stared, unable to play it cool. A member of Arabella's entourage noticed, tugged Arabella's elbow, and flicked her eyes in his direction.

Arabella's deep, dark green eyes met his sloe brown eyes for the first time. He did not look away. Silent communication continued until, at last, he flashed her the briefest of smirks, turned, and walked back to the main room, up to main bar, where awaited him a beer, smiles, and a fist-bump from the bartender. Holding his bottle, he stood like a statue before the stage, thighs against the velvet divider rope.

Several pretty girls materialized at either side of him, casting obvious glances of interest, which he patently ignored. He stared straight ahead at the empty DJ booth, awaiting the inevitable tug at his invisible fishing line, from the bait and hook he'd left in the anteroom. He felt Arabella's minions watching him. What he had seen in her eyes, he could not mistake for anything less than animal fascination with him. He played it cold, not cool. Until the recording artist from Scotland took up position at his DJ setup consisting of a laptop, booth monitors, mixer boards, headphones, and a turntable. The Scot kept his eyes fixed on his equipment. At no time did he cast a glance at the cheering, whistling room, as quickly now it began to fill up behind Jayden. When at last the artist looked up, his eyes fell on Jayden. He smirked, and with a thumb-jerk ushered Jayden up behind the booth to stand behind him. Jayden stepped over the vinyl rope and joined him on stage. The two hugged and exchanged words. Together they inspected all the pretty young female faces in the room. That was the second time Jayden's eyes met Arabella's. This time, she smiled.

The room erupted in the DJ's trademark deep, ominous thumping bass tracks. Multi-colored flashing show lights created movement and atmosphere. People started dancing. An hour into his set, the DJ said something to Jayden, who promptly strode down from the booth, walked along the wall to avoid the crush of the main room throng, aware of Arabella's eyes following him. He cut across to get to her. Eye to eye, gazing down at her, unsmiling, he extended his right hand, "Hi. I'm Jayden. It is an honor to make your acquaintance." Stunned, grinning self-consciously, she clasped his hand.

"Arabella. Why is it an honor?"

Still unsmiling, "Because, and I mean this like most sincerely, you are the most beautiful human being I have ever laid eyes on. The fact that you grace me now with polite cordiality is the highest compliment I have ever received."

Blushing, she said, "I'll bet you say that to all the girls."

Still unsmiling, he said, "If you believe that, then I shall trouble you no further," and turned back towards the wall.

"Wait!" she yelled. He stopped and turned. "I-I… I'm sorry, Jayden. That was presumptuous and rude of me. I didn't mean it. It's just that I get hit on by some of the most predatory males you can possibly imagine."

He closed the gap and faced her. Eight inches separated their faces. He glanced at the drama-absorbed, slack-jawed faces of her entourage as they raptly followed the intense exchange. "No worries. Listen, the DJ is a friend of mine."

"Are you serious? Who are you?"

He ignored the question, "He can't take you and all five of your friends up behind the booth with us, but if you'd like to come up, Arabella… and you," he said, pointing to the second prettiest girl, who also struck him as morally flexible, "then follow me." He let his gaze linger on her eyes for six more seconds. Again he turned his back on them and started his reverse course.

"Wait!" she said. She extended her left hand to him. With a momentary grin, he took hold. She grabbed her pretty friend's wrist, and the trio penetrated a night of exciting unknowns.

"I wonder how my friend made out with the DJ?" Arabella said, lying naked on Jayden's foam floor. Late-morning sunlight beamed in hot.

She pressed her hand flat against his hairless back, staring at the popcorn ceiling. He turned over, smiled, and wrapped her hands in his. "She learned how to play his bagpipe?" Laughing uproariously, she rolled on top and straddled his waist. "I'm starving. What are you making me for breakfast?"

He gazed up at her. "I realize we've only known each other for about twelve hours, so please forgive me if this sounds corny or trite, sappy, or silly: I feel like I could happily serve you three times a day for the rest of my life. Much more than nutrition. Can't see myself ever tiring of serving you. I mean, like…I could be your teddy bear, sort of. The one thing in your life that's reliable, comfortable, soft and welcoming. The one who makes you feel secure. Like you could squish me up into whatever you need me to be. Like…I'd follow you anywhere, or stay tucked away on your bed, or in your toy chest, and never make a single demand of you." He affected the most serious and sincere expression as he reached up to cup her cheeks. "With you, I feel different. Never have I felt so…I dunno, like, weak. Powerless. With no thoughts of myself. Does that make sense?"

Her eyes welled with tears. Lips pressed together, finally, she nodded. "Yes, Jayden. Nothing anyone ever said to me has ever made nearly this much sense."

He rolled back his eyes back, drew his closed mouth even tighter, and shook his head.

"What's wrong, lover?" she said.

"This probably can't work."

She appeared stunned. "Wait, what? Why? Oh my God! You're married!"

He shook his head. "Nope."

"Girlfriend?"

"Not even."

"Then why?"

Expression defeated, grim, "Because I'm poor, Arabella!" he shouted. "I come from a poor family. Paid for my own college driving a delivery van for a chemical company that offered tuition reimbursement. But the harder I work, for some reason I never seem to, like, get ahead financially. I'd be deluding myself to think that I could keep a real woman like you, keep you happy and safe from financial disaster, make it so you don't have to work if you don't want to. Women of your caliber require some measure of security. Kids are expensive, and if you wanted them, I would too, but like, I could never afford to raise them." He sat up, stood, and pulled on his boxers.

"Wait, hang on—what are you doing?"

"Getting dressed. I'll drive you home. I owe you that, and so much more. But that's all I can give you."

She leapt up and reached out. Both hands enclosed his face, "Jayden. Look at me." Looking down, he raised his eyes to hers. "Don't worry about money!"

He shook his head, "Pfft. Yeah, right. Sure, Arabella. I live in the real world. Everything runs on money."

She smiled. "I know this. I don't work. I spend from a trust left to me by my grandfather. Jayden baby, you may find this difficult to believe, but when my father passes, my net worth will be four hundred-seventy-five-million dollars. I'll make more in capital gains every month than most people earn in their lifetimes. Don't you see? I don't want your money."

She pulled his buttocks toward her. "I only want you. Silly boy."

"He's leaving it all to you?"

She nodded. "If I'm unmarried when I die, it goes to my older half-brother. If I'm married, it stays with my husband. Should my husband die, then it goes to my brother. He is very protective of me."

Jayden flashed a grin. Stoic expression restored, he said, "You didn't tell me you had a brother."

"Garrett Xavier Pendleman. I'll introduce you. He too has a cottage on the property. Mostly he keeps to himself. Sort of a recluse, OCD, germaphobe. I call him Howard Hughes. He writes software all day, video game stuff mostly, earning a good chunk of wealth all on his own. Nothing like the family pharmaceutical fortune, but he does okay. Not that he has to work. Daddy lets him want for nothing, but he's entrusting the future of family business to me. I don't know how to chair a board, but I guess he thinks I'd be the more serious of the two. Garrett is sort of the loser black sheep of the brood."

After a brunch of cheese omelets and maple syrup, followed by vigorous sex in the shower, he dressed in last night's ensemble, as did she. "You can drive me home now and meet my father."

"Oh geez, really? Like, must I?"

Laughing, "He's a softie. Had me late in life with his second wife. Garrett, he had in the first. He's seventy-eight."

Genuinely astonished, "Seriously?"

She nodded. "Eggs die away but not sperm. Well, sort of."

"What do you mean, sort of?"

"Well… advancing age has differential effects on DNA damage, chromatin integrity, gene mutations, and chromosome abnormalities in sperm. Like for example, Turner syndrome, a condition that affects only females, results when one of the X chromosomes is missing or partially missing. I hate telling you this…"

"No! Arabella please, if you want to trust me, now is the time to start."

"Failure of the ovaries to develop, and heart defects. Turner syndrome causes both… and, well…"

"You have both."

She nodded. "I do. I'm sterile. I can never have children. I really didn't want to tell you, but you're right: trust is everything. I suppose now you'll fuck me for a while longer, then blow away just as quickly as you blew in."

He took her hands. "Arabella, I'm not here for some distant, hazy, fantasy future. After death, there is only blackness, like, oblivion. But while I'm here, I need to serve something greater than myself. For some, that is children. For me, perhaps that something is… you. Do you really think I can love and grieve the loss of kids I'll never have? Want to know why I'm poor? Because I live for now, today."

Eyes sparking, heart thud-thudding so hard he could feel it against him, she stood on her toes and stole a kiss.

"You know, Arabella, I mean, like, one day, I'll be old. Chances are good that you'll throw me over for some young guy with a permanent hard-on. Turning over spouses runs in your DNA."

She gripped him through his pants. "Pills, baby. I and pills will keep you stiff for a lifetime."

"Tyler Pendleman, may I please introduce my friend, Jayden Bonner."

Jayden extended his hand first. The old blue-gray eyes felt to him like a vacuum, pulling him inside, vivisecting him. Cordially, the old man extended his hand and shook, but said nothing. "Well, now that you two have properly met, daddy, I'm going to show Tyler around the grounds, and let him freshen up at my cottage."

Voice stern and cool, "Will Mr. Bonner be spending the night?"

Jayden's gaze darted between him and Arabella. She grinned. "Yes daddy. I believe he might be spending every night at the cottage, beginning with tonight."

Later that evening, her phone buzzed. "Please come see me. Alone."

Twenty minutes later, she walked into her father's first floor study, eyes wide and curious, "Yes, daddy?"

"Come sit down. I'd like to discuss your friend, Mr. Bonner."

"His name is Jayden, daddy. He's with me now."

Face a mask of undisguised disappointment, he walked behind his desk and sat down. "What do you know about him, Arabella?"

"I trust my inner polygraph. He's clear. Green lights all the way. One of the good guys."

The corners of his mouth turned up. His eyes sparkled with barely restrained amusement. "Mr. Bonner was raised in the Norristown public school system. He graduated, barely, from an ill-regarded State college. He has not maintained a single job for more than ten months," he said, and tapped his computer monitor. "His driving record is longer than an unspooled roll of toilet paper. Both parents are dead. His father was a welder, his mother a book-keeper in a greenhouse. The instalment loan on his used Mercedes has 4.8 years of payments remaining, and he has missed several payments." Looking up, large and multi-pocketed bags hanging below them, wise old eyes pleaded with her. "Don't you see, honey?"

"See what?"

A wan expression. "Jayden is not your kind, dear. Unworthy of a Pendleman."

"And what kind is that exactly, dear father? Elitists? Pompous? High-browed social-climbers?"

He shook his finger at her, voice cramped and hissy. "He'll use you for your money then freeze your warm heart. I raised you smarter than this. Can't you see through this predator… this gigolo?"

"Wow, these grounds go on forever!" said Jayden, truly impressed by the expansive acreage and woods, clearings, buildings, surrounded by modern suburban sprawls yet only a short drive from Center City, Philadelphia. "Over there," he pointed, "is that what I think it is?"
Nodding, "The Pendleman family cemetery."
"Can we walk over and see? I've never seen a family cemetery." Taking his hand, she led the way across well-manicured lawns and white gravel paths. "What's that?" he said, pointing.
Smiling, "We call it The Labyrinth. It's the largest and probably oldest English boxwood hedge maze in the nation."
"Cool! Ever get lost in there?"
Laughing, "Yes! When I was a little girl playing with friends, a few times actually, after dark. My dad had to send servants in with flashlights to rescue us." They both laughed.
Pointing up at the tops of long aluminum poles, "I've seen cameras and LED motion-sensing spotlights on poles all over the grounds. Here too? Like, what is he afraid of, vandals? With that high-tech fence security system, why put cameras in a cemetery?"
"He is totally paranoid about intrusion."
"Has anyone ever tried to get in here?"
She nodded. "A few times. We're close enough to Philly that we're in the orbit of some very desperate lowlife types. The fence triggers alarms, and one of his full-time grounds staff is an ex-cop, super-scary guy, tough as nails. Killer with a badge. He takes a golf cart over, cuffs them, calls his old buddies at Five-O, and they come scoop 'em up. Rarely happens, though. I think the former cop wishes it would happen more often. He seems bored most of the time."
"Creepy!" he said. A few minutes later, on the western side of the hedge maze, they arrived at the cemetery. "Mausoleums. Like, wow. So many! Is there a space reserved for your dad… and for you?"
She nodded, pointing back toward the first, newest and shiniest of the tombs. "That one is for my dad, Garrett, and I. Every enduring branch of my family line is entombed here. We don't believe in burying underground."
"For poor people only?"
She gave him an understanding expression. "Something like that. Except that people with far less means do the same in some cemeteries, with cremation urns entombed in much smaller mausoleums. Sometimes I come here, open this crypt," she said, patting the carved granite wall,

"where my grandpa and grandma rest. I loved them very much, you see. There's a stone bench inside each crypt, so we can sit and talk with them."

"With them? You mean two-way communication?"

"I know. It's silly. When you're dead, you're dead. I believe that. After this life ends, there is perfect nothingness, like Nirvana in Buddhism, or Sheol in Judaism. There is no Heaven, no Hell," she said, and patted the warm stone. "There is only slow decomposition, even slower in one of these things. More like mummies. I imagine that if we would open my grandparents' coffins, they'd pretty much still look the same as when alive, maybe with longer hair and nails."

"Eww! Creepy as fuck!"

She squeezed his hand. "But still, I consider it therapeutic to confess the contents of my secret heart to those whom I loved most, even though they can't hear me. Nonsense, right?"

Striding over to face her, he took her hands in his. "No, Arabella. Not silly. We all need someone to trust with our secret selves."

"Jayden," she said, glancing down as she spoke, "do you think I could ever be someone that you trust enough to let me know you, I mean, really know you? As in, you'll let me inside that part of you that you would never admit to yourself even exists, lay yourself completely bare, and let me love your kinky, sick, twisted heart of hearts?"

Their eyes locked. Slowly he nodded for emphasis, though a large part of him authentically felt it. "Yes. I think maybe you already are."

"You are a sex god," she said. Blondish tresses covered the entirety of her pillow, eyelids and lips darkened, with the flush of climactic blood.

Propping himself on his left elbow, he smirked. "Aw shucks, ma'am. Tweren't nuffin'" he said, affecting a country accent. "Seriously though, Arabella—"

"Jayden, wait. "Everyone always shortens my name to Bella, which I guess I'm used to by now, but I don't much care for it. It's like… laziness. I know they think it's an endearing, familiar thing but my name has four syllables. In school they just called me 'Bels' and I hated it. Why haven't you shortened it, you know, the endearing-yourself-to-me name truncation routine?"

"Because Arabella is such a beautiful name, I cannot bear to part with a single syllable of it."

Tears formed in her eyes. She wiped them. "Okay, sorry, I had cut you off. What was it you were about to say?"

Leaning over, he kissed her with the artisanship of a well-practiced bee charmer. "Seriously, Arabella, as for the sex god comment, believe me when I say, truly, you haven't experienced anything yet. I will never let you get bored. Every time will feel better than the last, I promise. You make this possible. Like, you fire my imagination, get me all flustered, make my hormones run all helter-skelter. We have the whole rest of our lives to explore the innermost recesses of each other's hearts. Somewhere in there," he said, tapping her forehead, "you have fantasies so dark and so intensely personal that you have never shared them with girlfriends, or your diary, dead grandparents, or even your own self. I'll peel your silly onion until I get to the core of you and lay it completely bare. Then, and only then, will you truly trust me with your whole self. And for that, your reward will be grand. Magnificently, passionately, permanently so."

Unconvinced that her sycophant friends, suspicious father, board members, and distant blood relations were worth the planning of a full-blown bombastic wedding—she and Jayden eloped. They married in Las Vegas with borrowed local witnesses, and their honeymoon lasted eight months. They set a goal to have outdoor sex on every continent, also sex in the air, sex under the ocean, on a blue ice glacier, in jungle mud, and in full view of a large crowd of strangers. Goal achieved, they headed back to Gladwyne a few pounds lighter, deeply tanned, and exceedingly happy together.

"Today I'm going to go break my lease and arrange to have my gym equipment moved into the cottage."

Nods and smiles. "I'm sure you'll need a man-cave of your own. See that garage with the cupola on top? We've never explored the inside. Come on, let's see it." They held hands and walked to the white stucco structure. From a key on a ring in her purse, she opened the thick brass lock, entered, flicked on the lights, and showed Jayden around.

"Holy moly! Like, this is fantastic! I can set up the squat rack there, the calf machine in that corner, the dumbbell rack against the wall. Mirrors look easy enough to mount."

She moved in front of him, arms folded. "Only one condition, lover. Spend no more than two hours a day here. I want you inside me, on top of me, under me, or licking me the other twenty-two hours, three-sixty-five. Deal?"

Grinning, "Yes, mistress. I live to serve. I just don't want my pile-driving hips to lose their G-forces from lack of resistance training."

She laughed and threw back her head. "Take me here, now, on this dusty wood floor."

He did.

Back in the cottage under a warm shower, Arabella collapsed to the tiles. He turned off the water and knelt, gently holding her head, and repeated her name. Her eyes opened. She smiled. "Sorry, babe."

"What the fuck just happened?"

She affected a smile. "Nothing to worry about. Happens sometimes. See this scar under my chin?" she said, pointing. "Passed out sitting on the toilet, woke up in a small pool of blood."

"Arabella, people don't lose consciousness for no reason."

"Turner syndrome. My heart. In the past it happened rarely. For some reason it's been happening a bit more frequently."

"When was the last time you got checked out by a medical doctor?"

"Not since I met you, Mr. Swirly Tongue."

"Geez, this is my fault. Okay, make an appointment, I'm taking you."

She nodded once, then grinned mischievously, "Wanna play doctor?"

"I'll get the speculum."

It was a white Christmas, followed by one of the coldest, harshest winters Jayden could remember. Alone in the gym, central natural gas-heated air warmed the temperature to sixty-five. He felt like spending the entire night there to catch his breath, pull back, get some perspective. The sex was great, but her appetite was all-consuming. She allowed him so little privacy, for the better part of a year, now. Cloying, smothering. He felt a powerful need to recover his self-possession but reckoned that demanding a night off would freak her out, bigtime. If he even suggested it, she would psychoanalyze him all night. "She's like a tumor attached to me," he said aloud. "Easy duty, keeping her satisfied, but man, you are used to variety. I don't care if your favorite dish, the one you'd request on Death Row for your last meal is pizza: when all you eat is pizza three times a day for a whole year non-stop, you'll burn out. I don't care who you are, you'll grow sick of it. You'd start to feel like a soft-boiled egg would be a fucking five-star gourmet meal." *She has me talking to myself. Did I ever used to talk to myself this much?*

They showered together. "My friend from childhood, who would've been the best man at our wedding, I told you about him, David? He called. His wife left him for another man. He's a wreck, babe. I love the guy. I can tell he's spiraling down quickly. Would you mind terribly if I spent a few days with him at his place, help cheer him up? I've never heard him sound like this. I just want to be sure he doesn't hurt himself. Know what I mean?"

Her eyes narrowed. She turned off the water, opened the door, grabbed her phone, opened a browser, and tapped away until she stopped, wearing a satisfied smile. She held the phone up to his face. "I don't mind at all, if you'll wear this."

He stared at the screen, mouth agape. "Are you serious? A locking male chastity cage? Arabella—"

"If you mean well, to help your friend, then you won't mind this minor inconvenience at all."

"You don't trust me. Great. This is a test."

"I'm not testing you, Jayden. I only mean to test-fit the device."

He toweled off, grabbed clothes, and stuffed them into a rolling duffle along with his toothbrush from the bathroom. He stepped into boxers, socks, jeans, and a sweatshirt. He shot her with an angry glance backwards as he rolled towards the door. "You're crazy, Arabella. Hurting me like this. You'd throw away this beautiful thing we have over paranoid mistrust," he said, shaking his head. "Worst of all is that you don't give a shit if my dear friend kills himself." He gave her one final stare. "I think we really are done here."

Her face flushed as sanguine as a sunburn victim as he watched her collapse to the carpeting.

Her eyes opened forty-three minutes later. From their bed, she smiled up at him weakly. "You're still here."

"Of course, baby. Where else could I be but with you?"

"With your friend."

"Ah, yes. David needs me too right now. Too bad I can't clone myself. This was your worst fall yet. You still haven't seen a doctor. I'm taking you to the hospital now."

"Uh-uh, no way. It's snowing out."

"When isn't it snowing this winter, Arabella? You need to be seen. Let them run some tests. I'll spend the night at David's and be there to pick you up first thing in the morning. Please. You have me so worried."

After two full minutes of silent contemplation, "Okay. Because I love you, and don't want you to worry this much. I can see it in your face."

He smiled, hand on her cheek. "That's my girl. C'mon, let's get you dressed."

"Bryn Mawr Hospital, best in the area," he said, as he walked her up to the triage nurses for intake. Ninety-seven minutes later, Jayden staring at the analog wall clock, a blue-scrub employee entered through a door and said, "Follow me please, Mrs. Pendleman-Bonner." It was the first time since their wedding he had heard her ridiculous, hyphenated name spoken aloud. It felt emasculating. He blew her a kiss until she disappeared around a corner.

He practically trotted to the car, started it, and waited for the defogger to clear the windshield. He looked at his phone contacts. He called several old conquests in alphabetical order. "Whomever answers first and says yes, ding-ding-ding, wins." One he'd awakened. *Hungover*, he thought. She told him to swing by, pick her up, bring her home, and 'take her to paradise' she said.

And so, he did.

He brushed his teeth using her grotesque bubble-gum-flavored toothpaste. In the shower he used her weird flowery shampoo. Toweled off, he used her feminine deodorant spray under his pits. The morning after was cloudy, about eight degrees Fahrenheit, with at least one saving grace: no active snowfall. His car occasionally slipped on black ice as he bee-lined back to the hospital in time for visiting hours. In the waiting area, a nurse's aide pushed Arabella towards him in a wheelchair. "Hey look, it's my old lady!" he said, jokingly.

"Ha-ha, very funny." He helped her up from the chair and supported her during the walk to his car.

"You smell funny. What's that smell, Jayden?"

Sniffing his pits, he said, "What smell?"

"Like flowers."

"Oh. Yeah. Well, when at David's, you use what's available."

Eyes narrowed. She studied his face. "You didn't spend the night at David's, Jayden. I can see it in your eyes. Guys don't use flowery products."

"Good to see you, too," he said, and fired up the engine.

Riding in uncomfortable silence they drove up the long, winding driveway. Together they saw the ambulance parked in front of the mansion, lights flashing. Hands flew to her mouth, "Oh my God! Daddy!"

The servants struggled to direct traffic into neat rows and columns on the expansive grounds. The funeral of Tyler Pendleman was unlike any wedding, funeral, college graduation ceremony or private event that Jayden had ever seen. *So many people.* Local TV news vans arrived with parabolic equipment on top. Three news network helicopters hovered overhead. From the air, he figured the throng of people probably appeared like a giant inverted clamshell. In front of the granite tomb, he stood with Arabella, Xavier, and fewer than twenty Pendleman family members whom he never knew existed, along with two crucifix-wearing clergymen from which denomination he could not immediately discern. *Not Catholic. Episcopal, maybe?* Fanning out from that nucleus were rows of black-clad employees, supply chain vendor reps, and members of the press stretching out several hundred yards, most wearing boots in the muddy trampled snow.

Father McGuffin, confirmed now by Jayden as the diocesan bishop, along with a local Episcopal parish priest, read words from the Old and New Testaments on behalf of the deceased. Arabella wept piteously. Jayden could see now the extent of how deeply she cared for the old man. He felt only a measure of relief. *That icy blue stare of his; so judgmental. Never even tried to see things from my perspective or get to know me. Bye-bye, you miserable old fuck.*

Arabella collapsed unconscious. He caught her right arm, held up his left hand at everyone, gently tapped her cheek, and repeated her name. She was out cold. Jayden scooped her into his powerfully developed arms and easily carried her through the throng, which parted for them, back to the house, with every eye and camera lens focused on the couple.

In the mansion, a wake took place for the family, board of directors, and core C-suite employees. Arabella, recovered, escorted by Jayden, came downstairs to pay her respects to those closest to her father. "Garrett Xavier Pendleman," she said. Jayden eyed a five-foot-seven man is his fifties, balding, flabby, ruddy-faced, stuffed into an ill-fitting sport jacket with patched elbows, wide obsolete tie mismatched to the yellow shirt, and loose-fitting salmon pants over super-wide brown deck shoes with no socks. "My husband, Jayden Bonner."

Garrett offered a closed-mouth grin and his hand, to Jayden. "Thanks for taking my sister away from that sad scene out there."

Jayden nodded. "She would've done it for me, if her arms weren't twiggy little buggy whips." This made the siblings smile. "Good to meet you, Mr. Pendleman."

"Gary, please."

"Well brother, if you will please excuse us, I feel that I have reached my saturation point for the day," said Arabella. "Husband, please walk me home."

She slept away the afternoon and entire night, waking minutes before ten o'clock the next morning. Jayden, who had been up for hours had worked out, showered, eaten breakfast, and now heard her call his name. He came running into their bedroom. "Wow, babe. You must've been really exhausted. What did they say at the hospital?"

"Enlarged aorta and severe hypertension. My ticker is in somewhat of a precarious place lately. They tell me I need to get my blood pressure under control or I'm looking at a heart attack. Downstairs in my purse you'll find three medication prescriptions. Please go get them filled. I need to get busy living."

"Wow, babe, okay, I'm on it. Will you be alright for now?"

Nodding, she said, "Don't be long."

Searching 'hypertension' on his phone browser, he sat in his car waiting for the scrip fills. He read that certain common over-the-counter meds and supplements should be strictly avoided by those suffering from Turner's syndrome, as these can dramatically increase hypertension. In the vitamins and supplements aisle he found pseudoephedrine, yohimbe bark, and red Korean ginseng tablets, which he purchased along with the prescribed meds. In the car, he opened the three little brown opaque plastic prescription bottles, dumped the pills into the little white paper bag, and filled each bottle with the stimulant pills. Along the drive home, he opened the window to a cold blast of air, and emptied the prescription pills out onto the slush-covered road.

Seventy-two hours after the wake, Arabella started presenting viral symptoms; high fever, cough, nasal congestion, body aches, difficulty in breathing. She had lost her senses of smell and taste. Weakly, from the bed, she croaked his name. Wearing a blue medical-grade particulate respirator, he poked his head through the doorway. "Yes?" he said, voice muffled by the mask.

"I have Covid. Caught it from someone at the mansion. My chest feels like I have a gorilla sitting on it. My lungs feel gunked-up. I think maybe I had better go to the hospital."

"Nonsense, dear. It's only a cold, that's all. Nothing some chicken broth and rest can't knock out of you in a day or two."

"I haven't slept much since the morning after the funeral. I thought the anti-hypertension meds might calm me down a little, reduce anxiety, lower my blood pressure. I feel wired, loopy, like I'm dreaming though I'm conscious. Are you sure you got the right meds, lover?"

He nodded, gave her a thumbs up, and said, "Can I get you anything?"

"A pitcher of ice water would be nice. So hot and thirsty."

"Coming right up," he said, and returned minutes later with the pitcher and a coffee mug. He poured it for her. "Well, like, I know I told the Vegas guy 'in sickness and in health,' but one of us has to be strong to take care of the other, so, I'll ask the maidservant to fix me up a room in the big house. Text me if you need anything, I'll shoot right back here," he said, and closed the door behind him.

Moseying around the mansion, other than occasionally passing the maid, a short, stout middle-aged black woman named Alma, he had the place all to himself. Phil, the security guy worked alone inside a booth at the driveway's mouth, monitoring the security system. Inside the late Tyler Pendleman's luxurious office and study, Jayden stood in awe, taking in the thirty-foot high ceiling shelves spanning three walls crammed with thousands of thick hardcover books. *The old man's cave and happy place.*

He ran his fingertips over the hand-carved mahogany desk with lion's paw feet and rich black leather topper. He pulled the chain hanging from the green banker's lamp. He inspected the credenza covered in monitors. He sat and spun around in the sumptuous matching leather and wood chair. He stared at the dozen monitors showing live feeds from cameras at every sector of the property.

The second monitor from the left showed the cemetery and all the trodden snowy, muddy ground where mourners had stood. *We need another good snowstorm to brighten that view.* Each mausoleum, thirteen altogether, still wore a white hat of snow; icicles hung from each entrance like prehistoric Megalodon teeth. He imagined bird sounds, planes flying overhead, the occasional honk from a truck horn down slope on the Interstate. In here, it was all eerily silent.

He walked to the enormous professional-grade kitchen to fix himself a peanut butter and jelly sandwich, washed down with a glass of whole milk. Refreshed, bored, he returned to the clean, well-appointed guest room Alma had prepared for him. He laid atop the thick white down comforter and thought of the girl he had recently fucked. He texted her. She responded. He wrote, 'If it's okay with ya'll, they can come, too. Make it a three-way.' After he saw her thumbs-up and kissy lipstick lips emojis, he imagine a crappy car with three young girls pulling up to Phil's security gauntlet.

He called Phil at the security booth. "We're expecting a few friends of ours to arrive by rideshare early this evening. They'll likely spend the night. Please let them through. Three ladies. No ID necessary. Try to smile and be welcoming. They're important to Arabella."

With his phone set on vibrate, he missed three attempted calls and two text messages from Arabella. Lying naked somewhere in the middle of three dozing women, sometime after midnight in the peaceful quiet, sadly the text buzzes were unavoidable. He responded, "OMG, Arabella, so sorry. I passed out and didn't hear the alerts."

"Can barely breathe. Please call an ambulance."

"Be right over," he replied. His movements jostled awake his fuckbuddy.

"Jayd-baby, where are you going at this hour?"

"Urgent business," he whispered, so as not to disturb the other two girls. "Look around you! Do you think all of this, my empire, came without hard work and inconvenience? I need to deal with the Chinese. It's daytime there. Please get some rest," he said, pointing at his crotch. "You'll need it." She grinned slyly. "Seriously, go back to sleep, I won't be long." He pulled on his clothes, ran downstairs, donned his boots and winter wool coat, and headed out toward the cottage. Wide awake now, he considered his options. *Ambulance? No…*

Inside their cottage he shucked his boots and coat, snapped on his respirator, climbed the stairs, and slowly cracked open the bedroom door. What he saw inside, illuminated by the incandescent lamp on the nightstand, loosened his bowels. A hideous specter, lying upon a bed of suffering, every movement of her eyelids and limbs feeble. He sensed the nervous irritation of her temperament, also that she lacked the strength to express it. A deathly pallor had overspread her face. His reptile brain signaled a flight response, goading him to leave, though his feet carried him ever closer to his wife.

With a trembling hand he touched her forehead, then her exposed forearm. Color had disappeared from eyelids and cheeks, leaving an achromatic cadaverousness not unlike marble. Her once pink and eminently kissable lips had doubly shriveled, pinched up in the ghastly expression of death. A repulsive clamminess and coldness had consumed every inch of skin he touched. The room reeked of sickness and decay.

"Jayden, my love. Did you call an ambulance?" in a raspy whisper. Even through his respirator he detected the malodorous eye-stinging stench of feces and urine.

He nodded. "Yes, Arabella, my love. Any minute now. You need to rest. Are you able to swallow?"

She tried to shake her head, "Co-morbidities. Turner syndrome. Covid. I'm dying, lover."

"Pfft. You're the strongest person I know. Nobody's dying tonight, dearest."

"I haven't slept. Cannot rest."

"I'm going to get one of your sleeping pills and a glass of water. You need to rest, baby. Everybody knows it's key to recovery." Retracing his steps out into the hall, in the bathroom behind the hinged mirror, he shook out two of her prescription sleeping pills, and noticed the long-expired date, knowing psychiatrists and other medical doctors had stopped prescribing this med due to its addictive properties and side effects, including hallucinations. He filled a paper cup with tap water and brought them to her. He held her head, inserted the pills between leathery lips, and tilted water into her mouth. She swallowed and choked weakly.

"Don't leave me," she whispered. "Jayden, I am so scared."

He managed an affected smile. "Never. Wouldn't dream of it."

Thinking of the girls awaiting him in the mansion, he sent a text over, "Sorry little bee, I need you to fly on home, bzzzt. We'll pick this up another time." Then he texted Phil, "Our friends are leaving early due to another commitment, please let them out." Then he waited, watching Arabella's thin ribcage rise and fall more slowly as the sleep drug started to take effect.

In a deeply infected, phlegmy rattle, she whispered, "I love you always, Jayden. You saved me…in every way a person can be saved. Do you think maybe there really is a Heaven?"

He nodded. "Sure there is, Arabella. Sure there is."

He sat solemnly beside her bed of death. For the first time, he watched Cheyne–Stokes respiration, not knowing what it was but guessing what it meant. Peacefully, she breathed her last sighs. Arabella Pendleman's chest rose never again.

He waited in the cottage kitchen, until he saw the taillights of the vehicle disappear down the steep serpentine driveway, before calling 9-1-1. He called Phil, affecting a sound of panic, and alerted him to the ambulance on its way. Sitting in the dark, his conscious mind worked overtime to rationalize what he had done. *The pseudoephedrine and stimulant supplements were to help her breathe. If I had called the ambulance earlier, days ago, it still would've ended the same, except in a filthy-scary hospital, intubated, in an induced coma. Much worse than what I did for her.*

In the realm of human consciousness that exists during sleep but then lingers into the first few moments or minutes past awakening: this is where the essence of humanity most identify as the 'soul' gets laid bare. Jayden knew it. It's only that he had never given much consideration to his exposed soul in those moments, how it is rendered defenseless against the mind's endless pretzel-logic justifications and rationalizations for evil acts and intents. Jayden Bonner knew he was guilty of murdering his wife, through calculated and deliberate neglect commingled with outright poisoning.

He did not feel good. He had learned from a very young age to think through and absolve himself of every evil he had wrought against others, which mostly had consisted of coldly using naïve females. *They all call me a narcissist. Oh well. If there is a God, then He made me this way. Don't blame me— blame Him.* He vindicated his predatory behavior as natural and necessary to meet the primal objective: survival of the organism, Law of the Jungle. Seated in the kitchen, shrouded in shadow and silence, acutely aware of his decomposing victim only a short walk up the stairs, he found his usual rationalizations for bad behavior less convincing than ever before. *She trusted me with her life. But dammit—she had me boxed in! Caged! She even wanted to lock my junk in a cage! I'm not a breed fit to be caged. Could I have filed for divorce? Sure, yes. But then the organism would've ended up flat broke and homeless. It came down to her, or me.*

Arabella Pendleman's funeral came to pass, nearly identical to that of her father's except that today, Jayden Bonner stood by himself, wearing black sunglasses under a bitter cold, dark, and dreary overcast winter sky. At his request, the funeral director had arranged her body inside her silk-lined coffin wearing his favorite full-length white evening gown with puffy shoulders. At the viewing, he thought that she appeared as if she were still alive, only sleeping.

He followed six men, Garrett Xavier Pendleman and five strangers, who bore her coffin into the granite mausoleum. Carefully and with piqued reverence, working as one, they slotted Arabella's coffin into the yawning compartment beneath her father. He watched them carefully close the heavy, thick greenish copper or brass door. He studied Garrett's hands on the key somberly as he inserted it into the brass lock and turned it. This action brought with it an unpleasant squeaky squeal as ancient lock tumblers clawed into place, a sound Jayden knew he would never forget, a mournful metallic groan. The period at the end of Arabella's life sentence.

After the six filed out, Jayden remained, head bowed as if in prayer. He stared at the lock just below his eye-level. Soon, mounted above the lock there would be a shiny new brass plaque with her name, birth and death dates, and the family crest. Below her tomb was an unoccupied slot. This, he recognized, was reserved for him.

In the mansion, he found it difficult to remember all the names of distinguished-looking older gentlemen who introduced themselves and their wives to him, each hiding behind a well-rehearsed painted-on smile of comfort and condolence. Behind their eyes, he saw pressing matters of business flying. "As our de facto new Chairman of the Board, Mr. Bonner, have you given any thought as to whether you will take an active position as did Tyler, or more of a 'live and let live' passive approach?"

Jayden closed his eyes and shook his head. "Gentlemen, if you will please excuse me, I have not had like one moment's peace to contemplate life without my beloved Arabella. If you'll excuse me," he said and quickly stepped to the mansion's front door without turning around. Outside he inhaled deeply of the bracing-cold, sterile, steel-smelling winter atmosphere. Alone on the landing, his back against the door, Jayden wept. For the first time in his adult life, he cried as a child cries.

He sensed the door opening behind him. Felt the arm around his back and heard Garrett Pendleman's voice. "I know, Jayden. We had our differences, my sister and I. Different mothers and such. Didn't talk much at all. I'll never forget the day I first heard I was about to receive a baby sister, the feelings that ran through me. Thrilling, really. A new life, maybe like when a child receives a kitten or puppy as a gift from his parents. A certain sense of responsibility, and protectiveness," he said, patting Jayden's shoulder. "I never saw her as happy as I did when she introduced you to me. Just wanted you to know that."

Pulling himself together, Jayden blew his nose into a tissue from his pocket and glanced over at Garrett. "I don't know how to go on. All of this," he said, panning the property with a sweeping gesture. "I'm just a poor kid from Norristown. This is like an alien world, to me."

Smiling, Garrett redoubled his shoulder patting and switched to mid-back smacking. "No worries, little brother. I got this. The management part, I mean. It's all yours on paper. I'm familiar with the trust's terms and conditions. You just work on pulling yourself together. I'll handle the business aspects. I run a software business which is on par with pharmaceuticals in its global reach and regulatory oversight, and such. I'll get the hang of drug development and marketing. The board members are quite knowledgeable and talented. I trust this empire of yours will pretty much run itself, without need of much intervention from you or me. So. Will you continue to live in the cottage, or will you move into the mansion full-time? I can tell you mansion living is way better. I grew up here. Every luxury at your fingertips, like a cruise ship permanently docked."

He shook his head. "I can't even like set foot back in that cottage. Too many painful memories. I think it's better if I stay here."

"Smart choice. Of the indoor pool and hot tub, I suggest you avail yourself immediately, commencing this very night. You need to unwind, clear your mind, relax a little. The mansion has forty-seven separate bedrooms, along with my dad's master suite. Are you happy with Alma's choice of rooms for you?"

He nodded. "Yes. I like the location, proximity to the bathroom, the fireplace across from the bed."

Garrett grinned. "Yes. Tonight, build yourself a warm fire, it'll help get you off to sleep. I had one installed in every room of my cottage except for the kitchen. Sedatives, those things are."

"I take it your dad was a religious man? For the church to send a bishop—isn't that kind of a big deal?"

"Indeed, he was a very spiritual man, and very generous to the church. Are you?"

He shook his head. "Not so much. Arabella and I synced up in that regard. After this life ends, there's nothing."

"Hm. Well, I must respectfully differ with you on that point. I have been visited by spirits, mostly at night, sometimes in my dreams, but then too when wide awake. My father's, for instance. Walking alone in the cemetery lately, something I haven't done since childhood, it is there where I have heard his voice and have seen his form looking out from behind the glass of the mausoleum door. This is why I don't grieve his loss, Jayden. It might seem looney to you, but I know his essence goes on. And that he loves me still. We were close. Arabella and the family didn't think we were, but he and I would have high tea together almost every day. I've learned so much from him."

Jayden shrugged. "He didn't much care for me, I know this. Didn't think I was 'one of his kind.'"

"Nobody was one of his kind. I wasn't, either. A rare and radiant spirit is he. And yes, every bit the high-born, pompous, Main Line old-money trust fund elitist. You bleed red; he bled blue."

Looking over at Garrett, eyes pleading, "I don't want to go back in there."

"Hah, I'm sure you don't. I got this, kiddo. Go take a drive. Clear your head awhile. Come back in three hours. This place will be quieter than a tomb, by then."

"Oh good, Alma changed the sheets," Jayden said upon re-entering his bedroom. Taking Garrett's advice, he pushed some kindling underneath some very dry birch logs, opened the damper, used a wooden match, and watched flames instantly climb. Perhaps it was the fireplace depleting oxygen from the room, or the belly-full of delicious roast beef sandwiches and beer making him feel so incredibly tired. Lying on top of the comforter, he dozed, long enough to dream. Arabella's voice. "You killed me," it said. *The voice could have been hers*, his unconscious mind suggested.

Or any female voice, his mind answered.

"Together forever, Jayden," said the voice. It sounded like an Arabella, but as a ventriloquist, talking with her mouth closed. "I'm coming to take you with me. Life goes on, and on, and on," said the voice.

"What the hell?" he shouted, startled awake. "Whoa, dude. You need to get a grip." He shook his head and rubbed his face. The fire had rapidly converted the three logs into glowing embers. He got up and stacked more logs on top, something distracting and normal to do, though his mind continually replayed the voice from his dream. He sat on the edge of the bed, hypnotized by the flames, lost in the absurd shadows they cast. He felt himself merging with the darkness, felt his rapid descent into a new world of shadow and doubt from which, he now suspected, he would never re-emerge.

Swim followed by hot tub, muscles languid and loose, he decided to climb into bed and try to sleep through the night. *Tomorrow I'll have the girls back, and this time, for sure, they'll spend the night. Maybe the next, and the night after that.* He didn't feel that being alone right now is the best plan, with emotions running raw, and a seemingly ceaseless battle against unchecked guilt and remorse raging away within him. He dropped in five more split logs and climbed into bed. The room crackled with low light, pleasant smells, and seductive sounds of the fire. He watched it until his eyelids grew heavy.

"Tonight, I come for you, Jayden." His unconscious mind registered the same female voice as earlier. "We will make love, like before. Then, I must take your life, as you took mine. Together forever, Jayden."

His eyes opened. Seeing the fire had dwindled somewhat, he knew he hadn't been asleep for that long. Cursing his troubled mind, he dozed again. "I'm out of the coffin, now, Jayden. Turning the brass knob. Wait for me downstairs. Together forever, Jayden. Coming to make love to you, husband."

Fully awake now, recognizing no further sleep would be forthcoming this night, his conscious mind replayed her words, echoing still within his subconsciousness. He pulled on the thick terry bathrobe and stepped into the fleece-lined leather slippers Alma had provided. In the dark, he felt along the hallway to navigate his way back to the wide staircase landing. With a tight grip on the wooden rail, he descended, until he stepped onto the thick tiled first floor where natural light streamed through the front bay window. He walked to the window and looked out at the moonlight expanse of property. Then he remembered: the cameras.

Seated in Tyler's chair, he focused his attention on the second monitor from the left. In light cast from the monitors, his peripheral vision registered some new shadow on the black leather desktop. He leaned down and saw a thirty-eight-caliber snub-nosed revolver on the desk. "What the—" he said. He picked it up and saw that all six chambers contained brass cartridges. "How the fuck did this get here? Did Phil leave it?" He turned over the gun in his hand while his harried mind worked on solving the mystery of the weapon's sudden appearance.

But then movement registered in his brain. Still holding the gun, reluctantly and with blood pounding behind his eyes and deep in his ears, he returned his gaze to the second monitor from the left.

Arabella's crypt door hung wide open. He blinked. *No, it's not a trick of the light.* The open crypt yawned at him, tall and black. *There can be only one reason why I can see the mausoleum so brightly and clearly. The motion-sensing LED spotlight above the camera. Which means, something out there is on the move.*

Gone were the heavy wrought-iron bars affixed over thick panes of leaded glass. *No, this simply cannot be.* A war raged hot inside his mind. Part of him wanted to bolt—just run away far and fast from this macabre and incomprehensible situation. The rational portion of his brain stopped him from abandoning his new position in life of status and wealth beyond his wildest dreams. He thought of the three girls ornamenting his gilded bed.

Yet another facet of his consciousness busily asked urgent questions, the same old primordial human questions about life, death, and what might lie beyond. At no time did his eyes leave the monitor.

In the doorway of the crypt stood Arabella, of course still wearing his favorite white dress with the puffy shoulders, arms stiff at her sides like stalactites, one black shiny patent leather shoe partially sunk in semi-frozen muck. Right foot extended, knee unbent, an uncertain step down three inches from the granite slab to the mud. A teetering jerk forward with the right, followed by the left leg dragged stiffly beside it. Once as graceful as a jungle cat, his dead wife now rocked side to side, neck and head locked in one direction, inclined toward the mansion. Another lurching, unnatural goose-step from the extended, wooden-looking right leg, followed by the left. Then another. The figure started gaining speed, lurching forward, now almost to the camera's view limit, face as close to the lens as it would ever get before moving past it. In horror, he recognized the undertaker's work. Arabella's memorial green eyes glued shut, her once tasty, sensual mouth that so thrilled him now wired shut. *Like a figure in a wax museum.*

She—it—is coming for me! In my dream it said it will make love to me! And that it'll take me with it. It means to kill me! He thought of the physical strength it required to free itself from a granite prison. The front door lock won't stop it. These bay windows surely won't.

On another monitor fed from the CCTV cam covering the front door, from a distance, he saw the figure lurching forward. He laughed. Even to himself it sounded like hysterical, maniacal, and shrill laughter. "No-no-no, this isn't happening. I'm up there in bed dreaming all this. Only a nightmare, whew, what a doozy!"

The figure in the center monitor had grown larger, closer. Laughter turned into something like crying. Left hand over his face, he parted two fingers in time to watch the Arabella-thing jerkily ascend the front steps. Now it stood, swaying, outside the door. Reverberations, evenly spaced, like from a machine: Thump. Thump. Thump. It seemed to come from the front door.

Jayden Bonner's brain never heard the sharp explosion that pushed a copper-jacketed, hollow-point lead projectile straight through the roof of his mouth and his auditory cortexes. At six hundred ninety feet per second, the bullet had left no time for the organ to register pain, either. Here, then not here, quicker than a blink.

The mortician did as fine a job as she had ever done on the corpse of Jayden Bonner. The bullet entrance wound she plugged with wax and covered with cosmetics. It was that sweet potato-sized exit wound at the top of his skull that had given her fits.

On the Friday night following Jayden's funeral and his coffin's interment in the mausoleum beneath his wife, Garret Xavier Pendleman sat in his father's chair, just as he had as a young man. He admired the antique Ushak rug he had purchased from a dealer at the 'friend' price of only one-hundred-twenty-eight-thousand dollars, to replace his father's ruined, blood-stained modern forebearer.

He reminded himself to send the young actress who portrayed his deceased sister during filming an expensive shiny object—a new Maserati Quattro or Porsche 718 Cayman, perhaps—to ensure her continued strict adherence to their signed non-disclosure agreement, also as one final 'thank-you' for her Oscar-worthy performance that night. The night of the suicide, moments after he'd heard the shot through his hidden microphones, he had walked from his cottage over to the mansion and removed the mini speakers from under the bed in Jayden's former room, also the bass subwoofer speaker from the coat closet in the front hallway near the door.

Hacking monitors in his own childhood home to feed the pre-recorded footage of the actress, he felt, had been the least challenging part of the grift. The most difficult task had been auditioning female voiceover artists to closely approximate the pitch and timbre of his late sister. Worse, getting the talent to rearrange her schedule and record the sentences he had given her, dragging out consonants and vowels at precisely the right moments to sound spookier, like someone with her mouth wired shut might sound, asking her to imagine if an embalmed corpse were to attempt speech.

All things restored back to normal, he sat in his dad's command center and soaked in the truth of suddenly becoming truly, filthy rich. All of life's honors, pleasures, and rewards that had eluded him for a lifetime would all now be his. That also meant a new class of beautiful gold-digging women. He knew the fairer gender were attracted to extreme wealth—though not so much to a germophobic, out-of-shape recluse living under his father's shadow. He vowed to start using the late Jayden Bonner's gym across the compound.

Turning to the monitors he saw mostly blackness, save for the guard gate at the driveway entrance, where Phil's occasional movements outside the booth caused the overhead spotlights to pop on and remain on for twenty-minute periods. He laughed. "The perfect coup. Damn I'm good!"

He decided to soak in the hot tub. He clicked off the banker's lamp and pushed himself to stand. The second monitor from the left popped alive behind him. He turned just in time to watch his father and sister's mausoleum door opening from the inside. He collapsed back down and squinted. No question, it was open.

He reached into his pocket for his smartphone to alert Phil, but then he froze. A very tall figure in a black suit and tie over a white shirt stood in the crypt doorway. Hands grasped both sides of the doorframe as if for balance. The head inclined toward the light and camera. He stepped to the ground. A hand rose. It pointed at the camera. The man in the suit started walking, a normal two-mile-per-hour gait, head turned up to the camera. As the face came closest to the lens, Garrett gasped. Jayden Bonner's eyes, glued shut by the undertaker, were open. The eyelids top and bottom seemed tattered from glued flesh now ripped apart. The mouth, wired closed, was open in a malevolent grin, teeth missing from where pins and wires had torn them from their cold dead sockets when the jaw opened. It slowed to stare at the camera, revealing the sinister grin and dull filmy-eyed face of a living devil.

Fewer than five minutes later, Garrett felt the vibration of heavy footfalls outside on the wooden porch landing. There was no thumping sound effect this time, though he heard the locked doorknob getting jostled. And then, the summary explosion of splintering wood and bent hinges when the door imploded as if hit by a rocket-propelled grenade.

Garrett's feet pedaled air. Cold hands around his neck felt like a noose made of frozen steel cable. His nostrils recoiled at breath so bad that he could taste the formaldehyde and decomposing lung tissue carried with it. His scream sounded weird, even to himself, while his tongue got bitten off. The last thing he saw, before thumbs burst his eyeballs, were the cataract, dull filmy black eyes behind shredded lids, and the most avaricious, hateful smile of all.

The following morning, responding to Phil's call to his former detective cronies at the station, after taking Alma the housekeeper's hysterical report, investigators examined Garrett Pendleman's remains pinned underneath the corpse of Jayden Bonner. Pendleman's nose and ears were gone. The detective noted bite and rip marks around the head where these appendages had been detached. The throat, too, appeared to have been chewed wide open, revealing a severed esophagus. There was now dried goo in place of eyeballs, and everywhere pools of congealed blood. Seeing the victim's blood on the embalmed lips of Bonner, and the victim's eyeball liquid on Bonner's thumbs, the detective, a former associate of Phil's, admitted in 'squad car' confidence to Phil that this was the worst murder scene he had ever experienced. Shortly thereafter the detective launched a dragnet of the area to locate the sick, twisted, homicidal perp who not only killed Garrett Pendleman but abused and subsequently posed two corpses in a way that nauseated him.

The trust equally divided fifty-one percent of the shares in the Pendleman family holdings among all twelve board members. Of the remaining forty-nine percent, half was distributed across all employees globally, and the other half to the church diocese.

Once again, Jayden Bonner was interred under his wife, with Garrett Xavier Pendleman sealed in directly across from her, marking the end of the direct Pendleman line, forever.

Yoyo the Clown

At 9:57 a.m., on Friday, August 9, 2002, ten-year-old Pedro Pacheco shivered in the air conditioning. Artificially cooled air is something he had never experienced. The director of Mexico's Agencia Federal de Investigación, the premier investigative arm of the Attorney General of Mexico, sent Investigator Maria Padilla into the interrogation room, under the belief the team would achieve better results with a female interviewer. She changed from her official uniform into a simple peasant blouse, skirt, and flats before entering the room. She found the boy seated with his legs pulled up, arms wrapped around them. "My Lord, he's freezing! Diego, please get me a blanket and two cups of hot tea. Then leave us. I will speak with him alone."

Blanket around his shoulders, cup in his hands, she observed the change in the boy's body language as a measure of anxious edge drained from his body. She took a sip. "Good tea?" He met her eyes and nodded once. "Pedro, my name is Maria. I'm only here to help. You remind me so much of my son! He's just about your age and equally handsome. Will you speak with a mother?"

He took a sip, expression hopeful. He met her eyes. "Can you help me? I don't think it's possible. They shot my father dead. They arrested my mother. I have nobody else in the world but them." His eyes filled with tears. She could see him fighting against a full-blown cry. She reached out and cupped his hands in hers.

"My heart bleeds for you, Pedro. Please know that. And you're wrong about having no one else. Your mother's cousin, Monika Sanchez, legally immigrated to the USA fourteen years ago. We spoke with her and with U.S. authorities. How would you like to start over fresh in America? Leave all bad memories here, and go make new ones surrounded by kindness, love, and warmth?" She watched as it sank in. Eyes wide, he nodded.

"But before this can happen, we need you to tell us everything you know about Nuestra Señora de la Santa Muerte. Everything about your experiences growing up in Santa Muerte, the unholy death cult."

"No! No! They will kill me! They will hunt me down, cut open my belly and dance on my guts—it's what they do! No please! Please just let me go. I will live in the sewer if I must. If you send me to jail, they will get to me there. They'd get me in the States, too."

"Why would they risk so much to get you?"

His eyes grew dark. "Because I know too much."

Monday morning, August 8, 2022, one day shy of exactly twenty years since Pedro Pacheco first experienced air-conditioning in Mexico City, he wore a fleece hoodie inside his equipment warehouse on Main Street in Norristown, Pennsylvania. The sharp aromatic tang of heavy equipment hydraulic fluid and diesel fuel is something his brain no longer acknowledged; he had grown used to it.

He heard a vehicle pull into his gravel lot. His crew were out on jobs. He glanced at his watch: 10:23 a.m. He expected no deliveries today nor reappearance of his employees until late afternoon. He peered through the steel walk-in door's small wire-reinforced glass window. *Shiny black Lincoln. No bueno.* He grabbed his handgun, ran up the steps and out onto the flat roof. He watched four large men in suits pile out. He thought he heard the vehicle chassis groan happily when it rose two inches higher, now relieved of over a thousand pounds of human beef.

They spotted him. One of the two from the back waved up to acknowledge his presence. The man put his hands in his suit pants pockets. Pedro noticed his hair and necktie, both styled to perfection. "Good morning, Mr. Pacheco. I guess you know who we are and why we're here."

Pedro leaned forward. "Yeah. I know. I won the mall job fair and square. The union overbid. I bid it just right. I did not underbid it just to win it. The difference between you and me is that I'm not greedy. You should try it sometime. Your members would eat as well as you do."

The man below smiled. "Leave the job, Mr. Pacheco. This is your final warning."

Pedro held up his Colt 1911A semi-automatic handgun. "Or what?"

"Or we'll permanently put you out of business. Clear it up any?"

"¡Púdrete!" Pedro screamed. "I shoot you in face n' bury you in cement! Who you think you fuckin with?!"

All four men grinned. The spokesman removed his hands from his pockets and held them up dismissively. The four took up their seats. The car chassis sank. Pedro watched them crunch away from his lot. He returned to ground level, gun in hand. *They won't come at me during the day. Which means I need to spend every night here, for a while, anyway. Only go home to shower.* His crew returned then immediately left for home by 7:00 p.m. Pedro set up his cot and sleeping bag between his big front-end loader and his backhoe facing the roll-up doors. After a can of pork and beans heated on a camp stove and quick clean-up, he laid on the cot and stared up at the steel support beams and corrugated metal ceiling that he could not see in the dark but knew they were there. He drifted toward sleep. Tonight he skipped the Santa Muerte prayers his mother taught him.

He dreamed. His ten-year-old version had no choice but to obey the adults in the Nuestra Señora de la Santa Muerte group, which included his mother who was High Priestess up until her arrest, trial, murder convictions, and multiple life sentences in prison to run concurrently. What kept him from suffering ritual abuse and sodomy had not been his mother, as children of members are considered common property of the group. He was an effective recruiter, or 'roper' as they sometimes labeled him. Attractive, articulate, charming: Pedro had grown adept at recruiting kids his own age and younger, from poverty-stricken families, to take his hand and voluntarily accompany him back to 'church'—where he was forced to witness them suffer unimaginable sex enslavement for several days, culminating with the depraved tortures of the damned, unto death. Where children were used as human sacrifices to the Holy Saint of Death.

Tonight, perhaps because his waking mind now faced a potentially lethal show-down with powerful Philadelphia labor union thugs, on the anniversary precisely twenty years following the Santa Muerte's armed stand-off with Mexican authorities, something inside his dreaming, unconscious mind snapped. Like a brine shrimp egg desiccated and dormant for thousands of years, suddenly splashed with warm salt water. Soon after, out pops a living animal. Something dead in him, a hungry, obscene, revolting aspect resurrected itself this night in his sleep.

Kids today are different. Raised not to trust strangers. You're not ten anymore, Pedro. You no longer know how to talk to little kids; you don't speak 'kid' anymore. To 'rope' for us you'll need to remake yourself into an adult figure kids absolutely trust. Like a teacher. Like a policeman.

Like a circus clown.

He awoke early Tuesday to the sound of tires on gravel. He grabbed the gun from under his pillow, ran to the door opener and pressed the furthest left button. Finger on the trigger, he watched as the left-most big bay door slowly cranked up to the high ceiling. Seeing his crew, he tucked the gun in his waist and fluffed his tee-shirt over it. "Happy Tuesday, boys. TGIT," he said jokingly with a wave.

After they'd gone, he locked up and drove to his house a few miles east, in Plymouth Meeting. He showered, cooked and ate some bacon and eggs, cleaned up, drove to two big box stores and made purchases. He called a sub-contractor friend he had once used on a restaurant job who specialized in creating rigid fiberglass yard statues, glossy-painted and lifelike. All of this took nearly three hours. He drove his white Ford van back toward the Norristown warehouse. West on Main, on the left he glimpsed his building. His jaw dropped. All six of his bays were wide open. He smacked the steering wheel. "Los cojones! Fat rat bastards took everything but the toilet. ¡La madre que te parió!" he screamed.

He made calls to his insurer to get the claim going. He called his statue supplier and arranged to pay extra for a Saturday-morning meeting at his design studio. He waited for the crew to return, paid them, locked all warehouse doors as per ritual, and pulled out of the lot directly behind them.

Saturday morning, he awoke at 6:00 a.m. to bright summer sun. He spent an hour attempting to perfect the make-up and outfit, using safety pins in places. In costume he drove to the art studio. The contractor met him in the parking lot. "Pedro?" he said.

"No!" he said and honked his metal horn. "Yoyo is my name. Yoyo the clown! Pedro met with an unfortunate accident. I did however bring his checkbook and I've perfected his signature. Did you not know that clowns are natural forgers and mimics? We can be whomever you want us to be!" The contractor laughed. He ushered Yoyo inside.

Pedro spent the rest of the weekend driving near parks and playgrounds to observe. One seemed promising. Many unattended children. Few adults. Saturday evening, he returned to the small municipal park, parked in an empty professional office lot about five hundred yards away, and cut the engine. He used binoculars. Three tween girls seated on the concrete wood-slat bench with room for two more, smoking cigarettes, giggling, swatting at mosquitoes. He panned the entire park. *No one else. Only them. This is their safe-space hangout.* He waited until they stood and walked north through a narrow copse of trees. He started the engine. Three turns and a thousand yards later he stopped on a narrow road directly behind the trees used by the girls as a cut-through. *They live close. Maybe even on this street.* Slowly so as not to attract attention, he pulled away and drove home.

At home, he called twenty-one-year-old Monika, here from Mexico on an au pair visa during the summer. "Come over for a late snack?" He felt too worked up, head swimming with delicious possibilities awaiting him at the little park. Monika arrived. He mixed a pitcher of frozen salted margaritas. She drank until she felt loopy. She leaned on him as he walked her down to his basement sex dungeon. He took 'no' for 'yes please!' and pushed every limit she thought she had. Unshackled, she collapsed to the carpeting. He spooned behind her and tenderly dried her perspiration with his warm breath.

"Marry me, Pedro. When my visa expires, I want to stay here with you. I could be more than a wife to you. I'll be your slave, your chef, house cleaner, personal shopper and errand-girl. I'm studying accounting; I can even keep your books and file your taxes. Cheap labor. You want kids, I'll give you kids. You want to keep it simple, only the two of us: great too. I could be good for you. You could be good for me too, that is, if you keep me cumming every night just as hard as tonight. But only if you're up for it, of course. Absolutely no demands. I only want whatever you want to give me. Every man needs his space, his alone time. Truth be told, same with every woman. Well, every mature woman, I mean."

For a moment he considered it. The Catholic in him implored him to take Monika's offer seriously. *Truly beautiful. I can tell she'll age well even after childbirth. Brutally honest. There is no lying in her. No deceit, no clever manipulation. American girls are so silly, with more gross tats than MS-13 and Los Zetas. She's a good girl. Can't imagine me ever getting better.*

"When does your visa expire?"

"Two weeks after Labor Day."

"Give me time to think about it? It would be the biggest change in my life since moving here."

She smiled, white teeth, lips dark and full of arousal. "Thank you, Pedro. I'm not yet in love with you but I feel quite certain that if you would only seek me, you'd find me. If that ever happened—oh my God, yes! I know I could fall head-over-heels in love with you."

The malevolent spirit in him—awake, relentless, and with a hole running straight through its middle that can only be filled with human suffering—made its case using his mother's voice. *You're twenty years behind. Accomplish your solemn duties to la Huesuda with a wife at home? Loco. You are free. Free of the cartel. Free of the police. Free of debt. Freedom is your power. I gave this to you.*

"Perfecto! You are a true artist. Send the invoice to Armageddon Construction like last round," Pedro said. Together he and the subcontractor loaded the exact replica of himself made up as Yoyo the clown, first into protective bubble-wrap and cardboard, then into the van. Per Pedro's specification, it was formed in a seated position. The two shook hands on the deal.

It was Saturday morning, August 20, 8:47 a.m. when he arrived at the playground. *Empty.* He parked the van on the street behind the wooded berm. Without assistance it proved difficult to lug the awkward, ninety-nine-pound Yoyo sculpture a hundred yards through the scrub. He unwrapped it and set it on the far-left edge of the bench. He paced backwards for one quick look. He smiled. Quickly he paced back, started the engine, and drove to the empty office lot. He watched Yoyo through binoculars. He could see tiny kids getting excited by this new addition to the park, warming up to it, snuggling next to it, sitting on its lap. *Like it's been there forever.*

Three hours; three passes from police cruisers. They slowed not far from the clown but did not stop. *Will municipal authorities remove it? It's a gamble. Kids seem to love it. Word will spread. It'll become an unsolved mystery: Who made it? How did it get there? Law or Press might even trace the work back to the subcontractor and interview him...*

He dialed. "Hello?"

"Hey, it's Pedro. Listen: I donated the sculpture. Anonymous donation. This thing has your fingerprints all over it. Tracking me so far?"

"Yeah, uh-huh."

"Which means if anyone comes 'round demanding you ID the customer, what are you going to tell them?"

"Some clown in a clown car paid me cash to make this for him a long time ago. I reported the cash on my taxes, but I don't have a receipt or name. Sorry."

Pedro smiled. "I'll be feeding you work for years to come, my friend."

"You're a good man, Pedro Pacheco. Don't let anybody tell you otherwise."

Only la Hermana Blanca can judge your righteousness, Pedro. She and only she.

He went home to eat and take his siesta. Monika stopped over. "I only have time for a six-nine, Chica," he said. "Tonight I have a few things to take care of."

She smirked. "Is she pretty?"

"What? Oh. Hah-hah, no, nothing like that. One mujer loca is all I can handle, mami." Smiling, she undressed completely and eagerly settled down onto the familiar seat that was his face.

After a hasty dinner of birria tacos and chili relleno, he drove to the office lot, parked, shut down, and studied the lot. He watched moths and other winged creatures relentlessly bang against the bright LED spotlights surrounding the ballfield of the park. Very few lumens splashed into the shadows where Yoyo sat. He wondered if the three young girls would show up. *Please, Nuestra Señora de la Santa Muerte: make them come. I need to pay tribute.*

A few minutes later these same three girls arrived. Like little kids they seemed quite amused by Yoyo's permanent new residence. *Cops probably think that Rotary, Jaycees, Tall Cedars, Shriners, or the local Council put it there.* One of them straddled Yoyo's lap and bounced up and down on its crotch. Another girl replaced her with a reverse-cowboy crotch ride. Pedro grinned. *Filthy little demons, yes-yes-yes. Oh, thank you, Holy Mother, yes! Next Saturday night, one week from today, you shall feed again, I swear it. By Sunday night your heart will be filled to overflowing. After, I ask you to let Monika be. Oh, blessed Mother of the Most Saintly Death, this is my only request. Join her to me forever or send her away to safety.*

Saturday, August 27, 8:00 a.m., he exchanged the van's authentic Pennsylvania license plate with one he'd pinched two years back from a similar van in a parking lot far north in Wilkes Barre. He drove to a street in downtown Norristown. He parked along an empty stretch of curb. Eight minutes later, a young man approached his passenger window. "Yo. Help you find somethin?" He stared at the thick wad of hundred-dollar bills rubber-banded atop the center console.

Pedro leaned right. "I hear you're the man to see if I need something …strong."

The young man looked both ways. "You wit' da man?"

Pedro laughed. "I'm with Santa Muerte, via Mexico City, by grace of the Sinaloa. Maybe you've heard the name of my boss, Ovidio."

Pedro saw the recognition and momentary flicker of terror on the young man's face, like a cat realizing it just sneaked into a Rottweiler pen. "Shit, man. Why you here? I'm at the ass end."

"I've a strange request. Are you the man who can get things, or not?"

"Been known to. Whatchuneed, amigo?"

"A gram of midazolam hydrochloride and three syringes."

The man stroked his chin. "Man. Why don't you just ask Santa for a Bugatti? Shit."

"So that's a no," he said. He grabbed the roll, opened his vest and slipped the roll into the pocket next to his Colt .45 handgun. He made sure all of it was seen by the seller.

"Didn't say no, did I?" He rubbed his head. "Gonna cost you that lump in your pocket."

"When can you get it?"

He rubbed his head again. "Tomorrow noon."

Pedro shook his head. "Need it before sundown. For a friend."

The man smirked. "I got Ruffies. Twenty a pill."

"I need the midazolam hydrochloride and three syringes."

He shook his head. "Give me five Bens now to grease some wheels. The rest you give me at 5:00 sharp."

"If you're not here by 5:00 with the midazolam hydrochloride and three syringes, oh Holy Mother of Saintly Death. You'll refund my money or your future will be, how do you say: short. Ovidio has eyes everywhere." His grin was that of a demonic dog. There was no way for anyone to mistake the pedestrian, pitiless, remorseless thousand-yard stare in those cold eyes that died during childhood.

"I be here, chingon, with the stuff or with the refund."

Pedro pulled away. He glanced at his phone and smiled. *No pestering texts or voicemails from Monika. I could really get used to this girl.* He drove to the warehouse. Inside, he smiled. *Mm. Love that new-car smell.* All new heavy equipment awaited courtesy of the insurance payout. *The Sainted Mother is already blessing me.* He loaded the van with a large roll of moisture barrier wrap. He locked up and drove home. Down in his sex dungeon he spent the next two hours covering the floor and walls with the waterproof sheeting.

I haven't felt this excited since I was a boy. He fondled his crotch but suppressed the temptation to masturbate. *Save up every drop. Make tonight truly special.*

Repressed childhood memories floated up and bobbed on the surface of his thoughts. Lucid reason, along with deeply ingrained faith in Santa Muerte, felt clouded now. He suffered an annoying condition of conscience and doubt. Some remote voice within told him that it's not too late to turn back.

Is that my conscience? Mercy is for the weak. Pedro Pacheco is the son of a high priestess and cartel overlord. He does not suffer fools. Do not play the fool, Pedro. Be a leader for the Holy Mother of Death. Your parents did well until the silly laws of man defeated them. You're smarter. Stronger. Do what must be done, and all blessings shall be yours; power and strength multiplied for all time. You are an important man, Pedro. Go now to earn your place among the saints.

He pulled to the curb in Norristown at 4:59, parked, and kept the engine running. He placed the roll of hundred-dollar-bills on the passenger seat. He held his .45 semi-automatic handgun flat against the center console in his right hand. One minute later the young man appeared. In his hands, a plastic grocery bag which bore the name and logo of the small grocery store four blocks east. *Smart,* Pedro thought. *Hiding in plain sight.*

"Hola, chico!"

"Set the bag on the seat. Show me." The young man's eyes never left him. Pedro nodded, removed his right hand from the gun, and held out the roll of bills. "Grab it with both hands." When the man complied, Pedro's right hand shot out to grab and pull close the grocery bag. He watched the man thumb quickly through the bills to confirm all hundreds and not a sandwich containing singles in the middle. He smiled.

"Pleasure doin biz wid you, amigo. I'll be here if you ever need a friend."

Pedro nodded. "Put in a good word for you. Maybe you'll get a promotion. May the infinite blessings of la Dama Poderosa protect you." In his rearview mirror he watched the young man write down his stolen license plate number. He laughed. *Nobody gets leverage on me, kid.*

This train of thought led him back to the four labor union enforcers. He made himself a reminder to call in a favor from a former prison guard with police department connections, for whom he'd built a backyard water effect at no charge. *Trace their plate to where they live or work. Duct-tape a few sticks of dynamite underneath with radio-activated blasting cap. Tail them (but not too close, no) until the right moment. Kaboom! Union sent me a message; my reply will be louder and hurt worse. Nobody fucks with Pedro Pacheco. Nobody.*

Dinner consisted of a microwaved entrée inhaled within two minutes. He spent 5:42 until 7:21 perfecting his Yoyo make-up and costume. He finished it off with a spray bottle of scentless mineral oil to affect a glossy sheen. Carefully he inserted a syringe into the vial of midazolam hydrochloride. He pulled on the plunger until it was just over the point-two milligrams line. He flipped it upside down, squeezed out a drop, and capped the needle. He repeated this with two more syringes. Carefully he inserted them points-up into his clown costume pocket. "Showtime," he said. "Time for church. Long overdue, praise Señora de las Sombras."

Sunset over the park fell at 7:41 p.m. He drove from the empty office lot to the equally empty small road behind the park. He opened the empty van's rear doors before plunging through scrub separating the road from the park. He examined the sculpture carefully: its shoulder posture, head tilt, position of the hands and shoes. Satisfied, he scooped up the clown statue. *Not as heavy tonight. Must be adrenaline.* He carried it to the van, set it on bubble-wrap and utility blankets, set his long red clown shoe on the floor and stepped inside. He pulled the blanketed statue snug against the seatbacks up front. He unfurled more blankets until the floor was covered, stepped out, and shut the doors.

On the bench, he sat in Yoyo the statue's former spot. He spent the next quarter of an hour shifting ever-so-slightly to replicate the image fresh in his mind. He felt for the syringes and plastic zip-cuffs. He spent the next ten minutes palming one syringe in his left hand, two in his right, rehearsing in his mind many possible moves. He recalled past behaviors of the girls. Finally, he put his whole self into becoming as still as a statue. Breath control, resisting his body's involuntary need to blink, and to scratch itches. He transformed himself into Yoyo the clown statue. Just before nine, he smelled cigarette smoke. The three giggling, spitting girlfriends were close. *Constancy and predictability led you to me, and to your Santísima Muerte.*

They stood before the bench lighting smokes five feet in front of Pedro. He studied them insofar as park lights from a distance allowed. Brunettes all. One face vaguely reminded him of Monika. *All have yet to develop curves like hers. Boney little things*, he thought. He listened: he heard the word 'Twerk.' *I don't know this word.* He perceived the tallest one to be the leader. She demonstrated for her two friends, popping a squat and erotically thrusting her hips. *How do her jeans not rip? Fitted so tightly; painted on, like Yoyo's.*

"Let's see if Mr. Clown pops a boner. If I can make him hard, all must bow down and worship me!" This was met with loud giggles. The two watched as she paced to Pedro. She turned and shook her ass at him, gyrating closer, until her bottom grazed his knees. *Now or never*, he thought, and flicked the protective plastic cap from the needle hidden in his right palm. The cap fell silently to the grass between the wooden bench slats. Her tiny white sneakers stood a few inches right and left of his big red shoes. She meant to sit on his lap. Slowly, provocatively, she settled down straight onto the point of a needle as he squeezed the plunger. She yelped and spun around clutching her right rear cheek. "Oww, what the fuck!"

"What just happened, Emma?" said one of the others.

"I don't know! A bug bit me? Fuck! It hurts! And, oh my God, I feel strange!" She dropped to the grass on her knees. She stretched herself flat against the grass.

"Emma!" both friends yelled. They rushed to her prone body. They touched her back. "Emma! Are you okay?"

The girl on the ground moaned as though roused unexpectedly from deep sleep. "Oh my God! Maybe she got bit by some poisonous bug, or snake or something! We need to find it and kill it, then call 9-1-1!"

"Why?" asked the other.

"Because look at her, dumbass! If something bit her, they'll need to know what bit her, so they can give her something to counteract it! C'mon, grab your lighter."

"I'm scared!"

"So the Hell am I! If we see it, we'll step on its little fucking head."

Disposable lighter flicked on; Pedro watched the approach of the shaky flame. *They are so scared.* The flame came alarmingly close to his glistening lap. *Will they notice the ruse?* Both knelt before him. They passed the flame over his shoes and the grass under the bench.

"What's this?" said the girl holding the lighter in her right hand, in her left the plastic needle cover. Now or never. They lowered themselves to move their heads underneath the wooden slats; distance between the wood and the ground was about sixteen inches. He popped off the syringe covers in his left and right hands. In the flick of a scorpion tail, he whipped the needles into their backs and squeezed. He felt their heads bump up against the wood before he heard their piqued yelps. By the time they had backed out, Yoyo the clown's indifferent expression had not changed. *The ruse worked!* Noises diminished. The two joined their friend lying prone on the grass before him. *The kid in Norristown lives to enrich the Sainted Mother another day. Good work, ese.*

He searched for and found the three plastic caps which unfortunately blended perfectly with the grass. It took him the full five minutes required for the midazolam hydrochloride to reach full blood-brain saturation in the girls to find all three caps hiding in the lush green lawn. Completely sedated, each moaned groggily as one by one, he spirited them onto blankets in the van. He shut the doors, started the van, and drove home, careful to drive at exact speed limits and to use turn signals. *Get pulled over with this cargo? De ningún modo, ni de puta coña.* He backed the van over his front lawn and left only enough space between it and the house door to enable opening the rear doors. He carried each girl down to the dungeon, shut the van, and parked it normally.

Front door closed, he removed all his clothing except for his clown hat. He thought of removing the face paint and silly red nose. *I want them to know how they came to be guests in my church without words. The rites and rituals can be the only words spoken in the presence of Holy Santa Muerte.* He left his Yoyo head undisturbed. He closed and locked the basement door behind him. Down in his play space, he made his preparations.

Each girl regained consciousness in her own time within thirty minutes of one another; to find herself naked, suspended face-down inside a harness of nylon straps hung from chains attached to the ceiling. Each saw her two other friends in the identical position, as they formed a triangle, twenty-four inches between their heads, suspended three feet above the floor. One sobbed, "Who are you? Why me? I never did anything to you!"

The only words he spoke during their ordeal was his response: "I am Yoyo the clown. The Sainted Mother of Death requires me to take your souls into myself. When eventually the clown dies, your souls will become released to Heaven. This I promise." He wondered if Santa Muerte approved of his benison harvest.

He stepped through pools of diarrhea, urine, and vomit to stand in the middle of them. He knelt. "Santísima Muerte, Mother Death, beloved of my heart, do not leave me without your protection, neither by day nor by night. Illuminate me with your wisdom and comfort me with your love. And when my time has come, by your decree, take me into your arms and carry me into eternal life. Lady in White, Lady in Red, Lady in Black, I place upon your altar this sacrifice and plead for your blessing upon it."

Using the Emma-girl's lighter, he lit a votive candle. On the glass, a human skeleton dressed in a holy female robe, upon her dignified skull a gold crown; one skeletal hand clasped a scythe, the other palmed a gazing ball. "May this image of you be blessed to serve your child who trusts in you. May it bring me and my loved ones peace, prosperity, and hope, safety in our homes and upon our journeys. May we have always a roof over our heads and bread on our table, and all of our needs met. Free the prisoners, heal the sick, and comfort the forgotten with your holy love, O our guide upon eternity's path, and keeper of the doorway into the life eternal. Amen."

He reached outside the circle. His left hand returned holding a hunter's gutting knife. Candle flame glinted from its razor-honed edge. All three girls shrieked and wept piteously. "I believe in the power of Santa Muerte. She is the keeper of the living and protector of the dead. Who sees all things and forgives all sins. Whose authority is vast and her power absolute. I believe in the power of Santa Muerte; Whose judgment can be both swift and sure; I accept your power under the cloak of your protection and ask that you guard and guide me on my path now. Amen."

Pleas for succor fell on selfish ears. "Love has knocked on my door, dear and most holy death, but it has always behaved capriciously with me. I beg you with sadness so that you hear my prayer, feel how my being throbs when I speak to you. That is why I come to you, for only you are miraculous and kind. I want and wish that Monika corresponds to your love, as I love her. I will beg you for the time necessary for my wish to be fulfilled, while I will prove my loyalty offered for your grace with these three unblemished lambs, sacrificed in your holy name and in your honor and to your glory. So mote it be."

Screams grew deafening. *Now or never.*

"Holy Mother, La Flaca, please bless this instrument of divine deliverance." He kissed the knife three times. He stood before Emma, gut-hook knife hand. "I deliver you to Nuestra Señora de la Santa Muerte, with whom you will reign forever as a holy sainted daughter with the most high saint."

His left hand firmly gripped her hair. He pulled her eyes to meet his clown eyes. "Daddy save me! Mommy!"

He placed the knife tip just above her pubic bone and thrust upwards a full inch inside her abdomen until the gut hook was in position. The cruel little cutting cup or 'hook' of the knife was so sharp, meant to open the bellies of dead game without slicing into intestines, it required little strength for him to drag the blade up to her ribs. He studied her eyes. Brain overloaded from the cacophony of pain signals from thousands of nerves severed all at once, her agonized body and hopeless soul gave vent in the form of one long, desperate animal-like howl. Pedro's mind replayed every gruesome, unforgettable scene from his childhood in Santa Muerte, when he was a spectator to every depraved crime committed against children. Tonight, he was the adult in the room, and he executed the priestly role faithfully.

Forced to watch and listen to the sound of internal organs splatting atop the plastic sheet like a thunderstorm of pink-purple eels, expedited by his thrusts, Emma's two friends shook violently in their harnesses. Their piteous attempts to wriggle free of their impending destiny with the blade only fueled his fevered brain. As Emma's body quickly slipped into shock, with even the small mercy of unconsciousness denied by her tormentor's exertions, all heard her last audible words: "I'm sorry."

Sunday, August 28, Pedro awoke in his bed at 3:17 p.m. Vaguely he remembered the nighttime wrapping, the taping, and plastic take-down. He watched himself drive to the landfill in ebon darkness, an expansive, rat-infested gated property to which he held a mag-stripe pass-card thanks to his construction business. Now in bed, his mind relived the muscle-memory of the unceremonious tossing of three bodies, blankets from the van to which human hairs clung, and the trash bag that contained his Yoyo outfit with vial and re-capped syringes in its pocket. *Smart of me to cover the tightly taped packages with asphalt roofing construction debris. Four-dark-thirty, it was. How did I even manage it out there, half asleep in pitch dark with the van lights off?* He remembered the stink of dump on his clothes during the return drive. A fast-fading memory of restoring the original license plate to the van. The hot shower, where dried blood-spatter commingled with Yoyo the clown face-paint in the colorful maelstrom swirling down the drain. He could not recall the climb into bed.

He rose, tended to his oral hygiene, and returned to bed. He was starving. *Any loose ends? Well, there's Yoyo himself. Should I have left him under the shingles, too? Yes. So why didn't I?* He thought hard about the statue of the clown. *Couldn't bear to part with it. Why? Because now it is a Holy Relic? Does it hold three souls until the resurrection from Santa Muerte? I really should get rid of it.*

He called and ordered a large pizza, picked it up, took it home and ate every crumb of it. He washed it down with four cervezas. He went to the van and carried Yoyo to his couch. He rested the statue in the same left-most spot as he had in the park. He stood back to take it in. *What if Monika hears or reads about the mysterious clown statue gone missing the same night as three thirteen-year-old girls from the neighborhood? She's not stupid; in fact, I think her brain is more analytical than mine. Nope. Sorry, Yoyo. Can't stay here.*

With tremendous effort he carried it to the second-floor hallway. He pulled the chain which freed the folded wooden ladder allowing access to the unfinished attic. He worked up a sweat lugging Yoyo up the narrow stairs and pushing him through the narrow rectangular attic ingress. Warm afternoon daylight filtered in through the nine narrow slots of the gable vent. Among the forgotten items he'd stored here upon moving in was a hand-me-down wooden rocking chair. He stepped carefully, finding footing only upon ceiling joists to avoid his leg plunging through pink fiberglass batting like columns of cotton candy, covering weak half-inch ceiling drywall. He set Yoyo into the rocking chair, sneezed seven times, and buttoned up the attic.

7:30 a.m., Saturday September 3, Pedro awoke in his own bed on his left side, right arm slung over Monika's shoulder. He had loved her to completion nine times in four hours, a new personal record. He kissed her neck. Slowly she stirred and rolled onto her back. "Good morning, Chica," he said.

A drowsy smile. "Good morning, chico. Um, is that your hand on my thigh?" He wiggled ten fingers at her. Then he consumed her.

In the sex-filled couple's shower, with water streaming over his face as he got down on one knee: "Monika Pacheco. Will you do me the honor of joining me in holy matrimony?"

She giggled. A radiant white smile. "Mama, he proposed to me in a toilet."

He frowned. "At least I was squeaky clean when I did."

She laughed and pulled him to stand. "I will love you unto death, Pedro. I am the happiest woman on earth in all history, save for our Blessed Mother."

"Santa Muerte?"

"What? No, silly—Mary, mother of Jesus. She has reason to be even happier than I. But I run a close second!"

They made love again, toweled each other dry, and got dressed. "Let me make you bacon and eggs," he said.

She made a sad face. "No, prometido, I cannot stay. My host family are taking a day trip together. I must watch their kid. I'm an au pair; it's my job."

"When will they be back?"

She shook her head. "I asked the same question. They said sometime tonight. Gave me no time. Which means I do laundry, tidy up the place, polish the wood furniture, and deal with the kid until they get back."

He frowned. "Not for much longer. You'll be polishing my verga, mami."

She giggled. "If I can, I'll stop by later. They gave me last night off but I can't stay all night tonight. Maybe just enough time to give you one last polishing of the day so you'll have a better Monday. Everyone hates Mondays, yes?"

He grinned. "Nope. Monday is Labor Day. You must work but I don't. But I do need to see you tonight, and every night. Fingers crossed. Okay, see you when I see you. I'll be here polishing myself."

Giggles as she walked out the front door. "Save some for me, husband!"

He cooked himself bacon and eggs. *Is this what love feels like?* He was cleaning up when a loud sharp rapping at his front door disrupted his reverie like clicking off a light switch, plunging his brain chemistry into darkness. Like chickens when the fox chews into the coop, all happy chicken thoughts scattered. *Too early for Cub Scouts, missionaries or salesmen. What the hell?* He walked to the door and flung it inward. He faced three uniformed Plymouth police officers. One held the leash of a German Shepherd. One thrust a piece of paper in his face. "Pedro Pacheco: we have a warrant to search the premises. Please step aside."

His jaw dropped. "Um, officer? May I ask what this is about?"

"Mr. Pacheco, where were you last Thursday, first of September, between the hours of 7:30 p.m. and 7:30 a.m. Friday morning?"

He thought quickly. "Here, having dinner with my fiancé. She ended up spending the night. We never left."

The officer read him his stolen Wilkes Barre license plate number. "Is that your van parked outside?"

"Yes, sir. But that is not my registration number. Go check it out if you want. Why?"

"A vehicle fitting the description of your van, operated by a driver also fitting your facial profile was caught on security cameras leaving the site of union headquarters last Thursday. Friday morning at approximately 6:30 a.m., the same van and driver were caught on a traffic camera following a union-registered Lincoln Town Car moments before it exploded at an empty light, killing all four occupants. We know about the competitive bid. Who is your fiancé and how do we contact her?"

His eyes wide. "Oh my God, that's horrible! You think a Mexicano driving a white panel utility van is unusual around here? Okay whatever. Monika Sanchez is an au pair. You just missed her. She went to work at the host family home. Today she's alone with their child. I am not allowed to contact her until her employers return sometime tomorrow. Here," he said, and wrote her mobile number on a yellow sticky-note. Call her tomorrow."

"Detective, the dog came up clear on this floor and the second. I found a loaded handgun in the dresser drawer."

"For home-protection," said Pedro. "I'm sure when you did your deep dive into my life before deciding to visit, you saw that I also have a carry permit that's current. I'm a good citizen, officer. Pay my taxes, say my prayers, and I build things; build up this area that I love. You know I own a warehouse on Main Street. Feel free to search it for whatever it is you hope to find."

The officer gave a wan grin. "We already did. Warrant covers both properties. We know more about you, Mr. Pacheco, than you do."

I highly doubt that, praise Santa Muerte.

"We didn't check the attic or cellar."

"Please, if you will, follow me upstairs and I will take you to the attic. Getting inside is a little tricky." He led them to the pull chain. "Please watch your heads." With a yank, the folding wooden ladder unfurled with a clank and clong as its bottom hit the hardwood floor. "Let me poke my head up first in case animals or insects have made nests. Could be dangerous. I've not been in it since the original move-in years ago." He climbed up and looked around.

Yoyo the clown was gone. He stared at the empty rocking chair. "Sir? Please step down. Sir? Now, please." He climbed down. "What is it, Mr. Pacheco? You look like you saw a ghost. Well, sir? Are you ill?"

"It's nothing. I-I…I have a fear of heights. Makes me dizzy. Severe drop in blood pressure. It's fine. I saw no signs of life. Bring flashlights though and please, only step on the wooden joists. I don't mind you guys doing your jobs, protecting and serving and all that. But I swear if you step between the joists and come crashing down into my bedroom, your department, not my insurance company, will pay me a day's labor to repair it."

Four minutes later, the dog carefully scaled down the steep ladder head-first, followed by the officer. "All clear. The cellar, Mr. Pacheco?"

"Of course. Right this way. He led them to the door and flicked on the light. "Have at it." The dog and two officers descended. They were back in three minutes."

"Some kind of dungeon you have going down there, Mr. Pacheco."

He shrugged. "What can I say? Mexican girls like it rough. Which is why they generally don't date pasty-white boring vanilla boys whose hips don't move. No offense."

The Sergeant emitted air like a half-laugh. "Thank you, Mr. Pacheco. We'll be on our way. Don't leave town until we contact Miss Sanchez to establish your alibi."

"I live and work here, officer. Where the hell am I going to go?"

They left. He texted Monika. 'Do not answer calls from anyone except your host family. IMPORTANT. Long story, explain later. Not over phone.'

She responded. '??'

He replied, "Later."

He laid down his phone. "Where in the unholy Hell is the fucking clown?" Face red, fists balled, body hairs standing straight, he searched the house thoroughly from top to bottom. "Fuck! Did somebody steal it? Is someone fucking with my head?"

At 10:46 a.m., he stared at the ceiling above his bed. He found it impossible to hold a thought in his head. Mind awhirl, a sound refocused him to the present. What the hell is that noise?

'Squeeeek, squick… Squeeeek, squick…'

Whatever the source, the unnatural sound was coming from directly over his head. Once started, it did not stop. *Wood squeaks when rubbed under pressure, such as when someone sits in a chair and begins to rock. Not when its stationary, even if someone is sitting in it. But when the rocking begins, so does that hideous squeak. I'm not alone, am I? Whoever's fucking with me is up there right now.* He pulled his .45 and bright LED mini flashlight from the nightstand and tip-toed to the attic pull chain. *Uno, dos, tres*—he gave the chain a tug. Swift and sure, the ladder clanged down. He scurried up, light in his left hand, gun in his right. He peered just over the wooden edge.

The rocking chair was empty.

He killed every shadow in the space with his small but powerful beam. *No sign of life. Could've been wind through the gable vent slats?* He trucked down, slammed closed the attic entrance and returned to his bedroom to still himself, and listen.

"Squeeeek, squick… Squeeeek, squick…'

"Holy la Dama Poderosa, please! I sacrificed for You! I begged for Your blessing! Why? Why?"

'Squeeeek, squick… Squeeeek, squick…'

He laid face-down on the bed. He could smell Monika's presence, her uniquely wonderful pheromones mixed with soaps, body oils, botanical shampoo. He pounded the bed with both fists. "WHY? Why-why-why-why-why-why-WHY?" Her pillow slowly became saturated with his tears. "No! Santa Muerte, no! I asked You to bless our union! I delivered three lambs to You! Mightn't my actions save the idea of an earthly blessing, a normal life to aspire to? Eventually, to become worthy of? Mi Santa!

Whatever may be proven by blood sacrifice must have been proved by now. NO, I said no! No-no-no-no-no-no-no-NO!"

'Squeeeek, squick… Squeeeek, squick…'

Monika pulled into Pedro's driveway Saturday night at 10:09 p.m., exhausted from her day of catering to a spoiled rich little brat and filling her time with physical labor. Her sweaty, swollen feet ached. She felt salty and dirty from scalp to soles. She was about to knock on his door when Pedro opened it. Her eyes opened wide; hands flew up to cover her mouth. "Oh my God!"

He had grease-painted his face white with black eye sockets and black lines down his lips, the visage of a frightening skull. She'd seen plenty of this back home in Day of The Dead parades. But never on an entirely naked man sporting an erection pointing straight up at her. She giggled. "This is different. So, we're in for a night of cosplay. Got it. I'm dressed as a tired working woman in desperate need of a shower—"

He grabbed her wrist and pulled her inside. He shut the door behind him but was too worked up to remember to lock it. He led her to the open dungeon door and never bothered to close it. He pointed up and down, making a circular gesture of erotic impatience. She acknowledged the message with a sly grin. She toed off her shoes, pulled off her blouse and bra, and removed both jeans and underwear in one fluid motion. Naked, he pointed at the stairs. He followed her down. "Really, Pedro. I should shower," she said. "I'm gross."

Silence as he snapped her into the harness. He pulled the chains until she, like its previous occupant, faced down, arms and legs splayed wide apart precisely at the height of his crotch. "Why is there plastic on the floor and walls? What's that knife inside the circle?" More silence. He switched off the lights and lit the skeletal woman votive candle, dropped to his knees, and bowed to kiss the knife. She watched his lips moving but no sound came out. "Pedro, you're kind of creeping me out. Maybe you should let me out of this thing." He grabbed the knife and stood. Unwilling to look at her face, he moved behind her. He knelt and licked. Protest wriggles morphed to something else as his mouth worked its practiced magic.

Relief delivered, he stood and thrust them both to a crescendo from which there could be no return. Pleasure waves would wrack her body seconds from now; he stifled a groan at the earliest warning contraction of his own release. Under her, he positioned the gut-hook knife just below her bottom rib, precisely as he had observed in Mexico throughout his childhood. As they came together, he shoved it up inside her stomach, then smoothly drew it down to her public bone. Bladder and bowels released. Dark arterial blood, gobs of yellow fat, swollen fleshy filaments, and purplish ropey internal organs hit the plastic with an indifferent splat.

"Bless us, Santa Muerte."

8:29 a.m. Monday, September 5, two Montgomery County detectives knocked on Pedro's door. They knocked again, and again. "Mr. Pacheco, the judge issued a search warrant for a missing person, Monika Sanchez. Open up."

No answer. He tried the door handle. It opened. "Oh hell." The fetid funk of decomposition hit them both. Not unused to it in their line of work, yet not at all prepared, both blinked away tears caused by the hydrogen sulfide gases leeching up from rotting flesh. "Straight ahead. It's coming from down there." The lieutenant led the sergeant down the basement stairs, flashlights in hand. The sergeant flicked on the lights.

Neither had ever seen worse. An eviscerated Hispanic female on her back beside her own gut pile, Pedro Pacheco positioned directly over her, his own guts commingled with hers in a repulsive, ropey mass. The officer glanced at his sergeant. "At my niece's wedding, the happy couple each poured different colored sand into a jar and took turns mixing it up. Some symbolic shit, two becoming one flesh, or whatever. Maybe this right here is what passes for next-level love in 2023," he said with a shrug. "What do you make of it?"

"I think you need to lie on the department shrink's couch, is what I think. Seems to be clear what happened here: classic case of murder-suicide," said the sergeant.

The lieutenant shook his head. "Call HQ. Get the crime scene crew out here, stat. Even if they find dissociative drugs in his blood, there is no way any man would summon the strength required to completely disembowel himself like this, cut himself open from stem to stern. Stick himself—sure. But this? A clean straight very deep cut from sternum to groin? No way. This is homicide. My guess is cartel related. Fits their profile."

"You're the boss. I'd bet my pension against yours, but I'd rather just bet you a soda. I think forensics will find only their prints and their DNA, and nothing but. We'll check doorbell cams along this street and the one behind; I think we'll find only these two entered the house." The sergeant pointed to a rocking chair in the corner. "That wasn't here last time. What do you make of that? Creepy the way its eyes seem to follow us."

"You're standing in the worst crime scene we've ever walked into, and a stupid clown statue creeps you out?"

"Wanna hear something funny? When my kids were really little, we took them to a fast-food restaurant. Outside was a little play area. Sitting on a bench was a statue of the restaurant's trademark clown. I told the kids never to come here at night because, after midnight, the clown comes to life and eats children, alive and screaming. I was just joking around but hell if they didn't buy it! Holy crap—my wife still lays guilt trips on me about that.

They cried and lost sleep for weeks. They never wanted to come back to that restaurant. Oops."

Only half-hearing the sergeant's personal story the lieutenant shook his head. He stared at the creepy figure and stroked his chin. "I can't figure out why it's here either. Guess maybe one or both of 'em had some kind of a clown fetish."

Dog

Foreseeing no end to the apparent ceaseless rotation of your species, new physicians assigned to my 'case,' in the hope of possibly sparing myself the draining need of excessive repetition, and to potentially earn myself some hours of unmolested peace: for these reasons, I have decided to fully explain a detailed series of events that took place seventeen years ago, at the closing year of the third lustrum of my life, as I am now thirty-two. I was fifteen years old when it happened. The events are also why I'm locked in here. To save money, the Commonwealth of Pennsylvania wants nothing more than to release me into Section Eight housing on spirit-killing medications. In here, I cost them far more. Please add the recording to my case file, I beg you, so that I need not rehash this again with your replacements next year. It is painful for me to relive it repeatedly.

I will describe certain happenings which defy logic, reason, and all known peer-reviewed science, as well as natural laws. I and my three compatriots who, at the time, were at once participants and eyewitnesses and among whom I am the sole survivor, knew the corporeality of the events with absolute certainty. My recollections are clear. What follows is my eyewitness testimonial, so help me God, under penalty of death and eternal damnation.

I shared the home of my youth with my much older parents. I've since learned that I was the product of a late-in-life office fling between a star salesman and the pretty corporate secretary twelve years his junior. Both had been previously married and divorced. The colonial style two-story house, with brick exterior and two car garage, the home of my youth and, apart from this place, the only home I have ever known roughly divided two neighborhoods of nearly identical boxes. To our left, the Roman Catholic neighborhood, mostly Irish and Italian, with a few British and Polish family names. Every family to the right of our home were Jewish without exception. When I became old enough to ask what religion we were, 'Protestant' was the supplied answer, nothing further. We never attended any church, save for weddings and funerals on rare occasions. My parents never spoke of such matters.

Given the extreme age gap and emotional distance between me and my parents, in many ways, I became forced to raise myself inside that house, within the microcosm of that neighborhood. They never learned how to relate to me or talk to me as a unique individual personality. School, local parks, two indoor shopping malls, and a few outdoor strip malls of stores, punctuated occasionally with visits to a medical professional's office or hospital: such was the extent of my entire world outside the brick box.

Like every other human who ever lived, I wondered, who designed me? Who or what created this world? I believed that I was only just some happy accident of evolutionary forces. What happens when this mortal body dies? Does everything that I am become forever lost? Is it just fade to black, or is there life after death?

I was invited to Catholic 'Confirmation' ceremonies and Jewish Bar Mitzvahs and Bat Mitzvahs, which I attended in support of friends developed both to the left of the neighborhood divide and to the right. Still, I had no answers. I heavily researched Satanism. My parents had to have seen these books on the shelf in my room. If so, neither commented, nor about the demonic posters and blacklight lamps.

My best friends were a mix. I'm sure you can read all about them in my case file. For the sake of this narrative, I will refer to them now precisely as I did then: Johnny, Toadie, Fred, and Missy. They referred to me by my nickname, Juice. The sixth unofficial member of our friendship circle was my father's one-hundred-fifty-pound obsidian black dog, a male Tibetan Mastiff named BB.

Johnny was a big kid, so large and powerful that nobody in the ninth grade would dare mess with him. Toadie, Fred, and I were heads-down, aloof and reserved, rule-abiding, mouse-quiet academic types; skinny, unfashionably dressed, daily targets for school bullies. Missy was a pretty, precocious girl, going steady with different boys ever since the fourth grade. But her dad was dirt poor, and so she always wore ill-fitting hand-me-down clothing or thrift store numbers. Inevitably her cheap couture attracted the attention of the school's Mean Girls—that gender's version of the bullies I, Fred, and Toadie faced in gym locker rooms, boys' rooms, school buses, cafeteria, in classrooms, even down the mall. Bullies turned up everywhere, really, driven by some mean spirit to antagonize, goad, humiliate, and sometimes smack us around. Whenever Johnny caught them in the act he would use his superior size to quickly step in and end it, to protect us, but he couldn't shadow us twenty-four-seven. His interventions would almost always backfire on us. The harsh retribution we experienced caused us to politely ask our 'bestie' to save us no longer. The temporary juice was not worth the prolonged squeeze.

I had started lifting weights, eating protein supplements, and taking karate classes, with the singular goal of getting these bullies off our backs. They were deeply interfering not only with our self-esteem, but they made it nearly impossible to fulfill the purpose of attending school: to learn. At night, I would listen to music in my room and read about Satanic rituals— powerful events that could arouse and convoke eldritch spirits from another plane, invisible and unknown to mortals willfully ignorant of their existence.

It was then that an idea formed.

Fred and Joel, callow, highly intelligent and studious boys, quietly sat together on the bus, listening to a soundtrack of 'Kikes!' 'Heimies!' 'Dirty Jew boys!' 'Your ancestors killed Jesus!' Sometimes, the bus bullies brought blowguns: tubes of notebook paper rolled up and taped closed, along with a supply of paper cones with sewing needles or pins taped into the cone-points. I, Fred and Joel, often experienced the pain of dirty needles projected at high velocity into our necks, scalps, shoulders, arms, thighs. Sometimes the bullies brought large paper clips, which they would work back and forth until the metal broke, creating two 'U'-shaped projectiles, fired from large rubber bands. These mostly only stung when they hit, but sometimes the 'U' would turn mid-air and jagged prongs stuck into our skins. Bus drivers knew exactly what was going on. I'd catch their eyes looking straight at me through the big mirrors angled above their heads. None ever said a word.

The biggest and baddest of all antagonists was a thickly muscled, tattooed Italian kid they called Razz. Back then, no way could anyone under age seventeen get a legit tattoo, so he used a needle and India ink on himself. Second was a tall brown-haired boy who went by Ray-Ray. Third was a platinum-blond-headed boy named Roadie. They were my own personal devils throughout my youth. I think all three were hold-backs, meaning they had failed a grade somewhere along the line, maybe even two grades. Built like men, hairy like men, deep voices like men. They punched like men. Truly none had any business enrolled in a public school system. They vented their failures on us. I hated them with every fiber of my being.

I have since become a very sincere 'Born-Again' Christian, and I have forgiven them, along with everyone else who ever wronged me, including my absentee parents. It feels like some immense iron weight has been lifted from my soul. Forgive your enemies. Everyone should try it. Bet they don't preach that in psychology courses.

But at that time, learning of the three boys' painful, lingering deaths would've given me great joy—the more excruciating and torturous, the better. Each belonged in prison or in a grave, and mostly, either outcome is what I had wished for every single day.

I ran my idea past Fred and Joel. Initially, both seemed reluctant. I researched and informed them that within the Jewish Aggadah, a demon is believed to be a spiritual entity that may be conjured and controlled; a helpful, protective spirit to the conjurers. Between their doing some reading on their own and my incessant pestering, eventually they arrived at that same conclusion. Johnny, a devout Roman Catholic, expressed strong doubts. He was a confident, curious fifteen-year-old boy who never pretended to have all the answers, but about one thing he was certain. When I told him that Fred and Joel were into my idea a hundred percent, he declined emphatically. A very emphatic 'no' from the very Catholic Johnny.

"Pretty sure Jesus doesn't want me dancing with devils, Juice. Sorry. Can't do it. I'm out," decision firm. When I told Missy that if this works, she could be rid of the Mean Girls forever and have a bit of fun in a ceremony, she assented to my idea with zero hesitation.

I'd said to them, "First, we'll need a private place for a few hours. We'll need a few props. Hammer, nails. A wooden crucifix. Black 'Grim Reaper' cowled robes. Wafers made of turnip slices. Plenty of black candles and something to light them with. A wooden bowl. A gong. A temporary table with a black cloth on top. And music, preferably organ music, like Bach, or de Grigny. Right now, I have a hammer and nails, but that's it. I'm willing to go see if I can spend some of my lawn-mowing money on black candles and a wooden salad bowl. I'll check the mart and discount stores."

"Me and Fred are Jews," said Joel. "Crucifixes aren't exactly our thing, Juice. But mom has dark turnips. I can slice one and dry the slices. Also, she has a card table where she seats little kids during Thanksgiving and Passover Seder. I'll bring it."

Fred nodded. "I buy rock music every week down the mall. I'll look for cassettes with those names or ask for something similar. I have a portable cassette player. I'm a section leader in the school band. I'm sure the director will let me take home the small gong for one night if I ask."

"I'll ask Johnny to go the Catholic store where his mom hangs out all the time, and buy the largest wooden crucifix he can afford," I said.

"What about location?" Joel asked.

"Been thinking about that. You know the abandoned, dilapidated old house on the Pike with the 'Condemned' sticker on the door?"

"Dude, no way," Fred said to me. "Kids don't go there. It's supposedly haunted."

I smiled. "That's the point. Nobody ever goes there because they're afraid of it. We'll be completely safe."

"I heard from a friend, Jeff the druggie, who claims he and his buddies broke in there once to sniff glue, that the wood floors stick up in places from decades of water dripping in from the wrecked roof. He said if they had walked inside any further, they felt they might crash through to the cellar." Fred shivered. "God only knows what's living down there."

"I'll go in first, check it out. I'll walk BB over this weekend, bring a flashlight, and completely check it out top to bottom. Ought to make you feel better," I said. Fred nodded.

We four shook hands. My crazy idea had now morphed into a real plan.

The condemned house fronted a major four-lane highway. Built sometime in the mid-nineteenth century it had sat unoccupied for over a hundred years. Rotting clapboard over a crumbling, water-loosened stone foundation. Gray slate tiles made up the roof, most of them now smashed into bits on the firmament beneath the eaves; others had fallen inside through holes in the roof. Wood clapboards showed ghosts of ancient white paint peeking through the dense overspread of fungi and poison ivy. Entire board sections had peeled away in places. Some misshapen understory shrubs partially obscured the view from the Pike. There was no drive-able entrance. Any oil and chip driveway that may once have existed had disappeared long ago. The small, once-cleared area around the building long ago had become overgrown with wild and unchecked weeds, grass, and poison ivy shoots.

Amazingly, most of the windows still contained opaque, unmolested glass panes. The fact they weren't smashed was probably owed to the fear factor of the place, as in, to do so would bring only bad luck. To the right and behind, for several hundred yards stretched expanses of scrub woods ranging from wet and boggy to actual swampland. Once, I ventured onto that land with my friend to explore the bogs. The ill-conceived adventure was us lugging a molded plastic kiddie pool to use as a makeshift raft, and paddle across the swamp, for bragging rights. Kevin, my partner in this venture, stepped on what appeared to be leafy ground, but suddenly he disappeared instantly up the neck. Quicksand. Panicked, I pulled him out, and we ran out of there, never to return.

With BB leashed, that clear and starry Saturday night, armed with a flashlight, I walked him over to the Pike, then walked right. A minute later we arrived. The place was a five-minute walk from my parent's house. Windows stared down like vacant black eyes in the bleak gray moonlight. An air of stern, deep, and irredeemable gloom hung over and pervaded all. The quiet solemnity struck me: no nightbirds chirped, no insects ground out their lonely lover's chirps and buzzes. BB stopped, tongue out. Must've been hell for him on that warm July evening, trapped inside his exceptionally long, thick fur coat. I believe he stopped because even he sensed the unceasing, malignant radiation of despair that hung about the place like a black hole sun. He turned home and tried to pull us back in that direction. Nevertheless, mindful of the bullies, and my friends, I put the mission first. I tugged his leash, and reluctantly, he followed me onto the poisonous property.

I tried the front doorknob. Under me, it felt like the wooden stairs might crack. The door was locked and the lock appeared solid. Also, from where I stood, I would be easily spotted by drivers whizzing along the Pike behind me. "Let's go around back, shall we, boy?" I said to BB. There were two ingresses: the locked door I had just tried in front, and one around back. But near the back door, I spotted steel cellar doors rusted to an unusable, unsafe condition. I tried the back doorknob. No movement. I gave it a kick, with all hundred-seventeen pounds of me at the time. The crack of rotted wood echoed back a little way into the swamp, and the door exploded inwards without a struggle. I recall wishing my friends had been there to see my great strength, though a third grader could've done it with a doorframe so rotted.

Jeff the glue-sniffer, friend of Fred and Joel who had allegedly been here before, had passed along to them an accurate and just description. In the area penetrated by my flashlight beam, the wooden floor had suffered more than a century of water damage, parts of it split and sticking straight up like pungi sticks, just waiting for someone of dim eyesight or unsteady balance to step on them, become trapped, and die. All furnishings were gone. This room had once been the kitchen. Rusted steel cabinets underneath a rusted iron sink. I could see that treasure hunters had long ago stripped out all electrical and plumbing fixtures, copper water pipes, and electrical wires that could be sold for scrap. Plaster and wood lathe walls were slowly decomposing onto the floor in gray mushy piles, revealing behind them a skeleton framework of termite-infested wood.

The dank, oppressive atmosphere felt miasmal and molten, as BB and I breathed in dust, along with bat and rodent dung particles. At any moment, I expected to surprise some animal, but I knew BB would growl and bark if he heard any signs of life. His silence assured me that, for now, we were alone. Cautiously, I stepped around the sharp wooden stalagmites with BB in tow. I made my way into what was once the main living room. I could see the inside of the front door. Overhead, large holes in the ceiling revealed glimpses of a black sky over-sprinkled with star points. A staircase with entire middle risers and treads missing led up to the second floor. I decided it would be impossible and unsafe for me to explore up there. I checked out the room, tested every section of floor with my weight, and left footprints in more than a hundred years' worth of dust and desiccated rodent turds. I kicked aside fallen chunks of ceiling plaster and wood. I concluded that the room would suit our needs, safe and secure for our ceremony. We would, however, need to bring a folding table. "Okay, BB. Hate to say it, but we need to check out the cellar." If he had not been there with me, the place would be so scary that I could never have summoned the courage to enter.

Back in the kitchen, I shined my beam down the cement stairs into the cellar. The right wall was decaying stone, held together with a horsehair and limestone mortar. From behind me, ears perked up, BB moved to the fore, something dog trainers tell you never to do, something about you being the alpha out in front, and they must be taught to obey their beta follower place. Though in this case I believe, since Tibetan Mastiffs were bred eons ago for human protection and livestock herding, BB was going down first to protect me. He must have heard something. About halfway down, he started that low, menacing growl of his. Fear permeated my spine. Every hair on my skin stood straight. Three-quarters down, clear of the plaster wall to the left, my light perceived at least fifty tiny pinpoints of white light reflected from the tapetum lucidum, which helps animals see better in the dark.

Rats. I shivered as I panned the light around. Hundreds of them. Probably for the first time ever, BB and I disturbed their safe space, the local rat communal nesting and breeding environment.

When my dad had first brought home BB, before he sent him away to a professional dog trainer where he learned to obey German language commands, BB once crashed through our front screen door to attack the postman. Worse, before they started keeping him in the house all the time save for walks, BB chewed through his outdoor chain and escaped. Dad drove around for hours until finally a neighbor spotted him, called my house, and dad came and scooped him into the station wagon. But before he did, BB had killed every cat the neighborhood. Not killed: shredded. He was very gentle and tolerant of us, but we all acknowledged that our little protector also had a very dark aspect to him.

That night on the cellar stairs, I could feel him reverting to that vile version of himself. Before giving him the chance, I shouted, "BB! Geh raus!" His simple beastly mind obeyed without question. His jaws snapped shut. He pivoted and ran back up the stairs so quickly that I nearly tripped trying to keep up. It did feel empowering to know that no bully would ever hurt me with BB by my side. He would die before letting anything happen to me. He would never turn against me or my pack of familiars. This I believed without a worm of doubt.

It was a Friday night, September 22, 1989, under a Last Quarter Moon, only the left side lit, which gave my little patch of the world forty-six percent illumination. School had started weeks ago and with it, so had the bullying.

We had waited until this night, the Fall equinox, in the belief that it might be significant in the spirit world, if such a world exists. Halloween, which would take place five weeks later, was started in ancient Gaul by druid priests celebrating the Festival of Samhain, also the autumnal equinox, a time of magic when the spirit world moved closest to our world. Celtic timing was far off. My well-researched calculations were dead on.

Each of us had a later curfew if we all remained somewhere in the neighborhood, which was true—we were, sort of—in the condemned house on the Pike. Each told our parents we were heading to the other's house first and might jump between houses depending on what games we decided to play. Zero push-back from any parent. I had packed candles, wooden matches and bowl, hammer and nails, and the crucifix Johnny had supplied into my school knapsack, along with pieces of notebook paper where I had written down every correct word and deed required for the ceremony. Thinking ahead, I also packed a small straw whisk broom and bottle of rubbing alcohol. Fred brought the small gong, also the cassette player with music. Joel's parents had this light-but-sturdy card table with folding legs, not easy to carry, but he managed to schlep it to the mansion, baggie of dried turnip slices in his pocket. Missy scored four cowled robes from the drama club at school, also a black plastic tablecloth. She squeezed it all into her book sack, wrinkled but serviceable.

Missy was thoroughly grossed out by the filthy floor and interior of the abandoned house, as I had figured. Once the candles were arranged on what remained of the fireplace mantel, I bent and swept the dusty moldering rat droppings and plastered chunks out of the main area into a corner, then soaked the floor with the alcohol as a sanitizing agent, more for Missy, but I too was grossed out. At least the liquid partially reduced the volume of particulates from rat dung and mold making us sneeze.

"Unfortunately, we need to be naked under the robes, which means, barefoot."

"Oh, hell no—I'm not changing in front of you guys!" Missy screeched.

"Change outside behind the house, then come back in wearing sneakers. Take those off here in the safe zone. We'll change here. Say something before coming back in; we might not be finished yet."

Brows furrowed, she glared at me. I broke the stare and continued with set-up. With no further argument she grabbed her robe, a flashlight, and picked her way back through the kitchen, and out. Quickly, we three boys stripped off all our clothes and draped the robes over ourselves. "How do I look?" asked Fred.

"Like the grim reaper with albino salmon feet," I offered. We all got a good chuckle out of the simile. I set up the card table, draped Missy's black plastic cover over it, then stood back to take it all in. "Now we assign roles. Fred, you are Deacon. Joel, you are Subdeacon."

"What am I the sub?"

"You want to be the Deacon? You and Fred all say the same things. I don't care who's Deacon."

Joel looked at Fred, whose eyes dropped to his pale toes. "Yes, Juice. I'm Deacon," said Joel.

"Ready or not, here I come!" Missy called out from the kitchen. She joined us, slipped off her sneakers, and stood in our circle. "I was listening. So, Juice, what am I?"

"Nun," I said.

This really cracked her up. "Oh, if my granny could see me now. She always wanted at least one priest and one nun among her grandkids."

BB, obedient as ever, sat outside by the back door to keep watch. If anyone else should enter the property he would alert us with barks. I don't think he would attack without one my German commands. Animals, however much we wish their motivations were human-like, are unpredictable. In each, there exists a primal wildness.

"Okay guys, let's get serious, now. This is as no-nonsense as church, Missy. Or temple, guys." They copied my somber expression.

"The table is the altar. When I bow, you bow. Here—" I handed two of my papers to Joel. "Deacon and Subdeacon: when I look over at you, say the words together. If you struggle with the Latin bits, it's okay, but pretty much how it looks is also how it sounds. Got it?" All three squinted at my handwriting in the dim light. Each looked at me and nodded. "Ready?" I asked.

"Ready," all three answered.

"Tonight, we are too few and too inexperienced to call in the 'Big Guns.' I think we have a far better chance of calling on the pre-Islamic Arabian god, Yaghuth, god of strength and war, who had an idol that was a statue of a lion. We'll ask Yaghuth to send us a Jinn, to help us."

"Is that where the magic genie in a bottle comes from?" asked Missy. "Thought I'd read that."

I nodded. "Good, Missy—correct. The Jinn are supernatural beings who personify and control minor natural phenomena. These are spirits of the wilderness and the inhospitable forces of nature. Jinn inhabit stones, trees, the earth, space, the air, fire, the sky, animals, and bodies of water."

"We don't have three wishes for this genie," said Missy. "Only one."

"Get these bullies off our backs," said Fred. I nodded.

I caught Missy's eye and pointed to the gong: she hit it. I pointed to the cassette player; she hit PLAY. "Deacon to my left, sub to my right," I said, as we approached the makeshift altar. They took their cues from me, and thus we three bowed almost in complete sync. I said, "In nomine Magni Dei Nostri Yaghuth. Introibo ad altare Domini Terra."

Fred and Joel read from their sheets. "Ad eum qui laefificat meum."

I said, "Adjutorium nostrum in nomine Domini Terra."

They responded, "Ui regit terram."

I said, "Before the terrible and ineffable Yaghuth, and in the presence of the gods of the Ka'aba, and this assembled company, I acknowledge and confess my past error. Renouncing all past allegiances, I proclaim that Yaghuth rules the earth, to whom I consent, and renew my promise to recognize and honor him in all things, without reservation, desiring in return his manifold assistance in the successful completion of my endeavors and the fulfillment of my desires." I glanced left and right as a cue. "I call upon you, my brothers, to bear witness, and to do likewise."

Fred and Joel repeated what I had said, but added, "We call upon you, his liegeman and priest, to receive this pledge in his name."

I said, "Domine Yaghuth, tu conversus vivificabis nos."

The deacons said, "Et plebs tua laetabitur in te."

"Ostende nobis, Domine Yaghuth, potentiam tuam," I said.

They answered, "Et beneficium tuum da nobis."

I spoke at a higher volume, "Domine Yaghuth, exaudi meam."

In normal volume, they responded, "Et clamor meus ad te veniat."

Again loudly, I said, "Dominus Yaghuth vobiscum."

At normal volume they responded, "Et cum tuo."

I said, "Gloria Deo, Domino Terra, et in terra vita hominibus fortibus. Laudamus te, benedicimus te, adoramus te, glorificamus te, gratias agimus tibi propter magnam potentiam tuam: Domine Yaghuth, Rex Terra, Imperator omnipotens."

Pointing to the 'chalice,' which consisted of my wooden bowl filled with Joel's dried turnip slices covered with a strip of black plastic, I uncovered it. I held the wafers out in front of me at eye level. "Suscipe, Domine Yaghuth, hanc hostiam, quam ego dignus famulus tuus offero tibi, Deo meo vivo et vero, pro omnibus circumstantibus, sed et pro omnibus fidelibus famulis tuis: ut mihi et illis proficiat ad felicitatem in hanc vitam. Amen."

I dropped turnip slices back into the bowl. I held the bowl away from me at eye level. "Offerimus tibi, Domine Yaghuth, calicem voluptatis carnis, ut in conspectu majestatis tuae, pro nostra utilitate et felicitate, placeat tibi. Amen."

Respectfully I set the bowl back on the altar, my hands turned palms down. "Come, O Mighty Yaghuth, god of the Banu Madh'hij, of the Banu Khuza'a and Banu Quraysh in the Hijaz, bearing the names Abd-Yaghuth and Abd al-Asad in your honor, and look favorably on this sacrifice which we have prepared in thy name."

I turned the 'chalice' seven times counterclockwise and bowed very low before it. I raised it three times to the inverted crucifix nailed to the wall behind the altar. My glance at Fred and Joel hit the mark: we bowed as one. They followed me as I circumnavigated around the altar seven times counterclockwise until again, we stood before it in our original positions. I glanced at Missy, held up seven fingers and pointed to the gong, which she rang seven times, perfectly spaced. She allowed perfect vibration between each contact. Again, we three bowed low before the chalice.

"Yaghuth! Yaghuth! Yaghuth!" I yelled. I gave Missy three fingers, and she repeated herself perfectly.

"Therefore, O mighty and terrible Yaghuth, we entreat you that you receive and accept this sacrifice, which we offer to you on behalf of this assembled company, upon whom you have set your mark, that you may make us prosper in fullness and length of life, under thy protection, and may cause to go forth at our bidding thy dreadful minions, for the fulfillment of our desires and the destruction of our enemies. In concert this night, we ask thy unfailing assistance in this need. The students, Razz, Ray-Ray, Roadie…"

Fred first, then Joel, named their school antagonists, two apiece. Missy named eight different female students.

"We beseech thee, O Lord Yaghuth: we are strong of spirit but weak of body. Send us a Jinn, and bless your warrior with unfailing determination, and with might, and with courage. Defeat our enemies in your world. Render it no longer possible for them to harm us. In the unity of unholy fellowship, we praise and honor you, and all the nameless and formless ones, the mighty and innumerable hosts of your realm, by whose assistance may we be strengthened in mind, body and will."

I held up one finger to Missy, who banged the gong, I then extended my arms, palms down over the chalice, and said, "Hanc igitur oblationem servitutis nostrae sed et cunctae familiae tuae, quaesumus, Domine Yaghuth, ut placatus accipias; diesque nostros in felicitate disponas, et in electorum tuorum jubeas grege numerari. Shemhamephorash!"

The deacons said, "Shemhamephorash," which they seemed to recognize from their Jewish readings. Opaque recognition formed on their faces.

"Enlightened brother, we ask a blessing." Joel read notes I'd made and raised his eyebrows. He brought the chalice to Missy.

"Pee in it," Joel whispered. He handed her the bowl. Missy stared at me with a mixed expression of deep surprise, doubt, and mistrust. I narrowed my gaze, pressed my lips tightly together, and nodded once at her. Clearly, my leadership 'aura' made it an imperative for her. Advanced this far into the serious and somber ceremony, she refused to disappoint her alpha, and the powerful spirits a part of her hoped he understood. She squatted over the bowl and positioned her robe so that none of us could see anything. I could tell she was pee shy. Who could blame her? We three turned our backs to her.

"Deacons, join me here and face the altar, as I am." After twenty more seconds we heard the first squirts, then a good hard stream. "That's enough, sister," I said. "Deacon, bring the offering." Appearing somewhat embarrassed, Missy moved back and allowed Joel to grab the pungent bowl.

Chalice back on the altar, I said, "She maketh the font resound with the tears of her mortification. The waters of her shame become a shower of blessing in the tabernacle of Yaghuth, for that which hath been withheld pourest forth, and with it, her piety. The great Yaghuth, who is in the midst of the throne, shall sustain her, for she is a living fountain of water."

Joel said, "And the Lord Yaghuth shall wipe all tears from her eyes, for he said unto me: It is done. I am Alpha and Omega, the beginning and the end. I will give freely unto him that is athirst of the fountain of the water of life.''

Joel squeezed his eyes and held his breath as he reached into the bowl. He did not want to touch Missy's urine, that was plain. Dutifully he withdrew several turnip slices, reached under his robe, touched the dripping wafers to his boy-parts, then followed instructions perfectly. He shook droplets at the east, south, west, and due north toward the inverted crucifix. After each he said, "In the name of Yaghuth we bless thee with this, the symbol of the rod of life.''

Taking the wet unholy host from Joel in both hands before the altar, I said, "Hoc est corpus Jesu Christi''—the ultimate blasphemy and disrespect. It means 'This is the body of Jesus Christ.' I shudder now to think of this part. I was an ignorant kid armed with a bit of occult knowledge, yet I had zero insight into the source of real power. The Holy Bible contained all the power I needed but I'd never read it, thus I had zero baseline understanding of the true natures and depth of the powers I was invoking. Or more importantly of the loving God I so blithely blasphemed and disparaged.

I tore the wafers in half. "Hic est voluptatis carnis.'' I pointed. Missy struck the gong once. We circumambulated the altar seven more times, stopped, and bowed low to it.

All of us froze. What happened next made the blood in our veins coagulate. An infinitesimal, barely perceptible flash or brightening of candlelight. Pungent vapor of sulfur stung every eye—then gone just as quickly from the stale room atmosphere. From outside came an alien, unnatural sound. I remember the image of some extinct gigantic reptilian thing flashed to mind. Was it BB making such a frightful and odious growl?

I slipped on my sneakers, grabbed the flashlight, walked as quickly as I could through the dangerous minefield of spikey flooring until I reached the back door. I shined the light around the back door and property as far as the beam could reach in all directions.

BB was gone.

These events I have related accurately. I consider them the first milestone as they suddenly brought an abrupt close to the first great epoch of my life. I have heard it postulated that childhood is over the moment when you first realize you're going to die. I disagree. Mine ended September 22, 1989, at the age of fifteen. The first casualty was my father's trust, also a measure of his love for me—of this I am convinced. I arrived home to face parents who were still up watching TV in the living room. "Where's BB?'' my dad asked.

I told him that when we all walked the Pike over to the strip stores past the abandoned mansion, BB took off towards the swamp. We fanned out calling his name. Partially true story; I was able to look my father in the eye.

Face beet red he jumped up, cursed me out, and repeatedly jammed three fingers against my chest. He grabbed his keys, clawed my neck, pulled me into his car, and made me ride around with him searching for the dog. At two in the morning, he gave up. It was non-stop beratement the entire ride. I wanted so badly to sleep, but I felt so filthy inside and out. I had to shower first. After, pretty sure I was unconscious before my head had even hit the pillow.

The next morning, the moment I set foot downstairs he grounded me for two weeks. He removed my house landline phone, TV, and stereo privileges. He rode around alone, stapling photos of BB with our phone number, and drove a sheaf of leaflets over to the SPCA. He placed an ad in the classifieds. Not too many Tibetan Mastiffs in our County. My mother assured him daily that the dog would turn up. For me, life consisted of bullies on busses and in school, then solitary confinement in my room, which wasn't so bad: I had my school assignments, but then also I had my shelves of occult books and practitioner manuals. At school, Fred, Joel and Missy acted consolatory over my situation.

That first Wednesday following the ceremony, I came home with a black eye and bruised cheek. Ray-Ray and Roadie waited for me in the boys' room between classes. They each held an arm behind my back. Razz slunk out of a stall, grinning. "I told you last week to bring me twenty bucks or I'd kick your ass. Where's the money, Juicy freak?" I lowered my eyes. Razz wound up and uncorked a closed fist straight right to my left eye. My head snapped back. I semi-recovered my posture when he unleashed a roundhouse right to my cheek. I may have passed out a little, because when I came to, I was alone, face squashed against the filthy urine-soaked linoleum tiled floor.

I wept. Boys entering the bathroom stepped around me. No one offered to help. That night, my mother expressed sympathy and asked how it happened. "Elbow in gym class, no big deal."

Flash forward to the following Tuesday. Still no sign of BB. My dad grew increasingly morose, which of course set my mother on edge. I spotted Razz in the hallway but made a quick directional diversion to avoid him. His acolytes, Ray-Ray and Roadie, were nowhere to be seen. I found this odd, since they all had the same remedial-level classes together. Wednesday arrived. I had to go to the bathroom. It would've made me ten minutes late for my next class had I walked all the way over to the other bathroom located on the upper floor, so, I held my breath and went in, fully expecting to get jumped again. I had a Boy Scout pen knife in my pocket and clicked it open before the door fully closed behind me. Empty. Maybe things were looking up. If BB turned up, at least things would be stable.

My mother was in the kitchen. Every Sunday she cooked a pot roast with potatoes. Mondays would be leftovers from that meal. Tuesdays she'd fry leftover roast with onions and potatoes and call it 'roast beef hash.' Wednesdays would be leftover roast with mashed potatoes and gravy. No one could stretch a piece of meat like that woman. Wednesday, I ached for something to eat other than roast beef and potatoes. My dad, watching TV, called me over. "Did you know any of these boys?" Looking at the news alert, I saw an aerial view of a ballfield surrounded by trees and scrub which I recognized. A municipal park near our school. Yellow police tape, talk of 'murder scene,' what looked like a body under a white sheet.

Their full names rolled across the ticker at the bottom. I knew them as Ray-Ray and Roadie. Their bodies were discovered in the woods near the ball field. Likely time of death was sometime yesterday afternoon. And there it was. My worst nightmare, Razz, got himself killed today walking home from school. Homicide detectives asked for tips.

"I asked if you knew these boys," dad bellowed. Unable to speak, I glanced down at him, nodding slowly. "When your curfew ends, I want you coming straight home after school."

"For how long?"

"Until I say so!" he practically screamed.

The only opportunity to regroup with my deacons and nun would be at lunch. Typically, we'd split up and sit near 'cool' kids in a vague hope that it might increase our stations a little in the minds of our antagonists. Today, we huddled together as far from everyone as possible.

"Oh…my…God!" said Missy. She covered her wide-open mouth with both hands.

Fred and Joel appeared grim. "We did this," said Joel. "I know we did this. Somehow."

"How were they killed, does anyone know?" I asked.

Fred nodded. "This hasn't been released to the public. A woman in my dad's law firm is friends with the District Attorney. He asked me if I knew these students and made me swear to ultimate secrecy, but I must tell you two. All three had defensive wounds on their hands and arms from trying to keep dogs away. Keyword 'dogs.' They don't believe that only one dog could have done this. The first traumatic injury was to the face and throat. Most likely, Ray-Ray, Razz, and Roadie were pulled to the ground and mauled to death. Puncture wounds on their skulls align with animal bites. They are no longer treating this as a homicide case. They're casting a search for a pack of stray dogs, combing every wooded area, riverbanks, yards with junk cars and refrigerators—anywhere a pack of feral dogs could hole up."

Missy started crying. She covered her face. I grabbed her wrist and shook her arm until she turned her bloodshot eyes to me. "You need to focus. We all need to just calm the hell down!" I spoke softly but forcefully.

"I didn't mean for anyone to die, Juice! Swear to God, I never would've agreed to this—"

"Missy, but you did agree to this. We all wished death upon these enemies at one time or another, am I wrong? Search within yourselves, and don't lie! I know I did. I wanted these monsters dead. I wasn't willing to go to jail for it, but if I could've stoved in their skulls with a hammer in shop class and nobody would ever find out who did it, hell yes. I didn't know death would result from what we did but guys—I'm not entirely unhappy about it, either. I thought…well. Mostly I only wanted to scare them off. To get some revenge. It would've pleased me just to know they got scared and humbled by Yaghuth and his Jinn. Too distracted to beat me up all the time, and you too Fred, and you, Joel. I never expected this."

"Juice! I named eight girls! Eight girls!" yelled Missy. I noticed heads turn.

"We have to warn them," said Fred, voice tremulous, though I could tell he was trying to be the cool-headed voice of reason.

"Freddie, listen to me for a second. Are you listening?" Fred nodded. "One: nobody will buy our crazy story. It's like a fantasy. They'll only tell you to stop playing video games so much. Two: how could your warning keep them any safer or change their behavior any better than their own parents? My dad wants me coming straight home from school," I said, and looked at all three. "Don't yours?" They nodded. "Same with these girls. All parents are now scared for their kids because of what BB did."

Fred hitched a deep breath. "I didn't get to the worst part," he said. Joel, Missy, and I snapped to full attention. "Whatever killed them, ate them. The cop told my dad the bodies looked like a lion kill in Africa, or a piranha attack in South America. Plenty of skin and some organs are just gone. Not like vultures had time to feast. Whatever killed them…it also ate them, alive and screaming. Juice, I've known BB since he was a pup. Not the friendliest dog, but he'd let me pet him because I'm a member of your 'pack.'"

"Same here," said Joel.

"Right," said Fred. "We know BB doesn't have this in him. We're all assuming, based on identity of the victims and timing, that it was BB. Telling you, he does not have this in him."

I sighed. "Pretty sure BB isn't alone in there, if he's even still there at all. The thing running him *we* invited in. We invoked an old powerful desert god to send us whatever terrible thing now lives inside BB. My dog is no more."

"Well, what are we gonna do?" Missy asked. "We can't just do nothing!"

At that time, I knew nothing of Christianity, about exorcists and demonic possession. I was a boy and thought as a boy. "We need to hunt BB down and kill him before he hurts someone else."

"But you said he's not BB—"

"Yes, Joel, I know what I said. I'm hoping the thing inside BB will go back to wherever it came from when the host dies," I said. I buried my face in my hands. "I can't stand to hear myself say it, you guys. My dad freakin' loves that dog. So does my mom. You know I love him more than anyone. He's my sole protector. I feel like crying at the thought of killing him."

"*People* are dying, Juice."

"I know, Fred. I know."

"I have an idea!" said Missy. We all turned to look at her. "Let's find and capture him, you know, in a net or a crate or something."

Fred shook his head. "Maybe you weren't listening. He killed and ate the two biggest, strongest, and meanest guys in our school when they had the advantage of two-against-one. You want to get eaten alive?" Missy lowered her eyes and withdrew.

"When my curfew ends, my dad wants me home every night anyway. I'm out. Not unless I sneak out my bedroom window," I said.

"Borrow your dad's shotgun first. He's taken you shooting before. You know how to use it safely. Dude, I watched you kill squirrels and birds with your wrist-rocket. One look at that blood-soaked killing machine, I know you'll do the right thing when you—when we—find him."

"And how are we going to do that?"

As if waking from a deep trance, bashfully, as we had attacked her last brainstorm, Missy whispered, "Shadow the eight girls."

As I was sentenced to school followed by house arrest, I left it to my deacons and nun to follow around Missy's accursed eight. It took them three afternoons and evenings to nail down all eight predictable patterns. Never once did all these girls congregate together. Three had parents who carpooled them over to one house, where the two living nearby always walked home. After family dinners, three would meet up and walk to the popular ice cream hangout where high school girls went to flirt with older boys. They'd go there to watch and learn how by watching older girls. Wooded areas separated their neighborhood from the ice cream store.

Two girls played middle school sports and rode the after-school activities bus; it dropped them off about a one-fifth mile walk to their homes. The other three were party girls with same-age boyfriends, none old enough to drive, whose main activities involved bicycling to shadowy public parks and wooded overlooks to make out. I had to act. It was impossible for me to anticipate the next move of a dog that wasn't a dog. I sat near this cabal and listened carefully to them at lunch; I could see these foot and bike routes in my mind, each familiar to me. Where would BB find the least interference from potentially harmful adults?

That evening after another apathetic, sullen, testy dinner with my parents, I announced that I had a ton of homework and a few tests tomorrow, so if they call up and I don't answer I was either deep into textbooks or asleep. Enroute to my room, I slipped into their bedroom and snatched dad's twelve-gauge pump-action shotgun from under their bed loaded with eight triple-aught buckshot cartridges. In my room I discovered that the gun fit almost perfectly in my cloth hockey stick bag, which had handles. New-level nervous about the mission, yet my leaden conscience could not possibly support any more deaths, especially of girls. I opened the window, removed the detachable screen, placed the large aluminum hooks from the emergency fire escape rope ladder over the windowsill, remembering dad's one-and-only fire drill when I was twelve. Carefully, quietly, I lowered the chain ladder until taut. With stick bag in hand, I carefully made my way down and jumped off onto terra firma. It felt like a prison break. My lower belly and soles tingled with excitement.

I figured, since BB last struck during mid-afternoon daylight hours in a park near the school, he must favor wooded settings. I ran away from my house until I was clear of its sightlines, then walked on busy roads at a brisk four miles per hour until I closed in on Borough Hall. In a straight line it's not quite a mile from home, but unless I cut through an active farm and residential neighborhoods, I had to take the long way using roads and streets. The municipal building had a play area behind it with swing-sets and park benches. It was well-rumored to be a make-out place, hemmed in by Scotch Pines and dense evergreens.

I stood at the far back of the parking lot between two pines. From there I had a clear line of sight to the mulched playground about 150 feet ahead, well-lit under bright halogen lights. Beyond that tiny square of light, everywhere else, including where I stood, was jetty black. I found an old stump to sit on, eyes glued to the playground. I waited and swatted at hungry mosquitoes.

Soon I saw girls holding hands with boys, talking in a huddle. I heard giggles. They split up into couples. Two hid in the little plastic enclosed area at the top of the sliding board, two sat on swings pulled together to face each other, and two squeezed onto a little riding pony held aloft by a thick spring. The kissing commenced with enthusiasm. Hands grasped and pulled at each other's bodies. I felt a little voyeuristic at that point, having to remind myself that my presence was protective, not selfish. Briefly I thought of Missy and wondered what it would be like sitting with her on the swing set in a simpler time before our infernal ceremony.

Out from the blackness left of the playground, I saw what appeared to be a large moving shadow. From this distance it appeared filthy, ebon black fur matted and clumped with dried gore, mud, and sticks. Around its lion-like neck hung a simple thick metal chain.

BB's unmistakable neck chain, tattered leash still attached to it like a useless anchor. Even from this distance I recognized an aberrant new quality in BB's eyes: bioluminescence. BB's chilling eyes were fixed on the kids making out on the pony. This wasn't white light reflected from BB's tapetum lucidum: it was otherworldly blue, like dancing flames inside mini blue lava lamps. Slowly it crept toward them, muscles coiled like that of a large cat stalking prey. The gap between BB and the couple was now only thirty-five feet, and closing. No sound whatsoever, only lips peeled back to reveal canines and incisors, long and yellow.

Core animal fear infused me like at no other time in my life. For a few seconds I froze, until adrenaline kicked in. Bag unzipped, I pulled out the shotgun, racked a round and took off toward the playground. Too late: the dog covered the distance in a few bounding leaps and pounced on one of the couples. At night under halogen lighting, colors become distorted: black blood jetted from both throats. Screams. BB's unnatural raptor-like growls. He pulled the couple from the swings and chewed their throats wide open, then bolted up the slide into the five-by-five plastic square with large holes in the sides. I lost sight of him. Shrieks. The awful sound of flesh ripped and rived. Desperate gurgling. Too late to save anyone. I aimed the shotgun at the square, finger on the trigger. Blue, cold-smoldering eyes stared out at me. Gently like dad taught me, I squeezed. A mule kicked my right shoulder, yellow flash, loud boom. I knew echoes from the blast could be heard miles away under that cloud-shrouded atmosphere, could hear them ricocheting around.

The eyes disappeared after I squeezed off the shot. I distinctly heard a yelp, and police sirens. Nearby, six dead or dying humans. Self-interest got the better of me. Course reversal. I grabbed the stick bag and trucked as quickly through the pines as I could, bearing frequent whacks to the face and scratches on my arms until I came out the other side into a cornfield. Between the rows I traveled, until sirens faded a little. I hopped the farmer's wooden fence out onto the road, then followed a mazy course of residential streets until I reached my house. The ladder remained; relief swept through me. I clambered up, stowed the hockey stick back in the bag, hauled up the ladder, returned it to its box in my closet shelf, restored the screen, and closed the window. Some creative use of a flagpole and paper towels soaked in ammonia window cleaner made the gun seem unfired. I hid it under my bed.

I laid down but sleep never came.

At lunch the following day, I told them my story. They had already heard about the attacks at Borough Hall. I was past the point of panic. I felt emotionally drained and despondent. The yelp of canine agony still rang in my ears. "Also, cops found two freshly discharged shotgun shells at the scene, so now they are patrolling the area asking everyone if they saw someone last night armed with a long gun, asking for the public's help."

"But they didn't find a dead dog," I said.

I felt dizzy. Missy said, "Juice, there are the two neighborhood bus stops. One or both will get hit next."

"I can't bring a gun and can't clone myself. You three must pitch in this time. Fred and Joel, you two, cover one bus stop and follow behind the girl to her house. Missy, you come with me."

"If you couldn't kill the damned thing with a shotgun, what the hell are we supposed to use, Juice? Karate chops?"

"I hit him, Fred. Ever hear a dog yelp when you step on its foot? I heard that after the shot."

"But he walked away," said Joel.

"Right. It wasn't a kill shot. It was dark. I'd just witnessed him chewing six people. Maybe I only winged him." The thought came to me all at once. "Spears will kill BB. We can hang our school flags on them to divert unwanted attention. Dip them in holy water."

"What are you, a holy roller now? You're a Satanist, or have you forgotten?"

"Saw it in a movie. Many movies. Who knows if it'll help. Johnny gave me a small bottle once, told me to drink it if I ever felt possessed. He thinks I'm nuts regarding matters of faith and religion. Anyway, Fred, Joel: can you find some shovel handles and sharpen the ends into points? And Missy, can you go in the booster's or band's closet and pinch us a few school flags, and a roll of duct tape?"

When I got home from school that night, I told my parents that I had been up all night studying, and the tests sapped me of energy. I grabbed a banana, held it up, "dinner" I said. "Shower—bed—goodnight." I did shower. Then snuck out as I had before, small vial of holy water in my pocket. Slipped to the ground and met up with my deacons and nun at the agreed-upon rendezvous point. They had arrived slightly before me and taped the flags to the sturdy spears. Steel handles at the ends added leverage. I could sense everyone's nervousness rivaled my own. I dripped Johnny's holy water onto all four needle-sharp points. "How'd you do this?" I asked Joel. "These spear points are like needles."

"My dad's surform tool. Pretty sharp, right?"

I tapped a point, "Ouch! Excellent job, Joel!"

Each took a spear. Missy and I broke left, Fred and Joel headed straight. Missy knew the bus stop location and led me straight to it. A glance at my cheap chrome digital wristwatch. "Six o'clock drop-off, right?" She nodded.

"Scared?" I asked Missy. I'll never forget her eyes, so pretty, so vulnerable, as she nodded. I reached out my left arm; she moved against it. Tentatively I pulled her close. She rested her head on my shoulder. This was the first and only time I had ever been touched by a girl who was not my mother or a medical professional. It felt so incredibly good. Years later, at first, I tried to block out the memory. But as time wore on, I found it to be the only memory I still cling to when at my absolute lowest points. She and I stood like that, hearts thumping together like two pistons inside one engine, until we heard a bus revving up from first gear on its approach to the stop. We hid behind her flag to avoid getting recognized. We watched four girls deboard, "Which?"

"The two tallest are the ones I named in the ceremony."

We gave them a ten-pace head start, then I followed. Missy was behind me. I scanned everything. Spaces between houses, behind parked pick-up trucks and vans, rows of dense holly bushes—anywhere the dreadful miscreant could potentially lie in wait. It was still bright outside, though purplish colors of twilight formed in the western sky. I could hear blood rushing in my ears.

BB charged full speed at the girls in the middle of the street from the opposite direction. He launched. For a moment he appeared to fly, like bat or bird in a high arching slow-motion glide. He tackled both to the ground and quickly ripped open a throat before he pounced on the other and silenced her piteous, horrified screams. Missy cried out, "Stick it! Stick the fucking thing!" I screamed and ran directly at him. His movements were so unpredictably powerful and herky-jerky that, aiming straight for his chest I managed only to bury the tip of the spear in his meaty right rump. Like getting a needle at the vet, he barely seemed to notice. He froze. The big bloody head inclined toward me. A close look into its eyes revealed—there was absolutely zero question—that something blue and unnatural fulgurated therein. Our eyes locked momentarily in silent communication. The message I received curdled my blood. It ran off with the slightest right-favoring limp.

He was saving me for last.

The next day at our lonely spot in the cafeteria, Missy broke down in a violent spasm of crying. Everyone stared. Instinctively I came around to her side and draped my arm around her shoulders. I sensed adult lunch monitors were about to move on us and intervene, so hysterical was Missy. Perhaps they'd seen boy-girl breakups and drama before. They chose to leave us be. It went on for minutes. Finally, she said, "A minute before it got our two, it got the other two girls a few blocks away."

"I am so sorry, Missy. For everything. You can't know how sorry I am. I got you three into this but it's all my fault, not yours." I barely got the words out before she melted down. This time the lunch ladies descended on us. Missy managed to squeeze in one final statement before they carried her off to the school nurse.

"Juice—it also got Fred and Joel."

Home from school, I pocketed one of mom's larger kitchen knives from the wooden block, pulled my shirt out to hang over it, and called Missy's house. "Hiya, Juice. I'm in bed. My parents are worried that I'm sick or something. I lied. I told them I'm having really bad menstrual cramps."

"Uh-huh. Got it. Listen, Missy. I need you to forgive me. Do you think that maybe you can do that?"

She said nothing. I could only hear breathing. "Did you hear that?" she whispered."

"Hear what? No."

"I heard, or more like felt something move under my bed."

I whispered, "You're imagining things. We're under a ton of stress." Silence. "There it is again!"

"Look under the bed Missy, you'll see it's nothing."

I heard what sounded like a bare foot slap down onto wood flooring. Otherworldly growls. Screams. The sound a dog makes when it chews a bone. Phone clack as it hit the floor. Dial tone."

"Is everything all right?" my mom asked.

I affected a smile. "Sure is, ma," I said. I slunk out from under her suspicious gaze and up to my room. Thirty minutes later, I heard her scream. A round chambered into a shotgun, immediately followed by a blast. Demonic growls. My father's choking death-gurgle.

On numb legs I somehow managed to stand. I slowly cracked open my door. The eyes of a species not of this realm locked onto mine. Teeth bared, no sound. A dog's smile? Or the mirthless, sick smirk of a demon? It leaped. I held out the knife. It knocked me to the floor. Vice-like jaws snapped inches above my face and neck. I thrust the knife upward into his throat. I felt the blade part tendon and sinew, possibly bone. It must have nicked the brain. I pulled it out to make ready for another strike. As before when I wounded it with a shotgun pellet, and again later with a wooden spear, it did not yelp. It ran in circles. Eyes flickered between unearthly blue and the kind, dumb brown eyes I had once known, and loved.

I ran outside wearing only my tighty-whities, slamming doors behind me. The shotgun blast had prompted neighbors to call police; a cruiser screeched to a halt in my driveway. Behind it arrived four more, lights flashing. They saw a near-naked teenage boy grasping a bloody knife. Naturally they pushed me into the back of one of their cars. One officer remained outside while seven entered my home, guns drawn. Neighbors gathered to watch the show. Enroute to the station, I asked the officer if my dog was dead. "What dog?" he replied.

DNA criminal evidence usage was only four years old and not yet ubiquitous by the time of my trial in 1990, but they had it perfected just fine. The knife had contacted enough dried blood of BB's victims to help convict me of seventeen counts of second-degree murder, Dangerous Dog, and other felony and misdemeanor offenses. The police and court did not believe my story. I was a minor. A court-appointed psychiatrist watched my initial interrogation video and testimony under oath. He diagnosed me as criminally insane. The judge handed down a sentence of twenty years-to-life in Norristown State Hospital. I got to join the one hundred and thirty-five-patient forensic unit, where criminally committed patients live our lives, here in Building Fifty-One. They block the windows and skylights so we can't see the moon. But many inmates know anyway. Full moons here are predictably colorful. Until I landed here, I never knew that the ungenerous label 'lunatic' had everything to do with lunar gravitational pull upon diseased minds. Now I know.

You are here to evaluate me for a possible release in two years. They need to make room here due to budget cuts; I get that but know this: I assume BB died long ago, but the thing he carried inside him can never die. Once released into the world it travels through waterless places until it finds a suitable host and completes its mission. I am the last of its original targets. If you release me, I will die horribly, which perhaps I deserve, and that entirely will be on you. But there's no telling what my body would do to others with that thing pushing me out and exchanging itself for my spirit. I pray to the merciful God who lives in the perfect Heaven that bends above us to forgive me, show mercy on me. To take my soul unto Himself after the demon finishes me, and its diabolical calling.

Now that you have evaluated me, doctors: know that I have faithfully given you the whole and complete truth. I'd prefer to remain here, if preference matters. By reading this affidavit you very well might have inadvertently made yourselves part of the thing's orbit. I pray not, but please be watchful out there. Avoid dangerous dogs.

Casilda

Caracas, Venezuela
1631 AD

"You see, way off in the distance, the curved shape of the horizon?" Juan Ramos swept his hand from left to right and back. The air was a balmy seventy-two, still morning, hours before the sun would force them indoors behind thick stone walls and clay roof tiles. "You see twelve miles to the horizon. To that, add eight more miles, then square it in all directions. That is how much fallow farmland I own. The mountain, Avila, has washed gold down from the motherlode, but also so many nutrients to the plains that anything will grow here. I meant, farmland that *we* own, Casilda, my love."

Brown eyes, white blouse with gold-thread embroidery and Mandarin collar over bright and immaculate form-fitting red breeches, and thick brown wavy hair brushed to portrait-perfection made him appear regal in her dark blue eyes, so blue that they appeared gray, at times. The reality of it hit her for the first time: that this kind man pursuing her might also be powerful and connected. She knew him as the sweetest most charming man she had ever met, gentle to everyone, polite, articulate, educated, and worldly. A man loved and respected. A man used to getting what he wants. As the scope of it crept through her thoughts, her eyes opened wide and pale little hands covered her mouth. "Oh my God, Juan! You really *are* rich! You say anything that you sow will thrive here? What if you plant *me* in this dark, happy soil—will I grow up all over again? I do plan to live forever, you know."

With a smile he lightly tapped her straight and delicate European nose. "Land-rich, my love, only this and nothing more. I am an inheritor of my family's land and gold mine claims here, white Creoles a few generations back from noble Spanish families, like yours too at one time. With no prospect of inheriting a title themselves, bravely they set out to create titles for themselves here in the New World, in Venezuela."

He took her hands. "I don't care about titles, save for one: Mister Juan Ramos, husband and father. That suits me just fine. Soon the page will turn, and it will be the seventeenth century. The world is changing, my love. In Europe, they are growing quite infatuated with cocoa; next I am certain it will be coffee. I will bring forth the precious beans from every inch of our land. Europeans, especially Parisians, will pay us dearly for it.

"My family's gold claim is yielding less by the year. What I can pull from the ground just about covers the cost of maintaining the slaves, and myself. These magic cocoa and coffee beans that sharpen the mind and please the tongue are as precious as gold in Europe, and beans are a mine that will never run dry. Then, wife-to-be, we will become *truly* rich, wealthy beyond our wildest dreams. We will travel the world together, raise a family together, and give thanks to the Christ we both adore. We will live happily ever after, oh Casilda! New World nobility. I shall be king; you will be my queen. We will love no others, and be the strongest team there ever was. Nothing will stop us, God willing. You have my solemn oath."

A tear traced down her left cheek. Gently he wiped it away. She threw herself on him, buried her head against him, comforted by the heart beating soft and low behind his muscular chest. Twice her age, a girl of eighteen, she had never felt so safe and warm, not since her father had been murdered by the jealous mate of a teen girl from a local indigenous tribe, when she was eight years old. Her mother never spoke of it. Eventually, Casilda grew to understand the full meaning of her father's infidelity.

"Not that I care how she feels, but this would make my mother so happy, Juan. It was always her dream to see me married off to a good, gentle man," she said.

He hesitated before responding to a matter he knew was delicate. "It is unusual that in all this time, still you have not introduced me to her. It feels wrong, highly improper. Perhaps you feel ashamed of me."

She broke out in raucous laughter.

"What's so funny?"

Voice muffled against him, she said, "Maybe I am ashamed of her, have you considered? That witch believes I am cursed. That maybe a good man could help make me into a good woman. I never could make sense of it. I am chaste and virtuous. I have never been with a man. I've never even kissed a boy until you, that is. I did everything she told me to do, except go to church, I mean."

"Really? Why on earth would you not go to mass?"

He felt her shrug. "I don't know. I think it's boring. Their incense stinks; it makes my eyes burn and throat close. Their statues have scared me ever since I was little. She tried to make me go. I left home to live in your friend's home as a governess to escape her."

"Hmm. Disappointing. I never miss mass. I didn't know this about you, Casilda. I would not ask you to do anything you did not truly want to do. You will have to go to church at least once, of course, for our wedding ceremony."

Sighing against him, "Yes Juan. I know."

Silently he held her. "You do love God, too, don't you?"

"If I must share you with an invisible God, then so be it."

"And children? You will give me many sons and daughters, and we will dress them like little dolls and raise them in the church?"

"Many. Ten, twenty. Why not make it fifty? We will create our own village."

She could sense him smiling as he patted and soothed her back. "Maybe your mother knows you better than most. Maybe my skinny little queen has a big fat temper. But no worries, certainly you will not be the world's first temperamental royal elite, nor the last. Remind me not to spoil you. Which gives me an idea: perhaps I should put you to work alongside my house slaves, Dayhoo and Tanna. I need a wife with a strong back. Besides, you are so pale and thin. You could use a little sun on your shoulders and some wiry muscles."

Playfully she slapped his left cheek. "What was that you said…something about pleasing the tongue?" she cooed in her most seductive tone. She pulled his head into a very long, eager wet kiss. They stood exploring each other's mouths for many minutes. His right hand furtively slipped beneath the white folds of her cotton dress. Fingertips probed the satiny smoothness of taut leg skin as she respired into his mouth. Her moans emboldened and intoxicated him to a dripping froth. Up further his fingers climbed until the tips grazed the hair of her pudenda and then pushed further.

She jolted backwards and smacked away his hand.

"Not until I'm married, sir!" she said, straightening her dress, cheeks flushed, eyes misted from passion. She glanced down at the raging bull in his pants aching to burst through the matador's red cape with singularity of purpose.

Reaching down into his right pocket he withdrew his hand and closed it quickly before she could see what was in it. With Mont Avila to his left, the vast expanse of his lands spreading out before him to his right, nine o'clock sun in his face exposing all the little nicks where his African house slave, Dayhoo, had shaved him earlier, he got down on one knee. Yards away his white stallion whinnied, which Casilda took as a sign that the animal knew what was coming and was excited about it. He extended his right hand to her palm-up and flashed open his fingers. Looking down, she saw the most beautiful solid-gold ring she had ever seen, intricately tooled in the shape of two doves joined together in a golden eternity.

"Casilda, I waited this long to marry because I knew that one day, the angels in Heaven above watching over me would send me one of their own, whose innocence, charm, and beauty had never before walked this earth, a divine seraph at whose ethereal feet I would bow down to kiss and to serve. To give my life new meaning, whose life and honor I would spend all the rest of my days protecting with my own life, sacrificing to her every ounce of strength in my being. I love you with something more ecstatic than love, Casilda. Please make half a man whole, until the Good Lord lifts my spirit from this rock, only to await you on the other side where I will prepare a bed of clouds and a throne of gold and rose petals for my beloved queen in the next life, so that we may never part for but an instant. Will you marry me, Casilda? Tomorrow?"

Hands covered her mouth. She muttered something he could not hear.

"I'm sorry my love, what did you say?"

She burst into tears, smiling broadly, nodding rapidly. "Yes."

After making an immodest donation to the bishop to rearrange several schedules, the next morning at the Caracas Cathedral, together they blew out their unity candle, exchanged vows and rings, and the priest pronounced them man and wife. It was only the three of them, as Juan was the last in his line and trusted few; also Casilda seemed determined to estrange her mother from their new life together. They walked outside. "Casilda, there are two loves of my life that I would happily die for. One is God, the other is you. I gave you my heart today, entrusted it to you. If you should ever tire of it, then it is your property now. Do with it as you please."

After her father's untimely murder by the native boy, it had been a great struggle for his widow to raise a daughter alone, just the two of them living in the simple mud-walled house. Her mother earned income by hanging tobacco in barns at a nearby farm. Casilda left to work as a governess for a landowner's children. Today, leaving that entire scene behind, she felt overcome with the spirit of renewal, rebirth into a new and exciting life. "Your heart is my heart, Juan. And this ring, the most perfect ring ever in the history of the world, is also mine. Your lands, our future children, your beautiful home, your slaves, horses, everything is now mine. But I would gladly trade all of these for one thing right now," she said. She mounted her steed.

"Oh? You would trade my heart and everything I own in this world? For what?"

She did not smile. "Teach me to love people. I never learned how."

"Your slaves have homes somewhere?"

He nodded. I built quarters for my field slaves including a single unit for my overseers."

"What about the house slaves? Are they beautiful?" He ignored the question and rode quietly for a time. "You seem protective of these two. Maybe a little in love with one or both. Infatuated at the least."

"Casilda! Is this jealousy I hear?"

She pulled on the reins of Tigre, her Spanish jennet horse, compact and muscular with patches of spotted white, and so Juan did the same with his larger black charger. An abrupt stop in the middle of the earthen road. Riding side-saddle, she slid off and stood. "Juan, let me make one thing perfectly clear. Are you listening?"

"What is it, my love? I don't understand, you're scaring me a little."

It was her eyes, untamed, fixed on his. "You say your heart belongs to me. All your other organs are mine now too, Juan. If you ever so much as look at another woman with lust in your heart, if I ever catch you, I will burn you alive."

"Dear Lord! Who is this demon talking to me right now? Please, you should have introduced me to your mother before I wholeheartedly decided to marry the adorable angel I have grown to know and love. Whoever you are, go away."

Gradually, her face softened. "I just refuse to share you. I'm sorry if that hurts you, Juan."

He held her hand as she remounted. "Please believe me, Casilda, I am honored beyond words that you love me so fiercely. And we will never have to worry about anything like that, because there is room in my heart and my life for only one woman, now and forever. She is a gift from God, and I will always treat her as my saving grace."

They rode the remaining miles in silence.

Home, after a quick meal of oysters, bread, milk and coffee, he sent Dayhoo and Tanna off to the further reaches of his estate. "You sure you and the missus don't want us to draw you a bath, Master Ramos?" Dayhoo said.

He raised his hand. "No thank you," he said with a smile. "Come back in the morning to fix us breakfast." Casilda shot him a look. "Wait, Dayhoo? Come back Monday morning to fix us breakfast."

"Well sir, what do you plan to eat until then?"

With a wink at Casilda, "Each other."

Dayhoo burst into hearty laughter, thick jowls, pendulous breasts and tree-trunk arms jiggling and heaving along. She joined the far more diminutive Tanna at the mouth of the path that would lead them to their quarters for the next two nights.

"Well now, Master Ramos. You have me all to yourself. I remember a line from your Bible—"

"My Bible?"

"Wives should submit to their husbands in everything. Well, to what would you have me submit?" she said, chin down, blinking eyelashes as thick and long as miniature brooms.

Juan's sleeping brain heard the voices grow in volume as Dayhoo and Tanna walked the path back from the slave quarters. Spanish chattering, but then too some other language foreign to his begrogged, half-awake brain. Gradually it brought him to full consciousness. He was on his right side, Casilda's back curled against him. He smiled. *God, thank you, thank you so-so much for this gift rivaled only by your saving grace*, he thought. When the downstairs door slammed, he realized the bedroom door was wide open. With heavy regret, he decoupled from Casilda, jumped up and ran over to slam shut the door.

"Master Ramos, Missus Ramos, we're going to draw you a nice hot bath then while you two get yourselves a nice soak, we're going to empty the chamber pots and take that bedding down to the river for a good washing. Before that we'll fix you some bacon and eggs, buttered toast, some juice and coffee, and then you can decide where we go next. Is that good for you?"

"Yes!" he shouted down, more like a croak. His mouth and throat were bone dry. He glanced back at her, naked and curled atop his bed. He smiled. Hands in a prayer tent he jabbed them heavenward. "Thank-you my dear sweet Lord!" he said aloud. From below, he heard giggling. He felt the brief flush of embarrassment.

"Husband, come back to bed," said Casilda. "Your God can wait another hour."

Smiling, "Casilda, my love. We haven't eaten anything since Saturday evening. We are both filthy. Dayhoo and Tanna are back as ordered. Please be a dear. If I stand here watching you lying there for one more moment, surely, I will go crazy and leap back into bed."

"So then do it!"

"No! We must eat now, sorry, I insist. We cannot go on like this without food. Also, it's Monday; I must ride out to the slave quarters and set expectations for the week. They are used to seeing me every day."

"Send those two back to set expectations."

"My darling, if you only knew what it takes to get the best out of these Africans. Come on," he said. He grabbed a large white cloth from iron hooks set into the wall plaster and opened it like a flag to wrap around her. He then wrapped himself, and together they stood just inside the door, listening to the sounds of hot water splashing into the copper tub from buckets.

Their first bath together should have been long and luxurious. She could sense his unease, distracted by thoughts of business. Already she could read his body cues with the sensitivity of a house cat. Breakfast was voluminous, enough food to feed four, which the two scarfed down completely in under fifteen minutes. Casilda burped. They both laughed.

"I'm pregnant," she said, to which he broke out laughing.

"You're laughing? Why is that funny, Juan?"

Still snickering, he managed to say, "Because my love, it cannot happen that quickly. I have observed the slave women. They know when they are pregnant because their breasts enlarge, their taste sensation is different. They feel hot most of the time and they vomit frequently at first. All of this takes time; weeks after their bulls service them. We just made love for the first time twelve hours ago. That's why I'm laughing."

"I know things. Don't ask me how because I've never been able to figure it out, and I've never told anyone. I'm afraid they would think me a witch. I know with absolute certainty that I am pregnant. I can even tell you the sex of the child. Would you like me to—"

He held his right index finger to his lips, his left hand in the STOP position.

"So, then you do believe me, that I know things. Otherwise, you wouldn't care what I said next."

Shaking his head, he said, "No. I'm just…superstitious sometimes. I don't like to say things that could jinx the future. Does that make sense?"

"Not really. I've always known you and that I would marry, from that very first time that our eyes met at the Encinas estate, I knew. And here we are. Do you doubt me?"

He patted her hand indulgently. "I would never doubt you, my love. I hope your vision is true. I don't care if it is a boy or a girl, if our first-born is healthy and has ten fingers and ten toes and one beautiful head, and hopefully your amazing eyes, then all is right with the world. And Casilda, if your vision is wrong," he said, as he drew circles now on the palm of her hand, "then I promise you we will have fun as we keep trying to get you pregnant."

She did not smile back, nor did she blink. "I am right," she said. She arose and walked away.

He followed her upstairs. She paused at the landing and stared down at him. "Go do your business." She massaged her temples.

"What's wrong, my love?"

Her right hand shot to the balustrade to support herself. He could see a tremble in her legs. Quickly he bolted up two stairs at a time until he stood behind and supported her. It was then that she collapsed back against him. Hefting her eighty-five pounds was easy for Juan; gently he set her on the naked mattress as the slaves had taken the sheets and pillowcases down to the river.

"Close the curtain, the light hurts my eyes," she said, and he did, then rushed back to her side.

"What is it? Should I go fetch the doctor?"

She let out a groan. "No! Do not! Physicians have never understood what is wrong with me. Whenever this happens, they put leeches on my arms to drain away my blood, talking nonsense about body humors. It's awful. Don't ever let them do that to me!"

"Shh. My love, I would never. I only wish that I knew what was wrong so that maybe I can help."

"Pain, unbearable pain in my head, sometimes. It aches worse than anyone can imagine. I don't know what triggers these episodes. Sometimes it's only for a few hours, other times it lasts days. I've not had one of these dark episodes, that's how I think of them, since I've known you. Maybe it was our first argument just now, over my pregnancy, that triggered it."

"Shh." Lightly he stroked her taut forearm. "I am truly sorry that I ever doubted you. I will never doubt you again, my little witch."

Hearing that, she chuckled through the pain.

"Can I get you some spirits, perhaps? A bit of wine may help."

"No, please. Just go do what you must. Keep those slaves out of here. I mustn't be disturbed until this pain episode passes, however long it takes. When it's over, I'll find you. Promise me you won't stop loving me over this."

"Casilda, oh my dear Lord, I can never stop loving you, ever! You own my heart, remember?" For another minute he sat with her quietly, aching to touch her, soothe and comfort her. Seeing her like this, tortured and twisted by some unseen malady was driving him mad. He could not force himself to think about work, not now. "Whatever this is, your mother must have learned ways to help you through it. It's decided: I shall ride into town to introduce myself to her…I will elicit treatment advice from her."

Eyes squeezed tightly shut against the pain opened and stared. "Juan, I swear, if you go to her, I will burn you alive. Now get out!"

"Push now, Missus Ramos! I've midwifed for exactly two hundred and seventeen births and I ain't never seen one so well positioned, head down and ready to breathe. PUSH!"

She knelt between Casilda's spread legs. Tanna squatted behind her head, holding down her arms. "Breathe!" Dayhoo commanded. She rubbed Casilda's swollen belly in a loving, motherly fashion. Casilda obeyed, comfortable with Dayhoo.

"Let me go you bitch or I will skin you alive!" she shouted at Tanna who ignored her. Casilda's pale thin forearms remained clutched in powerful brown hands as secure as irons. Tanna glanced over at Dayhoo, who understood without words. Both women had participated together in many births among the slave community—this Creole birth serving as a first for both—yet neither could imagine such fixated anger on any person trying to help another.

Reaching into her apron pocket, Dayhoo secreted Juan's shaving razor down between Casilda's legs. In one deft move, she inserted the blade into her narrow birth canal and just as quickly withdrew it with just the right amount of downward pressure to make a cut so clean that Casilda did not scream. Dayhoo pocketed the razor and poked three fat fingers inside to feel the baby's crown. "Push girl, now's the time! Child's coming! Only just needs a little push from mama, now PUSH!!"

Casilda did push, pushed with every ounce of strength. She wanted it out of her. That quick, a baby along with an umbilical cord and bloody gore plopped into the practiced brown hands of Dayhoo. Again, using the razor, this time with Casilda watching, she cut the cord. Tanna released her vice-like grip on Casilda's wrists and handed Dayhoo the copper basin of water and clean cloths. "It's a boy, Missus Ramos! You and Master Ramos have a son! Master!" she screamed. "Come on up!"

Juan found Dayhoo and Tanna standing at either side of the bed, a wrapped bundle on Casilda's linen-covered chest, cradled in her arms. His mouth hung open. "Is everything… did everything…"

"Relax, Master Ramos, it was a perfect birth! Mother and baby are fine, just fine! Now, we two are going downstairs to give you three a little time alone. But I still have some work to do." She held up a small needle and thread. "Give you ten minutes then you call me back up, say yes, Master Ramos?"

He nodded, "Yes," he muttered, and slowly approached the bed. The two women padded downstairs carrying a basin filled with things he did not care to think about. He sat on the edge of the bed. Tenderly he brushed sopping wet hair from Casilda's eyes. She had locked eyes with the baby, dark blue like hers. "Son."

"I have a son!" he shouted, then heard the two women clapping and whooping down below. "May I hold him?"

Unsmiling, she nodded once. Gingerly he gathered the delicate treasure from her chest and pulled the bundled baby in his arms. Little blue eyes scanned Juan's face, which led to his first little toothless grin. "All of this is yours, my first-born son. You are a prince of men, born of a mother half human half divine, and your name shall be Hector Agustín Ramos. And you shall be called 'good' in the eyes of our Lord."

Juan handed him back to Casilda. She pulled down her linen cover to expose her left breast. Juan sat fascinated as the baby instinctively found the nipple and sucked away for the first time as if he had done it a thousand times before. Juan leaned down, kissed her forehead, and whispered, "He inherits my lands, dear wife. But you will forever own my heart."

"What name do you give your child?"

"Hector Agustín Ramos, father," responded Juan, speaking for both he and his wife, who seemed unable to find her tongue. Juan cast a panoramic glance around the interior of Caracas Cathedral. Before the main altar this early Sunday morning he and Casilda stood, along with his best friend and Casilda's former boss, Mateo de Encinas and his wife. There were also several local peasants kneeling and praying, strangers to Juan and Casilda, but on several levels it comforted him to have them there, witnesses to the baptism of his son. That Casilda's mother was not present gnawed at him incessantly.

"What do you ask of God's Church for Hector Agustin Ramos?"

"Baptism," said Juan.

"You have asked to have your child baptized. In doing so you accept the responsibility of training him in the practice of the faith. It will be your duty to bring him up to keep God's commandments as Christ taught us, by loving God and our neighbor. Do you clearly understand what you are undertaking?"

Juan glanced over at Casilda, whose mind appeared to be elsewhere. "We do," he answered.

"Are you ready to help the parents of this child in their duty as Christian parents?"

Mateo and his wife responded in perfect unison, as though they had practiced many times, "We are."

"Hector Agustin Ramos, the Christian community welcomes you with great joy. In its name I claim you for Christ our Savior by the sign of his cross. I now trace the cross on your forehead and invite your parents and godparents to do the same."

Juan traced the cross on his son's forehead. Casilda made no move to do the same. Mateo's wife went next, then Mateo. Visibly frustrated, Juan grabbed Casilda's hand, forced her left index finger out straight, and used it like a paint brush to trace the cross on Hector's forehead. Mateo and wife exchanged worried glances.

After the homily and litany, the priest called for a period of silence while all pray. Next came the intercessions which occupied several minutes of the priest's prayers and attendant responses in which all participated, save for Casilda.

It came time for the prayer of exorcism and anointing before baptism. "Almighty and ever-living God, you sent your only Son into the world to cast out the power of Satan, spirit of evil, to rescue man from the kingdom of darkness, and bring him into the splendor of your kingdom of light. We pray for this child: set him free from original sin, make him a temple of your glory, and send your Holy Spirit to dwell with him. We ask this through Christ our Lord."

Casilda shrieked, the sound of it unnatural to every ear. The priest repositioned himself momentarily, leaned over, and whispered to Juan, "Is there a problem here, Mr. Ramos?"

Juan appeared stricken. "No father, I apologize. My wife is having a difficult time lately. I fear that the birth of our son has somehow filled her with melancholy."

The priest narrowed his eyes. "Physicians can treat her for this. Mercury may help. Bleed off some of her black bile with a little bloodletting. If you really believe that melancholy is what possesses her."

Juan glared back. He spoke through closed teeth. "I'll see to it. Now please, can we get on with it?"

The priest resumed his position and glared at Juan, until he gathered himself. "We anoint you with the oil of salvation in the name of Christ our Savior; may He strengthen you with his power; He who lives and reigns for ever and ever."

"Amen."

After celebration of the sacrament, the priest turned to the font and said a prayer. Casilda coughed out an ear-splitting wail; everyone present found it jolting. After a full minute of staring at Juan, the priest resumed. "Do you believe in Jesus Christ, His only Son, our Lord, who was born of the Virgin Mary, was crucified, died, and was buried, rose from the dead, and is now seated at the right hand of the Father?"

"I do," said all, save for one. More words, more participant responses, then finally the priest said "Hector Agustín Ramos, I baptize you in the name of the Father," pouring holy water from the baptismal font onto the baby's head as he spoke, "and of the Son," again pouring, "and of the Holy Spirit," with a third and final pouring. As everyone said their 'amen,' Casilda screeched. She bolted from the altar out through the cathedral doors.

"Watch my son!" Juan shouted at Mateo as he chased her down. He found her across the street bent over in the shade of an arched doorway. "Casilda!" he called and ran across to her. Slowly she raised her head and let out a long hissing sigh through her teeth. "I know what you are going to say, Juan. My head is pounding. A dark episode is coming on strong like an earthquake."

"Casilda, I'm sorry this is happening to you. But you really and truly embarrassed me there. I have never felt such shame in all my life. How could you?"

Casilda stood. She rubbed her hand up and down the back of her neck. "The pain in my head makes childbirth feel like a stubbed toe, by comparison. Here's a question for you: How could I marry such a selfish, unsympathetic bastard? Excellent question. Let me know when you learn the answer. In the meantime, do not touch me, Juan, or I will chew off your bollocks and spit them right in your old man face."

In the bedroom, Juan drew the curtains and left his wife wrapped in her beloved darkness. Downstairs he ate the ham and bread Dayhoo had left out for him, and chased down the pink meat with two quarts of wine. "Nothing goes with ham quite like red table wine," he joked to himself. He felt the sweet anesthesia of the wine taking effect. He cradled Hector for a shady stroll through the trees behind the manor.

Outside he saw Tanna, not wearing her usual servant dress and apron, but rather tight, earth-colored breeches she must have worn for field work before purchasing her from another landowner. Her blouse was a stained beige cotton half-shirt that covered her breasts but left her neck, shoulders, arms, and midsection completely at the mercy of the unforgiving near-equatorial sun. A thick sheen of sweat on her mocha-brown skin reflected sunlight in a fascinating prism. She noticed him watching as she exercised. She stopped. "Master Ramos, forgive me, I was just stretching a little. Is there anything that needs doing now?"

He gathered himself. "No, no. Please continue, Tanna. Don't let me stop you."

Tanna smiled at him, but the smile disappeared when she looked up. He turned to see what had arrested her attention. A ghostly pale face peeked through the curtains of his bedroom window then faded back inside just as he turned to glimpse it. "Carry on, Tanna, he said, and turned back to the manor. Holding Hector, he leapt up the steps two at a time. Gently he opened the bedroom door. Ambient light from behind him illuminated the room, still mostly shadows, but the pale sheets and even paler wife lying atop them appeared to him in stark relief.

"Can I get you anything, my love? A drink of water, perhaps?"

Long thick hair cascaded around her face as white as the pillow. "You like her. That Tanna."

His jaw dropped in utter disbelief. "Why would you ever accuse me of such a thing? Because I didn't whip her for being out of uniform?"

"Get out," said Casilda.

"You are Missus Ramos?"

She nodded. "You are Brogoo, my husband's overseer?"

"Yessum. Sorry if I seem flustered, ma'am. I never expected to see you down here, is all. Mighty fine horse you rode in on, if I may say."

"Where is Tanna?"

"Why, ma'am, I expect she be up at the house. Master Ramos likes her there, not out in the fields."

"I will wait here. Go fetch her. Be quick about it. Take my steed."

Brogoo's bewilderment was plain. "Yes, ma'am, right away, ma'am," he said, forced to decide a best course of action, and hoped Ramos was home when he arrived to sort this out. He mounted her horse, did a double dig of heels into the animal's flanks, and was gone. Thirty-five minutes later he reappeared with Tanna's arms wrapped around his thick chocolate chest. "As you ordered, ma'am," he said. He dismounted and helped Tanna down.

Casilda approached Tanna until the two women stood facing each other. She studied the entirety of Tanna's lithe form, thin but highly toned legs, round shapely hips, clearly defined abdominal muscles, and strong wiry arms. A face some might consider pretty, small and perfectly even bone-white teeth, close-cropped African hair.

"I watched you in the yard the other day trying to seduce my husband."

"Ma'am?"

"Doing your little exercise routine in front of my house to coax him outside. I heard every word. I watched him watching you, and you him. The eyes never lie, Tanna. You see something in him. Maybe he has a history of fornicating with skinny little slave girls, I suspect he does. I also know you have the animal instinct to pick up on it."

"Ma'am, I would never—"

"Also, during childbirth, did I not threaten to skin you alive if you did not release me?"

"Ma'am, you were not in your right mind then. Scarcely can believe you remember all that."

"I remember everything, Tanna. My eyes see everything."

"Well ma'am I am sor—"

"Not yet. But you will be." Without breaking eye contact, she said, "Brogoo, get your whip and lead us to the whipping post."

"Ma'am?"

"DO NOT QUESTION ME!"

Wearing an expression of sadness and grief commingled with fear and nausea, Brogoo complied. He hung the coiled leather bullwhip on the waist loop there for the purpose and wrapped his enormous right hand completely around Tanna's thin upper arm until his fingertips met. He marched her back behind the long rectangular building that was the main slave barracks, to face two thick wooden poles planted five feet apart from which hung blackened iron chains and locking wrist clasps. Underneath was a five-foot square of sand, areas of which appeared darkened and clumped.

"Strip her completely."

"Ma'am I—"

"Another word out of you and I will tie you to my horse and drag you to Colombia."

Tanna stood bravely as Brogoo removed Tanna's shirt, breeches, and boots until she stood naked, hands over her crotch, on her face a pitiful expression of deep humiliation which positively delighted Casilda.

"Well? Fix her between the poles, Brogoo. No-no, not that way. I want her facing me."

"Ma'am, whippings go on their backs."

Casilda smiled. "Not today, Brogoo. Get on with it," she said. He grabbed Tanna's left wrist and clicked the iron manacle closed. He did the same for her right wrist. "Ankles, too. I want her nethers spread wide open for this."

Clicking the final manacle closed, Brogoo stepped back. A war waged within him. Having come up the hard way, the ascension to his current insulated position was made possible, he knew, by following one unbreakable policy: keep thy mouth shut and obey without question. He glared angrily at Casilda. She ignored him. She walked to the 'X' shaped woman close enough to smell her fear. She pressed her fingernails against Tanna's neck and dragged them down her entire torso like a cat sharpening its claws, down across brown areolas and undulating stomach. She stopped at the triangle of hair below.

"You are never to speak to my husband again. You are never to set foot in my house again. You will work in the fields under Brogoo. Or you will return to this very spot, where I will personally whip all the organs from your body and flesh from your bones. Nod if you understand."

A single tear rolled down Tanna's right cheek. She so wanted to explain that this horrible unjust persecution never needed to happen. But she was afraid of what she recognized in Casilda's eyes. She had seen it before. Part Nigerian, her people's belief system got passed down to her. She loved the Lord, Christ Jesus, indeed she did. Frolicking behind Casilda's childlike face and hypnotic blue eyes, she knew what it was. *Bad juju.* Evil spirits at work. The complete absence of love, or mercy. Tanna closed her eyes.

"Well, Brogoo? Do your job. One hundred lashes. I want you to pay particularly close attention to her bosom and pudenda. The next time she has sexual thoughts about my husband, I want her to look down and see mutilation, to remember this pain today. Chase those evil thoughts right out of her nappy little head. With your whip I want you to remove her evil, possessed bits. Ready? Begin."

"*You* are the one possessed by evil spirits!" Tanna screamed through her tears.

"Brogoo, make it two hundred lashes."

"She did WHAT?"

"That's right, sir, yes sir. I was praying you'd be up at the house to sort all this out. As you know I take orders from you, the missus, and God willing, one day little Hector. I ask no question. Brogoo just do whatever the Ramoses tell him to, yessir."

"Why did you not refuse her? Why did you not tell her that you only take orders from me? For God's sake, Brogoo, you nearly killed Tanna! I mean look at her! You permanently disfigured her! She is ruined for life. With that mess between her legs I can't imagine she'll ever be able to sit down and piss properly ever again."

"Sir? Begging for your pardon sir. The last time I saw a slave disobey a direct command from his master's wife, the master found out. He had that slave castrated while making us all watch. I was just a boy. And that slave? Sir, he was my daddy. The master took a wood-chopping axe to my father's man-parts all because daddy refused to kill a barking dog that was disturbing his wife. I did for your missus just exactly what I was told. I—we down here, we all love Tanna. She's like a daughter or little sister to us. My heart broke, sir, yessir, this broke it. Lord, please forgive me. But sir, you understand now why I did not refuse Missus Ramos?"

Reluctantly, Juan nodded. "Yes. Yes, Brogoo. I do. Now hear this because I'm only going to say it one time. If my wife or anyone else tells you to do something, you tell them you are under strict orders from me that I must first give permission. Understand? Because if you don't, next time it will be you between those posts so help me God."

"Yessir. I do understand. Thank you, sir."

"I'm sending Dayhoo down to tend to Tanna. She can stay until Tanna is up and moving again. I'll take care of the house chores myself until then. Extra rum rations for everyone until Tanna improves. I will pray for her, Brogoo."

"Yes, sir, thank you again, sir. Mighty generous of you."

"Remember on our wedding day, what I said?"

"Casilda, this is no time—"

"I warned you that if you ever so much as look at another woman with lust in your heart, if I ever catch you, I will roast you alive. Remember?"

Juan removed his thick leather razor strop from the bedroom hook. "Recall, during your last dark episode when you accused me of lusting after Tanna, and I asked why would you ever accuse me of such a thing? You never answered. Nor will I answer you now, except to teach you a lesson your daddy should have done over a decade ago."

Her hair was still wet from the bath. He tore away the cotton cloth she had wrapped around herself. "What are you doing—" He bound her wrists with cloth, looped them over the heavy iron wall hook, and kicked her knees out from under her. As she slipped and slid in her futile attempt to stand and run, he rained down blows with the thick leather razor strop.

"That's right, Casilda, scream! Scream louder! I want my slaves to know what happens to all who act without my permission." He avoided her breasts as his son still required mother's milk; not one inch of flesh below her neck escaped the blows. Wherever bathwater reached he turned angry red and welted. The screaming lasted a full hour.

He hung the strop back on the hook and released her. "You will never embarrass me like you did at the baptism again. You will have no contact with my slaves. You will submit to your husband's every whim. Obedience without question. And you will worship Christ. Nod if you understand."

She spit on him. He disrobed, then spent the next two hours viciously redefining his conjugal rights to obscene new levels. Slaves heard the humiliated screams from a distance. Dayhoo hugged and comforted Tanna. Weakly from her cot in the overseer's outbuilding, Tanna smiled and thanked God for justice.

"Where are you going, Casilda?"

"Down to the river with Hector for a swim, is that allowed?"

Juan shook his head at the impertinence. "I don't care what you do. Just don't let anything bad happen to my son." He mounted his horse and headed to the slave barracks to immerse himself in work. The cocoa crop that season had been magnificent. But a crop in the field did him no good; he needed every pod cut down, sliced open, beans dried in the sun, then sacked, loaded onto wagons and hauled over the mountain to Port La Guaira. If he did not hold Brogoo and his Africans to a timeline he would lose money. A loving wife he had already learned to live without, but to keep this business running, and to provide proper inheritance to his only son while hoping for a return to better times with Casilda, what he required absolutely was revenue.

Hector still wanted to be carried by his mother, so she slung him into a papoose and walked the narrow path through trees, plants, and boulders, in her hands a basket of linens. They arrived at the river's sandy beach. Naked, she and Hector splashed in the gentle currents, his little giggles audible for a distance in the still air. She felt relaxed, head pain diminished, until she heard the distinctive snap of a larger size branch in the woods. Alarmed, she trudged back to the beach and wrapped herself and Hector in linen. She stared into the woods. "Who's there?" she called. No answer. "I'll send my husband through these woods with a dozen armed Africans. Now just call yourself out so that I know you are not a threat."

Silence.

Fear tingled her belly and spine. She decided to cut short their day at the beach. She slipped her white undergarment over herself, pants and a blouse on Hector, grabbed her basket, slipped sandy soles into jute shoes and doubled back along the path, this time ears highly attuned to anything unusual. She heard nothing out of the ordinary, only birds and tiny skittering creatures enjoying their understory lives.

But she felt eyes on her.

Casilda had fallen asleep with her back to him, as was her usual behavior ever since Hector's birth. He stared out at the moon wondering how his marriage had possibly gone so far off track. An idea fomented. *Who knows a person better than her own mother? Well, God, of course. But for all my prayers I've yet to receive a sign, a feeling, a dream, or one single clue as to how to proceed. There are no answers to my most burning question: How can I possibly restore the unparalleled love and passion of our earlier time? Possibly, her mother holds the key to this mysterious woman who knew Casilda from inside the womb through young adulthood. Tomorrow.* He had decided. Sleep took him.

"I must go into town. I'll be back by lunchtime, hopefully," Juan said. She stood on the porch holding hands with Hector, who wobbled and weakly waved, having only recently learned to stand. Clip-clopping along, behind him the manor slowly grew smaller. He used the time to explore his mind for questions he might ask this woman. *Was Casilda always so mistrustful and cruel? Jealous? What of these 'dark episodes' of hers: how did you deal with them? Did you ever discipline her? Or did you spare the rod and spoil the child? After you two had arguments, how were you able to restore normal relations after? Why did you not take her to church? What is her aversion to all things Christian, did something happen to her as a child; was she attacked by a member of the clergy?*

These and many other questions whirled about his brain until he stopped to ask a local if he could point his way to the home of Casilda's mother. He thanked the old man profusely and pressed a gold coin into his shaky withered palm. As the village came into view, his mind once more reeled through questions he had for Maria, the mother of the woman he once adored, and wanted back.

In the back of his mind, he felt a sense of being watched. Thrice he turned hoping to catch someone following him but saw nothing out of the ordinary. Kids at play, cats and dogs. The feeling was eerie. He could not shake it.

Tying off his horse, he walked the rocky path up a grade to the mud-walled house, as indistinct and forgettable as all the unremarkable houses along this road, in this abysmally poor section of town. He wondered how his Creole people could have fallen so far from their New World energies but then remembered that the master of this particular house had dallied with an indigenous girl, resulting in his death under the point of a spear.

At the plain wooden door, he knocked three times. Nothing happened. He knocked again more forcefully. He spun around. Trees, bushes, horse troughs, outhouses. The sense of someone watching him sent tiny red flags popping erect in the proprioception sectors of his sensory awareness. From inside he heard a woman's voice. "Who's there?"

"Ma'am, my name in Juan Ramos. Husband of Casilda. Are you Maria?"

Moments later the door opened. Juan stood stunned. *My God, she's Casilda! Slightly older, possibly my age. One worry line across her pale smooth forehead that Casilda lacks, otherwise an accurate replica in every nuanced detail.* She smiled. "Won't you please come in, Juan?" She moved aside and closed the door behind her.

Cognizant of his own excitement, to calm himself he refocused his gaze to the interior of the two-room single-story structure. *Humble, yes—but also immaculately clean.* A small kitchen table with seating for two. Two chairs upholstered in leather, worn but also comfortable-looking and clean, between them a round table. A separate bed chamber. "Would you like coffee or tea, or some water to wash down road dust?"

"Water would be wonderful, Maria, thank you. Or should I call you mom?" he said with a sly grin.

"Call me that and I will be forced to strip you, bind you over the table and eat you for dinner alive and screaming," followed by an amused smirk.

From a ceramic pitcher she poured two cups of water, set them onto the round table, and took the seat that obviously conformed to her body. *Queen's throne*, he thought. He collapsed into the other and felt at home immediately. He quickly drained the cup of water. He felt her studying him with rapt attention.

"You are even more handsome than rumored." She bent her head to sip demurely from the cup.

His mouth opened. He blinked. "Thank you, very kind of you to say so, Maria. If I may say, you and your daughter could be mistaken for identical twin sisters." She smiled and pointed at a portrait on the wall. "A good likeness" he said. "Could be either one of you."

"That was me at twenty, close to my daughter's age now. Word reached me that I am a grandmother. Hector, is his name?"

"Hector Agustín Ramos. He'll be two years old soon. He's almost walking, stumbling around mostly, but this world cannot keep a good man down."

"I would love to meet him."

His face grew grim. "This is partially why I'm here, Maria."

"I know why you're here, Juan."

"Oh? Perhaps I should let you explain it to me."

She smirked. "Because that sweet little teenager you fell madly in love with has quickly changed into a loveless, hateful soul, existing rather than living, and seems well beyond your abilities to reach her. You believe you've committed no sin against her worthy of such horrible abandonment." She spoke with authority as if leaving no room for challenge because she knew none would come.

"How did you—"

"Wait," she said. From the cupboard she returned with a small cork-stoppered glass bottle. Reseated, cork removed, she tapped three drops from the bottle into his water cup. "Drink. It will relax you and better enable you to process the information I am about to give you."

He studied her face. "Are you sure? Is this safe, Maria? You wouldn't want to poison the father of your grandchild, now, would you?"

She giggled. "Who would raise him? A person needs two parents to be raised successfully, which is why we are here, to discuss the tragic result of a single-parent household. No, it isn't poison, Juan. It's a common relaxant among the local tribes. If it makes you feel better," she said, tapping three drops into her own cup of water," I'll join you. Better than wine, by far. Here's to Hector Agustín: may his days upon this earth be long and successful." Clinking cups, together they drained them. Immediately he felt different, languid and relaxed, yet at the same time his clarity of thought increased, perception of colors sharpened. His body felt wonderful, skin electrified. Again, he scanned the room hoping to spot a clue, something to help solve the burning mystery that was Casilda.

"Maria, I notice no crucifix or statue of Mother Mary in here. Casilda told me you were quite adamant about dragging her to church, but she refused."

"Ah, yes. Let us just say that my daughter was born with a naturally obstinate streak in her."

"I've noticed."

"Also, a disturbing and unnatural revulsion for all things Christian."

"Noticed that, too. Why is that? It's most unsettling. And you never answered my first question."

Maria uncrossed her legs; he tried not to look. His blood felt warm. He became aware of a tickle or pulsing beginning in his loins that quickly swept through his belly, feet, ears, fingers. "Gradually after my husband died, I lost faith. What can I say about that, Juan? Why did Casilda love you so fiercely then turn so cold toward you? It's along similar lines I suppose."

"You believe in nothing now? Worship nothing?"

"Au contraire, my good man. No—you are a great man. Caring and loving, hard-working and honest. I wanted this for myself once upon a time. I'm happy that my progeny has found it for herself."

"Please, I need to know. In what do you believe?"

She smiled. "The local tribes worship different spirits. Some believe in animal spirits, others in a single great spirit. Others believe the earth is everyone's mother. Me, I believe in the here and now, that after this life passes there is nothing. Utter blackness."

"Sounds peaceful."

"Yes! Doesn't it? An end to all suffering and injustice, to pain and grief and guilt."

He shook his head. "I believe in the next life as taught in church. Casilda's lack of faith has trapped her within her own little world in which, unfortunately, there is no longer any room for me."

"Did you notice anything strange about her?"

"Like what, for instance?"

"Foretelling future events before they happen?"

He thought back to their honeymoon. "Yes. Maybe."

"And where do you suppose that little gift comes from?"

"Let me guess. You?"

She grinned and thumped her bosom. "I said I don't believe in an afterlife. I did not say I don't believe in a spirit world. It's here, all around us all the time. If you learn how to get along with those spirits, you too can receive certain gifts."

"There are only three spirits that interest me: the Father, the Son, and The Holy Ghost."

"Stand here, Juan," she said, pointing at her bare feet. "I want to take a closer look at you. Would you mind? Promise I won't bite."

He rose and walked two steps. Soles against his breeched thighs arrested further movement. This close, he truly saw no physical difference between Maria and Casilda. *Even their voices sound the same, albeit Maria speaks with a mature woman's self-assurance and world-weary confidence.* "Give me your hand," she said. Hesitating at first, he complied. He stood over her joined at the hand as her feet massaged his thighs. "I know what you really want to know. I know the central question in your heart."

"Is that so? Tell me."

"I will answer, but first, tell me how are you feeling right now? Do you feel warm and relaxed? Better now than when you first arrived?"

"Yes. I feel deeply relaxed."

She smiled. "Before I tell you the question and the answer burning hot in your heart of hearts, feel my heart." She pulled his hand flat against her breasts. He felt transported back to a time when he would touch Casilda this way. "Casilda's heart is my heart. Now," she said. She pulled his hand down to her lap, lifted her dress, then guided him along the porcelain smoothness of her left thigh. He felt the old stirring in his loins burning hot. With his open hand, fingers outstretched, she slipped two of his fingers into herself. He tried to pull his hand back, plagued by a momentary sense of guilt, but using both hands she held him in place. Her eyes never left his, nor did the mischievous smile ever leave her face. Abruptly she released his hand. "Smell your fingers." *Enchanting eyes, dark blue almost gray, exactly like hers.* He complied. "She is me in every way, isn't that true, Juan?"

He nodded. "Amazing. You truly are like her."

"No. *She* truly is like *me.* Except that I know who I am and what makes me happy. She does not, nor will she ever. Kneel before me. For if I am not your true queen, who is? I made her. Am I not higher even than she? Kneel."

Juan knelt. Her toes explored and aggravated the swelling in his breech front. She lifted her dress, clutched his thick wavy hair and pulled his face down to her sex. "Please your queen, and I promise your wish will be granted," she said. Somewhere in his brain, a thought: *She even moans exactly like her.*

Breeches around his ankles, he took her from behind the way his wife likes it. Into Maria he hammered away with a fervor and delirium not felt in over two years, his tense body boiling from the soles of his feet to his tingling scalp. Maria grasped the chair leather as Casilda's sounds filled the room, which only heightened his pique.

After, collapsed into his chair, a now naked Maria curled up in his lap.

Absently she fondled his spent manhood. *The self-assured way Maria touches me there is different from Casilda.* "The question is, can you ever get the original Casilda back as she was." He nodded once.

"Sadly, Juan, the answer is no. Her dark spells only happen when the spirit of hate consumes her. Your wife was born with a giant hole running straight through her core top to bottom, a hole that can only be filled with other people's pain. She cannot be reasoned with. No matter how much love and tenderness you give her she will only deflect it. If you give her your misery, she will absorb it, magnify it a thousand-fold, and send it to back to you."

Replaying the first year of their marriage, he shook his head. "Maria, she is a completely different person now than the woman I married. Are you saying the young woman I married was an actress, a manufactured version, and that this woman today is the real Casilda?"

Maria nodded. "I'm afraid so. Sorry to be the one to tell you. Maybe she gave you clues and somehow you missed them. Or more accurately, you noticed but chose to ignore them."

He thought about her anxiety in the wedding chapel and again at the baptism. The raging jealousy expressed during the ride back home. "Damn it," he said.

"What is it, darling?"

"Yes. Yes, she did give me clues. But the passions of my forefathers live strong in me. I ignored all warning signs to get her right where I so dearly wanted her." He sighed. Whatever magic tribal potion Maria had introduced into his brain was beginning to wear off.

"No one knows a child like a parent. This is why she has kept us apart, Maria. Deep down she knows that you are quite possibly the better match for me. Same age, same shared experiences growing up here in the New World, working hard, maximizing whatever gifts we were given by God," he spoke in frustrated tones. "She did not want us to meet because you would have educated me straight away about her and kept me all to yourself."

It was Maria's turn to sigh. "I would not have married you, Juan."

"No? Why not, for Heaven's sake? What did we just do? There's warmth between us, you cannot deny."

She nodded. "There is that. I have never found myself so completely attracted to a man until this day. But no, because I would never bring your children into this dark world, nor would I worship your God."

"You'd find your way back to God, Maria. He is eternal. He has unchanged, only you have. All that is good in this world belongs to Him. You would bear me children and raise them with me in the church."

She fell silent. Her toying down low was having a rejuvenating effect. "Maybe, Juan. She knows what she is missing, though we can both agree she is not missing it at all. You're a strong man. Strong enough perhaps for me to follow."

He pushed her off his lap and stood. "This is wrong. Being here with you is the mother of all bad ideas. I should never have come. What we are doing here today goes against Christ."

This time they made it to the bedroom. The window curtain was open a crack.

Casilda fumed over the fact that Juan had broken his promise to return for lunch and now, mid-afternoon, he remained absent. She scooped up Hector and her linen basket and carried both along the path down to the river. Feeling trapped in the estate, she considered the slow, hypnotic action of river water somewhat of a balm.

Ears attuned to any sound that might not belong, Casilda and Hector made it to the little stretch of sandy beach. Unfurling a large linen square, she set the toddler upon it. Starting to pull off her dress, she stopped. Again, she heard the unmistakable sound of a dry branch crunching under a large animal's weight. "Who's there!" she screamed.

Emanating from some location just inside her forehead came the seeds of pain that she knew would, at some point this afternoon, develop into an epic whammer, and without Juan here to help take the pressure off by taking Hector or assigning Dayhoo to childcare duties.

"Hello!" a male voice answered back.

"Who are you? Don't you know you are trespassing on private land?"

"Apologies, Missus Ramos," came the reply, as the source crept out of the foliage within her view. A small, cowled figure enshrouded in a dark cloak too long for it jerked toward her in time-lapse increments. *No human had ever moved this way*, she observed.

"Stop right there! I don't know you are!"

"It's not important for now, who I am." Voice gravelly, tinny, inhuman.

"Are you the one who watches me here?"

"Yes," the figured hissed.

"I'm going to call Brogoo down here with his Africans. You'll rue the day you were born."

"Ah, born. Yes. Cannot recall when that was, or even if it was," said the robed specter as it advanced two more steps. "I assure you, madam, I am not here to hurt you, only to help you."

"I don't need help. Get away from us." The pain in her forehead now radiated clear through to the back of her neck, still not even a third of where she knew the pain would lead. "Why do you watch me?"

"Because I am interested in people, you and your husband, Juan Ramos, especially."

"Juan? What do you have to do with him?"

Another two fast-forward steps closer. Now the figure stood twenty feet away. "I have information about your husband that may change things between you. Are you curious what he is doing right now, this very minute, while you dutifully attend to his son, and his estate?"

"What are you talking about? He rode into town this morning; he'll return here any moment."

From eighteen feet now, she could make out skin so black and shiny that it appeared obsidian. *No African accent. Too small to be a runaway slave. His articulation and diction belie an education unavailable to slaves.* "You will be most interested to hear what I have to say. But nothing in this world is free, Missus Ramos."

"Money! So that's what you're after. Sorry, we don't keep any in the house. My husband uses banks."

"Not money, Missus Ramos. I will tell you what I saw of your husband this afternoon, but only if you agree to meet me back here tonight at midnight. At that time, I shall offer you the help you will most surely require. You can pay me then, if you think the information I am prepared to give you was important."

"I don't need anybody's help." The severe throbbing pain and pulsing sensation on the right side of her head caused her eyelid to droop. The first waves of nausea threatened to resurrect her lunch. So welcome on her skin earlier, sunlight now beamed straight into her head through her eyes like a red-hot poker.

"Missus Ramos, your husband went to visit your mother. I watched. Watching people is what I do, please understand. The bedroom curtain was open. I witnessed firsthand his remarkably enthusiastic pursuit of carnal knowledge with the lady Maria. It was special to watch. Your husband has a powerful appetite for flesh, Missus Ramos. Rare it is to see such passion. Maria is strong enough to meet his lusts with her own. If I may say, they seem very well matched."

Explosions in her head. Unimaginable pain. Blinding white and red lights.

Fire and fury.

"Midnight, please do not forget, Missus Ramos," said the little figure. It jerked backwards along its irregularly spaced self-same footprints until at length it faded back into the woods.

Juan and Maria, naked, uncovered, exhausted from their exertions, now asleep in each other's arms did not hear nor sense Casilda's stealthy approach. Hector, lulled to sleep by the lazy late afternoon sun and the rhythm of her horse remained attached to her back, safe in his papoose. Beeswax taper candle flames burned straight in the absence of any drafts, mounted in stands to the right and left of Maria's bed chamber. The flames did not even waver so stealthy was her entrance. The room reeked of sex.

Casilda positioned the tip of the blade less than half an inch from the furry opening of her mother's loins so much like her own. Without hesitation she plunged the wide blade nearly ten inches deep, using every bit of her considerable strength to push it past whatever tough cartilage or sinews slowed its progress. The tip came to rest within the uterus that once housed her for nine months. Jets of arterial blood cascaded onto the bed linen. Casilda studied her mother's face as the blade traveled its terrifying path. Maria's eyes flew open. No recognition at first, only a frozen fresco of shock as the animal brain struggled to process survival-level stress, pushing out all other thoughts. Casilda withdrew the machete and lowered her face to Maria's right ear. She whispered, "Burn in Hell, witch. But before you do, watch what I do to your lover."

Groggily, Juan regained consciousness. Casilda had already positioned herself between his spread legs, the machete's tip under his chin, balanced on his Adam's apple. She said, "You pray to Heaven, but to Hell you shall return." At the exact moment Maria bristled every neighbor's skin with her primal scream of agony and despair, Casilda gnashed her teeth down full force into Juan's scrotum. His body's attempt to recoil away from the trauma caused her to push the blade into the tender skin of his throat. She had trapped him inside a losing predicament of her dark design. The more he twisted his torso the harder she pushed the blade, forcing him to endure her teeth gnashing his most sensitive organs to pulp. His agonized screams commingled with Maria's; the space reverberated from the cacophonous din that would surely wake the neighborhood. Casilda wondered, *if Hell is real, maybe this is what it sounds like there.*

Hector awoke and started wailing, adding to the clangor, all of which caused the pain in Casilda's head to ascend to a theretofore unknown summit. Out of Juan's bloody, mangled scrotum leaked a pink jelly. His screaming subsided as his body entered shock, but there seemed no end to the horrified wails coming from Maria. Casilda spat pink goo commingled with chunks of dark skin and black hairs. It splatted against Juan's face like an obscene nightmare spider. With one ferocious thrust she pierced his lower abdomen until his spine arrested its progress. She unslung the papoose from her back, grasped the strap, whirled it around three-sixty like David with his sling about to release a stone into Goliath's forehead—and let go. She watched her son hit the baked-hard mud wall to Maria's right. *Ah, the crying ends, forever.* As the toddler's wrappings grazed the tapered candle it fell and set the low-hanging bed linen ablaze. Maria summoned the strength to get on her knees, hands clasped together. She pleaded with her daughter to stop, sheets beneath her entirely soaked in dark, pungent blood.

Machete tip resting against Maria's lower abdomen, Casilda thrust with all her might blade side up, ripping upwards, until sternum or rib bone prevented further travel. Intestines and severed organs spilled to the bed along with yellow bits of organ fat and dark blood. Deep red appeared brown in the fading daylight on the saturated sheets. Bed engulfed in flames just then Hector, apparently merely knocked unconscious, started crying. Casilda grabbed him by the throat and dropped him onto the burning bed. She backed away from the searing heat, unable to dissever her gaze from the gruesome scene she caused. Like sweet music, her soul absorbed their agonized screams as fire singed off eyebrows and hair, and blackened skins. Enraptured, she stared in fascination as fluids spurted up like geysers when body fat melted underneath and exploded out. Not one subtle nuance of exquisite torture escaped her notice. An accusative voice inside her mind, *Casilda! You just tortured and murdered your husband, mother, and son—and delighted at their final indescribable misery!* She nodded, inhaled deeply, and smiled. The cooking meat smell brought with it some fractional measure of relief from the magma chamber erupting within her head.

Midnight at the river, the waning moon cast a yellowish pale glow over the short stretch of beach. She watched the paroxysmal approach of the eerie little spy who had told her a true tale earlier, only this time, he twitched with more confidence.

"I am truly sorry for your loss, Missus Ramos."

"You watched? Then you'll know that I am no longer married. You will address me as Miss."

He moved to within two feet of her. *It is entirely black and shiny, like a beetle, like obsidian, down to its thin little lips and gums,* she thought. A peculiar stink greeting her nostrils in night air churned only by the river. The most relatable memory came forward: pig entrails left to rot in the butcher's mulch pit.

"Ah, yes, Casilda. Such a pretty name. You should know that, as we speak, the village authorities are making ready to come for you. They will take you back, and another will dress you and lead you where you do not wish to go."

"Lead me where?"

"To the Caracas capital dungeon, to take your confession."

The scent of her roasting family, echoes of their screams, a vision from all angles of what she must have looked like on her mother's street riding away on her unmistakable steed. "What if refuse to confess?"

She couldn't be certain, but she thought she saw a closed, black-lipped smile. "Oh, Casilda, they will torture you in the most atrocious, noisome ways until you confess. They will torture you nearly to the point of death. I expect the pain will be so unbearable that death would come as a soothing relief. A court of men will find you guilty of witchcraft and murder. They will pronounce your death sentence. From court, they will march you in chains to the village square. Many will gather to watch, and to mock you.

They will garrote you for what you have done. Villagers will stare into your eyes as the awful apparatus slowly crushes your windpipe. Your bladder and bowels will involuntarily release for all to see. Their angry faces will be the last vision you will see, until your spirit reawakens in the underworld. Are you prepared for this?"

She wept. Then she cried openly. The throbbing pain in her skull and anguish of her spirit poured from her in the presence of the stranger. "I don't want to die. Not like that. I don't ever want to die."

The cowled head nodded. "There is a way out of this, Casilda. As I said earlier you will require help, which I will offer you now. But only if you are interested. I can ensure that you will live a very long life, longer than you could possibly imagine, safe in a lovely place far away from people here who mean you harm. Far from all these painful memories. And that awful pain in your head? I will make it disappear and never return. But my help comes at a cost."

Naked, wrists pinned to the sandy beach, discomfited by the reeking, oddly formed figure on top of her, she closed her eyes as it indulged itself at her expense. Embarrassment and humiliation only added to the cannon-fire barrage of pain above her neck. She questioned her decision to consent to the discomfiting horror now befalling her.

She looked up at the moon as the shrouded stranger sniff-tasted her hairy, musky underarms and breasts with long-flat licks. Though robed, she felt herself getting pierced, not by a normal human male organ, rather by something long, steely and thin. To her it felt like a fireplace poker rod traveling up through her cervix as it pounded directly against her uterine walls. She gasped at the bizarre, uncomfortable intrusion. Nothing about it stimulated her in the normal sense, but gradually, the sensation deep in her belly she found to be decreasingly unpleasant.

A man pistoning himself at the impossible speed of hummingbird wings would at minimum respire heavily. There was no evidence of any breath at all coming from her sexual dominator. The thing inside her felt cold. Curiosity aroused, in a fit of pique she reached up and pulled away the hood. She gasped. Not the face of a man, but of something lower in the order. *A reptile? Possibly insect? Shiny black outer epidermis; iridescent eyes on either side of the head like a praying mantis giving it a 360-degree field of view. Hip thrusts unlike a man but like the vibrato of a fly's wings.* Black and forked was the tongue like that of a snake: it flickered down at her frightened face, up one nostril then the other. She turned her head right to escape this new probing assault. The tongue deeply probed her left ear. *Perhaps after seeing what I did to Juan, it fears my mouth and what damage my teeth might do,* she wondered. The horror, dreamlike, felt more chilling and repugnant than anything she had ever experienced. She wanted badly to scream, to physically give vent to the panic and terror consuming her.

The monstrous abomination continued to violate her in the obscenest, most sickening ways. Throughout the ordeal she wondered if death would not be preferable. She inhaled deeply, preparing to scream for help. *No,* came the response from her rational mind, one lucid thought born of deeply entrenched survival instincts forced her to remain silent. *The slaves will hear my screams. Men searching for me will hear. They will find me. And they will torture and kill me.*

The pain in her head occluded all further speculation about ending her immediate predicament. And then it was over. The entire intrusion lasted fewer than two minutes, though it had seemed like hours, until the rod-thing withdrew back up underneath the robe. It did not release her wrists. "In order for you to live," it hissed, "I must give you something."

Stiff black rubbery lips peeled back to reveal snake fangs. Pearls of venom gathered at needle-sharp points. Before she could object the points penetrated deeply into her pale, tender neck. Momentary flickers of pain quickly gave way to something pleasurable. Everything suddenly changed. Her five senses sharpened to a level she could scarcely accept. She thought she could see straight through the Milky Way galaxy of stars twinkling above to places far beyond the black tapestry. She smelled the faint aroma of a cat on the hunt across the other side of the river, could hear the frightened dying squeaks of the small rodent it captured. Her body felt more alive than ever before as warm night air and moonlight caressed her skin. With growing awareness of her sex, she felt the familiar blood-rush to her womanly organs, the tingling, an ocean wave warm and welcoming, cresting, seizing her entire body in the crash of a shuddering climax. Hips ground back against the sand; legs pinched together. *The most satisfying physical sensation of my entire life.*

All pain in her head completely vanished, like magic. Wrists now free, she felt around the neck wound site for tenderness and found none. She took full stock of how she felt throughout her body. She decided that not only did she feel fully recovered from her dark spell: she felt better, stronger, and healthier than ever before.

She heard it's hiss which she no longer found repulsive. "You must depart here immediately. Go barefoot. Wear only your white dress. Bring nothing. Follow the river. You will know when it is safe to regain higher ground. You will no longer require food for energy, not in the traditional sense. Travel to the Kogui tribe in the Sierra Nevada mountain range in Colombia. They will stop you. Say these words: Habá Hang éina. At the same time, wish for boils to rise on their skin until they let you pass. Do this, and you will live long and safe among the people."

"What are you?"

"Along the way your womb will fill once more. This will begin and end quickly, within a week. When labor pains come, squat in the woods. Whatever comes out, leave it where it lies and continue. Only then may you consider our account closed."

"What are you, I asked?"

"Something you can never understand. What comes forth from your belly, you must not look upon it. Like me, you will consider it…deformed. Delivery will be painless and quick. It will survive without assistance. You must leave it and walk away."

"You say I will not need food. How will I survive without clean water and nutrients?"

The dark robed figure absorbed moonlight like a sponge. To her, it appeared to be darting away in fits and starts, nothing resembling footsteps. From a distance, possibly from the woods, the familiar and final words she heard: "Our account will soon be closed."

She slept on the beach. When she awoke, the first birds awakened just before dawn signaled the abrupt end of her time there at the estate. *They will come for me at any minute. Perhaps they are already investigating the house and slave barracks. Before long they will follow my tracks here. I have to move quickly.*

The bank along the river was not traversable by humans. Inconsistent stretches of river rocks, sand, thick mud and overgrowth, steep banks. It seemed like a daunting path to her. People in the area would be on the lookout for a young woman traveling alone. A great many miles separated her from the mountains to the west where she knew she had to go. *Like a broken clock, that thing was accurate twice in the last twenty-four hours. The river truly is my only option.* She started running barefoot over the sand. Sandy silt changed to rocks, which should have hurt her feet if not sprained an ankle, but did not. She noticed that her breath never failed her, nor did she sweat, or thirst. Insects left her unmolested. She paused to look back and calculated that she had covered a distance of a mile in less than two minutes. She ran again, now slogging through mud with no loss of speed. She smiled. *I am invincible!*

At least twenty miles separated her from the village; she stopped to rinse her muddy legs and dress in the river. Effortlessly she leaped over a steep river embankment to the woods above and emerged on a road, just as the sky behind her glowed with the reddish tint of an impending sunrise pregnant with heavy rains. On the road, she walked. She felt movement in her womb. From behind, she sensed rather than heard an approaching cargo carriage. *Four—no six horses—probably carrying mineral ore to some distant drop point in the direction I'm heading: west.*

She walked at a normal pace along the road. The carriage driver leaned back on the reins of his animal engine, throttling them back to a slow amble. "Good morning, miss. Are you lost?"

She smiled. "Maybe I am. Are you married?"

"Ah…well. Yes, more or less."

"If I have sex with you, will you take me with you to wherever you're going?"

Avaricious eyes took in her innocence, youth, and stunning beauty. He craned around looking for the pimp, or the trap. Secure that they were truly alone, "Why, yes," he said, and patted the seat beside him.

"Take off your breeches," she said.

"Hm. Not much into foreplay and romance, I see. Right here, now, in the middle of the road?"

"Mm hmm," she nodded. Without removing his boots, he pulled his breeches down to his ankles, groin and thighs fully exposed.

She straddled him. Smiling, she reached down and stroked him to rigidity. "Ready?" she cooed. He nodded. Gently she grasped his hair, pulled back his head, kissed his neck, and chewed a large hole in his throat. A few ounces of blood gouted onto the leather-covered carriage seat before she managed to seal her mouth over the wound and consume the remaining ten pints. His abhorrent, initial panicked wail disturbed only a few nearby birds rustling about in the woods. No, it was her unnatural animal noises, high-frequency yips and snarls that sent a flock of powerful, bold, black-headed vultures flying away at full speed.

As her victim collapsed, Casilda laughed long and loud, overcome with a sense of joy, of deep and utter contentment.

She resumed walking, no longer in any hurry.

Death Macabre

Dr. Reynold 'Ron' Williams, M.D., Board-certified geriatrician and newest member of a larger medical practice, had only this morning received his assignment to the high-end assisted living community to make rounds, take blood samples, and provide whatever comfort he could to terminal residents. Sounded easy, but each Gen Z death took a small piece of him with it. He would dole out morphine and Tramadol, befriend them, and watch them slowly die—because someone had to—but mostly because of the love animating his heart. Williams's sole job here was to dispense pain meds and see them out as pain-free as possible. There was but one bright spot in this lachrymose routine, and he was looking at it.

"How do you feel, Dr. Tomkins?" he asked the eighty-four-year-old man in the bed. He inspected the morphine drip line.

Pale blue eyes, lucid and present, focused on Williams. "Earlier, I felt like exercising. Then I laid down until the feeling passed."

Williams laughed out loud. "You know, doc, I was beyond excited to get you as a patient! I was in med school from 2018 to 2022 when I studied your work, as we all did. Now today, all the schools offer entire courses dedicated to your research and discovery! I feel giddy having you as my patient. You know at one point I felt deeply torn between following in your footsteps doing cancer research and pursuing clinical."

Tomkins blinked in acknowledgement. "Perhaps I should have stuck with hepatology. Two of the cancers I failed to kill, liver and intrahepatic bile duct cancer would eventually get me. Life is nothing if not ironic. If I may, why did you choose clinical?"

Williams's face grim, "Yes, ironic. But your research spawned a whole new generation of biotechnology clinical trials. Eventually, soon I would think, they'll beat those too. I mean, with all the ground-breaking research in cellular pathways and stem cells going on all over the world, what's even more ironic is that smallpox, one of nature's worst viruses and the killer of so many humans across the millennia, with a bit of your incredible re-engineering would turn out to be the elegant hungry beast that gobbles up cancer cells like French pastries. You singled-headedly eradicated some of the worst indications: leukemia, pancreatic, esophageal, and the biggest killers of them all, breast, prostate, colorectal, and ovarian cancers. I recall reading an interview when the FDA issued your first treatment approval. The media-person asked how you alone were able to do what so many millions of molecular engineers, AI, and many billions of dollars were unable to. I'll never forget your response. Do you remember what it was?"

"Cancer, like the devil, is a bully. I never liked bullies."

Williams beamed. "Yes! That was *awesome!*"

Tomkins nodded. "I meant it. I believe a malicious and powerful spirit, the dark one, creates viruses and diseases. The ultimate biohacker. But sometimes the loving God intervenes, working through individuals that He finds useful."

Williams stroked his chin. "So, you're giving all credit to your God?"

Tomkins smiled. "Your God, too, Doctor Williams, believe it or not."

"Truth be told, I don't know what I believe about what happens after bodily death. I'm forty-eight years old—"

"Still a kid."

"Yes, I suppose all things seem relative to someone as old—I mean one with your experience." At this, Tomkins laughed. "So many important things I haven't figured out. To answer your question about why I chose clinical over research, the whole truth of it is this: I seem to have a high need for human interaction. Abraham Maslow's Hierarchy, his 'Esteem' and 'Self-Actualization' pyramid toppers yep. That's me. I don't particularly enjoy being alone trapped inside my own head all day every day. I mean, push comes to shove I will certainly do it. But such days seem to pass with agonizing slowness, just as time crawls by for the elderly, which is why I certified in geriatrics. My heart bleeds for the old, especially the terminal. They need compassionate care at their most vulnerable time. Does that make sense?

Tomkins closed his eyes. Closed lips moved as if in prayer. Williams sensed not to interrupt. A minute later, blue eyes opened. "When you've finished your rounds, Dr. Williams, if you have the interest and time, there is something I only hinted at with the reporter. Something I've never told anyone. My wife of forty-two years knows, because she's part of it.

"*You have a wife?* For as long as I've been alive? One of the best-kept secrets ever, wow. I am really surprised. Any kids?"

"Her body is incapable of reproduction. More about that later. Dr. Williams, please know that I have carried a bizarre truth with me now since age thirteen." A wan smile formed at the corners of his wrinkled mouth. "I choose you to be the one to trust with it. I sense the possibility that you can understand it, and profit from it. I just now prayed about it."

Williams's mouth hung open. "Really? I mean—*wow.* Okay. Give me maybe two hours to finish rounds and write scrips which as you know are now onerous, with all the Federal controlled-substance forms…"

Tomkins raised his right hand. "One day soon, I will check out of here. But not today. Take your time, young man. Rejoice that you have so much of it. I'll be here. I won't be exercising."

Beaming, Williams hustled away.

"I'm back! Still no appetite?"

Tomkins shook his head. "Not unless you happen to have a beef brisket platter and Johnny Ray's chocolate pie from Birmingham, Alabama. Or banana pudding. Best in the entire world, bar none."

"Johnny Ray's closed decades ago!" Tompkins said, tapping on his phone. "Nothing good lasts forever, but I'll see what I can do." He pulled up a comfortable vinyl and steel visitor's chair.

"My wife comes to see me every night to see me off to sleep. Until she arrives, I have time. Are you certain you want to hear this?"

"Oh yes, Doctor Tomkins. I am all yours, for as long as you like."

After taking a sip from a grape juice box, he set it down, folded his hands, and lightly rested them on his thin stomach. "Let's get something straight. I am not schizophrenic. You can dismiss me as insane—or believe me and be changed. I am possessed by two distinct states of mind forming the whole of my mental existence. There is the state of objective reason not to be disputed and belonging to the memory of events forming the first twelve years of my life. Also there exists a condition of irrational subjective bias describing the present, and of the years between age twelve and today, forming the second great era of my being. Therefore, what I shall tell of the earlier period, believe; and to what I may relate of the later time, I will not hold your doubt and rejection against you, for it is entirely phantasmagorical, and you will either find me senile, or a lunatic. Or you might believe it and allow yourself to be altered by it, as I did. Free will is yours."

Eyes widely attentive, Williams nodded.

"In my twelfth year, my father was driving me and my brother deep into the wooded heart of Pennsylvania, in the dead of winter, to a state park there for a bit of ice fishing and camping. Swerving to avoid hitting a kamikaze herd of deer, the car crashed in a ravine. My dad and brother died instantly. I suffered severe trauma and was knocked unconscious. Keep in mind, park officers and police don't patrol the area regularly in winter, because few people are crazy enough to camp in World's End State Park in January. When I regained consciousness, it was night, pitch black outside, as no ambient light reflected from manmade sources exist in such remote areas. I was accompanied by the mangled corpses of two people I loved more than the world.

"I crawled out. Mindless and numb, I crunched along a tunnel of trees weighted by snow up a steep firebreak and passed out again. When I regained consciousness, I was inside one of the park's rustic rental cabins. My wounds and other needs were being tended to by a little girl about my age, maybe a year older. Someone who had no business being there.

"Dear heavens, Dr. Tomkins, I am so very sorry. What a traumatic situation!"

He raised his hand. "Thanks entirely to Ariel, I survived and healed up nicely. She exercised a knowledge of naturopathic medicines. Somehow, she sourced dormant materials hidden under snow and found nutritious natural foods from the area. No infection, no fever, and my wounds healed wonderfully. She caught fish from the streams. Ariel did so many things over those weeks that I suppose to describe them all would fill an entire book."

"What would a little girl be doing alone in the winter woods, carrying all this deep survival knowledge?"

"*That*, Dr. Williams, is the right question. And here's where it gets even stranger. Weeks passed, and a series of unexplainable events began to affect me directly. Eventually, I gathered the courage to ask her. I will never forget her answer—every word of it, not one, not ever. Point blank, I asked her: 'Who are you, and why is this happening?'"

"She replied, 'Because Daniel. My equivalent to your birthdate happened five and one half billion, eight hundred seventy-seven million, three hundred and twenty-one thousand, two hundred forty days ago, at precisely nine o'clock ante meridiem using your Eastern Daylight Time. I am an ancient spirit injected into flesh newly formed for the purpose, which is to gain your trust and to not alarm you. I am assigned to keep you safe. The Father had to make me flesh to get you through this accursed episode—this unfortunate decision on the part of your earthly father to take you winter camping.' Her face and tone hinted at impatience. 'I volunteered to visit this sphere where you, Dan, are vulnerable to the Fallen One's control over lower life forms, animals, that are susceptible to programming by The Fallen, who wants you dead. None of these come for you in my presence, because any spirit from Heaven is more powerful than any from Hell, which is why you are safe only in my presence. Don't you want to know why the Fallen One wants you removed from this sphere?'"

Williams sat raptly listening. "Wow. I mean, how did you answer?"

"I nodded. 'Spirits exude their own colors in varying degrees of intensity, you know. Your spirit shines with love, Dan, more brightly than any I have seen. Humans cannot see love the way my kind does. Your spirit and mine are made of the same energy. Think of love as more than thoughts or actions. Love is a form of energy, the most powerful energy in all the universe! Love is creative. Love solves problems. Love makes stars shine because He loves this world. He wants to give people reasons to reach beyond. He seeks to be sought, reached for, understood, and loved. The Father *is* love and knows that love abolishes all limits. With love, one human can change the entire world which, to answer your question of why you, Daniel,' she said, staring intently into my eyes. 'Because He believes that one day you may change the world. Though you have free will.'"

"So, doc, what you're saying is, she claimed to be an angel? What happened to her?"

"You said angel. She claimed to be from someplace else. She knew that authorities had found the wreck with the bodies and that they were searching for me, which meant her time was up. Her spirit, her 'program' as she sometimes referred to it had to return to its point of origin." Tomkins stopped and choked up. Tears welled. "That this little girl body given to her was only designed to be temporary. But she promised never to leave my side. She drowned that body in the freezing depths of Loyalsock Creek so that no traces of her would remain. I loved her more than I had ever loved anyone, before or since. Losing her broke me inside. Then the men came and brought me home to my mother."

Inhaling deeply, Williams exhaled. "Whew. This is one wild story, Dr. Tomkins. You were right about it being hard to believe. I never expected any such words issuing from an intellectual giant, a lucid professional…"

Tomkins smiled and raised his hands. "Yes, which is why I've never told anyone, until now. If you like, I'll go on. But I must warn you, if you think the saga of the winter woods was tough to swallow, the next part might send you to the phone calling for psychiatric restraints."

Williams smiled. "Forget about consequences, there won't be any, I swear on my oath and licenses. Please continue."

"You're a good man, Williams, I can tell. Which is why I believe you are worth the telling. Call it a gut feeling."

"One year later, the anniversary of Ariel's passing, earlier that day I had found myself standing before a Juvenile Court Judge. Coping with the trauma in the woods manifested in dark, negative ways. Today they call it PTSD; back then they called it 'acting out.' Mischief, petty vandalism, blowing up mailboxes with home-made explosives—I was always pretty good at chemistry, you see, including home-made nitroglycerin—but it escalated. I got caught blowing up a small footbridge at night in a local park. Blew it to smithereens," he said, beaming proudly. "Anyway, given my academic excellence and no priors, the Judge sent me home with a slap on the wrist. By that point my poor widowed mother was powerless. I was essentially raising myself and not doing such a hot job of it. All the while I grieved for my dad, my brother, Barry…but Williams, no pain compared to the hole in my heart left by Ariel that could never be filled by another."

"Wow. One of the most famous physicians of all time has a criminal record!"

"I'm invoking doctor-patient privilege here, Dr. Williams. What is said here stays here and, in your brain, and nowhere else. Agreed?" Williams nodded.

"The promises of Ariel never to leave my side were not forgotten, for some nights I heard angel choirs. My nose detected wisps of nard having no earthly business in my hard city, which sometimes came floating past at lone hours when my heart weighed heaviest, carried by tendrils of breeze washing over my fevered face. Sometimes these nocturnal breezes were imbued with the softest whispers and murmurs in a voice that could only be hers. A weight, as if someone were sitting at the foot of my bed would rouse me from sleep. But the vacancy within my heart refused, even thus, to be filled. I longed for the spirit-lifting euphoria which so long ago, yet felt like yesterday, had filled it to overflowing.

"That night, lying in bed in my room, in the dim mental twilight somewhere between asleep and awake, a voice in the room called my name, a buttery soft, clear mezzo soprano voice. I wasn't at all frightened by it. In the light of the moon, commingled with the weak seven-watt yellow rays from a night-light, from out of the shadows stepped a young adult woman, wearing a black veil and black dress. I could see golden hair, and contours of the face behind it. Her beauty was stunning. The veil did little to hide the rarefied radiance emanating from behind. I found the solitary shape of her eyes pulling at memories stored deep within me, like magnets. I felt my blood pressure increase.

"Pulling the blanket up over my face up to my nose, I lowered it just enough to expose my mouth. I asked, 'Who are you?'

"'It's me, Dan. Ariel.'

I shook my head. 'No, you aren't. You're *old*!'

"She laughed, and it really was Ariel's special unique laugh all her own. 'I told you I would never leave your side, didn't I?'

"'Well, yes, but...'

"'Do you remember our secret code word? I do. Would you like me to say it?' I nodded. 'Ohkwari. From the native tribe. A word nobody alive in this time would know except me, and you.'

"'Oh my God! It really *is* you!'

"'Yes, Dan. I'm here with you only for a little while, in this new body, because The Father has given me permission to show you places only one mortal man, Yeshua of Nazareth, has ever visited while still mortal. Your body will remain in bed. It's your 'program' I'm taking on a quick little journey. Do you still trust me, Dan?'"

"I do. Always. Forever. Ariel, am I dreaming? Is this only just a dream?'"

"She smiled. 'Was the cabin a dream?'

"Sometimes, well, most of the time yes. I think it was only a dream. But then I look at my scars and read the newspaper articles about the 'Miracle Boy' surviving on his own against all odds. When I try to fall asleep, and when I first wake up, sometimes I cry. That's how I know you were real."

"'As real as real can be, Dan. So, will you come with me now, just for a bit?'

"Will I be safe?'"

"'Do you remember what I told you in the woods? All I can give you is an impenetrable wall against malevolent spirits and animal reprogramming by the Fallen Beast that will never stop trying to destroy you. But I cannot protect you from yourself. Tonight I will keep you safe. Every day and every night will I, until The Father chooses when to bring you back to Himself following your pre-programmed mortal death many years from now. I'm here to protect you, Dan. Your spiritual health is degrading.'"

"'I…I trust you.'

"She sat on the side of the bed, smiling through the veil, eyes shining with spectral radiance. 'Then give me your hand.'

"I did. Fingers longer than I remembered, but her skin still felt as soft as a new-born.

"I glanced at the glowing-hands clock on my dresser. Almost half past ten. What happened next, I can only describe it as the room rippling. Scant light and shadow rolled together like ocean waves, though I felt tethered to earth. I gripped the blanket like I was at sea holding onto a ship's gunwale during a hurricane. I sensed myself undulating like a cork in rough water. Can't say how long it lasted. Time had always felt very unnatural with Ariel.

"Suddenly the light grew almost blinding, like staring at a cold sun. The sense of movement ceased. Still clinging to my bedclothes and to Ariel's right hand, I looked at her. As if reading my mind, she removed her black veil, revealing the most beautiful face in all creation. The mouth and chin of a deity. Those eyes! —large, knowing and full. Liquid eyes that shimmered with an unnatural luster in colors that varied from pure emerald to intense and brilliant gold. A profusion of hair, colored somewhere between very light brown, golden yellow, and true Scandinavian blonde, which started relatively low on her forehead, incredibly thick and straight until it reached her ears, where then long gentle waves splashed down all the way down to her chest. A forehead of petite breadth gleamed forth at intervals, all light and ivory. She smiled at me, teeth perfectly even, straight, and white. I felt my insides loosen and tingle. I felt utterly powerless within her orbit. Her face at twelve or thirteen in the winter woods, redesigned for adulthood, retained all the earlier allure but with such greater character now. Inconceivably rare and radiant human beauty.

"It was a true struggle to tear my gaze from that face, but I hazarded a brief look around. It seemed like a normal room, white walls and floor, of a material foreign to my young mind, though recalling it for you now, I feel it may have been quarried from minerals not of this world, vaguely like slabs of the whitest alabaster, or perhaps quartz. Light streamed through a square opening where a window would be and sparkled off the ceiling, floor, and walls. The only color in the room, apart from white, was ourselves, me and Ariel. Thus far she had said nothing.

"Then she said, 'I am not permitted to bring you outside this room. But you may look out of the opening. Please do, Dan. Tell me what you see.'

"Reassured by her memorial emerald-gold eyes, and smile, still holding her hand, I allowed my bare feet to hang over the mattress. Taking a deep breath, my soles touched the floor, and I stood. It felt flat and yet slightly textured. She released my hand and remained seated on my bed as I padded over to the opening with no glass.

"What I saw beyond that room took the entirety of my breath away. Although she said my body was still home bed, I remained tethered to it, somehow, to all its frailties and functions. I had to consciously restore my breathing reflex, knees like rubber, fighting vasovagal syncope. This doesn't happen in dreams, now does it, Doctor?"

Williams shook his head. "Not that I've ever read. Sleeping people do not dream of passing out."

"Precisely, and I was passing out. Overwhelming sensory overload. But I fought hard, dropped to my knees, pressed my forehead against the cool white floor lower than my heart, and managed to come back to myself. Ariel helped me to stand, then assumed her exact position as before on the bed, though she pointed at the opening. Reluctantly, I stood and looked out once more at a world unlike the imaginative work of Hollywood's best CGI graphic artists.

There was the familiar: in the distance I saw fields of grass-that-wasn't-grass, tall and perfectly even, rolling gently from some unknown breeze, although I felt no circulation of atmosphere. I breathed air that contained more oxygen than I am breathing here now, with you. I felt neither hot or cold. The aromas I could not place. If you have ever spent winter months on the east coast where the air smells sterile, then after a two-hour flight walk outside in Florida where the air hits you with fragrant pollen—the delicious dichotomy of it—my olfactory senses felt overwhelmed at that moment. Seductive, alluring, soothing beyond anything I have ever experienced. One scent I did recognize: burning nard.

"The light was incredibly bright, soft and yellow, like sunlight except that its source gave no heat. Patches of flowers that had to be thirty feet tall, with sunny faces and colorful petals. Everything sparkled! Even the grass and flowers. It suggested that the basic elemental building blocks there, wherever we were, are not of earth. Streams, dazzling rivulets so clear and sparkling that even from this distance, I saw underwater beds thick with enormous amethysts, diamonds, emeralds, rubies, and sapphires. What I experienced in this place was energy and matter similar to what is of earth, but not exactly. All I can tell you.

"Behind all that stood a structure of such monolithic size and grandeur, nothing on our planet could possibly compare to it, just as our earthly mountains and volcanic cones pale next to the thirteen-mile-high Olympus Mons volcano on the planet Mars. This structure seemed to be made of the same white material as that of the room. I might call it a cathedral, a castle, a temple. You are aware of the Basilica de la Sagrada Familia?

"Gaudi's Cathedral. Yes, I've seen it."

"Imagine something like it only sized to hold three billion congregants, in which everyone gets their own room. Still, even this inadequate description falls limply against the splendor, the vastness, the majesty of it. From directly below I thought I heard voices. Looking down, I saw people.

"Except they weren't people, and I did not hear anything save for the murmuring from nearby streams and an underlying sound, as though every atom of this place sang together to form a harmonic more deeply satisfying than any music that has ever pleased you in this world. These humanoids were nothing like our carbon-based frame of reference, except in basic shape. I perceived that they were made of the same element as the cathedral, the room, the grass, the flowers—possibly. They moved like we do, skins of sparking gold, each the exact same height, size, and color. Each wore a long, flowing raiment, principally white, some with blue trim, some trimmed in purple. Gender? This I could not tell you, not from that distance, but one seemed feminine in facial features and bearing. Cradled in her arms was a silver cat. I could see and hear the cat's feelings! Utter contentment, found only in those particular arms. No energy in all the universe could have pried it away.

"They all looked up at me, smiling. Slits that may have been mouths never opened. I heard their thoughts—no, that's not right. I *experienced* their thoughts. This is most strenuous to explain—"

"Doctor Tomkins, please don't over-exert yourself."

"Afraid I might die?"

Doctor Williams closed his eyes; a wan grin offered for his own short-sightedness. "Forgive me, please continue. You could understand their thoughts without need of language?"

"Yes! Precisely! It was as though my thoughts and emotions were somehow dialed into theirs, simply because they spotted me and wished to communicate. Self-possessed, my most private thoughts inviolate, yet my immediate 'public' thoughts I shared with them, and theirs were shared with me. Now keep in mind, Williams, I am fluent in seven modern languages and Latin, enabling me to communicate effectively with people not of my nation. Here in this place, language is moot. Words are merely symbols representing images. When you dream, what spools across your unconscious mind: are these typically words, or scenes, like moving pictures?"

"Scenes," Williams answered without hesitation. "I remember my dreams, like movies spooling where either I am a participating actor or a passive audience member. I understand everything going on because I am a part of it."

"Precisely! No words needed. I saw myself through their eyes. Felt the equanimity, the loving warmth of their welcoming spirits. I was someone new for them to play with, to love. I felt special. I felt welcome. I felt wanted. Like I belonged here! Like I had come from here and had been away.

"Joy is a word we hear only at Christmastime here, joy to the world, blah-blah. Imagine if you were to roll up every ecstatic feeling and sensation you have ever felt. Security, winning hard-fought contests, acceptance letter, that first kiss, yes to the marriage proposal, pique romantic experiences, your newborn's smile, negative disease test result, job offer, paid-off deed, et cetera ad nauseum: roll all of that up and *still* you will barely have a glimpse of what 'joy' really feels like. In this place the feeling never leaves you! Not even for a moment! No anger or grief, no sadness—not a trace. Only kindness, mercy. And love."

Williams closed his ajar mouth. "Um, wow. That's…inconceivable."

"As good an adjective as any. No human can relate, and I'm not smart enough to translate the sensation there into words. Since you seem to like Maslow, I would describe it as place where 'Self-Actualization' is as basic as breathing to earth-bound mortals. I stood gazing out of that opening for I don't know how long. Could have been an hour, a day, a year. Time elapsed without any sense of its passing. I felt, for the first time in my life—and never again since—completely present.

"I turned back once to make sure Ariel was still there. She smiled. I took in one last look to lock it all into memory. Mountains of green that reached up into sparkling blue-green skies hundreds of miles high. Serene lakes that appeared bottomless, the size of oceans. None of this awe-inspiring, magnificent expansiveness measured much within me against feelings of indomitable joy, of love, of perfectly harmonious peace. 'Joy' is but a noun here, misused to describe a fleeting biochemical reaction in the human brain. There, joy is a force, sovereign and transcendent.

"A human voice penetrated my enchantment, voice gentler and more seductive than an aeolian harp. 'Dan, come back to bed. There's more I must show you before the night in Pennsylvania turns into day.'

"Unenthusiastically—but how could I risk disappointing Ariel? —I climbed back into bed."

"Once again, that perception of oscillation. Pulsating waves had me gripping the bed as the sparkling white firmament underneath rippled into something plastic, and the bright light that had so deliciously swathed me, in quivering waves, went dark.

"When the sensation of movement ceased, unlike in that beautiful place, darkness remained. Reddish-purple light seeped in through a rectangular opening. The walls and floor may have been charcoal gray or jetty black; it was impossible to discern in the dimness. Ariel, still holding my hand, said, 'Another window on another world. Will you take a look for me?'

"When I had arrived in that other place it felt as safe and soothing as in a loving mother's womb from the first instant. This dark place felt…malignant, somehow. That other place echoed with its own special music like nothing here on earth, as if the very walls, flowers, grasses, jewels, and waters sang together in an endless, perfectly fitted unanimity. Here, everything sounded wrong. Internecine. Creepy modulation, like from an accursed choir of fiends. It *smelled* wrong. Sewage, sulfur, decomposition. The acrid stench of human fear. I'm not certain those sources are accurate but that's how it strikes me now as I recall it to the fore. A fiendish malevolence thrilled my every molecule. If not for Ariel, I felt that in being here, somehow, I was committing a deadly sin that would so jeopardize my immortal soul as to place it—if such a thing were possible—even beyond the reach of the infinite mercy of The Most Merciful and Most Terrifying Father. I loathed this place with a hatred belonging more to demon than to man. I wanted to leave that awful place more than words can express.

"Only, my trust in Ariel was—is—marrow-deep. My feet touched the rough icy-cold floor and I stood. 'Please look out there, Dan.' At that moment I would have hiked that snowy firebreak at World's End barefoot rather than release her hand, but the love and power behind her eyes subdued my initial fear. Tentatively I shuffled toward the window. Looking out, it appeared to be earth-like, the time just before dawn when the eastern sky changes from pitch black to a dark purple, with the suggestion of orange and pink to follow, like a brightening layer cake. But here, it never changed. A melancholy place where daybreak never arrives, where darkness is the whole of it, with the tease that perhaps it might someday, some year, some millennium—lighten.

"There were illuminations of a sort. Imagine one of those artificial fireplaces meant to give the appearance of a real log fire except on a scale incomprehensibly colossal, flickering overtop a volcanic mountain over a dozen miles high. It cast an orangey-red, mirthless glow over all things below. The surface of the place was impossibly rough and craggy, of a terrain that would be impossible to travel by our standards, narrow ravines and crevasses plunging down into total shadow, a hundred feet or ten miles deep. It was impossible to discern.

"In that other place, I had experienced the thoughts of others: here I heard voices emanating up from beneath my window, just as plainly as you are hearing mine. Leaning over the ledge of the window-like opening, I chanced a look straight down. The ground there seemed flatter than the rest yet made of the same exceedingly dangerous sharp volcanic glass and rock. I saw people like us, but not exactly like us. I saw a nude female figure whose head seemed nearly normal size, but its gelatinous corpulence spread about beneath it, making the head appear like a pea balanced atop a foothill. On earth, such adipose would weigh as much as a tugboat. Unmoving, it appeared to be gnawing on a lean, roasted human leg.

A thin man-thing stood staring at the volcano, so gaunt and narrow that I would accurately describe him as a skeleton wrapped in obsidian-hued, charred-looking skin.

Left of all this, I watched a red-eyed, pink-tailed sewer rat the size of a city bus, bloated from pregnancy. I knew rats birth live young. Long, spear-like whiskers twitched as it rhythmically pushed out egg sacs, as it goes with insects such as queen termites, ants, bees. Some sacs were moving. Odious pink rat-lings the size of Saint Bernard dogs chewed themselves out of gelatinous membranes. Each mewled out the most abominable, revolting sound, as huge front incisors snapped open and closed. There were so many of these things that the noise from them became almost deafening. I looked upon this pestilential death-scape with unutterable loathing. My mind and spirit recoiled from the horrid scene, as from the breath of a contagious disease.

"The creepy hum of high-pitched discordant voices I had heard from a distance had edged closer. Rising from came the unmistakable sounds of humans crying, and English-language pleas for mercy. To the right, I saw two human-in-every-way women whom I would place in their early twenties, similar in appearance, one dark haired one light, emaciated and reedy. They were completely nude. Pale skins were covered in many tattoos. They were getting pulled along by their wrists.

"The thing doing the pulling…I confess, Dr. Williams, that the sight of it caused me nightmares at least weekly for the next seventy-one years. A human skull, carbonized to black, with live black adders writhing atop the pate in a preposterous approximation of hair. The body was at least seven feet tall. Save for well-muscled humanoid arms, its form consisted of a man-like ribcage, skeleton and spine from the waist up. Shadows behind the ribs struck me as desiccated withered organs, maybe. On the thing's back, I glimpsed movement. As it turned its back to me, I saw the source: spiders, the way a mother wolf spider carries her young on the top of her abdomen. If these spider-things were the offspring of something larger, then by earthly standards the relative dimensions of the mother creature would necessarily be larger than a cow.

"From the waist down, it appeared to be animal legs: rump, thigh, hock, hock joint, fetlock, and hoof of a horse. The dock led to a curled tail lifted from the ground. In moments when the tail became fully extended, I guessed it's length at seven feet, proportionate to the creature's height. Its hands, if we were to call them such, consisted of three claws of equal length. Each claw tightly clasped the wrist of these crying, protesting girls.

"It hauled them down onto the jagged ebony bed of jagged glass, lying flat, face up. In a blink, the tail whipped around its left flank and pressed against the throats of both girls, not quite choking off their piteous entreaties. A voice came from it, otherworldly, like a low-pitched boom, gravelly, as through a torrid throat of broken glass, directed at the young woman on its left: 'I will torture you now. If you resist or wail, I shall kill your friend.' To the girl on its right, it said: 'I'm going to torture you now. If you resist or wail, I shall kill your friend.'

"It had promised life for each other's friend in exchange for silence. Using its six powerful opposing claws at precisely the same instant, it severed the left arm below the shoulder of one woman, then quickly the right arm of the other. Black liquid burbled from the wounds as struggles weakened. I could see them struggling not to cry out, but then the agony of their souls found vent in two loud, long, and final screams of despair. The creature's claws then eviscerated them, vivisected them organ by bloody organ. It punished them with their love, as if to teach them a lesson: that love has no home here. Love here only gets you dead, or deader. Only the most hideous and horrifying human appetites get rewarded in this realm.

"It picked up the two severed arms, trotted over horse-like to the misshapen, obese woman-thing, and handed them over. Normal-sized hands, set at the ends of dolphin-thick, flabby arms, took them. The creature dropped the now picked-clean leg bone and immediately set about eating the tattooed limbs raw. It consumed them greedily, grunting and grinning, black liquid shining on its teeth.

"The skeletal horse creature with snakes for hair, covered in spiders larger than baseball mitts faced the wall under the window. Slowly, it raised its skull to look straight at me with eyeholes that contained no eyes, only black crevices with what seemed like two tiny red laser-dots where eyes would have been, or once had been, maybe. It had no lips, so to say it was smirking at me would seem redundant, but that's how it felt to me. Something about body language told me that it was. It raised its powerful right arm to point at me. In the approximation of a 'come-hither' motion, it used one of its three raptor claws to beckon me. Clearly then I heard, 'Join us,' drawing out the 's' like a hissing snake.

"The two girls entirely regenerated. Life had returned. Whole again, they sat up and stared at me. Both princess waved. 'Join us!' together they said in jovial tones. 'You look so tasty,' said one. 'I'll make a man out of you!' said the other. I was so very done with this place, a world built upon dissimulation. Dr. Williams, again I find myself struggling to form an adequate description. Suffice it to say it is a dismal, dreary, terrifying place where the worst nightmares of mankind all come true."

"Christ Almighty," said Williams.

"You know Him?"

"Of him. Go on."

"The blob-lady thing spoke. It sounded like a human female gargling jelly into an amplified microphone. 'Hungry,' it bellowed. It pointed at me. 'You come down now, bad boy. Useless boy. I give you purpose.' Sometimes, even still, I have nightmares about the sound of the blob-thing's voice. Awful beyond description.

"This was the only time in my life that I ever vomited from fear. I projected out of the window-like opening; watched and heard my stomach contents splatting against the sacrificial rock. Just as I pulled myself back inside, the final vision was that of the cadaverous charred man staring at me, immobile and silent throughout the ordeal, who suddenly sprang into motion with speed rivalling a cheetah chasing prey. It slammed itself down onto my vomitus and greedily consumed it. The dog-sized rat-lings came skittering over to lick the rocks clean after the charred man had satisfied himself. Or more accurately, itself.

"There was more. Foulness even worse—but let me hurry to a conclusion. I ran back to my bed, leapt in and wiped my mouth on the blanket pulled up to my eyes. Ariel reached down, took my hand, and said, 'Thank you, Daniel. Let's go home, shall we?' I nodded vigorously.

"The darkness shivered and trembled; with it, that queer sense of falling. Moments later, I saw my rock-and-roll band posters, model rocket I'd been building, my baseball glove, bookshelves, all bathed in the warm vividness of my nightlight. The time on the glowing hands showed half past ten exactly. I said to Ariel, 'You mean, we've only been gone one minute?'

"She smiled. I'm telling you, Dr. Williams, if she were to smile at you, your life would never be the same afterwards. She said, stifling back laughter, 'Your species holds only the most basic understanding of the force you call time. Yes, we were only gone a minute.'

"But it seemed like hours!"

"'Rest, now, Dan. Tomorrow is a new day.' I felt her grip on my hand loosen. Terror seized me.

"You're leaving me? Again? Ariel, I love you! Don't you see? Can't you understand why I do messed-up stupid things? Because I can't forget you! I can't move past these feelings I have for you! Don't you remember what you said to me before you left? 'Dan, if you allow me to shed this body and return to my true form, I promise never to leave your side, but you won't see me,' is what you'd said. You pressed your hand over my heart. 'I'll live here, inside of you day and night. I'll visit you in your dreams. I will never age in your memories. Maybe you'll forget all about me and take a human wife, telling yourself none of this was real; that you hit your head inside the car and came to, and found this cabin on your own, and all things that happened next were simply hallucinations accompanying your body's shock.

Maybe that's the truth, Dan. Consider, maybe I am only a figment of your imagination, like a dream. Maybe I am a character your sleeping mind has assembled from random images and sound fragments. Do you believe I'm real, Daniel Tompkins?'

"And now here you are, Ariel, one year later, as real as real can be. Or am I dreaming? Is all this only just a nightmare within an otherwise perfect dream?

"'Only you can decide what is real from what is make-believe, Dan.'

"At this point, Williams, I wept. 'I love you with all my heart. You're leaving me,' I murmured, half awake. 'If you could stay here with me again, for the rest of my life, would you? Would you leave Paradise and come back to me someday, if you could? Would you come back for me again, Ariel? Will you come back to stay? Will I ever see you again?'

"'I want to,' she said, 'I'm here now. And no, this is not a dream. Whether or not I return depends on the will of The Father, and on you, Daniel Tomkins. You were saved for some great purpose; I know not what; such is not given to me or my kind. Only The Father moves forward and backward through time. I will say this: that tonight you received an extraordinary, priceless gift. I hope you learned that everything you are— this life—from the moment your eyes open each day until they close is but a series of small and large decisions, each with a consequence. At the close of your mortal journey, your program will live on. Where, and with whom, is entirely a cumulative result of all your decisions. You may believe that you are following The Father's will, but you may only be obeying your own wants. The desire to please Him does in fact please Him. I hope, Daniel, that you keep that desire in everything you do, and that you will never do anything apart from that desire,' she said, and laid her baby-soft hand on my cheek. 'His Spirit will lead you down the right path, though you may know nothing about it.' She kissed my forehead, long and lingering. 'I love you, Dan. I always will.'

"She held my cheek, then lightly stroked my forehead. Previous exertions had sapped all strength from me. I fell asleep.

"Sunlight and bird sounds jolted me awake. I was alone. I lost her for the second time. Thumping my heart I called out, 'Are you in there, Ariel? Were you ever real? Of course you were. I trust in my own level-headed, objective brain more than I trust in anyone or anything else. Except you, Ariel. You, I trust with all my heart. I love you every atom of my being. I could never love another. For what woman of earth can substitute? Who can own my heart when you occupy all of it?' Deeply I sighed.

After a time, I had decided the prior night's ethereal journey had been a dream, nothing more. From then on, I resigned myself to despair. But across the years, despite myself, when my soul had descended into shadow and doubt from which it felt as though it may never again rise, I called out to her. 'You kept your promise made in the woods and visited me in my dreams. During the worst nights, I laid awake and was certain I'd felt the press of spiritual lips upon my cheek, the weight of you on my bed.' With tearful eyes, I spoke far too often to Ariel, though unrequited.

"My childhood, Dr. Williams, was unlike any other. Brief—inarguably so. Even if I had only dreamed it, I took Ariel's prayer for me to heart, not wasting time establishing a sequence of cause and effect, of disaster-atrocity-potential salvation or questioning the rationality, the validity of these two 'visitations.' Reading The Holy Bible helped put things into perspective and brought a good measure of comfort. I studied ferociously while other kids played sports, dated, went to movies, read fiction, engaged in hobbies, and went on family trips. A complete ascetic was I. My undergrad, graduate, and post-grad history I probably don't need to relate, as you seem to know much about that second great epoch of my mental existence."

Williams nodded. "Except the part about your wife that nobody knows about."

Eyes shining, Tomkins said, "Yes. I did tell you I would get to that. What time is it?"

Flicking a glance at his watch, "Your dream-girl was correct; our species seems to have no sense of the force called time. 5:57!"

Tomkins smiled. "You're in luck, Dr. Williams. In a few moments, you shall be one of the few people to meet her."

"Whatever had passed between us, this force to which nothing else compares, was ours and ours alone, mine and Ariel's. It could never be replicated using a stand-in replacement actor. There was unique and special magic to it. Alluring and attractive women had tried over the years to get at that part of me. The harder they tried, the more protective and closed off I became until they quit trying and gave up. The eternal spirit, the program driving this fragile bag of blood, the core of everything that I am will forever belong to Ariel. This is what I learned about myself before the age of fourteen. By the time I had reached age forty-two and achieved my first breakthrough cancer cure, I felt as alone and emotionally isolated as a man can feel. God knows, my spirit had sunk to a new low I never would've thought possible.

"One cold, drizzly winter's day after giving a speech in Philly to an auditorium of oncologists, I drove back to the cabin in World's End where it all started hoping, I suppose, to somehow reconnect with Ariel. I hoped that maybe there, she might feel safe to give me a sign from that other place; to prove that she was in fact real. It failed. I should have felt some measure of joy from my professional triumphs, but I was positively despondent. In a mood of sheer desperation I decided to go talk to my dead parents and brother. Several hours later I arrived at the Washington Memorial Chapel Churchyard off Route 23 in Valley Forge National Historical Park, where they are interred.

"Certain that I was alone in the cemetery, I spoke aloud to them. I stood like that for what seemed like hours. The trees sheltered me from the worst of the drizzle and there was no breeze. I did not move. Stuporous, I followed my mind down into the many dark holes it was leading me.

"Out of the corner of my eye, I sensed that I wasn't alone. In my periphery, I spotted this figure dressed in black standing before a grave marker shaped like a crucifix. A woman. Approximate age was indeterminable. Face covered by a sheer black mourning veil. Black knee-length trench coat, looked to be a Burberry London from the ruched sleeves, tight around a very slim waist. Black boots, small black handbag. The figure stood before the cross and stared at it, unmoving. Not an unusual sight in a cemetery. Soundlessly she had appeared not twenty paces from me. You could hear a pinecone fall in this outdoor echo chamber, and mine was the only vehicle in the tiny parking area, yet somehow this visitor had escaped my notice until now.

"Thinking about this brought me out of my dark reverie and back to the present. I wondered how many of my words she may have heard and how long she had stood there. I looked myself over self-consciously. Was I even presentable for public consumption? I surely didn't feel it.

"It was not my intention to stare and risk making her uncomfortable, but I could not help myself. Something about this person commanded my full attention, I cannot say what. Maybe it was the dichotomy of her seemingly unshakeable placidness, statue-still in a way unfamiliar to me, which seemed incongruous against what I took to be a relatively youthful form and posture, and fashionable couture. Something in this picture did not fit. Her body faced the crucifix grave when her head turned to look at me. I looked away fast but knew I was caught. I cast a furtive glance at her. She was now staring at me. I stared back. Neither moved. We stood like that for a full minute. Hands in pockets, I took a few paces in her direction until we were about ten feet apart. 'I'm sorry, really. I didn't mean to stare. I meant nothing by it. I was just startled to learn that I wasn't alone. And here I am talking to ghosts. I'm more than a little embarrassed.'

"Her body then turned to face me. I could not see her face behind the veil, not well anyway, but I did see a slim waif, a tiny pixie compared to my six-plus feet. 'It's quite alright, sir,' she replied in a buttery soft, clear mezzo soprano voice. Articulate and highly educated, this I could tell.

"'Thanks,' I said. I removed my right hand from my coat pocket and extended it as I paced over to her, crucifix headstone to our left. 'Dr. Daniel Tompkins.' Slowly and without any unnecessary body movement, she raised her gloved hand, which I took and gently pumped twice.

"'It's quite alright because I could not help but overhearing every word you said. Congratulations on your achievements, doctor. You have changed the world. Made it better.' I didn't know how to respond to that. 'I sense you expect me to give my name. I do have one, but no one has spoken it aloud in nearly three decades.'

"I puzzled over this. Her words failed to register. As any man gets in the presence of an exceedingly beautiful woman, my mind journeyed to many places at once. I don't know if I blushed just then, but it sure felt like I did. My face, really my entire body suddenly felt warm. 'Call me Dan, please. And thank you, um…'

"'You don't know my name, yet you feel like you know me somehow. Is that not true?'

"Startling. Perhaps that is why I had stared, trying to figure out if I had met her before somewhere. Her voice sounded familiar yet irritatingly abstruse. Could she have been one of my post-grad students? Something about her veiled face, the pale skin. 'Maybe,' I said.

"'I think it would be nice to know you even better,' she said. I was close enough now to see the basic shape of her face through the veil, golden hair done up under the hat. Her beauty was stunning. The veil did little to hide the rarefied radiance emanating from behind it. I found the shape of her eyes pulling at memories stored deep within. My body felt like a furnace. It had been such a very long time since any woman elicited that effect. Twenty-nine years, to be exact. Then she said, 'I should probably be going. Perhaps we will see each other again somewhere, in the ether.'

"I closed my mouth, then nodded. 'Sooner rather than later, I hope.' Was that an appropriate and smooth response? I asked myself. Turning, I paced back to the Tompkins family plot and stood before Barry's stone. I kept glancing up, craving another look at the veiled stranger who now knew more about me than anyone else alive, based on the overheard one-way conversation with my dead family. I watched her bend and pick up a fallen branch from the Scotch Pine above her. I watched as she used the branch to carve something in the muddy earth before the cross-shaped grave marker. I looked one last time at my family's markers and said farewell. Didn't know when I would return here or where I'd go from here today, tomorrow, the rest of my days.

"When I looked up, she was gone. I moped over to where she had stood, her boot prints still clear in the snow. The moment reminded me of age twelve, trying to locate a young woman's prints on that fateful morning when I woke up alone, the first of nearly eleven thousand lonely mornings since. I saw the stick she'd used with mud clumped on the end. Then I looked at the earth, curious about what she had carved into it. It appeared to be a single word. I bent to study the letters.

"Ohkwari."

"Ohkwari ohkwari…seemed familiar somehow. Where had I heard this word before? A buried word, around which my brain had formed a sort of mental callous to shield me from pain. Not English, for sure. A primitive sound. And that thing with her name, saying she has one, but no one uses it: I'd heard all that before somewhere eons ago, in another place and time, in another life.

"Suddenly then it hit me. What I had repressed, now I remembered. Ariel's word. *Our* word. The secret word she gave to me just before she disappeared into that stream, gone from my life as abruptly as she'd entered it. An ancient word that exists in the modern world only between Ariel and me. 'No, it can't be.' My brain whirled through all possibilities.

"The woman whose hand I just shook, could it be? When I last touched Ariel, I dwelled within a child's body. Ohkwari. How could it not? The fervor of hope, the delirium of a love that was more than love, so immediately and completely intoxicating that it transformed every lonely corner of my being all at once. Feelings I had repressed; nocturnal dreams where I had felt the press of spiritual lips upon my cheek and forehead; countless waking fantasies I had grappled with and so adamantly denied for a lifetime suddenly flooded back and bewildered my brain. I felt my spirit lifted—transported— by the possibilities of holding my beloved Ariel again! First as a girl-child, second time as a mature woman. And possibly once more and for all time—at least through the rest of our time on earth? My aloneness and isolation from other hearts, whether by conscious decision or owed to the ethereal, inimitable link forged between us so long ago in the cabin along Loyalsock Creek, probably equal parts of both—hurt less, now. I felt some impossibly heavy load I had lugged uphill day and night for so long, I was about to, at long last, just set it down.

"Ariel couldn't have gone far this time. So I ran."

Ron Williams, medical doctor, geriatrician, did not know what to think, even less what to say. He sat in stone silence trying to process all that the celebrated and esteemed Dr. Daniel Tomkins had just candidly and confidentiality shared with him. It was then that the perception of a third presence in the room interrupted his deep reverie. Toward the doorway believing it to be a nurse, he shot up his hand. "Not now. Come back later."

The presence remained. He turned to behold a young woman, face covered by a sheer black veil, wearing a knee-length raincoat with ruched sleeves, tight around a slim waist, black boots, holding a small black handbag. Williams stared, mouth agape. Daniel Tomkins raised both hands, his left pointed at the woman, his right at Williams. "She is the only person listed on my HIPAA form as legal authorized representative with full Power of Attorney, also co-signer of my living will, also my last will and testament."

"Ah, I see. She's your attorney."

"No, Dr. Williams. She is my heart, my love, my lady. My guardian across all time. For all intents and purposes, though never formerly, legally married—my wife. Dr. Ron Williams, may I introduce you to Ariel Tomkins."

Pale, delicate, unblemished young hands slowly lifted the veil. Wide set emerald-green eyes with flecks of gold, luminous and opalescent, belied a depth of wisdom and self-possession like nothing of earth. She offered Williams her right hand. Reflexively he stood, then realized he had stopped breathing. She smiled. At this, his knees felt unsteady. Tentatively he touched her hand. It reminded him of his brief rotation of obstetrics long ago, holding newly born babies, skin softer than buttered velvet.

"Dr. Williams, you really must sit back down," she said, placid voice as soothing and captivating as the Sirens. "You appear most unsteady."

In a bid to restore his doctor's bearing and civilized manner. "Please," he said and pointed at the still-warm seat, "I insist. Been sitting for hours listening to your husband. I need to stretch my legs." Still smiling, she acquiesced and primly sat in the visitor's chair. "My-my, this is a puzzle. Dr. Tomkins just explained your history together. May I ask, what was your age when you visited him in his bedroom, when he was thirteen?"

"Referring only to this body: sixty seconds."

His eyes narrowed. "He said you appeared in your mid-twenties?"

"The body formed for me at that moment was, by all earthly appearance and measure, twenty-seven years old."

Williams rubbed his face. "I see. Forgive my curiosity, I am not usually this direct. Please help me understand. You have remained with Dr. Tomkins in a forty-two-year relationship commencing when you were… twenty-seven? By all outward appearance you are still in your twenties, not just south of seventy. Your body does not age? Is your body…human?"

"Yes, it is the normally functioning body of a human female. The Father presented me with this opportunity, the human experience, three times, to keep Dan safe from evil powers beyond your comprehension. To keep him healthy in mind, spirit, and body, enabling him to complete his important work."

Beholding her husband, shoulders bent double with decrepitude, shriveled dry skin mottled and brown-spotted, the eyes of Daniel Tomkins glistened with the rheum of years. His lank hair was thin and snow white. She said, "Though it was not given to me to conceive and bear him children. Only The Son was at once mortal and divine. Of the eyewitness record of His visitation, I expect you are aware of Yeshua. Nevertheless, I have experienced human love, desire, passion, grief: a singular gift never bestowed upon one of my kind. It has been the most magnificent departure, one that I shall hold close for eternity. A part of me will dearly miss this world, now that I have deeply lived the human experience. I'm sure it required far more strength for The Son to leave here than it will be for me, but it causes me pain, nevertheless. Tonight, Dan's spirit returns to its Creator, as will mine. A drop of sadness in an eternal ocean of joy. Dan and I have loved with a love that is more than love. A higher love. This connection will never be broken. Our joy together lives on. Please do not grieve, Dr. Williams."

"No! I mean please…I have a thousand questions to ask you!"

Smiling, "Yes, I know. I hear them. It is your intellect, natural curiosity, and warm loving heart that has earned you the revelation from Dan and I tonight. The Father wishes for you to pick up the research where Dan's ended due to his body's natural expiration. I hope you do not believe your assignment to this place, on this day, was accidental or random, nor that mere caprice led Daniel to offer you, of all people, his life's work."

Tomkins reached over to the nightstand and eased open the drawer. He grasped a spiral-bound notebook. He closed the drawer and held it in his hands. He turned it over. He thumbed through the pages. He offered it to Williams. "Herein contains the keys to the kingdom of oncology research. I cannot say with certainty from where the ideas and notions originate. The truth can only be found through hard work in the lab, testing, failing, testing some more and sometimes succeeding. There can never be a replacement for good old-fashioned hard work.

"You are chosen, Dr. Williams," said Ariel. "Humans are given freedom to obey their own wills, or to obey the will of The Father. It has been that way since the beginning and so it shall be until the close of the age. You have chosen not to believe the eyewitness evidence of the supernatural visitation two millenniums ago; also, you may choose to disbelieve your own eyes now, at this moment."

Her eyes enthralled him. After minutes of silent reflection, he said, "I believe. In both. God knows, after my own eyewitness of supernatural events and testimony today, I believe. The truth of this day I can share with no other, for it is too fantastical to believe. I will lose all credibility. I suppose that somehow, I must teach myself to learn to live with this knowledge in solitude."

She smiled. So did Tomkins. Williams did not avert his gaze from her. "May I ask, will you remain together? In that… next place?"

"Marriage is not given to my kind—soon to be Dan's kind. There it is not necessary. True intimacy is but a thought away."

Tomkins interjected. "If you had experienced what Ariel gave to me when I was thirteen, perhaps you would understand why it is not so. The cat—think of the cat. Utter contentment in the arms of a familiar spirit, equanimity and fulfillment for both spirits. As it shall be with Ariel and I, as we continue to love one another throughout all eternity, never apart through all of time, at peace in the loving protection of The Father."

"What will happen to you…to this—lovely form?"

She shot a knowing glance at her husband. "I expect Loyalsock Creek in World's End State Park will, by tomorrow morning, have washed away all evidence of its existence. To this world, I was never here."

"What will happen to me?"

"That," said Ariel, "remains entirely up to you. Remember: human life is but a string of decisions large and small. Your body will end as Daniel's body now ends. Between this day and that, you might consider embracing all things that you believe in doing, asking yourself if doing them will please The Father."

"After this body ends, what then?"

"Your program will sleep—for how long I cannot say—for such information is not given to my kind. Think of it much like now, when you rest, your spirit remains active though your mind is not conscious. You dream, and when your body and conscious mind re-awaken you have no sense of eight hours passing. Time elapses in a blink, for spirits. So it is for disembodied human spirits. Each will one day awaken in a new form, in a new conscious mind, with no sense of whether eight hours or eight-thousand years have passed. Some mortal programs reawaken in the next realm immediately: special programs, like Dan's. Perhaps yours might. Most spirits will remain in stasis awaiting judgement from The Son. Depending on the result of the judgement, eternity awaits every spirit assigned to one of two realms.

"I showed young Dan the eternal places, for it was The Father's will that Dan be given these unique glimpses, which he has adequately described to you. A tremendous gulf has been fixed between the two realms, so that life existing in one can never cross over to the other. Ever since the war fought in my realm, a rebellion on an epic scale that, for a time, terribly disturbed the harmonious and loving peace—the finality of this separation is absolute and eternal. Where your program will go is not mine to know, Dr. Williams."

"Will a spirit protect me as you protected Dr. Tompkins?"

"This also is not given for me to know," said Ariel. She arose and moved to the bed, where the tired chin of Dan Tomkins rested against his bosom. He held the book on his lap. Once again, he offered it up. "Now, Dr. Williams, if you would kindly give us some privacy, my husband and I must go on our way." She turned her hypnotic gaze to Daniel.

Sensing his presence there was no longer appropriate, Dr. Ron Williams left without a word. He closed the door behind him, notebook in hand.

ABOUT THE AUTHOR

John James Minster writes horror drawn from nightmares both waking and sleeping. A Pennsylvania native, he launched a successful international career in technology during the 1980s while publishing horror short stories in anthologies.

His works include the middle-grade horror novel Dreamjacker; the acclaimed religious horror The Undertaker's Daughter (Hellbender Books, 2022); the short story collection The Vengeful Dead (2023), which drew attention from Hollywood producers; and Second Coming (2024), hailed by readers as his finest work to date. Across all titles, Minster's fiction has earned widespread praise and five-star reviews from horror fans around the world.

As a child, he often sleepwalked—once nearly leaping down the stairs, convinced he could fly. Even now, he thrashes and talks in his sleep, describing his nightmares as "nightly mini horror movies." He credits them with keeping his imagination sharp and his stories flowing: "No writer's block on the horizon; no chance I'll run out of tales."

Learn more at https://linktr.ee/johnjamesminster